RED SKY AT MORNING

Konner Glick

For Haley—my greatest adventure and the one who inspires me to do hard things.

Once a seafaring vessel has entered international waters, it becomes free from national laws and is only expected to abide by international guidelines and treaties.

The human crewmembers, however, fall under the jurisdiction of the vessel's "flag"—or the nation in which the ship is registered. When a crime is committed at sea, prosecution, defense, and potential incarceration of the accused take place in the ship's flagged nation once the vessel has returned to port.

While still at sea, the accused are under the immediate supervision of the ship's commanding officer. For that reason, most large ships are equipped with a brig or other secure holding area. Smaller craft are generally unable to have such facilities, making the apprehension and detention of potential criminals complicated and difficult—especially when the nearest port can be over 100 miles away.

On average, Earth and Mars are approximately 140,000,000 miles apart.

CHAPTER ONE

It was enormous, all of it, and it made James feel both incredibly small and infinitely insignificant in spite of the importance of his undertaking. *How the world would change if everybody on planet Earth could see this,* he thought to himself, his eyes raking over the star-filled void. One of those stars—probably that bright one just aft of the engines and rear solar panels—was planet Earth—its colors, clouds, and continents combined into one glowing pin-prick of light cast against an ink-black blanket of space.

James let out a small sigh of awe, one of many that had already escaped his lips during the past eight and a half months. Seeing the Earth like this, from millions of miles away, would change things—change everything—for people, regardless of race, religion, or status, but right now the view belonged to him. And what a view it was!

It was all enough to take James' breath away, but not necessarily because of its desolate beauty. Earth was at least a hundred million miles away by now, and James knew that the only thing between him and his home planet was a merciless, destructive vacuum. James shivered—his suit was starting to feel cramped and claustrophobic, and the composite glass of his helmet—a defense against death less than a half-inch thick—seemed closer to his nose than ever.

"Hey, Lake," a voice said over James' headset, referring to him by his last name. It was the always-cheery voice of James' mission commander, Commander Alejandro Gonzalez. "Hey man," he continued. "Houston wants you to check on terminal C to try to isolate the problem. They think that's where power is getting cut off."

"I tried that already, Gonzo," replied James, grateful for the sudden distraction. "Five minutes ago. It looks fine—I thought I radioed that in."

"You probably did," replied Gonzalez. "I guess we'll just sit and wait for them to reply while our systems slowly die out, leaving us to suffocate and die in the abyss of interplanetary space. You hear that Houston? We're all going to die. This is your fault, dammit!"

It was an old joke, one that still made James grin in spite of how annoying hearing the same joke was. Gonzalez, who the entire crew just called "Gonzo," seemed to take sick pleasure in the fact that he could get away with saying just about anything since the radio transmission back to Earth wasn't live. In fact, a one-way message from *Perseus* back to planet Earth could take almost ten minutes, with the return transmission taking just as long. Any reprimanding from Houston would come almost twenty minutes after the fact, and after all, what would they do? Order Gonzo back to Earth?

"You keep talking like that and they won't believe us when something serious actually *does* go wrong," said another voice, this one belonging to Aaron Samuelson, the mission's flight engineering specialist. "But in all seriousness, James, I think we should go ahead and move to terminal A instead of waiting for Houston's response. That *must* be the problem, we've tried almost everything else."

"Concur," replied James, not waiting for permission from Gonzalez to carefully unclip his safety harness and connect it to the next handhold over. He'd already been outside *Perseus* for three hours now, and he was eager to get back inside and out of his bulky extravehicular suit. *"Three damn hours,"* he muttered under his breath. Three hours just to find the glitch that was keeping electricity from flowing between the starboard solar panel and *Perseus*.

What made it all the more frustrating for James was the fact that he was out here instead of Aaron. Aaron was the engineer—he was the one who could figure this out in less than an hour. But Houston wanted to limit radiation exposure, and James was next on the rotation. He knew he shouldn't complain about the opportunity to float out in space, but *anything* could get tedious when you could only act every twenty minutes after Houston gave the all-clear. And tedious could turn to terror awfully quick when in space.

"Almost there," reported James, clipping his safety harness onto another rail and moving slowly towards the next terminal.

"I'm here now," a third voice, this one belonging to a woman, said over James' headset. "I'll proceed to remove the main panel on terminal A."

"Roger, Nikki," replied Gonzalez. "Lake, get over there, you've got the voltage meter."

"Roger," James replied quickly, taking a brief second to look up towards where terminal A would be. Sure enough, Nicole Prince was already floating next to the terminal, identifiable in her otherwise nondescript EMU suit by the orange stripes of color around her knees and elbows. She was already at work silently unscrewing the panel with one of NASA's overly-expensive space drills. By the time James arrived at her side, the task was already done.

"About time you showed up," Nikki mumbled, barely glancing at James from behind her helmet's visor as she carefully flipped the panel open.

"Better late than never, right?"

Nikki just nodded somberly behind her helmet's glass.

"I was just kidding," James said quickly, slightly annoyed at Nikki's odd dismissiveness. "Sorry, I was caught looking at the view."

"Some of us are just more concerned with electricity getting to the CO_2 scrubbers and oxygen systems," shrugged Nikki inside her suit. "We can't all just float around aimlessly."

James chuckled at Nikki's pointed humor. "I get it," he said as Nikki smiled weakly. "It won't happen again, I take full..."

James trailed off awkwardly—something else had already caught his attention. Nikki's drill was floating on its own in space about a foot behind her head.

"What is it?" Nikki asked, twisting her body so she could see what James was looking at.

"You'd better grab that," James quickly said, pointing towards the floating drill. Nikki rotated around quickly, reached out to grab the drill without letting go of the spacecraft, and snagged it. James watched as she carefully tucked the tool into her EVA bag and re-clipped the drill's attached carabiner to the bag.

"Sorry," Nikki said, shaking her head to herself. "Forgot to clip it in. Gotta' get my head in the game here."

"Is everything ok?" asked James. "You seem stressed."

"Just don't want to lose a thousand-dollar drill, that's all."

James didn't reply right away. Nikki seemed slightly on edge, though he didn't blame her. "No worries," James said, pivoting the conversation. "I once lost two of those drills during the same mission in the training pool."

"I thought it was three?" joked Gonzalez over the radio. It *was* three, but James didn't feel the need to correct himself. Instead, he got right to work looking over the terminal box.

It only took a few seconds for James to spot what was going wrong, and he didn't even need to use his tools. One of the large coils of wire in the box was disconnected from its port, the small plastic clip that should have held the coils in place clearly broken off. It was probably from the extreme temperature swings and constant radiation, but even then, NASA should have known better than building such a flimsy connector.

"You reading my visual, Aaron?" asked James. "I'm going to plug the unit back in and secure it with electrical tape."

"Hold on a second," Aaron said quickly. "This time I do think that Houston should have a chance to look it over."

"I don't think that's necessary," Gonzalez overruled. "But I do think that thing needs to be secured tightly. Houston, I've given Lake and Specialist Prince permission to remove their helmets and apply their chewing gum on the loose wire connection, over."

"I really think we need to check with Houston," protested Aaron, but Gonzalez quickly overruled him.

"Let's just get this over with," the mission commander said. "We know the problem, let's fix it."

James agreed—he was ready to go back inside to the relative safety of *Perseus*. He carefully plugged the wire back into place before using his meter to check the connection. Sure enough, the once-dead panel was now coursing with electricity. A multipurpose clamp and a copious amount of electrical tape later and the job was done. Gonzalez was quick to voice his approval, and Aaron reluctantly concurred after James used his helmet camera to give him a good look at the repair.

Nikki immediately got to work screwing the panel back into place—but after three bolts she suddenly stopped. "Damn," she said, spinning around to look for something. "I lost a bolt. What's with me today? Don't say anything, James. I'm not in the mood."

Nikki's brief lapse of focus was curious for James, but it wasn't a big deal. It just wasn't like the mission's geologist to be so careless, that was all. That said, spacewalks *were* outside of her general repertoire. She was much more suited to playing around in the dirt, and proud of that fact.

"Three bolts should hold just fine for now," Aaron said after letting out a sigh. "I'm showing good systems from here. Nice work out there you two. Gonzo says you're good to come in."

"After you," James said to Nikki, who responded to the affirmative. She paused to unclip her harness and attach it to the next rail over as she moved towards the airlock. James took the moment to gaze out towards the front of *Perseus*. They were only a week away, and sure enough, Mars, once just a point of red light, was growing bigger and bigger. James couldn't wait. What a privilege it would be to be one of the first people to set foot on Mars! His name would go down in the history books along with his other six crewmates.

"Hey, Lake," Gonzalez said suddenly, his voice channeled into James' helmet. "Houston says you should check out terminal A. They did want to see visual before you do anything though. What do you think?"

James couldn't help but roll his eyes at the absurdity of the communications delay. At least it was only ten minutes each way—depending on the two planets' positions it could be much longer. "Better to ask forgiveness than permission," James finally teased back as he followed Nikki towards the airlock. "Why don't you just pretend that we're still out there? It's not like they'll know the difference for another ten minutes."

James didn't think his comment was that funny, but it was enough to elicit an audible snicker from Nikki as both she and James pulled themselves into the open airlock. Once the hatch behind them was closed, Nikki reached out to pressurize the airlock, filling the relatively small space with oxygen, nitrogen, and noise. James liked hearing noise from outside his suit—it meant he could take it off.

Repressurization took a minute or two, and James took the time to gaze out the airlock's window. The airlock module itself connected to the bottom of the ship, but the door faced aft—towards the engines and service module. It was a novel design choice that allowed for a more spacious entrance and exit—and another view of Earth for James.

A friendly-sounding computer chime indicated that pressure was equalized, and the astronauts could take off their suits. James started with his outer gloves, then proceeded to remove his helmet—an immensely satisfying feeling he found comparable to taking a big breath after a dive in the pool. Next came his under-gloves and his "Snoopy cap," then the entire top half of his suit. With his arms and torso completely free he was then able to slide out of his EMU suit's pants, leaving him floating comfortably in his socks, gym shorts, and "Captain America" t-shirt.

Nikki was having a harder time. The suits were tricky, and sometimes James struggled too, even after doing it dozens and dozens of times. "Can you help me take my pants off?" Nikki asked, struggling to get her legs out as she slowly spun around in zero gravity. "Don't get too excited," she joked quickly. "Just hold on to the boots so I can get some leverage. Yeah, just like that."

"Damn, it's good to be back inside," said James as he watched Nikki free the rest of herself from the suit. James could tell she was relieved to be back inside too.

Nikki smiled. "Still smells bad in *here* though," she joked before unceremoniously adjusting her bra and giving her breasts a quick scratch. "Sorry for being so anal out there, James."

Nikki reached down to itch one of her long, bare legs without waiting for a response from James, who instinctively looked away and got to work opening the interior hatch.

It wasn't that James didn't want Nikki to catch him looking at her, it was that he didn't want his mind to wander—a very real threat. Nikki was by far the prettiest woman in NASA's astronaut corps, and her official photo was no doubt already a screensaver for hundreds of computer nerds and astronaut wannabes throughout the world. Her long, blonde hair highlighted her youth—she was barely twenty-eight—and her still-tan skin only accentuated her perfect physique. It didn't help that her favorite thing to wear around the ship was a pair of spandex shorts and a t-shirt.

James was happily married to a woman he considered to be just as beautiful and far more desirable—the only problem was that Claire was one-hundred-million miles away. Nevertheless, James swore to himself he'd be perfectly faithful to her his entire life, even in thought, and that wasn't going to change now. Whether by unconscious instinct or conscious effort, he wasn't going to let anyone get in between him and his wife, even if it was a woman eight years younger than him who clearly didn't have any romantic inclinations towards him anyway.

With Nikki behind him, James floated through the hatch and into the main truss of *Perseus*. *Perseus* was like a flying space station, consisting of an engine and service module in the back, followed by a node to which the airlock module was connected on the "bottom." Two rigid compartments in the middle came next, then a second node in the front. Connected to that forward node was the Mars descent vehicle—the MDV—at the nose of the ship, its landing gear and heat shield facing forward towards Mars, and the Orion+ command module, which was connected to the bottom hatch.

Fortunately for the crew, there was even more space on board. Four enormous, inflatable modules lined the "top" and "bottom" of the ship—two coming out of each rigid center module—giving the ship the outward appearance of some kind of frilled serpent, and the two sets of large solar panels—two pairs, extending from the left and right sides of the ship both in the back by the engines and towards the front—only furthered the image. The panels faced back towards the steadily shrinking sun. It wasn't as elegant looking as spaceships from the movies, but James didn't care—the original plan didn't have the four inflatable modules included. *Perseus* was still small and cramped, but that would have been hell.

Upon floating into the first central cylindrical compartment, James' nostrils were struck with the visceral scent of fresh human sweat. It was obvious where it was coming from—Jordyn Marx, the mission's pilot, was running hard on the specially designed treadmill that was connected to one of the module's walls, and her dark brown skin glistened with moisture that was flicked into space by her bouncing black hair. Jordyn was nearly as pretty as Nikki was, but James felt far more comfortable around her. Maybe it was the fact that both Jordyn and him served in the Air Force, maybe it was that both had spouses waiting back home, or maybe it was the simple fact that she was far more serious than Nikki was. Regardless, James held her in very high regard.

"Hey, watch it!" snapped Jordyn as James accidently brushed up against her as he floated past in the confined module.

"Weren't you getting ready to run when we started our walk?" Nikki asked incredulously, pausing to slap a floating drop of Jordyn's sweat out of the way. "Damn, girl."

"Today is the Boston Marathon back on Earth," replied Jordyn, not slowing her pace in the least. "And I'm running it too. I'm on my last mile—so don't touch me again, James."

"What's your time?" asked James.

"Three hours thirty-five," responded Jordyn simply. "Gonna' be the first woman in space under three hours forty-five."

James was impressed. He wasn't much of a runner—he vastly preferred team sports—but he knew enough to understand that Jordyn was keeping a fantastic pace, especially for someone held to a space treadmill by elastic straps at the waist.

"We oughta' get this on camera for this week's recording," Nikki said, referring to the weekly videotaping the crew did for the news media back on Earth.

"Gonzo already did," Jordyn said, this time sounding more out of breath. "He also said that he wanted the crew to eat dinner together today at o'nineteen. Now let me finish."

Not wanting to ruin Jordyn's focus any more than he already had, James silently pushed forward, passing the laboratory between the exercise equipment and the kitchen module while simultaneously checking his watch. NASA already had all of them measuring time by the Martian day—or Sol— but the concept of hours and minutes was still the same. Dinner would be in only fifteen minutes.

Sure enough, much of the Ares I crew was already in the central module in preparation for dinner. Aaron floated in the far end of the room, staring intently out one of the few small portholes, absentmindedly running a hand through his blonde hair. Mike Syracuse, the mission's red-headed, fair-skinned biologist and botanist, was busy gathering food packets from a storage compartment and floating them across the room towards Harrison Larsen, a burly, muscular man from Georgia who was the mission's payload specialist. Harrison was busy putting the packets in the ship's food heater, but he stopped long enough to take a long glance towards Nikki as she and James entered the room. "Hey guys," he said pleasantly with a hint of southern drawl, clearly struggling to pull his blue eyes away from Nikki.

"Hi, Harrison," replied Nikki with a smile, grabbing him by the arm to stop her momentum. "Hi, Mike."

"You're back!" Mike exclaimed energetically. "It's about time, too. Gonzo made us wait for you before we could start eating, and NASA has us scheduled for pork chops today. Pork chops! Real, pre-cooked, frozen chops!"

"Really?" James asked, genuinely excited. Most food on the *Perseus* was pretty bland, but every couple weeks NASA would schedule in some real food for morale purposes. The thought of a solid chunk of meat made James' mouth water.

"That's not even the best part," Harrison said, still floating alongside Nikki. "Tell 'em Mike."

"I've made my husband's BBQ sauce again," Mike said excitedly. "The one we had three months ago."

"I've gotta' meet this guy," Nikki said quickly. "His recipes are the absolute best. Seriously."

"It's too bad Aaron won't be allowed to eat it," said Mike. "He can't eat anything."

"Why wouldn't I be allowed to eat it?" asked a puzzled Aaron.

"I heard Mormons couldn't eat stuff made by gay people," Mike deadpanned. "I heard it sends 'em to hell."

James turned towards Aaron, curious as to how he would respond.

"Guess I'm going to hell," shrugged Aaron. "I'd sell my soul for that sauce in a heartbeat anyways."

The five crewmates shared a good laugh, including James. While living in close quarters for such an extended period of time could make tempers run high, Mike and Aaron seemed impervious to the pressure. The only thing funnier than Mike's constant ribbing of Aaron was Aaron's witty responses. The two were complete opposites—Aaron, the conservative Mormon from California, and Mike, the homosexual from Massachusetts—but the way they got along was a perfect example of the comradery necessary for a seven-person crew to survive a year-and-a-half mission to Mars and back. James knew the two men disagreed on practically everything, but that didn't stop them from being the best pair of friends on the ship.

James thought it was funny how things worked out. The Ares I crew was hand-picked by NASA psychologists to be as compatible as possible—especially considering the fact they'd be sharing a ship no bigger than a couple of RVs for such a long period of time—but Aaron wasn't one of the chosen. He was actually on the "B-team"—part of the backup crew that would go on to fly the Ares II mission later next year—but when Lipinski got pneumonia a week before the already-late launch, their positions were swapped. James considered it a happy accident—Lipinski was a jerk.

After a few minutes of conversation, Gonzalez entered the compartment from the direction of the Command Module, followed shortly thereafter by a still-sweaty Jordyn. Jordyn was happy to report a time of three hours, forty-two minutes and twenty-two seconds.

12

Dinner was fantastic. The pork chops were every bit as good as James had envisioned, and Mike's sauce was as delicious as advertised. Even Harrison, who usually complained the most about the ship's food, gave it a seal of approval, flashing a simple thumbs up so as to not interrupt his ferocious eating. Once everyone was finished, Gonzalez cleared his throat.

"I wanted to congratulate James and Nikki on their successful EVA today," he said, pausing for a brief moment of polite applause from the other crewmembers. "It was...well, it was adequate," he joked. "Anyways, I also wanted to remind you guys about the new sleep schedules. We'll be on Mars in about a week and a half, and we need to be ready to take advantage of the daylight we get there. You saw the schedule, please stick to it."

"There's no need to call me out in public," Harrison groaned. "We already talked about it."

"It's just a general reminder," Gonzalez explained quickly—though he wasn't hiding anything. "Ok, everyone?"

"Got it, sir," replied Jordyn.

"Good," nodded Gonzalez. "Last of all, I know you're looking forward to tomorrow night's data dump, but make sure you have the scheduled tasks done first, ok? I don't want a replay of what happened two weeks ago, got it?"

"Sure thing, Gonzo," James said. This time it was his fault the crew was getting this lecture—he'd taken some shortcuts so that he could see a video of his young son's preschool graduation.

"Alright," Gonzalez finished with a grin. "Now, what's for dessert?"

"Tiramisu," replied Mike. "Don't worry Aaron, I made you some plain chocolate pudding so that there's no coffee to worry about. I've got your back."

"Thanks," Aaron replied, sounding equal parts grateful and unenthused. "I'm glad NASA thought of-"

A sharp cry of pain suddenly filled the room, cutting off Aaron and making James flinch. Panic, however, was unnecessary.

"Sorry," Jordyn winced, floating backwards as she grabbed at her right calf. "Bad cramp, that's all."

James quickly stuck his fork to the Velcro on the wall before pushing himself gently towards where Jordyn was floating. He grabbed her by the leg, stretching it out and pushing the ball of her foot back towards her body while simultaneously massaging her smooth, toned calf. "Ow," she groaned. "Not so hard, James. No, don't stop either, it's helping."

"Don't get all hot and heavy while we're still here," teased Gonzalez. "Or Houston will hear about it."

"Shut the hell up," retorted Jordyn. After another couple of seconds, she motioned for James to let her go, which he promptly did. "Damn that was bad," she said, testing out her leg gingerly. "Thanks, James."

"You just ran a marathon," replied James. "Your body is low on nutrients, so it's to be expected that you'd cramp up. You should probably take some ibuprofen for any muscle inflammation, and you really ought to have another portion of food. Can we make that happen, Gonzo?"

"You're the flight surgeon," he replied. "Your wish is my command. Well, actually, it's Mike's command. Get the girl some more food please, Mike."

James returned to his dessert, feeling invigorated and truly useful for the first time in a while. He was sick of running standard health screenings for his crewmates, and even a simple cramp was a nice change of pace. He knew, however, that no unexpected health challenges for him was a good thing. He wouldn't want someone to be seriously sick or hurt, not here in space. A cramp was better than appendicitis or something like that any day.

"Well, that was exciting," said Harrison sarcastically as he finished his dessert. "Anyone up for a game of *Madden* on the PlayStation?"

"Just keep the volume down this time," grumbled Nikki.

"What's gotten into *you*?" Jordyn asked bluntly. "It's never bothered you before."

"I'll play," Aaron said quickly, saving the crew from confrontation. "What about you, James? Last time you crushed both of us."

James would normally say yes in a heartbeat, but today he just wasn't feeling it. He was still stiff and sore from his spacewalk, and he wanted nothing more than to take a hot shower—even if said shower was more of a sponge bath. "I'll pass," James said. "But I'll take you up on it after the data dump tomorrow. Sound good?"

"Sure thing," replied Harrison. "We'll just win then. Let's go, A. And yes, we'll keep the volume low."

Nikki just sniffed.

James stuck around just long enough to help wipe off his fork and stick it to the Velcro near the galley, then left the others and headed back into one of the large, inflatable modules that was above the compartment with the exercise equipment. That's where the shower and toilet were, and James was planning on taking plenty of time with each. After pausing to look at himself in the mirror, he climbed into the bathroom and was about to shut the flimsy plastic door when Nikki suddenly appeared at the end of the module.

"Sorry," she said quickly, floating towards him. "I just had a quick, uh, health question."

"What's up?" asked James. Questions from the crew were routine, but Nikki's timing was inconvenient.

Nikki paused for a moment. She opened her mouth to say something, then closed it again. "Sorry," she said finally. "I just, uh, wanted to know if you thought it was ok to take a sleeping pill. I'm worried about the coffee in the Tiramisu."

"I'd give it an hour or two first," replied James. "But that should be fine, yeah."

"Thanks," replied the geologist, forcing a smile. "Sorry to take up your time."

"It's fine," James said with a wave of his hand—a wave which made him rotate slightly in zero gravity. "But hey, Nikki..."

"What?"

"Is everything ok? You seem a little..."

"High strung?" Nikki asked with a smile.

"It's just not like you," admitted James.

"Just problems at home," dismissed Nikki. "And no, Vic and I are fine, so don't start your psych spill."

"Alright," responded James. "Just trying to do my job."

"You're being a good friend," said Nikki, her voice sincere. "Thanks for asking, I mean it."

James replied that he was happy to help—which of course he was—then watched as Nikki headed back the way she came. Her blonde hair floated behind her gracefully, framing her tight butt and long legs as she left the module. James quickly looked away.

Problems at home, eh? James knew how that could be. Problems cropped up with his wife and kids at home, too—problems he couldn't help with from millions of miles away. Still, something seemed odd about the way Nikki was acting—but it wasn't enough to overly worry James. Everybody acted odd on occasion, especially when they were crammed into a tight ship in the vacuum of space, isolated some hundred-million miles away from home. It was to be expected.

CHAPTER TWO

James' shower was unsatisfying—just as it always was on board *Perseus.* With no gravity and limited resources, showers on board were little more than a trickle of water from a hose, followed by the tedium of collecting the leftover blobs of floating water with the vacuum hose. Using the restroom wasn't much better. James would have killed for the simple pleasure of relieving himself on a normal toilet in complete privacy.

That would have to wait. The slight cough of someone entering the restroom module was signal enough that someone else was waiting their turn. James dressed quickly and headed towards the module's "sink"— another water and vacuum hose. Gonzalez was already waiting outside.

"Sorry, James," he said. "Mike's sauce is getting to me. You'd think being a Mexican I'd be used to spicy food, but damn."

"I'll clear out quick then," replied James. Unfortunately, it wouldn't matter much. The ship was so small that the smell would spread everywhere anyway.

"Sure thing," said Gonzalez. "Oh, I have one more assignment for you before you hit the sack, James," he continued, lowering his voice. "You need to talk to Jordyn about yesterday."

James sighed. "Can't it wait? We're less than a week from Mars. All this stupid stuff will go away as soon as people get some space."

"Some space from space," joked Gonzo. "But yeah, you need to talk to her. It's an order."

"Well, yessir then," answered James as he gave a mock salute. "I'll go track her down."

James pulled himself from the restroom module and down into the ship's lab and exercise unit, dreading yet another awkward conversation. As the ship's flight surgeon, James wasn't only in charge of the crew's physical health—he was also in charge of their mental health. In general, everyone seemed to be doing fine—better than fine, considering their circumstances—but being stuck in such a confined space would get on anybody's nerves after a while. For James, that meant that he didn't only play the role of doctor, but that of peacekeeper too—if it didn't require intervention from Commander Gonzalez, obviously. He hated it. Sometimes it was hard enough to take care of himself.

Fortunately—or perhaps unfortunately—James didn't have to wait long to confront Jordyn. She was already strapped into the treadmill, walking briskly.

"What are you doing?" James asked, a tad exasperated. "You just ran a damn marathon, Jordyn."

"Pacing helps me think, you know that," she replied. "It's better than just floating around or something. I just want some gravity, you know?"

"I hear you," agreed James. "But that's the point. We'll have plenty of work to do on Mars. We agreed you'd take it easy if I let you run the marathon."

"Fair," sighed Jordyn, reaching for the controls and turning off the treadmill. She unclasped herself from the elastics, then floated to face James.

"You excited for the data dump tomorrow?" asked James. "Last one before Mars, eh?"

Jordyn shook her head and laughed. "Cut the crap, James," she said. "I know Gonzo wants you to talk to me about yesterday. Let's get this over with. I know neither of us wants to do it."

"I'm like space HR," shrugged James. "It won't be a big deal. Can we go to the auxiliary lab?"

Jordyn nodded, and the two friends descended into the inflated auxiliary lab connected just below the exercise room and the restroom module above it. The auxiliary lab was more of a glorified Kevlar balloon filled with rows of storage and equipment. The only interesting things the room contained were a large window to the outside, and a small compartment containing live plants underneath a row of growing lights. James stopped himself before he floated into the window—it was certainly strong enough to take a little bump, but it still made James nervous.

"Alright then," said James. "I know you want to get to writing Derek before the data dump, so we can be quick. How are you two by the way?"

"We're doing fine," nodded Jordyn. "It's just like a deployment—you know that. And my father in law's cancer has us all worried. How is Claire doing?"

"She's doing as fine as she can for being outnumbered by our kids," laughed James.

"You two are crazy for starting so early," teased Jordyn.

James smiled. While he didn't necessarily enjoy playing psychologist, talking with Jordyn was like a breath of fresh air. She was probably the only person James could talk openly with on the ship, and James knew she'd always tell him exactly what she was thinking. He wanted to talk with her about the upcoming Mars landing—Jordyn undoubtedly had special insight as the crew's pilot—but he had to get business out of the way first.

"So, yesterday," he began awkwardly. "I assume Gonzo has already dealt with things?"

"There's nothing to deal with," Jordyn replied with a roll of her eyes. "I snapped at Harrison, big deal."

"Everyone in the ship heard it, Jordyn. It was more than a snap."

19

"Ok, a shout," Jordyn said, smirking mischievously. "I just got sick of him always using my towel after he exercises. It's gross. I lost my temper."

"Is that all it was?" inquired James, pressing for more information. He much preferred his role as doctor, but he knew that his assigned psychologist duties were necessary and important.

"Oh come on, James," Jordyn said defensively. "You're a doctor, not a shrink."

"I've actually been trained in both," replied James patiently.

"Well it doesn't take either to know that everyone on the ship has cabin fever," responded Jordyn. I got mad. I'm sorry. It won't happen again. Maybe if I was allowed to jog more, it wouldn't build up so much."

"You're sure it was just the fact that he used your towel?"

Jordyn rolled her eyes again. "Of course not. You know how it is. I'm sick of bumping into people, smelling people, and literally drinking filtered piss. I'm also pretty damn sick of being in this sea of testosterone!"

"I can understand that," nodded James.

"Look, you're one of the good ones," Jordyn said, her volume dropping from its crescendo. "But you don't get it. I've caught everyone eyeballing me—yes, you too, and no, that's not an attack. It's just how it is. Harrison is the worst. I'm sick of his eyes on my chest and legs."

James bit his lip. "I'm really sorry," he said slowly. "I-"

"You're not the problem," Jordyn explained quickly. "I really mean that. We're friends. But look, there're two fit women and five men on board—and guess what? No one's had sex in a damn long time—hell, Aaron's still a virgin. That just means little things that I might even consider a compliment on Earth are super grating out here."

"I still don't want to be *part* of the problem," James said somberly. "Do you think this is something we need to take up with Flight back in Houston?"

"No, James. Please just drop it. I'm fine. We're all fine. We've just all been in everybody's space for 9 months. It's part of the job, and I lost my cool. That's on me."

James nodded thoughtfully. His psychology training told him he should press Jordyn a little more—but his role as a crewmate and friend told him that now wasn't the time. "Alright," he said finally. "I trust you, Major. But I am serious about what I said. If this goes on, or gets worse, please talk to me. I'll tell Nikki the same."

Jordyn sniffed, once again casting her eyes upwards. "Good luck with that," she muttered. "She's part of the problem lately."

"What do you mean?"

"She's been acting like a drama queen," Jordyn shrugged. "Speaking of shrink time like this, she's the one that needs to be talked too. She's been acting super weird lately."

"She *was* pretty...stern today," James agreed.

"That's not like her," Jordyn said. "Come on, she's like the bubbliest person on board—except for maybe Mike. You think something's up with her and Vic?"

"That's not my place to say right now," answered James. "But last I heard he was doing fine back home. Maybe she's just feeling the same thing you are."

"Maybe," grunted Jordyn. "But I'm not the one being a bitch about it."

"She's not the one shouting at everyone over a sweat rag."

Jordyn stared at James, her eyes nearly bulging from their sockets. James instantly regretted what he had said, but before he could apologize, Jordyn's lips cracked into a smile.

"Very funny," she said. "Now am I free to go, Doc?"

James nodded. Jordyn smiled again, and actually reached out to put a hand on James' arm.

"Hey," she said. "In all seriousness, I'm glad I have someone on board I can talk to. I hope you feel the same."

"Thanks," replied James. He knew Jordyn was being sincere, but that didn't change the fact that she had gotten snippy with him.

Jordyn left James alone with his thoughts in the module. She was certainly right—about a lot of things. James knew that everyone was struggling with being in the same confined space for so long—he was struggling with it too. No amount of preflight training or psychological evaluation could prevent it—people just needed to deal with it.

James let out a sigh of concern. He felt a little guilty about what Jordyn had said about the men of the ship looking at her, but that wasn't his number one worry. No, James was more concerned about what Jordyn had mentioned about Nikki. Nikki *was* acting strange lately. As Jordyn had said, Nikki was generally happy and bubbly. She was talkative at meals, chipper during exercise, and she made a point to ask everyone about their families on a regular basis. But lately she seemed wound up like a coiled spring. Her impatience with James during the spacewalk and her relative silence the rest of the evening only served to make James feel more uneasy.

It would be solved with time—James knew that. Mars was just days away. Pretty soon *Perseus* would enter Mars' orbit, and the only thing visible through the auxiliary lab's window would be the planet's red surface.

James pushed himself back towards the exercise module, throwing himself into a lazy, weightless summersault just for the fun of it. He pushed off that module's wall with his feet, propelling himself through the main lab and into the ship's galley. Aaron shouted something about a touchdown as he and Harrison played in the rec module above.

While the thought of decompressing with a video game seemed appealing—NASA had allowed video games for just that reason—James was truly exhausted. He had plenty of tasks due tomorrow, and he wanted to finish them so he could dedicate his time to his incoming mail. Instead of pushing himself up into the rec module, James headed down into the sleeping compartment.

The sleeping section was another inflatable module, made of Kevlar and other advanced materials just like the auxiliary lab. The individual sleeping compartments—nothing more than glorified closets with flimsy accordion doors—were assembled by the crew while *Perseus* was still in Earth's orbit. At the very least the compartments blocked most noise and allowed for at least a little privacy.

Two of the three compartments closest to the module's entrance were open, each revealing a sleeping sack stuck to the wall with Velcro and a few storage compartments. The compartments were just big enough for an astronaut to sleep with their arms floating in front of them—the typical position in zero gravity.

James' attention wasn't drawn to the two open compartments. It was drawn to the one that was still closed. The name "NICOLE PRINCE" was printed in bold letters, with a smattering of random stickers stuck below it.

James caught one of the handholds and paused outside Nikki's door. He was concerned about her—and it was clear he wasn't the only one. Jordyn was concerned about her too. James briefly considered knocking—but he didn't want to wake her if she was sleeping. No, he'd talk to her tomorrow. Just to make sure everything was ok. Once they were on Mars, things would get better. There'd be more space, more things to do, and something to explore.

James looked once more at Nikki's door, then pushed himself down to the lower row of sleeping compartments. He pulled himself into his own tiny room, slid the flimsy door shut, and took a deep breath. It was the first time he had really been alone all day.

CHAPTER THREE

It wasn't a particularly loud noise that ripped James from a pleasant dream. The ship's alarms weren't even as loud as a typical smoke detector back on Earth, but this one's tone and repetition were enough to instantly alert James' mind to the severity of the situation—even as he fought his way out of his sleeping bag in a groggy daze.

James fumbled for a moment with the simple lock on his sleeping closet's flimsy door, but he was soon floating in the middle of *Perseus'* sleeping module and its rows of sleeping closets. He quickly grabbed hold of one of the compartment's many handholds and launched himself forward towards the module's computer station, barely missing Harrison as he swung open his room's door and poked his head out in a panicked daze. "What the Sam Hill is goin' on?" he asked, but James was too busy to answer.

It didn't take long for James to figure out what was going on. The computer screen was illuminated in red, and bold white letters spelled out the warning.

EXTERNAL AIRLOCK MALFUNCTION

"Well that can't be good," Gonzalez said bluntly as he arrived at James' side. Gonzalez quickly cleared the message from the screen and silenced the audible alarm, then input a command to close the door again. The warning message instantly popped back up, and the alarm began to sound again.

"Aaron!" snapped Gonzalez. "Get back to the rear node and figure out what the hell is going on!"

"I'm already on it," Aaron shouted back, already shooting out of the sleeping module, into the kitchen, and out of sight.

"It's saying there's a leak," James said, pointing to a section of the screen that showed air pressure. Sure enough, the air pressure reading from the airlock read zero—it was a complete vacuum in there.

"Marx!" Gonzalez barked.

"Yes sir." replied Jordyn, wrestling a shirt on as she emerged from her own sleeping compartment.

"Get to the command module *now*," ordered Gonzalez. "If we've been venting oxygen we could be way off course. Nikki, I want you on the radio with Houston ASAP. Everyone else I want in the kitchen right away. Let's move people!"

James didn't waste any time following Gonzalez' orders. He was the first to arrive in the kitchen, followed immediately by Mike and Harrison. The initial panic of the alarm was starting to wear off, but James knew that they could still be in serious trouble. A malfunctioning door could easily be the result of an electrical shortage, which could easily lead to a fire. *That* would lead to a very quick death.

"I've got a visual on the exterior door through the window!" Aaron shouted from the rear node, his voice carrying easily through the modules that separated him from James and the rest of the crew. "I can't get it closed from here either. The door is jammed open!"

"What do you mean it's open?" Harrison asked incredulously. "Why the hell would it be open?"

"It's about halfway open," reported Aaron. "It looks like it's physically jammed on something that won't let it close. The computer isn't giving me any electrical warnings other than the failure to close."

"That makes no sense," Harrison muttered. "It had to have opened itself."

"It sealed just fine when Nikki and I got back yesterday," James said, equally puzzled. "Maybe a hatch broke, or a seal. The pressure could have blown the door open."

"We'll have to look at it from the outside," said Gonzalez. "James, I want you and Aaron suited up and outside in fifteen minutes. We'll seal off the back node and use it as an airlock—it was designed for that use in an emergency anyways. Can you do that? You were the last man in."

"Sure," James replied, his body instantly growing tense with stress. "But don't you think we should talk to Houston first? I mean, what's the immediate danger if it's just a stuck exterior hatch?"

"I agree with James," Mike said, floating next to the compartment's tiny microwave. "We need to be controlled with this, we need to be ca-"

"If the airlock had an explosive decompression we could be looking at exterior damage," interrupted Gonzalez. "The exterior airlock door faces back towards the main engines and service module, and damage there would mean we're screwed. That's not to mention the fact that we may have been thrown off course. We're nearly to Mars and we're not going to lose it because of some damn-stupid problem. And if something outside is about to fail and make an even bigger damn-stupid problem, we can't afford to wait twenty damn-stupid minutes for Houston to respond! They probably haven't even gotten the emergency signal from *Perseus* yet, and Nikki won't hear back from them for another ten minutes after that!"

"Fair enough," Mike answered tensely, swayed by Gonzalez' reasoning.

Gonzalez started barking more orders, instructing the rest of the crew to empty out the rear node while Aaron and James hurriedly put on their EMU suits. Thanks to NASA's cerebral way of planning for every possible occurrence, Two of *Perseus'* EMU suits were always stored in the rear node, just *outside* the interior airlock door.

A decade or so ago, James would have spent at least a half hour breathing NASA's special mix of almost pure oxygen before sitting through an airlock's half-hour-long depressurization cycle. Fortunately for the crew, however, *Perseus'* EMU suits were brand-new, state of the art pieces of equipment that allowed the astronauts to have a fully pressurized atmosphere while still providing full mobility. That meant that the only limit to how fast James and Aaron could get outside was the amount of time it took them to get their suits on and depressurize the node.

Even though they were rushing, James double checked every single fitting on the suit. There could be no room for error. His radio connected to *Perseus*. Check. He could hear and talk to Aaron. Check. The suit was good to go. Check. Gloves sealed, cap on, helmet sealed. Check.

Mike gave the two men a thumbs up before closing the hatch between the rear node and the rec room that Jordyn was jogging in just six short hours ago. A split second later and air was hissing out of the node as *Perseus* slowly vented air directly outside, unlike the airlock which would have pumped air back into the ship. Only a minute or two later the sound was gone, and James and Aaron found themselves staring into the star-dotted blackness of space.

"For the record, I think we should have waited for NASA, too," Aaron said, clipping his safety harness to one of the external handholds before carefully pushing himself outside. He sounded breathless and nervous.

"I heard that," Gonzalez said over the radio. "And I get where you're coming from—this one's on me. Let's just take a quick look at our situation, and then beers are on me. Err, I guess a cherry Kool-Aid for you, Aaron."

James followed in Aaron's steps, carefully clipping and unclipping his safety harness as he moved from the exterior of the node onto the outside of the airlock. The two men moved slowly, carefully examining each inch of metal in search of damage. Everything looked ok, even the delicate solar panels that extended from the ship's sides. They'd have to check those up close later, James knew, but things were starting to look more minor than he originally feared.

"Hey you two," Gonzalez said after a minute or two. "Jordyn just told me that we're still on course. We're barely a meter off, and most of the added momentum is straight ahead."

"That would imply that the decompression wasn't totally explosive," deduced Aaron. "That's good news."

"So, we just need to figure out the airlock hatch," added James.

"Roger that," answered the mission commander.

Their quick external inspection complete, James decided to move towards the actual airlock door. His helmet's heads-up display showed that he'd only been outside for ten minutes or so—which meant that he'd only been awake for almost twenty. They would be hearing Houston's freak-out session any second now.

"I've disabled any automatic controls on the exterior hatch," Harrison said over the radio as James and Aaron drew nearer. "It's all manual—all dead. It's not going to open up or close on you guys unless you want to muscle it."

"Thanks, Harrison," Aaron said simply. "I'm still concerned it's a software thing—not a hardware one. Let's be careful, James."

"You don't need to tell me twice," mumbled James as he reattached his safety harness for the last time before pulling himself over the edge of the airlock and coming face to face with the rear-facing hatch.

James was surprised to find that apart from the half-opened hatch, nothing at all seemed wrong with the airlock module. There was no damage, no chipped metal, no scouring around the rim of the opened door. In fact, it looked no different than it did the day before when James entered in behind Nikki and looked out the window. Things looked so normal that James was honestly surprised when the hatch didn't budge in the least. He gave it a solid tug and a strong push, but it didn't even twitch either way.

"Could be a burned-out servo or something," Aaron said. "But it was designed to be operated manually even if that were the case."

28

James nodded thoughtfully inside his helmet as he carefully reached out to get a better grip. He wanted to inspect the hinges, just to see if there was some bit of debris wedged inside.

"Hey guys," a voice belonging to Jordyn said over the headset. "Houston's tizzy-fit just came through on the main radio. Just so you know, it appears we have some sort of problem with the airlock."

"So maybe five, ten minutes until we get some real answers," Gonzalez replied. "Jordyn, Nikki, patch it through to everyone when their response comes through."

"Roger," one of the women replied. James couldn't tell which one, he was too busy focusing on the hatch. Something was off.

"That's not normal," Aaron said from James' side.

It wasn't normal at all. There was something metallic jammed in the hatch's hinge. Unlike the surrounding metal that looked polished and clean, this piece was darkly colored and almost rough looking. James carefully reached a gloved finger out and prodded it. It was definitely stuck fast.

"Can I see that pair of plyers?" James said, reaching a hand out towards Aaron, who readily responded to the affirmative.

It took a few tries, but James was finally able to get a good grip on the foreign object. With Aaron helping to apply leverage to counteract weightlessness, James pulled firmly back on the object. It gave slightly, and after another two tries the object came free. The source of the malfunction removed, the hatch swung open slightly.

"Hey," Harrison said over the radio. "The alarm in here just went off. The computer is telling me I have remote control again. I'm going to try to close the hatch, stay clear guys."

Sure enough, the hatch silently closed like normal, the noise of the servos lost in the vacuum of space.

"That's great," Aaron replied happily. "I think we're done out here, don't you think, Gonzo? We'll wait to re-pressurize until Houston can go through the numbers and check the software for bugs. Sound good?"

"Roger," replied Gonzalez. "Come on in, guys. I'm sure we'll be out again later once Houston gets their shit together."

Aaron gave James a solid pat on the back, barely noticeable through the bulky EMU suit. "James?" Aaron asked when James didn't reply right away. "Hey, nice work man. You ok? James?"

James didn't answer. He was too surprised by what he held in his gloved hand. It was a bolt. Not just any bolt, however. James had seen three other ones just like it, only yesterday.

"No way," Aaron said, also recognizing the bolt that belonged to the electrical box that James and Nikki were working on yesterday. "What are the odds of that? A little bolt like that, stuck right in the hatch. Maybe Nikki had it on her the whole time. Stuck in her work bag or something."

"Maybe," James replied. But something still seemed off. "Even if the bolt got stuck there by chance, how did the hatch open in the first place?" he asked, repeating the same question that was assuredly on everyone's minds. "You really think a software glitch would just open a hatch? If that's the case, we could be seriously screwed. I know you've seen '2001, A Space Odyssey.'"

"Hal didn't have to compete against me and everyone back in Houston," Aaron joked. James could tell that he was trying to sound optimistic, but if there was anyone on the crew who realized the gravity of the situation, it was Aaron.

Their work outside *Perseus* done for now, James followed Aaron back to the node's hatch, taking it slow just to avoid any accidents. James' stress levels were only just starting to drop back to normal levels—but with the ship looking unscathed and their course unaltered, he knew they were out of any immediate danger. Sure, the idea of a software glitch opening hatches was worrisome, but James had absolute trust in Aaron and the scientists back in

Houston. He was just hoping that he could get back to bed while Aaron had to deal with the twenty-minute communication delay. The poor guy would probably be fiddling with this for the next seventy-two hours—and if it wasn't fixed the Mars landing would probably be pushed back a few days. James groaned, his breath momentarily fogging up his helmet. The crew needed to get off this ship.

Minutes later, James was hanging on just outside of the node's hatch, watching as Aaron carefully entered the makeshift airlock. Once he was inside, James entered, feet first, so that he could close the hatch manually. He didn't want to do it automatically.

"It's been, what, ten minutes since Houston's last transmission?" Gonzalez said over the radio as James pulled the hatch closed and began to spin the wheel that manually sealed the door. "Nikki, how long ago was your transmission?"

The hatch completely sealed, James pointed for Aaron to re-pressurize the node. Soon, James began to hear noises from outside his suit—the hissing of air, the chirp from the computer indicating full pressure, the dull "click" from Aaron as he detached his helmet. James eagerly followed suit—he had an itch on the back of his head that was driving him crazy.

"Hey, Nikki," Gonzalez said again. "Hey, are you reading me? When was your-"

James quickly removed his headset, cutting off Gonzalez as he got to work scratching his itchy head. James wondered why no one at NASA had figured out a way to put a head-scratcher in one of these things. The EMU suits had a straw for water, their own climate control, and everything else they'd need to keep someone alive in the vacuum of space, but there was no way to scratch a bad itch. Or a way to take a proper piss for that matter.

Once again, James beat his spacewalking companion out of his EMU suit. He carefully secured it with Velcro straps in its customary place just outside the malfunctioning airlock, then got to work opening the hatch to the main interior of *Perseus.* He was sure that Gonzalez would be waiting for them, probably with a bag of Kool-Aid as a joke for Aaron, ready with a few more orders to get the ship back in perfect condition. What James opened up to instead, however, was chaos.

"WHAT THE HELL DO YOU MEAN SHE'S NOT IN THERE WITH YOU?!?" Gonzalez shouted furiously from his position way up towards the nose of the ship. He was yelling into the command module where Jordyn must be, but his voice easily carried through all of *Perseus.*

Harrison suddenly crossed in front of James' path as he shot from one of the upper inflatable rec rooms, across the kitchen, and into one sleeping module. "Nikki!" he shouted. "NIKKI!!!"

"What's going on?" a confused Aaron asked from behind James.

"GET IN HERE!!!" Gonzalez shouted as he saw James and Aaron. "Get over here, now!"

"What's wrong?" James asked, his insides tightening into knots as he propelled himself forward. Just when he was crossing the exercise room he was suddenly struck by Mike, who shot out of the lower auxiliary lab in a panic.

"Dammit!" James cursed as he spun into the side of the module, whacking his head painfully. "Would someone tell me what the hell is going on in here?!?"

"It's Nikki," Jordyn said, suddenly appearing at James' side. "She's, uh…"

"Is she conscious?" James asked quickly, his medical training kicking in. "Where is she? Is she breathing?"

"No-" replied Jordyn quickly, but James was already talking over her.

"Where is she then?" he demanded. "How long has she been unconscious, where is she at?"

"Just shut up and listen!" shouted Jordyn.

"WHERE IS SHE?!?" James shouted right back. There was no time to waste.

Jordyn paused, locking eyes with James. James quieted down instantly—something was wrong, very wrong.

"She's gone," Jordyn said softly.

James took a deep breath, gathering his thoughts as he tried to figure out his next move. He had been trained for this, sure, but he *never* thought it would actually happen. "Let me look at her," he said weakly. "Maybe it's not too late."

Jordyn shook her head, her jet-black ponytail waving behind her face in zero gravity. "No," she said forcefully. "You don't get it. She's gone, James. Nikki isn't on board *Perseus*."

CHAPTER FOUR

"NIKKI!!!" shouted James as he flew from module to module, crashing against walls as he ripped open the bathroom dividers, then the sleeping closet openings. "NIKKI!!!"

He paused for a moment after checking Nikki's compartment for the umpteenth time just to catch his breath. Everyone had already checked here at least a dozen times. They had checked everywhere.

James slammed his fist against the wall. He knew every nook and cranny of *Perseus*—he and the other crew members had already spent nearly nine months on board. That was a lot of time to be crammed in here, time spent staring at the same walls and people day after day. James was even to the point where he could tell who had eaten lately just by the position of their spoon on the Velcro board. He could tell who had exercised recently by the last treadmill pace. He could even take an educated guess on who was in the bathroom at any given time. Nine months in the same ship with the same people had made him pick up on every little thing.

None of that could help him now. There wasn't a single module that held Nikki, not one. The inflatable module with the bathroom—empty. The exercise room and science module—empty. The sleeping module, kitchen, and auxiliary lab—all empty, just like the Orion+ capsule and the Mars Descent Vehicle, or MDV. There was nothing in Nikki's sleeping compartment—nothing unusual other than the obvious lack of the woman whose belongings were still here. It was probably just his mind playing tricks on him, but James could have sworn that Nikki's sleeping bag—still stuck fast to the wall—held a bit of warmth from the woman's body heat.

"Everyone in the galley, *now*!" ordered Gonzalez, authority dripping from his voice. "Everybody over here. Come on!"

"I'm still looking," Harrison replied weakly, shock still apparent in his voice's timbre. "I want to go check the command-"

"I've already checked it twice!" exclaimed an exasperated Aaron. "She's not here."

"GALLEY!" bellowed Gonzalez.

James ripped his eyes from Nikki's sleeping compartment and pulled himself towards the kitchen module just as the others began to congregate. Shock was apparent in each of their faces—and the eyes of those who weren't crying were cold glass.

"What do we do?" asked Mike to nobody in particular. "What does Houston say? Do we go outside and look?"

"We were just out there," Aaron said shakily. "I didn't...we didn't see anything, right James?"

"That's enough," Gonzalez said, almost whispering. His voice was dangerously quiet, and it instantly commanded obedience.

Gonzalez looked at each of the remaining six crewmembers as he chewed on his lower lip. "She's not here," he said simply. "So, what the hell happened?"

Nobody answered.

"Who saw her last?"

Silence.

Gonzalez chewed on his lip a moment more, a vein on his forehead starting to throb. Suddenly, he lashed out with his fist, ramming it against the module wall. "WHO SAW HER LAST?!?" he shouted.

"Stop shouting!" Jordyn responded. "We all saw her last night at dinner—I saw her go to her sleeping module. Everyone else was asleep when the alarm went off."

"Someone had to have seen something," Gonzalez said, his voice cracking. "Wasn't anyone up?"

"It's like 0300," Mike said. "No."

An awkward silence fell over the crew. Harrison sniffed audibly.

"Is Houston going to order another spacewalk?" Aaron said, his voice cracking too. "I mean, if she's not on the ship..."

"What does Houston say?" Jordyn said. She was clearly the coolest head in the room. James' head, on the other hand, was spinning.

"How the hell should I know?" Gonzalez replied, his frustration clearly meant towards the situation, not the crew. "They're still ten damn minutes behind us."

There was another awkward pause. Aaron, who was clearly crying now, cleared his throat to speak.

"She's got to be outside," he said softly. "I mean, the airlock alarm—there's really no denying it. Do you think she was in there when the error occurred?"

"What error?" challenged Harrison.

"I don't know, a computer glitch. An automatic opening."

James pursed his lips. A computer glitch wasn't out of the question, but it seemed unlikely. Was it some other kind of accident? Had Nikki gone to the airlock and unintentionally started a decompression? Why on Earth would Nikki even be in the airlock at such an unusual hour. None of it made any...

36

An invisible hand seized James' throat, freezing him where he floated. It all made sense. Nikki's change in behavior. Her sudden stress. Her short temper with crewmates who were generally friendly with one another.

James wanted to speak, but he couldn't. It was all he could do just to look down from where he floated, down towards the sleeping module and its rows of compartments. Nikki's door was open. It hadn't been open when James decided not to check on her last night.

CHAPTER FIVE

After the initial, panicked search of *Perseus* revealed nothing, James and the rest of the crew endured hour after hour trying literally everything they and Houston could possibly think of. Mike and Jordyn were tasked with a spacewalk outside, finding and seeing nothing. When that failed, NASA suggested using *Perseus'* wide band radar to scan for objects in near space—but that too found nothing. The airlock faced aft, towards the back of the ship—a blind spot to the radar due to the location of the engines and service module. If Nikki had been ejected that way her body was likely trailing *Perseus'* exact trajectory, the distance between the two bodies increasing by the minute.

From the constant, delayed communications reaching the crew from Earth, it was clear that NASA was still trying to locate something from their end. Unfortunately, James knew that finding a small human body in the vastness of interplanetary space was like finding a needle in a haystack, only at one-thousand times the scale. No Earthbound telescope or radar system would find her, not without exact coordinates. It was clear from the stunned-yet-calm attitude that had taken over the crew that the others knew this, too.

With the immediate recovery of Nikki's body clearly impossible, NASA quickly had the crew turn to matters of their immediate safety. There was still a chance that the airlock had malfunctioned somehow, and Houston was already having Aaron comb over as much data as he could muster as mission control did the same.

The crew all had the same questions. Why was Nikki in the airlock in the first place? Why hadn't she been sleeping just like the rest of the crew? James knew the answer, though he couldn't bring himself to say it out loud. He knew what had happened.

"I'm just going to say it," Jordyn said, arms folded across her chest as she floated in the kitchen module, across from James and the remaining members of the Ares I crew. Several hours had passed since the alarm, Nikki's disappearance, and the crews desperate search. The eyes of James' crewmates were bloodshot from fatigue and stress. James could tell that they were all on a knife's edge.

Jordyn paused, clearly hesitant to say what she was thinking. "Go on, Major," said Gonzalez.

"It was suicide," said Jordyn bluntly.

"We don't know that," argued Mike. "We don't know anything yet."

"Yes, we do," Jordyn argued. "We're not stupid. Nikki's been acting odd for a while now, and I know that all of you noticed it, too. Airlocks don't just open by themselves, and even if she was using the automatic controls, it's a four-step process. She snapped, she went to the airlock, and she-"

"Shut up," snapped Harrison, whose blue eyes were still red and puffy. "We don't know that. Come on, we all knew her. She'd never..."

"I wish we'd have noticed something was wrong earlier," Mike said, still crying. Aaron was next to him—he reached over and gave Mike a reassuring pat on the back.

James floated in complete silence. He was grateful that Jordyn had said what he was thinking, but that didn't make him feel any better. It was clear to him that his crewmates were struggling with the early stages of the grieving process—including denial, anger, and even some limited acceptance. James, however, felt guilt. White-hot, searing guilt.

"Alright everyone," Gonzalez said finally, running a hand through his black hair. This was the first time since calling the meeting that he had spoken, and he sounded exhausted. The tan Hispanic skin on his forehead was crisscrossed with lines of concern, and his eyes were bloodshot. "Can I ask everyone to just quiet down for a moment?" he asked. "Thank you."

"Not like we're talking much anyways," Aaron mumbled with somber sarcasm.

Gonzalez paused again for a moment to regain his composure while James stifled an unintentional yawn. There was no sleep in his mind, but his body was clearly exhausted. The stress of losing Nikki like this was too much. James knew that nobody, including himself, had ever considered this contingency. Not in their minds, not in the simulator, not ever.

"I'm not going to agree or disagree with anything that has been said," Gonzalez continued carefully. "The fact is we don't have any clue what happened. All we know is that our friend has...passed away."

The crew nodded somberly. Harrison began to cry again, doing his best to stay silent. This time it was Jordyn who reached out to comfort her crewmate, though her face was completely blank.

James couldn't stop thinking about the prompting to check on Nikki that he had ignored. He was well aware that Nikki was acting strange yesterday— and for the past little while—and he was also well aware of the fact that he basically chose to ignore it.

It was still hard for James to mentally comprehend suicide. Sure, he understood the cold science of mental illness, but it didn't feel right to have it happen to someone he knew so well—someone so generally happy. He just couldn't make the connection between Nikki's behavior and something like suicide, even if, as a doctor, James knew better than most how effectively mental illness could be hidden. He just couldn't believe it, even as he knew it to be true.

There was no denying that Nikki wanted to talk to him last night when she had instead asked him about the tiramisu. Was it a final effort to get some help? James wanted to believe that he had missed the signs, but he knew he hadn't. Instead, he had missed his chance to help.

Gonzalez cleared his throat to talk but didn't say anything. James could tell he was rattled like the others. There had already been several heated conversations in the last few hours—this current meeting was already much calmer than the others. Gonzalez and Jordyn had been especially on edge. In the chaos of the alarm, Gonzalez had assumed that Nikki would have followed Jordyn into the command module so as to use the main radio to contact Houston. Jordyn figured that Nikki was probably using one of the computer terminals in either the rec room or the kitchen. Neither of the two—or anyone else for that matter—realized that Nikki was simply gone until James and Aaron were back inside.

"So what do we do now?" Aaron asked, breaking the latest round of silence.

"We don't really have a choice, do we?" Harrison said abruptly. "We abort. We're missing our geologist—our friend."

"Don't be ridiculous," Jordyn said dismissively. "The whole mission is designed with a three-month stay on Mars. We can't just zip around Mars and go home, the orbits don't line up. You know that."

"That's enough," Gonzalez interrupted before the conversation could get out of hand like the previous ones. "Look, Major Marx is right—we can't just turn around. We've got our orbital insertion burn coming up in less than forty-eight hours, and we've got to do it if we want to get home."

"Couldn't we just swing around Mars and return to Earth directly?" asked Harrison.

Gonzalez shook his head. "That's why I called another meeting. I just got a message from Flight. Basically, they've offered the option to sit in this can for three months in orbit around Mars instead of going down to the surface. That way we'd still hit our correct trajectory for return to Earth. It's really the only abort option—we don't have fuel for a direct abort."

"Ugh," groaned James. The thought of staying cooped up in *Perseus* sounded horrible.

"Look," Gonzalez continued. "I won't lie. NASA wants us to go ahead with the mission. I feel like we should too. But I wanted to put it up to a vote. Does everyone understand our options? It's simple. We keep going, or we sit in orbit."

"Let's finish this thing," said Mike quickly. All the others, including James, nodded in agreement. Only Harrison seemed hesitant, but he still voted in favor.

Gonzalez nodded approvingly, albeit wearily. "I'll let Flight know," he said. "Honestly, that's all I've got. I don't really know what else to say other than today has been hell. I think we all just need some time to process things, and we all need some sleep. I'm giving you all the rest of the day off, I'll take care of Houston."

"I'll stay up," Aaron said, stifling a yawn. "I'm sure Houston will want to go through the computers and electrical systems with me. Besides, I'm sure you could use the company, Gonzo."

"I'd appreciate it," replied Gonzalez gratefully. "Now go get some rest."

James was about to leave when Mike cleared his throat and made an odd, yet fitting, request. He wanted someone to pray for Nikki, and he asked if Aaron—easily the crew's most religious member— would offer one. Harrison, the crew's skeptic, shrugged noncommittally, but he didn't complain as Aaron offered a simple prayer asking God to look out for Nikki and the surviving members of the crew. James wasn't excessively religious, but he found the occasion calming.

It also seemed to diffuse the tension among the crew. Gonzalez apologized to Jordyn for the way he acted, and Jordyn even started to cry a little. The remaining six members of the Ares I crew took turns embracing, then they headed their separate ways. Aaron and Gonzalez headed to the command module, Mike headed off to take a shower, and Jordyn, Harrison, and James all headed towards the crew quarters to get some rest.

James was the last person to enter the sleeping module. He arrived to find both Jordyn and Harrison floating just outside Nikki's compartment, both staring inside with tears in their eyes. James stopped to see what they were looking at—the compartment looked the same as always.

"What should we do with her stuff?" Harrison asked quietly.

James paused for a moment, wondering the same thing. It was likely that Houston would have them pack it up tightly in order to make room for something else. The thought made James uncomfortable—he didn't want to go through Nikki's stuff, not soon anyway. When neither Harrison nor Jordyn said anything further, James carefully reached over, grabbed the flimsy plastic accordion-style door, and pulled it shut with a click. "Let's not worry about that for now," James said sorrowfully.

"I just can't believe she's gone," said Harrison. "She was my best friend on the crew. Never judgmental, always having fun. I can't believe I didn't see this." Harrison finished, banging his hand against the wall. He quickly gathered his emotions and bid James and Jordyn a quick "good night" before pulling himself into his own sleeping compartment and shutting it without another word.

James didn't try to say anything—he had always suspected that Harrison harbored feelings towards Nikki, and that would only mean that Harrison was in a lot of pain.

"You ok?" Jordyn asked, pulling James into an embrace.

"I could have talked to her," James said softly, fighting off his own emotions now. "Right after I talked to you last night."

"It's not your fault," Jordyn said simply, her tone still indicating understanding. She gave James a quick kiss on the cheek and then released him. "I'm going to get some rest now," she said. "I'll see you in a few hours, I'm sure. Please don't blame yourself."

"Yeah."

Jordyn grimaced, pulling James into one last embrace before heading to her own compartment. She shut the door without looking back.

James returned to his own sleeping compartment, tired, confused, and sorrowful. It had been a horrible day, both for the crew and for manned spaceflight as a whole. Nothing had ever happened like this before, and it was sure to have repercussions for the future.

His door shut, James took off his sweatpants and replaced them with a fresh pair of gym shorts for sleeping. He climbed into his sleeping bag, zipped the side up halfway, and double checked that his tablet was secured to the wall charger.

He didn't know how he'd even be able to sleep, but James knew his body still needed it. He engaged in his regular pre-sleep routine. James washed his face with a wet wipe, put in some special eye drops used to try to preserve the astronauts' eyesight after months and months in zero-g, and finally tucked his floating sweatpants into one of the storage compartments—though not before retrieving a small plastic baggy from one of the pockets. Finally, James flicked the main light off, but left his reading light on. He wanted to ponder something.

James' tablet, still stuck to the side of the compartment with Velcro, suddenly illuminated as a new notification came in. It was the planned data dump, still taking place in spite of the day's events. James' data package surely contained video clips from his wife and kids, as well as his parents, and maybe even one of his brothers or sisters.

James, however, was too focused to even notice the tablet light up. He was too entranced by the plastic baggy that floated in midair, right in front of

44

his eyes. The baggy contained a small piece of metal, not much larger than his pointer finger. It was the bolt that was jammed in the airlock hatch, safely stowed away in a plastic baggy and stuffed in his pocket the second James was out of his EMU suit earlier. James wasn't sure why he kept it, or why he didn't tell any of his crewmates about it. Perhaps it was because it was something he could remember Nikki by—yes, maybe that's why he had kept it.

James shook his head to himself, then reached out to put the bolt in the same compartment as his underwear. The bolt seemed important for some reason, and not just because Nikki had handled it. It represented some form of random chance—an act of God, something to remind James to never make the same mistake of procrastinating help again. The fact that it had stuck itself right in the hatch that Nikki disappeared out of made it special. It was almost like a cold, metal embodiment of Nikki's death.

James turned off his reading light, closed his eyes, and, surprisingly, quickly fell into a deep sleep, his arms floating weightlessly in front of him in his sleeping compartment.

CHAPTER SIX

"Hi baby!" said Claire, obviously trying her best to seem upbeat. "I just got back from taking Jane to that new nursery—you know the one I told you about last week? The one Sarah Muller runs? It seems really nice, but I guess I told you about it last week, didn't I? I'm a horrible mom, but I just needed some time off. I can't believe a ten-month-old could be so crazy after Carter was so mellow. You're lucky you knew her when she *only* pooped herself and cried."

"Fair," said James, who couldn't help but grin at his wife.

Almost two full days had passed since the accident involving Nikki, and James was just now finding the time to go through his emails and video messages. A lot had occurred since Nikki went missing, but at the same time nothing had really changed. There was still no trace of her, *Perseus* was still scheduled for an orbital insertion burn in the coming hours, and the crew—following orders from both Houston and Gonzalez—was already back in a routine, albeit a modified one that accounted for the geologist's absence.

"...so that's what Carter has been up to," continued Claire, her recording still playing on James' tablet. Only her beautiful face was visible on James' screen. It was her eyes—both a gorgeous blue-grey steel—that James had noticed when he first met her, those and her hair that couldn't be defined as either brown nor blonde. With time her kind smile and inviting eyes had become James' true home. It was so hard being away from her.

"Look James," Claire said, her voice growing stressed. "I need to tell you something. Carter got in a fight on the playground yesterday. Some older kids beat him up. Don't let it worry you—apparently he got in a few good punches."

James winced. It was hard hearing bad news from home when there was nothing he could do about it. Especially hard was the feeling that he could have helped if only he were home. There was no way to get this time back— even if he was confident that he had made the right decision in pursuing this mission.

Claire continued, now sounding artificially upbeat. "His teacher says that he's the smartest kid in kindergarten, just like his dad. Well, *she* didn't say that. I am. I mean, I don't know how smart you were in kindergarten, but...oh screw it."

James actually laughed out loud, the absurdity of his wife's humor briefly cutting through the cloud he carried. He quickly stifled it so as not to bother his crewmates—James' sleeping compartment was lined with sound-absorbing materials, but he knew from experience that noise could easily escape. There was nothing worse than being woken up in the middle of a nap by loud talking or laughter, and James knew that Aaron—who had been awake for hours and hours working with NASA—was fast asleep in his own compartment, right next to his own.

Aaron hadn't found anything wrong with *Perseus'* computer systems. There were no glitches, no viruses, and nothing that would make a hatch open itself. The computer showed that the airlock began its five-minute depressurization cycle at approximately 0201 hours, but the hatch was opened manually from the inside about fifty seconds later at 0202 hours. Opening a hatch at that point would lead to a rapid, but not explosive, depressurization that would almost instantly burst eardrums and carbonate blood—Nikki would have died painfully within sixty seconds, especially after already enduring fifty seconds of more controlled depressurization. She probably just wanted to end it.

The warning alarm began to sound the moment the door was opened. *Perseus,* recognizing the abnormal depressurization, instantly began trying to close the exterior hatch automatically, though it obviously couldn't do so due to the stuck bolt.

Perseus had a number of cameras throughout her modules, but these cameras were used infrequently. Part of it was for psychological reasons—NASA didn't want the crew to feel like they were under constant surveillance. It also didn't make sense to beam video back to Houston, not when it would take ten minutes to get there anyway, so they were usually left off unless the crew was filming something for the public. There was a camera in the airlock, and a few outside as well, but these would only be set to record manually when there was a planned spacewalk. There was no recording of Nikki to be found. What bothered James more than anything, however, was the fact that Nikki's body was probably still fairly close to the ship at the time he and Aaron were outside looking for damage, perhaps even in visual range. Had they only known, they might have been able to at least identify the body floating behind the ship.

Information was limited, but NASA and their team of psychologists had concluded the same thing as James—that Nikki had likely had a mental breakdown. She had entered the airlock without a space suit, sealed the interior hatch tightly, then began a suicidal depressurization. Then, either by design or by an urge to end it all faster, Nikki had manually opened the exterior hatch. Her body would have been propelled into space by the leftover air in the airlock, and she would have died quickly. It was suicide.

"...thinking of getting a part-time job at the school," continued Claire, her two-day old recording oblivious to what had happened. James wondered if NASA had even told her and the other families yet.

"Anyways," sighed Claire, her beautiful eyes locked onto the camera. "I know you're busy up there being an American hero and all, James, but I wanted to tell you one more little thing before I let you go. You know

Saturday is our anniversary, and I just wanted to tell you how much I love you."

Saturday was tomorrow, and James hadn't forgotten. He had actually recorded a special message last week and sent it back to Houston in the most recent data-dump so that they could send it to his wife on the actual day. He missed Claire, now more than ever.

"And I have a surprise," Claire continued. She stood up quickly and backed away from the camera, revealing her entire body. James instinctively checked to make sure his compartment door was shut—Claire was wearing nothing but lingerie.

"I've lost ten pounds since you've gone," Claire said proudly, putting her hands on her hips. There were still some stretch marks visible from her pregnancy, but she was looking fantastic. "I'd show you more," she said mischievously, "but I don't want some NASA intern accidently clicking on this, so there you go. Well, I guess I'll hear back from you soon. Gosh, I just want you to be home. I think by next time we talk you'll be on Mars!"

Claire paused thoughtfully before continuing. "Please be safe," she said softly. "I need you to come home to me. I love you, James. I miss you."

"I miss you too," sighed James. Claire blew him a kiss, and just like that the video was over.

It was enough to make James want to cry. He missed his wife and kids more than he had ever imagined when he first joined the astronaut corps, and it only reminded him of how Nikki's family must be feeling. Nikki was always coy about her personal life—she rarely spoke of her fiancé Victor and her immediate family. James could only imagine the pain they would be feeling—and James could imagine a lot. Nikki was a good friend, and her death tore at James' insides.

James wondered if NASA had let the families know about what had happened—they would have had to, right? Claire did an admiral job of hiding her concern about James' impending descent to Martian soil, but if she knew what had happened she'd be a nervous wreck. Yes, it was far better if NASA didn't say anything until they were down safely. Then again, the world expected to see seven Americans on the surface of Mars, and if one was missing someone would surely notice. James was just glad he didn't need to make those decisions—he'd gladly let the NASA bureaucrats deal with that any day.

James placed his tablet back on its Velcro patch on the side of his sleeping compartment, then slid the door open and pushed his body into the main body of the module. The orbital insertion burn couldn't be more than an hour away, and James wanted to grab a cup of coffee before he had to go strap himself into his seat in the command module.

As James exited the sleeping module and entered the kitchen compartment he was almost struck by Jordyn—who was on her way to the sleeping module herself. "I was just about to come get you," she said, quickly grabbing a hand hold to stop herself from colliding with James. "Houston moved up our burn time by five minutes or so—something about less mass in the ship."

James nodded. He was well aware that that was simply technical speak for the fact that Nikki wasn't on board anymore. Jordyn, being the pilot, would obviously know that too.

"How was your family?" she asked finally when James didn't say anything.

"I see you're the one making small-talk now," joked James weakly. Jordyn just grimaced. "They're good. Parents are doing great, so is Claire. I don't think they know yet. My guess is they'll hear once we've landed. Anyways, that's grim. How was *your* fam?"

"Derek just got a promotion," Jordyn replied happily.

"That's awesome!" James said, and he meant it. Derek was Jordyn's husband, and he and James had become golfing buddies. "So he's what now, Captain?"

"Still outranked by me," Jordyn grinned. "But that's not even the good news. I guess my father in law's last screening came back clear. He's officially cancer free."

Now *that* was really good news. James knew full well that Jordyn had been worried sick about her husband's father, and anytime that someone was able to beat cancer it made James happy. As a doctor he'd had to give out that horrible prognosis more than once.

"We're really relieved," Jordyn beamed following James' heartfelt congratulations. "So at least that's something we can focus on after a rough week. Speaking of which," she continued, lowering her voice. "How are you doing, James? Everyone else has obviously been upset, but you've really been simmering on this one more. I can tell."

"I'm alright," James replied. He meant it, but he also knew for a fact that Jordyn had him pegged. His other crewmembers had cried and mourned, but James' grief had been a little more subdued. It was hard to be sad when he was so angry at himself.

"We both know that's bullshit," said Jordyn, her voice understanding despite her words. "But I won't press you on it. Anyways, I'm going to go get Aaron up. I'll see you in a bit."

James nodded politely and headed straight for the coffee machine. He placed his typical bag into the machine and pressed a button, then watched as the bag slowly filled with lukewarm coffee—they couldn't risk having boiling blobs of water flying around in weightlessness. James eagerly took a sip—it was straight black, just how he liked it—and headed towards the command module. By the end of today *Perseus* would be in orbit around Mars, and James was looking forward to the break in the routine.

The Orion+ command module looked different than any other part of the ship. Unlike the rest of *Perseus*, which was designed for *relative* roominess, comfort, and efficiency, the command module was tight, cramped, and stuffed with hardware, screens, and analog controls. This was the module that was designed to get seven people back to Earth safely after carrying them through an atmospheric descent so violent that it would melt unprotected steel. The seven seats formed a circle around the floor of the module, all facing outward towards various screens and windows. One of those seats—Nikki's—had a few thoughtful letters and pictures from the crew taped to it, destined for Nikki's parents once the crew was home. It was the least they could do.

"Hey man," Gonzalez said tiredly from the Commander's seat. "Glad to see you're up. I for one wanted to do the burn while you were sleeping, just to hear you freak out, but Jordyn wouldn't let me."

"After the past few days I'd probably sleep through it," James replied quickly. "And I'm sure it's worse for you and Aaron."

"You can say that again," nodded Gonzalez grimly. "I haven't slept since it happened, at least not soundly. I feel like I blew it, man. I really do."

James opened his mouth to say something, but no words came. None of this was Gonzo's fault—it wasn't anyone's fault really. It was just...sad.

"You know what kills me the most?" Gonzalez continued when James didn't say anything. "It's not even what happened. It's the fact that she's still out there, you know? Nikki's still out there, all alone. Hell, she's probably closer to us than we think—her body probably has the same momentum as the ship. She could be following us right into orbit, just out of sight. How the hell has Houston not been able to find her?"

"Beats me," James said, putting a hand on Gonzalez' shoulder. "But Gonzo, you can't blame yourself for this. You know that."

"I know," Gonzalez replied weakly before turning his attention back to the monitor in front of him. James thought that Gonzalez looked pretty defeated—though most of it was probably just exhaustion. The doctor in James hoped that Gonzo would get two nights of good rest before the descent to the Martian surface two days from now.

Gonzalez didn't say much else, and that was fine by James, who floated sipping his coffee while contemplating the fate of Nikki's body. Soon Harrison came into the command module, followed by Mike, then Jordyn. Aaron, his eyes bloodshot and shadowed by fatigue, was the last to arrive a few minutes later, greeting everyone pleasantly before sliding into his seat next to Nikki's empty one.

"Final maneuver calculations look good," Jordyn said, tapping on a touch screen in front of her. "Houston approves. T-minus five minutes until the burn. You sure cut it close, Aaron."

"I know," Aaron replied, his answer turning into a broad yawn as he buckled himself into his seat. "I just wanted to double-check that airlock hatch again."

"Still good?" Gonzalez asked quietly.

"Roger," answered Aaron.

With the burn time fast approaching, James reminded everyone of what direction the acceleration forces would be coming from. The seating arrangement was meant to protect the crew from g-forces endured on launch and landing, but it meant that some people would be pushed sideways during orbital maneuvers. Acceleration in space was gradual, however, and it was nearly impossible to be harmed unless you were caught completely off guard.

"Thirty seconds," Jordyn said. "Houston, I am ready to take manual control if need be, and the ignition safeties have been disabled."

"Gonzalez verifies," said Gonzalez, voicing his approval as mission commander.

"Fifteen seconds," Jordyn said. "RCS thrusters enabled. Manifold pressure optimal. Let's spend some delta-v."

James turned his head to look at Jordyn, but something caught his attention instead. It was the window across the capsule, visible where Nikki's head should have been. Instead of the eerie blackness that James had grown accustomed to, the window was full of red. It was Mars, looming large.

"Ignition," Jordyn said.

James felt a slight tug of acceleration, but he didn't turn his head. He kept it locked so that he could look out the window at the rusty planet below.

CHAPTER SEVEN

There was plenty of work to be done.

Perseus' orbit around Mars was right on track thanks to the vessel's telemetry computer and Jordyn's careful eye. The descent to Mars would proceed as scheduled tomorrow morning, which meant that the crew had to make sure the MDV was packed, cleaned, and ready to go. It was careful, methodical work, which meant that James had plenty of time to think. He thought about his wife and kids back home, and the magnitude of being one of the first people on the red planet. He did think about what had happened with Nikki, but he tried to suppress it and not let it bother him—for now. There was a mission to be accomplished, and James had to be ready.

"I'm not going to do it," Jordyn said, raising her voice slightly towards Gonzalez as she shoved one of tomorrow's flight suits into the MDV. "It's stupid. It's because I'm black, and I have a vagina. That's it. It's a publicity stunt."

"That's not fair," Gonzalez began to say defensively, but Jordyn was building up a head of steam.

"I want to be known for my actions and my expertise, not some stupid PR garbage," Jordyn remarked angrily. "Besides, we all know it should be you, Gonzo. You're the mission commander."

"But it *is* him," Aaron said from his spot inside the MDV. "At least, it was. Hey Mike, can you hand me that checklist? Thanks mate."

"What are you talking about?" challenged Jordyn.

"Someone's gotta' tell her eventually," Mike said as he helped Aaron.

"Tell me what?" Jordyn said, clearly confused.

"Gonzo said he didn't want to do it," said Harrison, just beating James to the reveal. "He put it up to a vote."

"You did *what*?" Jordyn asked dangerously, her eyes narrowing towards Gonzalez.

"I'm the commander, I can do what I want," replied Gonzalez. "Honestly I don't want the infamy. It's not my style. Hey, don't look at *me* like that! I ran it by the others and put it up to a vote. You won. You deserve it. No one has worked harder than you, and you're going to have a hell of a time piloting us down tomorrow."

"It was almost unanimous," Mike added. "You only had one person vote against you."

Jordyn stopped what she was doing and looked around at her fellow crewmembers. She opened her mouth, closed it, then opened it again. "Thanks," she said, her voice cracking slightly. "I mean, really. What a huge honor."

"You deserve it," Aaron said, repeating the sentiment.

Jordyn smiled broadly, barely containing her excitement before getting things under control. "Who voted against me?" she blurted out.

"Harrison did," James said quickly, shamelessly selling out his crewmate. It was all in good fun, and he knew it wouldn't upset Harrison.

"What can I say?" Harrison shrugged. "Harrison Larsen, first man on Mars had a nice ring to it—I'm not going to lie."

The entire crew genuinely laughed for the first time since Nikki's death, even James. It was just in time, too. James knew that the crew needed to be as loose and collected as possible for the following day's descent. It would be stressful enough—even under normal circumstances.

Loading the rest of the MDV only took an hour or two, and both Aaron and Mike stayed in the vehicle to make sure it was balanced and ready to go. Jordyn and Gonzalez both headed back to the command module to make sure that Houston was comfortable with everything, including that status of the habitation module and the ascent stage waiting on the Martian surface. A serious problem with either system would mean scrubbing the mission, but James wasn't worried. NASA had spent decades preparing for tomorrow, and it was going to go fine.

Surprisingly enough, James suddenly found himself with nothing to do. All of his belongings that would be going down to the surface had been loaded, and everything up here would just stay on *Perseus* as it orbited autonomously. James figured that it was a good time to send a last quick email off to his wife congratulating her on their 10th anniversary, so he decided to head towards the sleeping module after making a quick trip to the restroom. At the very least he wanted to let Claire know how much he loved her—just in case something happened tomorrow.

What should he say? He didn't want to worry her, but he didn't want to leave anything left unsaid—just in case. Should he be frank and upfront about the danger tomorrow—easily the most dangerous part of the entire mission—or should he downplay it? The puzzle filled James' mind to the point that he almost didn't notice the sound of rummaging going on in Nikki's sleeping compartment.

James knew he had heard something, but he wanted to ignore it and head straight to his own compartment. The second sound of rustling and a muttered curse word, however, made it impossible to ignore. Curious, James pushed himself towards Nikki's compartment, stopping himself on the frame of the sliding door. The door was open, and sure enough James heard the cough of someone inside.

"Hey," James said, knocking on the flimsy accordion door. "Someone in there?"

"Just me," replied Harrison hurriedly from inside. "Sorry, I was just...uh..."

James slid the door open just in time to see Harrison stuff a piece of paper into his pocket. Caught red-handed, Harrison's face instantly turned beet red under his five o'clock shadow.

"What's going on?" James asked, slightly taken aback.

"I...uh...hell," stuttered Harrison, his face turning an even brighter shade of red. "I'm sorry, James, I know this looks weird."

"Yeah," James nodded, his suspicion building. Why was Harrison rummaging around Nikki's quarters? What was on the paper?

"Look, just promise not to tell anyone," Harrison said, his voice suddenly hushed. "Please, James, just don't tell anyone."

"What are you talking about?" challenged James. "Spit it out quick."

"It's just, I had a thing for Nikki," Harrison explained quickly. "I liked her a lot, and, uh, I'm pretty sure she felt the same. I wrote her a letter about it..." Harrison trailed off, gesturing vaguely towards his pocket before continuing. "We all know she had a fiancé at home—I didn't want to...you know, ruin her reputation or something."

A quick flash of anger filled James. Inter-crew romances of even the most minor sort were strictly prohibited, even if a simple letter was all that connected Harrison and Nikki. Hurt feelings, a falling-out, or any sort of romantic escalation could lead to psychological hell for the entire crew—and that wasn't even mentioning the potential consequences of a physical, sexual relationship. It was something that simply couldn't be risked in the vacuum of space.

James' anger, however, was quickly tempered by the fact that there was no danger of anything more between Harrison and Nikki. Nikki was gone, and it probably hurt Harrison immensely. James knew this, and he took a deep breath before continuing. "Don't worry about it," he told Harrison coolly. "But seriously, man. You know that stuff doesn't fly in this ship."

"I know," Harrison said, lowering his head in shame. "Nothing physical happened though, I swear. Just words and-"

"You don't need to tell me anything," James interrupted. "I don't want to hear it. It's done."

"Done," repeated Harrison.

Satisfied, James floated away from the door, making room for Harrison to exit. Harrison thanked James again before pulling himself up towards the kitchen, disappearing around the corner. James just shook his head in disbelief. Harrison was a consummate professional—what had gotten into him?

It was a question that quickly left James' thoughts as he entered his own compartment and shut the door. His tablet was still in the room—another one was waiting for him down in the habitation module on the surface—and he had a letter to write to his wife. There wouldn't be any time tomorrow morning.

With the accordion door shut, James powered on his tablet and entered his email app. It was a marvel of technology that James was able to read letters from home and even send video—he couldn't imagine how past explorers like Columbus and Polo would have survived their voyages without a single letter from home for years at a time. And here James was, scrolling through new emails—NASA must have allowed a final data dump—from his mom, his brother in Memphis, and even the president of the United States. He didn't care to read any of those ones now—James just wanted to read the two emails from his wife. One was labeled "To the Love of my Life," the other was titled "Happy Anniversary!" Odd that she would send two—and only five minutes apart.

James tapped on the "love of my life" one first and was pleased to find a very heartfelt letter from Claire that included pictures of her, their children, and a bonus picture of Claire in a very skimpy outfit. Simultaneously pleased and homesick, James eagerly tapped on the next email from Claire. Something, however, was different.

James Lake, the letter began.

Strange that Claire would be so formal. James continued after only a brief hesitation of thought.

James Lake,

Apologies for spoofing your wife's personal email account. This is important—please keep reading.

I don't know if you remember me from the crew bbq a few weeks before launch? My name is Victor Patterson. I'm...that is, I was...Nikki's fiancé.

NASA told me what happened to Nichole only yesterday and I'm obviously devastated. Words can't come close to describing the pain that I feel. I'm being eaten alive. NASA tells me she committed suicide—that she threw herself out of an airlock after some kind of psychotic episode.

That's bullshit.

Nikki would never do something like that. She's...she was the happiest person I knew. Our relationship was better than ever before she left, and being selected to the first mission to Mars was the proudest moment of her life. Why on Earth would she do something like this only days before your landing?

NASA assures me it wasn't an accident. They say that they've checked everything a hundred times over. That leaves me with only one conclusion.

Nikki was murdered.

James' heart stopped, and his vision constricted. A suicide was impossible enough. But *this*? He quickly re-read the last paragraph and then continued.

I realize that I might sound nuts, but this is all I can think of. I'm a local police officer from Hancaster, just months out of the academy, and I just see too many parallels to what I'm learning and reading about.

I don't know who to trust, and maybe you're not the one. I figured that out of everyone there, the doctor/flight surgeon would be the soberest, and have the most respect for human life. And frankly, if you and I are going to figure out what happened to Nikki, we need someone with your skills and an eye for detail.

Nikki was murdered, and you and I are going to get to the bottom of this. I hope I can trust you. Maybe you and I can start out by-"

James abruptly stopped reading and turned off the tablet's screen. No. This was ridiculous, this was outrageous. Why on Earth would someone be contacting him, how in the world would they even know how to in the first place? This was all crazy—of course someone close to Nikki would want to deny that it was suicide. Of course they would want to exhaust every possible resource. But this was a manned mission to Mars—the very first of human kind. The crew had spent 9 months in near total isolation, crammed inside of a small spacecraft, under constant threat of death from the icy vacuum outside. It would be illogical to assume that someone simply couldn't snap under the pressure. But yet...

Something tugged at the back of James' mind, something that pulled lightly yet firmly. There *was* something strange going on. Nikki had been acting odd, he couldn't deny it. But the way she had disappeared without a trace, leaving nothing behind, not even a note, seemed odd. And then there was the behavior of the crew. Everyone seemed absolutely devastated, but yet there was something wrong. How was it possible that everyone had simply assumed that Nikki was on the radio in a different module? And what about Harrison just now? James had caught him rummaging through Nikki's stuff in search of a letter. A letter involving intimate feelings. A letter suggesting that something scandalous was going on between an engaged woman and a member of the Ares I crew.

James sat floating for a moment, arms folded in front of his chest, the tablet floating gently in front of him. The gears of his brain struggled and churned, producing a novel idea that quickly took hold. What if Patterson—if it *was* him—was right? What if James' hadn't missed any signs of mental instability? What if Nikki hadn't committed suicide after all?

What if Nikki was murdered?

CHAPTER EIGHT

James ripped open the sleeping sack and began rummaging furiously in search of something, anything. There was very little time, and his window of opportunity was rapidly closing.

"James!" Gonzalez shouted from somewhere far away. "How long does it take you to get a single picture of your wife?"

"I've almost got it, sorry!" James lied, checking to make sure the picture of Claire was already in his pocket before getting back to his hurried search. There was nothing in the sack except for a mismatched sock and what looked like a wrapper for a tiny feminine pad. The sack still smelled like Nikki—it was easy to identify anybody's smell after nine months in close quarters—but there was nothing useful there.

James had already searched both storage drawers and the tiny Velcro bags stuck around Nikki's empty compartment, and he hadn't found anything that would support Patterson's claim. He wondered why he was risking everything for a man he'd barely met back on Earth. Perhaps it was because he'd want someone to do the same for him if the roles were reversed.

James needed to hurry. He made one last attempt to access Nikki's tablet—it was locked, just as he expected—turned out the light, and left Nikki's sleeping compartment. There was nothing there that would give any credence to the idea that Nikki was murdered. Absolutely nothing—and James was thankful for that.

Not wanting to press his luck any further, James grabbed a handhold and launched himself up towards the kitchen module. He was nearly there when Aaron barreled around the corner.

"Hey, James," Aaron said awkwardly, rubbing the blonde hair on the back of his head. "Sorry, Gonzo sent me back here to get you to hurry up. You all done?"

"All set," replied James. "You ready to make some history today, man?"

"Heck yeah I am," Aaron replied, a smile spreading across his face. "You know what? I'm honestly just excited to feel some gravity again, even if it's only a third of what..." Aaron trailed off suddenly, his eyes looking behind James and towards the sleeping compartments.

"What is it?" James asked quickly, his voice betraying him more than he would have liked. He didn't want Aaron to suspect anything, especially considering that *if* Nikki had been murdered, anyone could be the...

James quickly shook his head to clear out the ridiculous thought. He still hadn't found any evidence of Patterson's claims of foul play, and he was being stupid buying into them so much. Besides, out of everyone, it'd never be Aaron. Right?

"Sorry," Aaron said, also shaking his head before focusing back on James. "Sorry man, I just thought I shut all the sleeping compartment doors per Gonzo's orders. Nikki's is still open."

"That's my bad," James answered swiftly, figuring a tweaked version of the truth was better than an outright lie. "I opened it," he continued. "It just felt weird to be going down without her."

"I know," nodded Aaron somberly as he pushed past James and stopped to shut Nikki's accordion door. He paused for a moment, peering inside. "It sucks," Aaron concluded, shutting the door softly.

"GET THE HELL UP HERE!" Gonzalez shouted again. "We've got to be undocked in an hour or we'll miss our landing site! And I for one am *not* eating potatoes grown in crap."

"We're on our way," James laughed awkwardly, grabbing a handhold and following Aaron towards the MDV. Aaron paused to turn out the lights, casting *Perseus'* sleeping quarters into a darkness that was only punctuated by small lights on the electronics. James didn't look back—he was grateful to be leaving the cramped ship behind for a while.

The rest of the crew was just outside the MDV's hatch. Harrison, Gonzalez, and Jordyn were all busy putting their M-suits—slang for the only EVA suits they'd be wearing on the descent, the ascent, and on Mars itself. Mike already had his on except for his helmet, which floated just next to him as he flexed and moved, testing the suit's feel. The bright colors on the suit—meant to provide contrast against the constant redness of Mars—juxtaposed curiously with Mike's thinning red hair.

James had a love-hate relationship with the M-suits. Unlike any other space suit he had used, the M-suit was skin tight, very light, and specifically customized to fit every individual astronaut perfectly. It was designed to maintain pressure by relying more on the material's tensile strength than on the force of the air filling the suit. It all made for a suit that was mobile, flexible, and tough—perfect for the Martian surface. They also had the added benefit of being flattering on nearly anyone who wore them—*if* they could get them on in the first place. James was sure he'd get faster with practice, but it took a full ten minutes to get his on, and then another ten to correctly attach the rigid composite vest-backpack combo that rested on top of his shoulders. The helmet, at least, was blessedly easy to put on.

The entire crew now suited up, Gonzalez ordered everyone to their seats before sending a transmission to Houston. Everything was still on schedule, but they needed a final go-ahead from mission control before they detached from *Perseus* and began their descent. It was time that James was doomed to pass sitting awkwardly in his seat, his helmet keeping him from turning around to look at the other members of the crew.

Time passed slowly, with only Gonzalez and Jordyn speaking as they went through the checklist. The other crew members were clearly nervous, and so was James. James, however, carried an additional burden. What if this Patterson guy was right? And why had he contacted James?

James was still skeptical to the idea of foul play, but the idea haunted him even more than the idea of a suicide. It would mean that someone sitting next to him was a murderer, someone who posed a very real danger to the rest of the crew. The good news, at least from James' point of view, is that no one seemed to have any reason to attack Nikki. There was no motive, and James knew that that was important—at least according to television.

For the umpteenth time since receiving the mysterious email, James ran through the list of potential "suspects," starting with the highest rank. Gonzo had no reason to harm Nikki—in fact, he had gone through more psychological evaluations than anyone else in the crew. As mission commander, his sole focus was getting everyone to Mars and back alive. Gonzo had a wife and kids at home—there was no reason to jeopardize that.

Jordyn was beyond suspicion. James felt that he knew her better than anyone else, and he trusted her completely. Just like anyone else on the crew, she had no beef with Nikki—nothing to gain. Could it be some attention thing between the two women? No, that was absurd.

Aaron was also devoid of suspicion. The guy was religious to a fault and wore his heart on his sleeve. He was one of only two single men on the crew, but that was meaningless. The guy was a straight arrow, and James knew from experience that any guilt—regardless of the severity of the "offense"— would easily be identifiable in Aaron's actions.

Mike seemed to be faultless as well. He was everyone's best friend, and he wouldn't hurt a fly—not that James had even seen a fly in over 9 months.

Plus, Mike was gay, meaning that any sort of sexual motivation to a killing was nonexistent. No, there was no way it could be Mike.

That brought James to Harrison. Yes, James had caught him going through Nikki's compartment in search of a letter, but James felt that Harrison had been upfront with him. A potential romantic entanglement certainly seemed suspicious, but James just didn't buy the thought that Harrison would do anything this rash. In fact, Harrison seemed to be one of the crew's most level-headed individuals, and the fact that he took Nikki's death so hard only seemed to reaffirm his innocence.

"Roger, undocking now," said Jordyn, yanking James back into the present as the ship shuddered slightly. "Clear. Computer has activated RCS, and we are separating at point two meters per second and accelerating."

"Confirm," added Gonzalez. "All systems nominal. Crew ready, right gang?"

"Right," James replied, adding to the chorus of affirmative responses.

"Don't blow this for us, Jordyn," teased Mike.

"She'll do great," Aaron replied quickly. "This will be just like landing at JFK."

"Well, at least Mars will be nicer than JFK," deadpanned Harrison. "The people are probably friendlier there than back in New York."

"Cool it guys," admonished Gonzalez as he tried to fight back a laugh. "Remember that we're on camera for the descent. You know, for posterity and all."

"Or for the NTSB report," Jordyn said. "Either or."

James laughed nervously, though he was cut off by a sharp pain just between his pecs. The rest of the crew had a good laugh as well, though it was quickly cut off by a sudden roll and translation from the MDV.

"Relax everybody," Jordyn said reassuringly. "I've got this."

No one said anything else as the craft descended towards the red planet. James tried to take a deep breath to ease his nerves, but he was once again cut off by pain in his chest. James considered trying to adjust his suit, but he didn't want to give anything away.

It was the bolt. Nikki's bolt. The one that was blocking the exterior hatch from closing. James didn't exactly know why he had brought it with him, stuffed in between his undershirt and his M-suit, but he knew one thing: he wasn't going to be able to relax until he was completely, totally, and unequivocally sure that Nikki's death was just an accident.

CHAPTER NINE

Red and orange flashes illuminating the cockpit and casting spontaneous shadows all around. The shocking strength of g-forces crushing his body into his seat after 9 months of weightlessness. Creaking metal, constant shaking, and two rough jolts—first the parachutes deploying, then the heatshield being jettisoned by small explosive bolts. A sudden, firm deceleration from landing thrusters. The feeling of gravity, one third that of Earth's. And then...

Touchdown.

It was far less red than James had envisioned. Sure, he had seen picture after picture of the Martian surface, but in person the rocks, the sand, and even the sky itself looked more like a muted brownish-orange than anything.

James was third off the ladder, right in the middle. Jordyn had already spoken the words that would be remembered for centuries to come, and Gonzalez was already a few meters away setting up the camera for when the stars and stripes would be planted firmly in the ground. James made sure to step on virgin Martian soil that was untouched by the others. His first footstep was ill-defined, the texture of his boots erased by fine grained sand. The second step was on flat rock. Overcome with emotion, James mouthed a silent prayer of gratitude, then took a shaky step backwards to watch the others come out.

Aaron was next. He immediately dropped to his knees and ran his gloved fingers through red dirt before mumbling something about God's creations over the radio. Mike followed, and after quickly testing Mars' gravity he decided to leapfrog Aaron as he kneeled, clearing him easily. Harrison, the last to emerge, took his first few steps carefully. Even through his helmet James could tell that he was crying from emotion.

The rest of the sol passed quickly. There was plenty to be done, and if the astronauts wanted to sleep somewhere other than in the lander's chairs they needed to make sure that the semi-inflatable habitation module—which had been landed autonomously months prior—was functioning properly.

It was. The module, which everyone at NASA had taken to calling the SIM, responded immediately to Harrison's command to inflate—though it took over three hours for the two inflatable sections to extend to their full inflated size. While the SIM carried some oxygen on board, much of the breathable atmosphere that inflated the Kevlar-composite domes was drawn and converted on the spot from Mars' super-thin atmosphere by the module's advanced equipment.

The SIM looked like a giant plus sign from above and consisted of a rigid center module that contained the lab, kitchen, and life-support systems. The two large inflatable rooms branched off each side—one for sleeping, the other for meeting, exercise, and work. It was the latter inflatable room where James found himself now, seated around a folding table with the other members of the crew.

"A toast!" Gonzalez said happily, raising a glass of distilled water in the air. "To the finest crew of astronauts in the world! Let's make the next three months count. It's what Nikki would've wanted."

"To Nikki," Harrison said, also raising his glass of water.

"To Nikki," James echoed, throwing back a swig of water before taking one final bite of his reconstituted peach cobbler. It was super weird getting used to eating food that could fall off a fork and towards the ground.

"What time are we supposed to be up tomorrow?" asked Aaron. "I know we're setting up the auxiliary solar panels and starting some surveys, but you didn't say what time."

"I hope we get to sleep in," muttered Jordyn. Mike nodded quickly in agreement.

"Sorry," Gonzalez replied. "We need to film a team broadcast from the SIM in the morning. I'm thinking 0600. And we all still need to keep our exercise schedules. The gravity is only a third of what we'll head home to—you guys know that."

"Damn," laughed Harrison. "No rest for the wicked."

"Don't talk to me about rest," said Gonzalez. "You guys haven't even had to deal with gravity for almost a year."

"And you haven't had to deal with real work since you were made the damn mission commander," Jordyn teased sharply.

"We've barely adjusted to sols," added James, coming to Gonzo's defense. "If we throw off our sleep schedules we're gonna' be miserable. And Gonzo's right about exercise—unless you all want to have heart problems back home?"

"Listen to Doctor James," Gonzalez said with a hint of teasing. "Oh, and speaking of which, Houston says first round of Mars physicals start tomorrow, so make sure you've shaved and washed your privies."

"Ugh," scoffed Jordyn. "Gonzo, you're disgusting."

"I don't like it any more than you do," replied James with an awkward laugh. He didn't enjoy doing physicals at all. Sure, years of being in medicine had numbed the awkwardness of it all, but that was only the case with strangers. There was no way to do medical tests on his crewmates without it being extremely uncomfortable for both parties. "On that note," James said, rising from his seat, "I'm going to call it a night. Can I be dismissed, Gonzo?"

"You got it," nodded Gonzalez. "I'd actually like to play a quick round of poker if anyone is game. Winner gets to collect the first real sample."

"I'll play," Aaron said quickly. "I'm not very good though, you know that."

"Never heard that before," grunted Mike jokingly, rolling his eyes. "Prepare to get hustled."

James grinned as he walked away from the table and towards the SIM's rigid center room. He had to step carefully to keep himself from tripping. As he had mentioned to the crew, Mars' gravity was significantly less than that of Earth's—but it was still gravity nonetheless, and James had been floating for 9 months. His two-hundred-pound frame weighed more like seventy-five here. It would take getting used to—and by the time he was comfortable, their time on Mars would probably be up.

James entered the center module and headed towards the opening to the second inflatable room that served as a sleeping quarters. He really was exhausted, and he knew that tomorrow was going to be even busier. James sighed as he looked down at his loose t-shirt and sweat pants—tomorrow he'd spend another ten hours in that uncomfortable M-suit. At least he wouldn't have that bolt digging into his ribs.

The bolt. The thought made James pause before entering the sleeping room. Still unsure about the merits of his rudimentary plan, James backtracked towards the lab and paused in front of one of the lab's electronic microscopes. They were primarily designed to observe Martian samples, but they couldn't be much different than medical microscopes used back on Earth. Sure, he'd have to read up on the intricacies of the machine, but he was pretty sure that he could make it work. Using his fingers to mimic the general size of the bolt, James put his hand under the microscope to check for fit.

"Thinking of filling in as the geologist?" a voice said suddenly, startling James. It was Harrison, who stood in the middle of the kitchen looking towards James curiously. "Seriously though," he continued. "Who's gonna' check out the samples we get tomorrow?"

"No idea," James said uncomfortably, unconsciously putting his hands in his pockets. He knew being seen by the microscope wasn't a big deal, but he didn't want to arouse the least amount of suspicion, not when there was a chance—however remote—that someone on the crew had committed an act of violence.

"It ain't gonna' be me, that's for sure," laughed Harrison. "Hell, I wouldn't even know how to tell an alien cell from a grain of sand. I'll stick to making sure the SIM doesn't spontaneously combust."

"That would be a bad day," answered James, doing his best to force a laugh. "And I'm already concerned it's going to be a bad *night* sleeping with gravity again. It's going to suck."

"Yeah it is," Harrison agreed good-naturedly from where he stood in the open doorway leading to the sleeping compartment.

James stepped away from the microscope and took a few steps towards the doorway to the sleeping compartment. When he reached it, however, Harrison didn't move. He just stood there, contemplating James.

"You sure you don't want to come back and play cards?" Harrison asked, not moving from where he stood.

"Yeah, man," answered James, gesturing towards the door so that Harrison would get the hint to move.

"Oh, sorry," Harrison said oddly, stepping away from the door. "Sorry," he repeated, now gesturing for James to pass through. "Lot on my mind, I guess. We're the first people on Mars! Still hasn't sunk in yet. I'll catch you later."

Harrison clapped James on the arm before heading back towards the card game in the other room, leaving James standing with his lips pursed in thought. Surely Harrison had nothing to hide, but why was he acting so strange? Did he have something to hide after all?

James shook his head to clear it. He was still considering Patterson's request, but he wasn't going to buy into paranoia—not yet. Still tripping on his own feet, James headed into the dimly lit inflatable module that housed the crew's sleeping arrangements.

Unlike *Perseus* and its private sleeping quarters, the SIM contained a folding cot for each crew member as well as a comfortable sleeping bag. Two pop-up dressing rooms that the crew had placed near one of the walls were the only source of privacy in the whole room. That meant that the only area in the whole base that had any real sort of door was the tiny bathroom and shower room back in the rigid center section. That was ok with James. He'd trade privacy for space at the moment.

There were a number of plastic shelves and storage closets on the sides of the inflatable module—they had been intricately designed to unfold as the module inflated—and James headed towards the one where his tablet was currently charging. He unplugged it quickly, paused to glance out the tiny window that looked across the dark Martian desert, then headed straight towards his sleeping bag. He didn't bother changing before he climbed in—he knew there wasn't much time before the others started trickling in to go to sleep.

James powered up his tablet and quickly plugged in the SIM's network code. The tablet connected to the SIM's network, meaning that he had access to nearly everything in the module's computer, including his password-protected email account. Just like *Perseus,* the SIM would transmit and receive information in large data dumps. Those would now be taking place daily thanks to the power and communication systems that were landed with the SIM before the crew arrived.

A quick scroll through his emails showed that James hadn't received any new emails since he'd left *Perseus.* However, his outgoing email to Nikki's fiancé Patterson—if it *was* him sending the emails—had sent successfully. *I know we've met,* James had written. *But how am I supposed to trust you on this? What you're alleging is serious to the utmost degree, and if you're a police officer you should know that. Have you talked to any superiors? Have you thought to talk to NASA?*

James stared at his old email, his questions still unanswered. He was about to power down the tablet when his foot brushed against something in his sleeping bag.

It was the bolt from *Perseus*, tucked carefully into a small plastic baggy for protection. James couldn't think of a safer place to put it, so there it was. Its presence was enough to make up James' mind.

I still want answers, and I'm not buying this. He typed simply. He paused before adding one final sentence and hitting the send button.

How do you check for fingerprints?

CHAPTER TEN

The reply came in sometime around 0300 hours. James was pretty restless anyway, and his tablet's slight vibration was enough to wake him up entirely. Careful to keep his sleeping bag over his head, James opened up his email. There were now several emails from a variety of people, all of whom were offering congratulations on the landing. but just like before there was a strange duplicate email from Claire. James was peeved that this Patterson guy was spoofing his wife's email account, but he understood the logic. Emails from spouses and family were considered one of the few truly private things that the astronauts had.

James quickly read through his wife's real email—she was obviously relieved that he had landed safely—and made a quick note to reply to her when he had some real free time. Then it was on to Patterson's email.

James,

Thanks for taking me seriously. It means more than you know.

I'm sure there're a million questions you have for me. I'll do my best to answer them. I hope that you'll trust me. Oh, I also wanted to apologize for "using" your wife's email account. It's just a fake email account that mimics your wife's. I promise I haven't hacked or anything like that. Just wanted you to know.

I've attached a picture of my badge and license, though I know that's not terribly convincing. You can also look up Hancaster PD's website and see my name there.

James had an idea. He made a quick mental note to consider asking Claire to double-check Patterson's story. He didn't want Claire to worry, but if there really was foul play going on he'd have to let her know sometime down the line. He'd save that, however, for when—*if*—he found some real evidence.

I went to NASA right away. I was told not to worry, that they were doing everything in their power, but that it looked like suicide. I begged them to reconsider. I told them everything I told you. They didn't believe me, and I've got no evidence, no suspects. I've got nothing but my feelings, and I've pressed my luck enough. We can't go public on this, not when you guys are out there, not with the consequences of me being wrong. Or even the consequences of me being right.

While I don't believe it, I sincerely hope that it really was suicide, or at least an accident. But I can't shake the thought that it was something worse. Your reply tells me you feel the same.

Anyways. Let's get started then. We need the clichés: motive, means, and opportunity—and then we need hard evidence. I'm sure means are plentiful in space. Any ideas of motive? Did anyone have it out for Nikki? I can't seem to think of anything obvious. And opportunity? You know better than I how Nikki must have died...all I know is that her body was blown out of an airlock. But how long was she alone in there? Can you prove she was alone?

Fingerprints, eh? I'm not sure what you might have that has fingerprints on it. Just be careful... just because someone has fingerprints on it doesn't mean that they're guilty. Lots of people touch lots of things.

James knew that this was a wise comment, but he also knew something Patterson didn't know. The bolt—his initial target for his fingerprint search— had been in space for almost a year, and it hadn't been touched by human skin since its creation. If—and that was a big "if"—the bolt had fingerprints on it at all, they would have had to be made in between the time Nikki recovered it outside and the time James found it jammed in the hatch. It would mean that Nikki had brought the bolt inside, even if it was unintentional. The only

77

prints that could conceivably be on the bolt would have to be from either Nikki, James, or a potential killer.

The odds were slim that James would find anything conclusive—he knew that. Finding no prints or prints from only Nikki wouldn't prove anything, and besides, the bolt could have miraculously floated to the perfect spot in the airlock door at the perfect time, the likelihood of that be damned. But what if there *were* prints from Nikki and someone else? It would mean she had shown something to someone that hadn't been reported to anyone else. It could have been the last person she had seen. And maybe, just maybe, Nikki had jammed the bolt in the hatch intentionally as she was ejected. *If* she was ejected, James reminded himself.

James huffed to himself. It was a hell of a construct he was coming up with. But still, he couldn't shake the urge to investigate, at least a little. He had little to lose if his weak suspicions were unfounded—as he expected. But if there was a killer on board...

James continued reading.

Start with keeping the object safe. You don't want to ruin any existing prints. Even if you can't see any visually, that doesn't mean they're not there. There are a couple of tricks to help see if prints are there—you can look through a piece of angled glass, or a microscope or something—but they don't always work. I know the crime scene guys here have some chemicals and lights, but I don't know much about that. I'll ask.

You'll need to "lift" the print to compare it. You could just use a piece of clear tape, but that doesn't always lift it right. It'd be better to use some ultra-fine powder like talc if you have it. Spread it over a potential print. Brush it off gently as can be, and if there's a print the powder will stick to the oils. Then do the tape thing, but this time you'll get a better print. Does that all make sense?

That brings me to the problem with fingerprints. You need to compare them to other prints for them to mean anything. We could probably figure out a way to get me images of prints if you can get them, but that doesn't do much good considering none of your colleagues would have their prints in a police database. No, what you'd need to do is somehow collect prints from your team and compare them to what you get. That'll have to be done by me somehow—no way we can get you software like that up there.

I guess that's as good a place as any to get started. Just do the best you can. And be careful. If someone up there has done something to Nikki, they won't take kindly to being investigated. Feel free to ask any questions you like.

I'll do more digging on my end and check in soon. -P

James re-read the letter to make sure he had absorbed all the information, then paused, his finger hovering over the 'delete' button. Patterson's word of caution only motivated James to be more careful than ever with this unofficial investigation. It was unlikely that NASA would go through personal emails, but James knew they had the ability to do it. As far as the crew was concerned, Gonzo technically had rights to everything as the commander, and Harrison and Aaron where both computer-savvy enough to hack a simple email if they wanted to. James was convinced—he deleted the email, then tucked his tablet away for the time being.

CHAPTER ELEVEN

Two hours of sleep passed by fitfully for James. Before he knew it, Gonzalez was waking up the crew by blasting some old David Bowie song through the SIM's speakers. James rolled over in his sleeping bag, his muscles aching from gravity's fresh embrace. He was first up on the exercise equipment this morning—that was going to suck.

It did. But James powered through it before heading to the central part of the SIM to take an honest-to-goodness, gravity-assisted shower. It was the exact opposite of exercising with new gravity—it was blissful. He had forgotten what it was like to have water run freely down his back and into a drain—no vacuum hose required.

It was the crew's first real sol on Mars, and there was plenty of work to be done. After each of the six astronauts had a chance to take a short shower and shave, they gathered around the folding table in the inflatable module that the crew was already calling the "dining room." Gonzalez had already picked out the exact spots for the crew to sit as they recorded a message to Earth. The room's tiny window and its view of Mars behind him, James sat down and awaited his turn to speak.

The entire world would be watching "live"—which meant fifteen minutes late after the data had traveled to Earth and been parsed by Houston. It was a moment that James had been eagerly anticipating—for a moment, James forgot about Nikki and the bolt. He was positively giddy to be on Mars—it had been his dream ever since he was a kid, and here he was. He even got emotional talking about it to the camera.

Once the recording was finished it was time for the first round of Mars physicals. They were quite similar to a physical done on Earth, but with a few extra tests. James weighed every crewman and adjusted their weight according to Martian gravity, measured their height—they had each grown slightly taller after so much time in space—and tested their vision. Then there were the typical awkward tests—hernia checks, breast exams, and asking about any new moles or bumps. The exams didn't stop there—in addition to other, smaller tests, everyone submitted a blood and urine sample, and the men submitted a semen sample to test the effects of radiation and microgravity on the reproductive system. Once James had given the crew a clean bill of health, Mike, the mission's biologist, would run the samples through the lab in search of further scientific knowledge.

James did his best to minimize the awkwardness of the exams, which meant keeping talk to a minimum and doing his best to remain absolutely professional at all times. He had earned the complete trust of the crew when it came to medicine and health, and he would not put that in jeopardy.

He was, however, cognizant of the opportunity that the physicals gave of looking for possible clues to Nikki's death. James was looking for anything that might point to signs of a struggle—like cuts or bruises—but neither Gonzo, Aaron, nor Harrison had anything that might be construed as such. The three men looked to be in excellent health—for which, as a flight surgeon, James was thankful for.

Jordyn came next. Keen to get the only female physical over with, James moved quickly through the list of NASA-mandated checkups. He saved the most intrusive parts for last and made sure to be as fast as possible while still being thorough. After a rapid breast cancer screening, however, James paused. There was a large, fresh bruise on Jordyn's left ribs, about three inches below her breast.

"What happened, Major Marx?" asked James, being sure to use her title to preserve the atmosphere of reverent formality. "That's quite the shiner you have there."

"I know," replied Jordyn as she tugged her bra and shirt back down. "I...well..."

"Yes?" inquired James.

"I tripped last night and hit the lab table pretty hard," Jordyn replied sheepishly. "Not quite used to the gravity yet. It's just a bruise, Doc. Am I done yet?"

"Just about," answered James as he gestured for Jordyn to take a seat on the chair in the lab. The responsibilities he held aboard *Perseus* still applied on Mars, and James had been tasked with running a quick psychological evaluation on every crewmember during every checkup.

James paused. The evaluation wasn't much more than asking how each crewmember was doing, but James had suddenly had an idea. He was kicking himself for not thinking of it earlier, before he had completed the other crewmembers' exams.

"What is it?" Jordyn asked impatiently. "C'mon James, you know I get to fire up the rover today. Ask your stupid psych questions."

"I will," answered James as he moved to one of the medical cabinets. "But I just remembered that I need a hair sample. Here," James continued, tossing a small pair of scissors to Jordyn, who caught them easily. "Clip off just a single strand. That's all I need. Maybe two inches?"

"This is new," Jordyn said as she picked out a target. "Is this more radiation testing?"

"Yeah," lied James as he rummaged through the section containing bandages and athletic tape. Finally, he found what he was looking for: clear tape.

"Go ahead and press the hair into the tape, then fold it over itself," James said. "So it doesn't get lost. I'll have you write your name on the edge there with a sharpie. Perfect, just like that."

Jordyn did as she was told and handed the hair sample and tape back to James. Sure enough, a partial fingerprint—certainly enough in James' uneducated view—was encased in the tape along with a strand of jet-black hair. It was only part of what he needed, but James felt himself grin ever so slightly at his cleverness.

"If you're not going to ask me your stupid shrink questions I'll have to do it myself," Jordyn said with just a twinge of annoyance.

"How are you feeling?" James asked quickly, using the same, obvious first question that he did every time.

"Well, I'm more isolated from humanity than I've ever been, my friend was sucked into space, and today I exposed myself to a man who isn't my husband. So I guess you could say everything's fine."

James just raised an eyebrow.

"Oh come on," laughed Jordyn. "It's a joke. Come on, James, you know me. I'm alright. Besides, you're the person I trust most on this ship. If I have a problem, psychological or whatever, you'll be the first to know. OK? Now can I be done?"

"Yes, Major," answered James.

"Thank you, *Doctor* Lake," replied Jordyn, mimicking James with mock formality as she rose to her feet. "Now hurry up and finish. We can't go outside until everyone's done. I'm going to go put on my M-suit."

With that, Jordyn was gone, leaving James with an unneeded strand of hair and a potentially valuable fingerprint—although it came from someone James considered to be the most unlikely culprit.

Mike came in next. James did all of his examinations but left out the part about needing a hair sample. Mike would know that NASA didn't need anything of the sort, and asking him for one would just arouse suspicion. Mike was in excellent health, so James was soon on to the psychological questionnaire, which he began with the same tired question.

"Honestly," Mike began thoughtfully, running a hand through his sandy-red hair. "Not so good, James. It's been a rough week, obviously."

"Tell me about it," James nodded as he cleared his mind. Mike needed him to pay attention—it was his duty. "Rough for sure," James added.

"I'm ok," assured Mike. "But it's been pretty hard on me, probably for a lot of reasons. I don't want to talk about it, but things aren't going so well at home, for a couple of reasons. I guess my dad had some chest pains last month, and Cameron seems a little more distant than normal…"

Mike trailed off, but James didn't say anything. He just waited for Mike to continue, which he did after a moment.

"Sorry," Mike continued. "So yeah, that sucks. And Nikki was obviously a good friend to all of us, especially me. It hurts, man. You know it, just like me. I've seen it in your eyes, too. Aaron's been telling me about God and heaven and stuff, but it still sucks. It sucks bad."

"We're all here for each other," James said tentatively once it was clear Mike wasn't going to continue. "And I'm here for you. Is there anything I can do to help? As a doctor, or a friend. I just want to be here for you."

"I really am ok," Mike said, clearing his throat. He opened his mouth to say something else, but closed it suddenly. "Well, actually…"

"What is it?"

"James," began Mike, who lowered his voice unexpectedly. "I'm haunted by the idea that it wasn't suicide."

James' stomach dropped instantly. Could Mike have the same suspicions that he was having? Did this mean that Mike was to be trusted? Should James tell him that he agreed?

"I mean, what if it was an accident?" Mike continued. "But it couldn't be, right? I mean, how would you accidently open a hatch? It was suicide. I know it. You know it."

James looked at Mike carefully. There didn't seem to be any indication that Mike legitimately imagined foul play, but then again, he might just not want to say it out loud. After all, James hadn't said it out loud yet, and he didn't intend to now.

"I don't know if we'll ever truly know," James said cautiously. "And that sucks, like you said. And it's ok to hurt because of it. She deserves to be mourned."

"You're right," Mike said, smiling weakly. "I like that, James. Thanks for that."

"We're friends," James affirmed. "Of course. Is there anything else you want to get off your chest?"

"I miss fresh fruit," Mike said, simultaneously sniffling and laughing. "Seriously man. I'm sick of all the freeze-dried or flash-packaged stuff. It's the worst, and I just want something fresh, you know? Something that'll make me..."

Mike continued to talk, but James wasn't quite listening anymore. He was thinking. Mike might not have mentioned foul play, but he wasn't convinced of suicide either. That added another person to the list of skeptics. James needed to figure this out, but he needed fingerprints from everyone first. But fingerprints weren't everything. James needed what Patterson called the clichés: motive, means, and opportunity.

"Are you even listening?" Mike asked.

"Yeah," lied James. "You just have me thinking about food, too."

CHAPTER TWELVE

"This…is…heavier…than I…expected!" grunted James as he, Harrison, and Aaron wrestled with the heavy airlock adapter. "Holy smokes," James gasped, his breath echoing around his helmet. "We're not even lifting it straight up!"

"It was 500 pounds back on Earth," Aaron groaned back. "That makes it, what, a little less than 200 here?"

"That's still like 80 a man," grumbled Harrison. "Damn I'm out of shape."

The three men paused for a moment to catch their breath, then counted to three before jostling the airlock into a better position with the help of the rover's crane. This airlock was different than normal—it was a specially shaped adapter that connected exclusively with the rover. The airlock was connected to the SIM's rigid center module by a soon-to-be-inflated tube—Kevlar-composite like the others—that was strong enough to resist anything Mars could throw at it. The system would allow the astronauts to transition from the SIM to the rover without having to put on their M-suits.

"Looks good enough to me," Gonzalez said over the radio as the men finished the adjustment. He was in the rover's passenger seat next to Jordyn, his helmet off, his boots visible on the dash in a pose of mock relaxation. "I don't want to be the first to try it though," he laughed.

"I'll do it if you let me drive," Aaron said eagerly. "Houston doesn't have to know, right?"

"How about we arm wrestle for it?" Jordyn shot back mischievously.

"In all seriousness though, I can do it," interjected Harrison. "Setting up the Mars habitat is my job, and if I don't do it I'll be relegated to repeating the computer or something."

"Maybe you *should* be relegated the way your CO2 levels are spiking," joked Mike from the SIM. Although he'd been out of the SIM plenty of times in the past three days, most of Mike's work would take place inside the SIM's lab. He was also tasked with monitoring the crew's life support—which just gave him an excuse to tease anyone anytime their heartrate went above 80 beats per minute.

James laughed under his breath, then took a deep breath of recycled oxygen from his M-suit as he looked around at the surrounding land. It was a view that was already starting to look monotonous, yet it was infinitely interesting.

James turned away from the SIM and towards the vast expanse of Martian desert that lay before them. They had landed in the southwestern quadrant of what was called Amazonis Planitia, a zone selected because of its closeness to the Martian equator, the relatively level topography that made landings and departures easier, and the plenitude of interesting geological features that were within the mission's 200-mile exploration zone. The mission's primary target, Marte Vallis, a sea of plains punctuated by hills, craters, and potential water erosion formations, was a mere 10 miles to the southwest. Most of what James could see was the same: flat plains of brown-red dirt, punctuated by the occasional rock or boulder. In the distance to the south, James could make out the ridge of a crater or formation, one of many that were out there to be explored.

James took another breath and looked to the sky, his inhalation sounding tinny inside of his advanced helmet. The sun, far weaker here than it was on Earth, was starting to get low on the horizon. The Martian sky, which was generally a dusty orange, was fading into black, and the sun was starting to take on a bluish tinge. It was a reminder of just how thin Mars' atmosphere was—any accident here would kill you just as quickly as one in deep space.

87

James took another breath, and this time he savored it. His M-suit was a modern marvel, capable of filtering his every inhalation and supplying hours of breathable, life-sustaining oxygen. As much as he hated its tight fit, the suit was an incredible piece of engineering that allowed him to do something that only he and five other human beings had ever done: walk on Mars.

A quick glance at his wristscreen told James that it would soon be time to head back inside for another night, and truth be told, James was looking forward to taking another shower. Even more present in James' mind, however, was the chance to collect a few more fingerprints. Up until now he had obtained three of the five he would need—Jordyn's on the tape, Mike's on one of his vials in the SIM's lab, and Gonzo's from his personal tablet. So far it hadn't been much of a problem—James' presence in the lab wasn't unexpected, and Gonzo had actually just given James his tablet when he asked to borrow it—but James still felt he was pushing his luck. The last thing he wanted was for his crewmates to think he was acting strangely, especially if one of them was guilty. It'd probably be even worse if someone discovered what he was doing, and no one was guilty of anything.

"It's gorgeous, isn't it?" Aaron said, clapping a gloved hand on James' shoulder. "Absolutely incredible."

"Crazy to think that this place might have once looked like Earth," answered James thoughtfully. "NASA thinks this whole area could have been underwater once."

"Speaking of water," Harrison cut in with his light southern accent, "I've gotta' get the drill rig up and running tomorrow. Houston wants some core samples."

"That'll have to wait until tomorrow," said Gonzalez from the rover. "I'm calling it, guys. Let's go get some dinner. We've worked hard today."

"Your heartrate hasn't passed 70 all afternoon, Commander," Mike joked dryly over the radio.

"Someone's got to supervise," Gonzalez joked back.

James took one last look at the empty Martian horizon before turning back towards the SIM. The little establishment of humanity that had been dubbed *Unity Base* was starting to look like a proper base. The SIM and its inflatable modules were completely set up, the solar panels and instrumentation were assembled, and Jordyn was carefully driving the rover up to the brand-new airlock and tube. A few hundred yards away to the northeast was the MDV, and another hundred yards north of that was the Mars Ascent Vehicle, or MAV, which would return the crew and their samples to *Perseus* after about three months. It had been remotely landed along with the SIM a few months before *Perseus* had arrived in orbit.

James went over to help give Jordyn some final guidance as she successfully docked the rover to the new hatch, then watched as Harrison slowly pressurized the system. The tough tube gradually inflated until it had reached its full, seven-foot diameter. James watched through the windows of the rover as Jordyn and Gonzalez, both with their M-suits fully on, opened the hatch and stepped inside. Everything was working properly.

"Nice work, Harrison," said James. "Everything is looking great."

"Thank you," answered Harrison. "I honestly feel like a glorified balloon-blower, but hey, as long as I'm not responsible for killing any of you guys I'll have done my..."

Harrison trailed off suddenly, his mind obviously connecting his phrase to what had happened aboard *Perseus*. "My job," he finished weakly. "Sorry, that probably sounded flippant."

"Not in the least," reassured James. "Personally, I hope you don't kill us too."

James was *mostly* joking.

With another day's work outside completed, the remaining Ares I crew headed back towards the main airlock, each astronaut pausing to observe the blue Martian sunset before ducking inside. James was the last man in, so he sealed the airlock behind him and initiated the pressurization cycle. Air hissed in, filling the compartment with noise and amplifying the sounds that his crewmates were making. Unlike empty space, sound could travel through Mars' thin atmosphere, but every noise outside of a M-suit was dull, muffled, and quiet. Inside the pressurized airlock, however, noise penetrated the M-suits easily.

Pressure restored. The SIM's computer chanted pleasantly.

"Gosh, it's good to take this off," Aaron sighed as removed his helmet and placed it on top of his locker. He proceeded to remove his gloves, then reached for the airlock's small compressed air hose. James watched as Aaron used the hose to blow the red Martian dust out of his M-suit's connectors. The dust and sand got everywhere, and the crew had to be painstakingly careful about cleaning important equipment. They had already had to clean off the solar panels twice.

James reached up to remove his helmet, but he had a quick idea. "Hey Aaron," he said as Aaron was passing the compressed air hose over to Harrison. "My helmet's a little stuck, I think I might have some sand in here. Can you give me a hand?"

"You got it," answered Aaron, stopping what he was doing to come to James' aid. "Is it the latch or what?"

"Just seemed to stick when I was twisting it off," answered James, raising his voice so that Aaron could hear. "I just wanted someone to try it while they could actually see it."

Aaron placed his bare hands on James' helmet and twisted carefully while manipulating the latch. The helmet twisted off smoothly, leaving James inhaling the airlock's sterile air.

"Looks ok," Aaron said, pausing to look at the helmet's seal before passing it back to James.

"Sorry, A," James said, doing his best to sound sheepish. "Maybe I should just have you dress me too, eh?"

"I accept VISA," Aaron replied.

James placed his helmet to the side, then proceeded to take off his gloves. Next, he unfastened the hard shell that housed his life support and radio equipment. It unclipped in the front, then opened towards the back like a pair of wings, but remained connected to the top part of the suit, making it awkward and difficult to remove. Finally, James was able to tug off his boots and his M-suit pants, leaving him in his tight gym shorts and undershirt. He instantly got to scratching every itch that had been bothering him during the day.

Aaron finished undressing, and soon Harrison followed. That left James alone in the airlock, sitting on one of the changing benches. He stood up and put his M-suit back on his assigned rack, then reached for his helmet. He paused to check it closely and smiled. Sure enough, Aaron had left ten perfect fingerprints smudged on the helmet's glass.

That just left Harrison.

CHAPTER THIRTEEN

James wasn't going to wait any longer.

He didn't want to worry anymore—didn't want to be constantly stressed. With partial fingerprints collected from nearly every member of the crew, James had decided that tonight would be the night. All he needed was to collect Harrison's fingerprints off of his coffee cup. Then he could at least get started, even if he needed to collect a few more prints.

It all made James nervous. He sat at the dinner table that night, trying to act normal while feeling on edge. He didn't want to get overly optimistic, but he felt that he was nearing some closure. At least, he hoped he was.

While James had gotten a fingerprint or two from nearly everyone, he knew full well that that wouldn't necessarily lead to a match with a fingerprint on the bolt—*if* there was a fingerprint on the bolt. He had peered through the plastic bag in the safety of his sleeping sack, but couldn't detect any fingerprints visually. He was going to have to use one of the SIM's microscopes, and he would have to do it in secret after the others had fallen asleep. James was praying that he wouldn't find any prints on the bolt, because if he found any prints other than his and Nikki's, that would mean...nothing good. The thought quickly reminded him that he didn't have any of Nikki's prints.

James quickly swallowed a sigh before the others noticed. If there were any fingerprints on the bolt that didn't match up with the ones he'd already collected, it meant they were from Nikki or one of the crews' uncollected prints—after all, James only had a single print from Jordyn, not one from all ten fingers. Plus, there would be no way to know if any fingerprints matched until after James had sent all the scanned prints back to Patterson. Patterson had the software and the expertise to match prints—James had no such ability. This was quickly becoming more tedious by the minute.

"James, you seem awfully quiet," Harrison mentioned in his barely-there southern drawl. "What's up?"

"He's probably disgusted by the rehydrated potatoes," Mike said quickly. "Who can blame him?"

"I'm just thinking of home," James lied, though his thoughts did legitimately turn back to Claire with the lie. "I kind of wish that my wife could experience this. It's going to be hard to describe space...Mars..."

"I hear you," Jordyn added with a laugh, her mouth full of food. "Derek still asks me about how water floats in space. He also keeps asking about what sex would be like in zero gravity, which explains why I'm the one NASA selected and he's the one stuck in the Air Force."

"Good thing they didn't pick both of you," deadpanned Mike.

"What about you three?" Jordyn asked, ignoring Mike's comment and gesturing between Harrison, Aaron, and Gonzalez with her fork. "You three never seem to talk about home."

"Not much to talk about," shrugged Aaron. "You guys know that. My parents have been gone for five years now, and there's not really anyone waiting for me back home other than my siblings."

"Aaron, the thirty-two-year-old virgin," teased Gonzalez. "Maybe I should pick up the movie rights. Or maybe I should line you up with my friend Jessica. She has a bit of a...loose reputation."

"Aaron would just try to convert her to Mormonism," Harrison joked under his breath.

"Alright guys," Aaron laughed good-naturedly. "I promise you guys I'll try to get married within a month of getting home. Is that good enough?"

"Make it a week and we might be satisfied," Jordyn teased.

"Hey, didn't you live in Nicaragua for a few years?" continued Gonzalez, clearly relishing the chance to tease Aaron. "I'm sure those Latinas would love some time with a blonde-haired Adonis like yourself. Hell, I can barely contain myself around you. There's got to be a lady back there, right? There's no way there wasn't someone…"

"I was a missionary," Aaron interjected weakly.

"Wouldn't have stopped me," joked Harrison. The crew laughed, but Aaron just grimaced. James could tell that his patience was growing thin, but Aaron would never crack.

"Alright," James said, stepping in to take the heat off of Aaron. "I think the roast is ready to move on to Harrison, our other bachelor."

"Let me stop you there," Harrison said with a smile. "Ok, ok. I don't have many prospects back home either. But yeah, my parents and siblings can't get enough of my being here. I've practically made them celebrities back in my home town. They got to ride in a Corvette during the fourth of July parade."

"Maybe if you're lucky they'll erect a statue of you in the rodeo grounds of that tiny town in the sticks," teased Aaron, who was obviously pleased to not be the center of attention.

"You're not that far off," grunted Harrison. "I'm the only person from Marlette to really amount to anything of consequence. It's a small town."

"How's Estefani?" Jordyn asked Gonzalez, abruptly shifting the conversation to the mission commander. "What's your son's name again? Seriously though Gonzo, you never tell us anything."

"It's to protect the innocent," Gonzalez said, raising his hands in mock defense. "Fernando's his name—remember him from the tour of the assembly building? He's doing great, just finished 6th grade. Estefani is doing fine too..."

Gonzalez paused for a moment as if contemplating his family back home. He had a faraway look in his eyes that every member of the crew had had themselves at some point during the mission. The crew jokingly referred to it as the million-mile stare.

"Unity base to Gonzo," teased Jordyn, snapping her fingers. "Come in, sir."

Gonzalez shook his head to clear it and laughed. "And on that touchy feely note," he said, "I'm going to go hit the showers. We're heading out to Barret crater tomorrow and I want to make sure we have plenty of daylight, especially with the boys back in Houston riding our asses. I think we should all get some rest."

With that, Gonzalez stood up and left the table. The rest of the crew sat in silence for a brief moment before following in Gonzo's footsteps. James caught a glimpse of the million-mile stare in the eyes of a few of them, including Jordyn.

James remained seated for a moment, watching as the others cleared their dishes and took them back towards the SIM's kitchen. They'd load the dishes into the SIM's small dishwasher, but they wouldn't start it until James had brought his dishes in too, which was James' plan. The dishwasher was only to be run when completely full, and the water used to run it would be filtered and recycled. It was a small convenience for the crew, one that had doubtlessly cost NASA thousands.

In the meantime, James sat pondering Gonzalez' limited answer about his family. James knew from his own experience that time in space away from one's family was rough, and that was with a near-perfect woman like Claire running things back home. James had only briefly met Gonzo's lovely wife— Estefani was a first-generation immigrant from Honduras—but he hoped that her relationship with Gonzalez was rock-solid, for Gonzo's sake.

The clattering of dishes subsided, and the friendly banter of the crew moved out of the SIM's core and into the inflatable sleeping and rec room. James heard the familiar noise of a video game starting—this one was NBA 2043—and the sound of the shower starting up. The SIM almost felt like home, except for the near-vacuum of Mars that surrounded it.

James was ready. He picked up his plate and walked confidently towards the kitchen. Sure enough, it was empty, and the small dishwasher had its door left open for him. Being careful to be as quiet as possible, James loaded his cup, plate, and spork, then paused to look over his shoulder. He was alone.

The role of tape was in his pocket, and James pulled it out silently. He tore a large strip off, then proceeded to adhere it to the side of Harrison's labeled cup. He repeated the process with another four strips of tape, moving around the cup clockwise until he was confident that at least *some* prints would be acquired. James then carefully removed each strip of tape, adhering each to a small piece of microscope-mounting glass that he had borrowed from the lab. The job done, James bent down and placed the cup back in the washer.

"It'd be hell to wash everything by hand," a muffled voice said suddenly behind James.

James jerked backwards, nearly losing his balance in the low Martian gravity. Gonzalez, who stood by the door to the bathroom in a towel, snorted in laughter.

"You scared me," James said, hastily shoving the glass into his pocket. How much had Gonzo seen?

"I can tell," chuckled Gonzalez, his voice garbled as he returned to brushing his teeth. "Damn, 'ames. I 'ope no 'un scares you 'uring my nex' physical."

"I didn't even hear you come out," James said, slightly reassured by Gonzo's attitude. If he had seen something, he would have asked about it. Gonzalez had no filter.

"Bafoom ninja," Gonzalez shrugged, turning back toward the small bathroom to spit into the sink.

James hurriedly shut the washer and initiated its cycle. He didn't stop to chat with Gonzo, he just left and headed towards his sleeping bag in the sleeping and rec room. He passed Mike as he entered, who said something about taking a shower, then made a beeline for his cot. Before getting there, however, his mind caught up to his racing heart. He couldn't just shove stuff into his sleeping bag now, not with everyone in here. He had to act normal. He had to chill out.

Aaron and Harrison were sitting in front of the SIM's large TV, in the middle of what was already an intense game of virtual basketball. The men on the Ares I crew took their sports video games seriously, with full-length quarters and maximum difficulty. The Utah Jazz, controlled by Aaron, were up 23-20 on Harrison's Atlanta Hawks.

"I'll take the winner," James announced, taking a seat next to Jordyn, who watched the game with a bemused look on her face.

"That'll be me," Aaron said quickly, not looking away from the screen. "Unless Jordyn wants to take you on first."

"It'll be 2300 by the time this is over," answered Jordyn. "I'll pass tonight, boys."

"Suit yourself," replied Harrison, not breaking his concentration either. "But she is right, James. When I win we'll have to play a half game. Deal?"

"Deal," answered James, fingering the microscope glass in his pocket.

The game ran long, with Harrison winning in overtime. Just like Jordyn had predicted, it was past 2330, which meant that James and Harrison had to play an abbreviated game with the volume turned down low. They saved it after the first quarter—Harrison led, 22-15—and got ready for bed. All the others were already asleep.

Harrison left to use the toilet, giving James the chance he needed. He quickly put the piece of glass into a plastic baggy, then shoved the baggy into the bottom of his sleeping bag, checking to make sure the other bags with the bolt and other print samples were still there. Tonight would be the night James checked the bolt, and if a print was found he'd scan and upload the other collected prints soon.

James had to stay up so that he could use the SIM's lab when all the others were asleep, but that proved to be the easy part. His nerves were so frayed from being surprised by Gonzalez that he had no trouble staying awake. The hard part was managing the tension and nervousness. James was terrified that he would find something on the bolt, something that would imply foul play aboard *Perseus*. Scenario after scenario ran through his mind, ranging from finding nothing on the bolt, to finding a perfect match with someone on the crew. And if there was a match, what then? Was it enough to accuse someone of murder? Would it be enough to convince the others?

Soon enough, it was time for action rather than pondering. Being as silent as possible, James extracted himself from his sleeping bag, the bolt baggy clutched tightly inside his fist. He made his way to the SIM's center module, quietly sidestepping his crewmates' cots and keeping the lights off.

The science part of the center module was at the far north end. The kitchen was in the middle, and the bathroom at the opposite, southern end of the module. This made for a U-shaped lab with equipment lining the walls from floor to ceiling. The general optical microscope, the simplest scope and the one James would be using, was against one of the side walls, meaning the kitchen was on James' right.

Double checking that the coast was clear, James clicked on the tiny workstation light and booted up the microscope's accompanying computer. He then put gloves onto his shaking hands, and carefully extracted the bolt from its baggy, placing it silently on the illuminated glass below the microscope's lens.

It was a remarkably ordinary looking bolt. The steel—or whatever alloy it was made of—was a cold grey with a dull shine. There was a slight dent in the threading where the jammed hatch clamped down on it, but otherwise the bolt was in pristine condition.

James pondered the bolt for a moment longer, wondering where to begin. Maybe there were prints on the threads, but those would be almost impossible to get and even more difficult to analyze. No, the best place to start would be the six-sided head of the bolt. There was nothing visible to the naked eye, but maybe with some powder and a microscope...

James silently opened one of the medical drawers and extracted a small container of talcum powder. Patterson had said that a light dusting of the powder could stick to oily fingerprints, and it was worth a shot. Lightly holding the end of the threads, James tapped the white powder over the rest of the bolt, shaking the excess off gently.

Using the limited light supplied by the workstation, James carefully examined the bolt again. The white powder filled the grooves of the bolt's threads, and a small amount seemed to stick to the head of the bolt, right on the top. His heart suddenly racing, James took a closer look.

It was just a smear. There was no obvious fingerprint or anything of the sort. Just a smear of talcum powder that had stuck to the bolt. It wasn't quite the damning evidence James feared to find, but maybe the sticking powder meant something. Unsure of whether to be relieved or terrified, James reached out to adjust the microscope for a closer look. Just as his fingers touched the cold metal knob, however, James heard a slight cough from the sleeping quarters.

He had been planning for this, and he wasn't going to let someone sneak up on him again, especially after being surprised by Gonzalez earlier. In a flash the bolt was back in its protective baggy, and back in James' pocket. The talcum powder went back in its drawer, and the computer terminal was shut off. James clicked off the science station light too, but only after turning on the light above the fresh water station. He was just in time. Just as he grabbed his clean cup from the dishwasher, Harrison entered the kitchen, rubbing his eyes.

"Hey," whispered James as he filled his cup with water. "Sorry man, I hope I didn't wake you up."

"No worries," yawned Harrison. "I woke up on my own. I think we had the same idea," he finished, gesturing towards the water station. "I swear, the air here in the SIM is dryer than the air on *Perseus*, and that's saying something."

"Seriously though," agreed James, collecting himself and taking a sip of water. "It doesn't help that the air in M-suits are the same way, either."

"And all the damn sand and dust everywhere," continued Harrison as he bent over and reached into the dishwasher for his own cup. "It's already getting everywhere inside, even just from the airlock. I just wake up freakin' parched."

"I just want a soda sometimes," whispered James. "A Dr. Pepper, or just something carbonated."

"I want a beer," Harrison laughed softly, filling his cup at the water station and taking a big gulp on the spot. "Or a nice shot of whisk...hold on, what the hell is this?"

James froze, staring at what Harrison was looking at. There was a small strip of tape stuck to the outside of Harrison's cup.

"What is it?" asked James, fighting to keep himself composed.

Harrison peeled the tape off slowly, took one glance at it, then rolled it into a little ball and tossed it aside. "How did I get tape on my cup?" he asked to himself.

"Maybe it came from the table?" James offered. "Or maybe something else in the dishwasher?"

"The bigger question is why the hell the washer didn't take it off," replied Harrison as he crouched over to examine the inside of the washer. "Damn thing only costs fifty-thousand, you'd think it'd get a better clean. I mean, the food specks are enough already. Oh well, I'll look into it later."

"Sorry man," James said calmly. "More for you to do, huh?"

"It's all good," answered Harrison, refilling his cup. "I didn't do squat on *Perseus*—this is my job, managing the equipment on Mars. I just thought I'd be wrestling with drills and fixing rover wheels. All I've done so far is clean dust out of the hatches and now do dishes by hand."

"Let's just hope those are our only problems," James replied. "It's a long way back home."

"I'll drink to that," Harrison smiled, raising his cup in a mock toast. "Anyways, I'm going to hit the bathroom. I'll see you in the morning, James."

With that, Harrison finished his water, put his cup on the counter, and headed towards the bathroom. When the door had shut, James looked around the lab. He hadn't left anything out of place except for a little talcum powder on the floor, which he quickly brushed away with his socked foot.

James cast one last glance towards the microscope. He'd have to try again, and soon. But he'd have to be more careful. He was getting tired of almost getting caught investigating a crime that might never have been committed in the first place.

CHAPTER FOURTEEN

"Lake, do you have that beacon up yet or what?" demanded Gonzalez, his voice clearly stressed. "We're already fifteen minutes behind schedule, team. We're going to lose our sat time."

"Still working on it, sir," James answered. "We're still getting it in position. Hey, A? Do you think you could find a big, stable rock or something?"

Aaron stopped his work on the beacon and looked up at James, small beads of sweat forming on his forehead from exertion, just visible behind his helmet's glass. "It's a good idea," replied Aaron. "But if it's too big we'll have to unhitch the beacon from the crane and use that. I'll take a look."

"What if I rotate it?" asked Jordyn. "Maybe if we get the legs right it'll be enough."

James took a step back and put his hands on his hips as he looked over the situation. He, Aaron, and Jordyn were atop a relatively large hill that NASA had named Mount Vespa. Most of the mission's exploration zone was flat and gentle, but there were plenty of craters, including some very large ones surrounded by a massive, raised ring of dirt, with massive hills of ejecta surrounding the main crater. Mount Vespa wasn't really a mountain at all, but rather a high point on the rim on one of the larger craters within the exploration zone.

"James?" Jordyn nagged again.

"Hang on just a minute," James said, struggling not to snap. The whole crew was getting a little frustrated.

They were a long way from *Unity*. Eighty miles away to be exact—a three-hour drive, plus another hour as they carefully navigated up NASA's predetermined path to the beacon's deployment area. It was supposed to be a fairly simple job—the beacon was already linked to *Unity*, and all the 3-person team had to do was set it up on flat ground. That was easier said than done, however, especially when the increasingly frustrated Harrison and Gonzo were snapping at them over the radio.

"Yeah, I don't think the rock thing will work," Aaron said, returning to where the beacon hung suspended by the rover's crane. "Also, be careful going that way. There's like a ten-foot cliff where the crater begins. It's all loose sediment too. I gotta' tell you though, it's a heck of a view. I think it'd be worth it, Jordyn."

"No thank you," answered Jordyn from inside the rover. "Now can we just get this thing placed? I don't want to be driving down this ridge in the dark."

"Aw come on, Marx," chided James. "All you need to do is put your helmet on. We all managed to do that inside the rover somehow."

It really was that simple. The rover was pressurized, so the crew was able to ride without their M-suits fully on until they got to the work area.

"Come on, team," Gonzalez said over the radio from his location back at *Unity*. "Please? Can we just get this done?"

"Roger that," James replied, squatting back down to see how the beacon could be placed. He thought he found a spot, but he wanted to be sure—damaging the beacon would be bad, especially if they damaged the tiny nuclear core that powered the thing. The beacon was one of three that had been landed with the SIM, and the second that was being placed by the crew. The beacons did a little of everything—they helped improve location tracking, they served as weather stations, and they could even transmit directly to Earth if a relay satellite went down. The problem was that they could only function if they were properly level. The legs were adjustable to three degrees each, but the closest they'd gotten to vertical thus far was still five degrees off. The fact that it was such a small margin made it all the more annoying.

James sighed, then stood up—too quickly. The blood rushed out of his head, and his vision clouded momentarily. Mars' gravity was having strange effects on everyone, especially after so much time in weightlessness. James took a few deep breaths, the noise echoing slightly around his helmet, and waited for his vision to clear. Once it had, he decided to give it a shot.

"Let's rotate it about ten degrees clockwise," James said. "I think that'll get us close enough."

"I still say we just move it to a different spot," Jordyn whined.

"This is the most stable rock in the area," Aaron replied. "Moving it would put us on sediment, which would mean shifting, which would mean coming back out here tomorrow. I'm not Nikki, but this is the most stable area for sure."

Jordyn sighed audibly over the radio, but sure enough, the crane began to move, rotating the beacon slowly and methodically. James watched for it to line up with where he thought the legs could go, then called for Jordyn to stop.

"Let it down," he said, grabbing on to one of the legs to keep it stable.

Jordyn let it down slowly, while James and Aaron kept the beacon steady. James caught himself breathing heavily—whether it was from exertion or stress, he couldn't tell.

"Contact," said Aaron as the legs reached the ground. "James, what do we got?"

"Three-point-five degrees," James answered as he checked the instruments. "That'll do—the legs can be adjusted to account for the difference. *Unity*, we have a stable position. We're adjusting the angle now."

"About damn time," Gonzalez said, clearly pleased.

James pulled a wrench out of his work bag and got busy adjusting one of the three legs. It would take some fiddling, but they were almost done. James was relieved—he was tired, and he wanted to get back to his cot in *Unity*.

It had been nearly a week since James had last tried to analyze the bolt, and he hadn't been able to get back to it. They had been incredibly busy—two one-hundred-mile-plus rover trips, hard, manual sample collecting, and even some hasty repair work on a malfunctioning solar panel meant that the crew barely had time to sleep and eat at all. It was all the same to James. He hadn't heard from Patterson in a couple days, and to be honest, he was enjoying not having it press on his mind as much.

"Hey James," Mike said over the radio from his position back in the SIM. "Can you do me a favor and give me a quick suit check? Your heart rate and breathing are elevated."

"Of course they are," grunted James in reply as he gave the adjusting bolt another hard turn clockwise. "What do you expect?"

"My mistake," apologized Mike. "You just seem pretty winded for twisting in a bolt."

"Ha ha," replied James flatly.

"I mean, more winded than normal," Mike explained quickly. "Please, just humor me."

"I'm fine," James answered sharply, pausing to check his suit's readouts to be sure. "I'm all good here."

"Copy," Mike replied flatly. James felt slightly bad for snapping at him—he was just doing his job.

James finished adjusting his bolt, then moved to help Aaron. After a number of small tweaks and adjustments—and a number of jokes from Gonzalez and Harrison about James' apparent lack of fitness—the beacon was level and ready to go.

"We're all done up here, *Unity*." Jordyn said over the radio.

"Set up looks good from here," Harrison said over the radio. "We'll just have to wait for Houston's confirmation. Sit tight for twenty minutes. Enjoy the view."

"I'd rather enjoy getting my helmet off," remarked Aaron. "I'm heading back to the rover. You coming?"

James looked at the rover, then at Aaron, his face now slightly obscured by the gold sheen on his visor. "I actually think I'll go check out that view you mentioned," he said. "Over there, right?"

"Yeah, maybe fifty meters," answered Aaron. "It's a great place to do some pondering."

"Glad to see that word has survived from the 1800's," joked James. "I'll be right back."

James headed in the direction Aaron indicated, pausing to take a swig of water from the straw inside of his M-suit. Truth be told, James did feel a little gassed—there was no denying that he was getting older. He'd have to increase his daily exercise—especially when they were back on *Perseus*—or Earth's full gravity would be hell.

After cresting a small hill, James walked the remaining thirty meters to the ridge that Aaron had indicated. The rover was no longer visible, but Aaron's footsteps remained on the dusty, rocky ground. It was weird to be alone— even for just a moment—but it was worth it. The view from where the footprints ended was truly remarkable, just as Aaron had promised. It was quite literally breathtaking.

The crater was massive. James knew that it sprawled nearly twenty miles in diameter, and it filled most of his range of vision. It formed a giant, dusty bowl, with a small hill rising up in the middle. Half of the crater looked to be filled with sand dunes, no doubt blown in by the weak Martian wind over the millennia. A small breeze blew now, leaving thin, light tentacles of dust twisting through the distant air like smoke. James coughed, perhaps instinctively.

James took a step further than Aaron had gone, being careful to avoid the precipice that he had been warned about. It wasn't a huge drop, but it could be enough to damage critical equipment on his M-suit. The others might not be able to reach him in time to save him. James wasn't worried, however. He was careful, and far too busy marveling at the view. The sun, far weaker here than it was on Earth, was almost directly overhead, perfectly illuminating the crater. James wished he had a camera.

What was he thinking? Of course he had a camera, the one mounted to his helmet. He raised his left arm to type on his wristscreen, but had to pause for a minute. The sheer size of the crater was giving him vertigo, and James had to step away from the edge. He took a step back, then tapped on the screen. It illuminated, but James was having a hard time reading anything. He quickly brushed the screen off, thinking it was dust, but it didn't improve.

"Any word from Houston?" Jordyn asked over the radio.

"Negative," replied Harrison. "Probably another minute or two more until we get their signal."

It was probably time to head back. James turned around to go back to the rover, but the movement made his head spin. He paused again, putting his gloved hands instinctively on his helmet as a wave of dizziness enveloped him. He tried to take a deep breath, but it didn't help. Something was wrong.

"Jord...ston?" James slurred as his vision narrowed. "Hey, uh..."

"Say again?" someone answered, their voice sounding tinny and far away in James' helmet.

James tried to breathe—something entered his lungs, but it didn't satisfy. Sheer terror filled the parts of James' brain that were still working.

Darkness enveloped James as he lost consciousness. He started to fall forward, but his extended right leg, still stiff from his brain's last impulse, twisted his fall. James' limp body fell backwards and to the side, landing hard on the Martian sediment. It started to give way.

James, now blissfully unaware of anything that was happening, tumbled off the ledge and over the lip of the crater.

CHAPTER FIFTEEN

James didn't dream—in fact, he wasn't cognizant of anything at all. There was nothing but blackness and silence for what seemed like quite a long time.

The first thing that James was conscious of was noise. It was a strange, electronic noise, four ascending notes that never quite reached resolution. He listened to it for a moment, the tones coming in louder, clearer.

WARNING...OXYGEN LEVEL EIGHT PERCENT, said a grating women's voice, practically shouting. *SUIT BREACH DETECTED.*

James heard the words, but it took him more than a second to understand them. His brain was plodding, his thoughts tedious. Suddenly the words started to take on meaning.

Then came the pain.

James was slammed violently into full consciousness, his mind flooding with thoughts. Where was he? He was on Mars, he was installing a beacon, he was...

Another wave of crippling pain hit him. His head felt like it was in danger of exploding into a million pieces. It was as if a concussion had combined with a hangover, then drove nails into his skull. His lungs burned too, as if he had stood over a campfire and inhaled deeply—repeatedly. What the hell had happened?

WARNING...OXYGEN LEVEL SEVEN PERCENT, shouted his suit's computer. *SUIT BREACH DETECTED.*

"Hello?" James breathed into his mic before choking and coughing. He was having a hard time inhaling, much less speaking. Nobody responded.

Everything was dark around James. He was lying face down in red dust, which was just barely illuminated by his helmet's quivering, malfunctioning heads-up display. He rolled his body over just a bit, and sunlight streamed through, temporarily dazzling him.

"Hello?" he wheezed again. Again, there was no response.

James slowly pushed himself to his hands and knees, checking each extremity for injury. The dust and sand he was lying in gave slightly underneath his gloves and kneepads, and James even started to slide backwards a little. Forgetting about taking it slow, James rolled onto his butt and stuck his boots and hands into the ground to arrest his slide. His headache throbbed as punishment.

James suddenly became aware of a new noise, one different than his suit's alarm. It was a hissing sound, one that on Mars could only mean death. There was no secret where it was coming from either—James' helmet, though not entirely punctured, was a spider's web of cracks and fractures in the composite glass. He was lucky it hadn't blown out entirely and killed him already.

WARNING...OXYGEN LEVEL SIX PERCENT...SUIT BREACH DETECTED

James still didn't understand exactly what had happened, but he understood one thing extremely well. He needed to get back to the rover, or he was going to die—and quickly. Once his M-suit ran out of the fresh oxygen that it was using at five-times its normal rate to keep him alive, his suit would lose pressure, and he would either suffocate or lose consciousness from vacuum exposure, whichever came first. With that thought pressing relentlessly on his consciousness, James—struggling to fight off the welling panic—stumbled to his feet, being careful not to lose his footing.

He was at the base of the drop that he was only just now starting to remember. Like Aaron had said, the drop itself wasn't too high, but it had been enough to damage James' helmet and destroy half of its electronics—as evidenced by the failing radio and malfunctioning heads-up display. The base of the cliff was fine sand, sloped up towards the precipice by years of wind and accumulation. If James wasn't careful, he'd tumble further down into the massive crater, and the slope of the sand didn't start to diminish for a good 200 meters.

"*Unity* in the blind," James said, his voice shaky from fear. "Jordyn? Aaron? I've fallen off a ledge near the rover. My suit's been breached."

No response.

"DAMN IT!" James cursed, his voice really trembling now. He looked at the cliff, then back at the slope behind him. He had to climb, he had to get up. The cliff itself was only about twice his own height, but it looked unstable. Big flat plates of what looked like sandstone jutted out from the crumbly cliff wall, providing tempting but fragile handholds.

ALERT…ALERT, the M-suit computer chanted. ***OXYGEN LEVEL CRITICAL. FIVE PERCENT. SUIT BREACH DETECTED.***

"This is Lake in the blind, I'm going to try to climb," James stuttered, doubting that anyone was even hearing him. He stepped up to the ledge and tested a flat rocky plate, hanging his entire body off of it before deciding that it would do. He held fast, then reached up with his left boot, testing another plate of rock. This one held too.

James took a deep breath and stepped up, reaching for another ledge with his free hand. Surprisingly enough, this one didn't break either. James found another handhold, then another foothold. He was a few feet up now, maybe a quarter of the way…

…***OXYGEN LEVEL CRITICAL. FOUR PERCENT…***

Suddenly, James' left hand began to lose its grip. The rocks were coated with sand and dust, and despite his best efforts, James couldn't recover. He lost his grip, the stone he was stepping on with his right foot cracked in half, and James fell hard. He slammed on his back, knocking the wind out of him and making his suit chirp another alarm. In horror, James watched as one of the cracks in his helmet spread ever so slightly.

James gagged for a moment, choking on his own shock.

...THREE PERCENT...

His vision narrowed and his mind clouded, but it wasn't because of a lack of oxygen. It was fear. Raw, primal fear. James was going to die, and he knew it. And it was going to be painful.

For a brief moment James considered just lying there, but something yanked him to his feet. Maybe it was the omnipresent fear of death that all humans share, or maybe it was the thought of his wife Claire and the two kids he shared with her. Either way, he wasn't going to die on his back.

James clutched at another jutting rock, putting all of his weight on it from the beginning. It pulled out of the soft cliff wall and fell, slamming painfully into his shoulder and just missing his damaged helmet. James didn't quit. He found another rock and then repeated the process. This time the rock simply snapped in half, crumbling into tiny pieces in his hand.

...TWO PERCENT...

Frustrated, James slammed his fists against the cliff wall and shouted. He looked to the sky to curse God, but just as he did so he caught a glimpse of movement.

It was Aaron, recognizable from the bright blue stripe above the bronzed visor that was peeking over the edge of the ledge above James. Aaron gestured towards his own helmet, making the emergency signal for oxygen that they had learned in training with his gloved hand.

"Two!" shouted James, who stuck out two fingers as he realized that his shouting was useless. He had to slow down his breathing, he needed to conserve the air he had left.

Aaron acknowledged with a hand signal and disappeared from the edge before James could signal that his suit was damaged. What the hell was Aaron thinking? Was he trying to get Jordyn? The rover? There was no time!

"Come back!" James shouted, not caring about his oxygen levels anymore. "Aaron, please! Come–"

Aaron reappeared suddenly, but this time it wasn't just his helmet peeking over the ledge. James watched, mouth agape, as Aaron lowered himself over the ledge as if intending to climb down, then let go of the edge, tumbling backwards and falling towards the ground. He landed a few feet away from James, feet first, knees bending as he expertly rolled backwards to spread the impact of his fall. James tried to reach for him, but it was too late—Aaron was rolling, tumbling down the dune of sand, arms flailing wildly.

It was a good fifty feet before Aaron's tumble came to an end. He was up in a flash, scrambling up the hill, sliding one step backwards for every step forward.

James stood still in shock, but only for a moment. He had no idea what Aaron was up to, but he was his only chance. Being careful not to lose his own balance, James stumbled down the hill towards Aaron as fast as he dared.

They met mere seconds later. Aaron, his face grim with determination, gestured for James to sit down.

"Just hold still!" James heard Aaron shout. His voice was incredibly faint and shrill, barely making it through his helmet and the thin Martian air before reaching James' ears, significantly distorted. Aaron started fumbling for something in his tool pouch, his gloved hand emerging seconds later with what looked like a red garden hose. James recognized it instantly as a "buddy tube." He, and all the members of the Ares crew carried one just like it on every Martian spacewalk.

Aaron hastily plugged one end onto the hard chest plate of his own M-suit's life support and power system, then reached to connect the other end to the same adapter on James' suit. James reached up to help, but Aaron quickly brushed his hands out of the way. There was a scraping noise as Aaron attempted to plug the buddy tube into the socket, but James' suit gave a negative sounding beep.

"Sand!" shouted Aaron as he hurriedly worked to clean out the socket with his fingers, his voice extremely faint. James could do nothing but look at Aaron as he worked to save his life. Panic and worry were apparent in his furrowed brow, and sweat was dripping from his face onto the inside of his helmet as he worked desperately. It really was getting hard for James to breathe now.

"GOT IT!" Aaron cried triumphantly, immediately punching a command into his wristscreen. A new hissing sound suddenly filled James' ears—this time the sound of air entering the suit rather than leaving it. The alarm that had been blaring in James' M-suit this entire time finally ceased.

"You OK?" Aaron panted, his voice still somewhat faint, but now coming through the buddy tube that connected their suits' life support systems.

"I think so," replied James, his voice quivering. "I...uh..."

"What happened?" Aaron said, double checking the tube's connection before examining James' near-shattered helmet. Air was still leaking from it, but with Aaron's fresh life-support system connected they had plenty of time before they ran out of air.

"I don't know," James said, still in a bit of a daze. "I think I passed out, I think I fell."

"What?" shouted Aaron.

"I fell!" James yelled back, instantly regretting it as he lungs screamed in pain.

"Yeah, you fell," Aaron laughed nervously. "What about injuries? What's your suit's status?"

"I'm fine, but the suit is on the fritz," answered James, checking his dead wristscreen. "I've got no readouts."

"*Unity,* Houston, I've got Lake here, alive," Aaron said into his radio. "I've got him buddy-hosed, his visor has a lot of cracks and fractures—we need to get this done soon. My suit's already expending a lot of oxygen. I've got maybe twenty minutes, a half-hour if we sit still."

Aaron paused for a moment, listening for a reply that was inaudible to James. "Sounds good," he said finally. "James, Jordyn is going to pull up to the edge with the rover, we're going to use the crane to haul us back up. Are you good to climb back up to the base of the ledge?" he asked, gesturing up the hill of sand.

"Yeah," James answered, his eyes nervously locked onto the spider web of cracks in his visor.

"I'm going to run a quick systems check here before we climb," Aaron said, punching another command into his wristscreen. "We'll take it slow, we don't want any mis..." Aaron trailed off suddenly, staring at his wristscreen.

"What is it?" James asked nervously.

"Damn."

Aaron never swore. James knew this was serious. "What?" he repeated.

"James, your suit CO_2 levels are off the charts," Aaron answered. "They're dropping now, but your suit diagnostics said that you spiked at 18%. Didn't your suit give you a warning alert?"

"No," James said softly. "Damn, no wonder I passed out."

"That could have killed you," said Aaron. "James, if your suit hadn't been feeding in extra oxygen to keep your suit pressurized you'd be dead already. It must've flushed out the excess CO_2."

James nodded inside his helmet, his lips suddenly feeling very dry.

The climb back up to the base of the precipice was slow and tedious. With every step upwards in the fine, dusty sand, the two men sank a half step back. What should've been a quick, 30-second climb turned into five minutes of arduous scrambling made all the harder by the short, three-foot hose that connected the two men.

Jordyn and the rover reached the top of the ledge at almost the exact same time Aaron and James reached the bottom. It took a few minutes for Jordyn to attach the right hook to the base of the cable, but soon enough, James and Aaron were hooking their carabiners onto the attachment point. The two men had to go up at the same time, and they had to go slowly so as not to affect the rover's already precarious position. After two full minutes of being suspended, the two men reached the top of the ledge. Jordyn, her eyes wide behind her helmet's glass, helped them inside immediately.

The rover was surprisingly spacious on the inside. It was large enough to carry four fully-suited astronauts up to five hundred miles on a single charge, and with its tiny airlock it could be fully pressurized for more comfortable travel. The second the three astronauts were inside Jordyn initiated the pressurization cycle and backed the rover away from the ledge.

Breathable air filled the inside of the rover as it pressurized itself. The pressure pushing in on James' helmet made the cracked grass bend and pop ominously as the glass actually started to bend *towards* James' face. The second the computer indicated safe pressure, James twisted his helmet off. He was safe.

"God, James," Jordyn said, reaching back from the driver's seat and putting a gloved hand on his face. "You scared the shit outta' all of us. You didn't say anything, you just...disappeared."

"We thought we lost you," added Aaron as he removed his own helmet. "And I'm sure NASA was having an aneurism."

"What the hell happened?" Jordyn asked, turning her attention back to the rover's navigation equipment.

"He passed out," Aaron answered for James. "Fell off the ledge. He's lucky his helmet wasn't totally punctured. In fact, he's lucky it cracked, too."

"CO2 poisoning," James said, his heartrate beginning to come down for the first time in the past twenty minutes. "Something malfunctioned in my suit. I...I..."

James broke down and trembled for a minute, the realization of his fragile mortality overcoming him for a moment. He was alive, and he knew he was lucky. Aaron and Jordyn had saved his life.

"Thank you," he stuttered, tears starting to come now. "Thanks, you two."

"It's ok, James," Jordyn said—rare, genuine concern in her voice. "Really, there's no way we'd leave you."

"We're family, man," nodded Aaron. "There's no way we're going to lose another one. Not after Nikki."

James nodded, his quick moment of weakness ending. He sniffled loudly, and paused to wipe the tears from his face with his gloves, smearing red dust all over his nose and cheeks.

"*Unity,* we're coming home," Jordyn said simply over the radio. "Tell Houston that Lake really is alright. Can you update our waypoints from there?"

"Thank goodness," Gonzalez replied, breathing an audible sigh of relief over the radio. "Damn, James, you had us worried. Mike didn't want to become the doctor."

"I didn't say that," objected Mike. "James, seriously, are you ok?"

It was all James could do to nod, so Jordyn answered for him. "He's fine," she said.

The rover lurched forward, heading towards Mars' weak afternoon sun and down the crater rim towards the flat Martian midlands. James sat back in his seat, letting the emotions wash over him and then drain from him. He was lucky to be alive. He was going back to base. He was safe.

Or was he?

A thought entered James' mind and took root instantly. It wasn't a thought anymore. It was fact. Plain and simple.

Someone had murdered Nikki.

And someone had just tried to kill him too.

CHAPTER SIXTEEN

The Martian sun had been set for over an hour by the time James, Aaron, and Jordyn arrived back at *Unity.* The rover slowed down gently, pitching slightly forward as the rover's big, squishy shock absorbers took on the momentum. The light movement was enough to wake up Aaron, who shook his head quickly and rubbed the sleep out of his eyes.

There was no fatigue in James, not even a trace of it. His body ached, his head throbbed, and his lungs still burned—but there was no sleep in his eyes. His mind was running a million miles per hour, but he was no closer to consolidating his thoughts.

Everyone was a suspect, but at the same time, no one was. James had spent years with this group of people. He could finish their sentences and read their thoughts. None of them were capable of such a barbaric act.

Harrison was particularly suspicious. James had seen him rummaging through Nikki's stuff, and Harrison had caught James looking at the microscopes and seen the tape on his cup. But that didn't explain Harrison's very real grief at Nikki's passing. Besides, James was now looking for someone that was after him too, and Harrison hadn't done anything, *anything,* that seemed suspicious to James in that regard. He'd have to keep an eye on him though.

Gonzalez had caught James in the lab too, but that didn't seem like a big deal. Besides, any problems with the mission would fall on his head. James knew that Gonzo was already in trouble with Houston for somehow missing signs of Nikki's suicide—as if *he* were truly expected to know something like that.

Mike seemed detached from this all somehow, even though he had brought up the possibility of Nikki's death not being suicide during their brief chat after his physical. He had also mentioned something about relationship strain back home though, hadn't he?

Jordyn was James' closest friend on the crew, and the two were confidants—to a point. Why was it then that James couldn't bring himself to mention his suspicions to her? Then there was Aaron, who seemed to have acquitted himself after risking it all to save James today. Or had he?

No one could have done any of this. No one.

But someone had. This wasn't coincidence. James couldn't trust anyone. The pounding of his headache only drove that point home with every throb.

It took only moments for Jordyn to dock the rover to the pressurized tube that would connect it to the SIM. After the computer voiced the safe docking, James grabbed his badly damaged helmet and followed Aaron out of the rover's small hatch and into the tube. A few damaged pieces of metal and glass from James helmet fell down onto the reinforced weave, which Jordyn bent over and swooped up.

"Thanks," James said weakly.

"Try not to dwell on it," answered Jordyn. "What happened out there. You made it, and you're ok. We're ok here."

"Yeah," nodded James. He could tell that Jordyn was worried that he'd be terrified of going outside again, or something stupid like that. That was the least of his worries. He was more terrified of going *inside*.

The three emerged into the SIM where the rest of the crew was gathered to meet them. James was instantly accosted by hugs from all three of the other crew members. Gonzalez seemed especially relieved, and Mike was already shoving a warm cup of coffee into James' free left hand.

"Damn," Harrison said simply, looking at James' helmet with wide eyes. "Can I see that?"

James hesitated, his helmet clutched in his right hand.

"Oh no," laughed Harrison uncomfortably. "I'm sorry—that was some serious shit out there and here I am obsessing over your gear. Are you alright, James? Thank God you're alright."

"I'm fine," James answered flatly.

"Come have a seat," said Gonzo. "Take a minute to talk things out with us. Houston wants you to make a recording afterwards to debrief. They've put a freeze on EVA until Harrison's gone over your suit."

"I'd like to look too," Aaron said quickly. "Could be a software glitch if his alarms didn't go off."

"Done," Gonzalez nodded. "Now come on, James. Mike's got a dessert ration ready for you that I think you're going to like."

"I'll take that off your hands," Harrison said, reaching for James' helmet. James recoiled backwards, and Harrison stepped back in surprise, his hands shooting into the air defensively. James could see in his eyes that he looked totally bewildered.

"Lay off him for a second!" Jordyn snapped, pushing her shorter frame between James and the rest of the crew. "Give the man some damn space! He almost died out there!"

"Relax, *Major*," Harrison said defensively. "You're right, you're right. Sorry."

There was a short moment of silence as the crew took a collective breath. With the exception of the day Nikki went missing, this was the first time anyone on the crew had raised their voices in true contention. It was clearly uncomfortable for everyone.

"It's ok, Jordyn," James said softly, taking a step forward and clearing his throat. "It's OK, everyone. Thanks for looking out for me, I mean it. I clearly gave you guys quite the scare. It's like you guys care about me or something."

"Don't go getting all big-headed," quipped Mike. His bit of humor landed with perfect timing. Despite his worries, James couldn't help but laugh, and the tension amongst the crew eased slightly.

"I am sorry," Harrison said quickly, rubbing the back of his head awkwardly. "I really was-"

"It's all good," interrupted James, reaching out and handing his helmet to Harrison, who took it sheepishly.

"Come on then," Gonzalez said good-naturedly, reaching out to slap James on the back before stopping due to a withering glare from Jordyn. "It's peach cobbler."

"How about we all get some, eh?" suggested Mike. "I'll go heat up some more."

"That sounds good," James said, his voice shaking again for some reason. He paused to take a sip of hot coffee, then followed Gonzo towards the large table that the whole crew could sit around.

Everyone was intensely interested in what had happened, and they all listened to James in rapture as he recounted everything that had happened at the crater. By the time he had finished and Jordyn and Aaron had taken to telling their side of the story, James' cobbler and coffee were cold. He didn't care, and dived in immediately—he was starving.

It was interesting to hear the others' perspectives. Apparently they were all oblivious to what had happened with James until NASA had replied saying that the beacon was functioning properly. Gonzo had given the group the all clear to come back to base, but James hadn't replied to Jordyn's command to come back to the rover. By the time Aaron found the ledge barren, James had been unconscious or fighting for life for nearly fifteen minutes.

Aaron had indeed acted heroically when he jumped down to save James. Gonzalez, who had to act quickly without any word from Houston, had ordered Jordyn and Aaron to use the rover to recover James so as not to risk anyone else's lives. It was a fact that made Gonzo visibly uncomfortable when he admitted it, but James understood entirely. Still, had Aaron not disobeyed orders, James would likely have been dead.

Harrison's telling of NASA's full on freak-out was almost funny in hindsight. The second the crew had realized what had happened, Gonzalez had sent an emergency message to Houston. That meant that James was recovered by the time the radio waves reached Earth, so the crisis had already passed when the resulting barrage of panic came back from NASA. There were five straight minutes of sheer terror from Earth, then a pause as Gonzalez' message telling NASA that James was safe made it to Earth. Finally, Julianna Scoville, the mission's flight director, sent back a single, relieved message that must have been mashed into her keyboard: "askdofhsdjona." "That's a lot more g-rated than what I would have said," laughed Gonzalez as he related the story. James forced a hollow laugh.

The others were still eager to talk with James, but he was finding it hard to talk with any of them. Not only did his lungs and head still ache, but his trust and confidence in his crewmates was completely shattered. Finally, Jordyn seemed to get the message and bluntly told everyone that they should give James some space and privacy. It was exactly what James needed. The SIM, which for a few weeks seemed large and spacious compared to *Perseus*, no longer seemed safe.

James filmed his debriefing video for Houston, made sure it sent, then hit the SIM's shower and helped himself to double the standard allowable time. He let the hot water run over his body, washing away the sweat and grime from the day. It did little, however, to alleviate the tension James was feeling.

James paused on the way out to gaze at his reflection in the mirror. He looked hammered. His eyes were bloodshot, and dark circles were underneath both of his eyes. He was also getting older—there was no doubt about that. New wrinkles were forming on his brow, perhaps accelerated by the physical and emotional stress he'd been under for a while now. His dark hair was also looking a tad thinner—could it be the radiation that he'd been exposed to almost constantly since he'd left Earth? He had known about the risks when he accepted the assignment, but it had mattered little at the time.

There were fresh bruises all over his body from the fall he took earlier, and a small cut on his thigh. His arms were sore from everything that had happened, and his hands and fingers were particularly ravaged from his desperate attempts to climb to safety, even though he was wearing gloves. James examined each finger absentmindedly, then set to work brushing his teeth. He was only ten seconds in when he paused and looked at his fingers again.

There could be no more wasting time.

James dressed quickly and left the bathroom, stopping only to throw his sweat-soaked EVA clothes into the SIM's chemical washer. A quick glance at the digital clock in the center of the room said it was 2402 hours—a time only possible on Mars. The crew should be settling down now, though there wasn't much of a rush considering that tomorrow's EVAs had been cancelled until Harrison and Aaron could look into James' suit "malfunction."

James walked through the kitchen and into the inflatable sleeping and rec module, his mind churning. So much had happened. It hadn't even been a month since Nikki's passing—the crew had only been on Mars for about three weeks, and they still had almost two months left before they departed for *Perseus*, and then Earth. James had a sudden realization that he would be back on Earth in just less than a year now, but that seemed like an eternity away. Two more months on Mars, nine more months in space. All with a murderer somewhere in his presence.

Jordyn, Gonzo, and Harrison were already in their sleeping bags, and Aaron and Mike were sitting on their individual cots, scrolling through their glowing tablets. James' fear and suspicions were tempered just a bit as he remembered that none of his fellow crewmates seemed violent or murderous. Perhaps there was another explanation? Someone from Houston tampering with systems, maybe? No, that wasn't likely. Then again, none of this was.

James sat down on his cot and pulled out his own tablet. He accessed his email account and went straight to his inbox. There was nothing new from Patterson, nor anyone else for that matter. NASA wouldn't have told Claire about what had almost happened today, not yet.

James stayed up on his tablet until his crewmates had gone to sleep. He'd wait a little while longer yet, but tonight he was going to scan all of his collected fingerprints and send them back to Patterson. He'd go over the bolt again, seeing if the smear was indicative of something, anything that could be matched to the fingerprints that he had collected. He only hoped Patterson had access to some sort of software that could do the analysis. James knew there was no way he'd be able to find a match from Mars.

Mind roiling, James crawled into his sleeping bag and prepared for another sleepless night of sneaking around. Then, repeating a nervous tic that he had developed over the past couple weeks, he reached towards the bottom of the sleeping bag with his toes, just to make sure the little baggies and samples he'd stealthily collected were still there.

James' toes felt nothing but polyester and fleece.

He was already awake, but James' faculties jerked back into overdrive. He sat up quickly and pulled his legs from the bag, swinging around to stick his arm deep into his sleeping bag. He groped around for a moment or two, then swore under his breath.

There was nothing there. No plastic baggies, no fingerprint samples, no bolt. They were gone. Stolen.

Someone knew what he was doing.

CHAPTER SEVENTEEN

"So that's what happened," Harrison concluded, placing the small piece of green plastic down on the table. "A single wire came unsoldered—that's why it took us and the boys back in Houston a whole day to figure it out."

James stared at the tiny piece of electrical equipment that had come from the bowels of his dismantled M-suit. It was strange to think that such a little wire on such a little computer chip could have such deadly effects.

"Wait a second," said Jordyn. "That's it?"

"That's it," nodded Aaron, who sat next to Harrison. "That controls the rebreather filters—the things that remove excess CO_2. There's one just like it in all of our suits, and the spares."

"It's a total fluke, really," added Harrison. "And Houston agrees with me. There's no inherent weakness in the soldering, no electrical issues. The wire just came loose, simple as that. It's an accident." Harrison looked to Aaron, who nodded his agreement.

James nodded too, though inside he didn't buy any of it. Someone had been through his things, and someone had doubtlessly tampered with this tiny piece of equipment. He had suspected as much ever since last night.

James hadn't slept, mostly out of sheer terror. He sat in his violated sleeping bag all night, his eyes wide open as he contemplated his next move. Initially he had decided that he would let the crew know of his suspicions and tell them that he was convinced that one of them had murdered Nikki—and had also tried to murder him. After an hour of toying with the idea, however, he had thought better of it. Alerting the crew now, without any real evidence, could be disastrous. It would likely make the real killer panic and do something rash, putting the entire crew in jeopardy. And even if it didn't, it would tear the crew's comradery apart at the seams, something just as deadly in the vacuum of space, millions of miles away from home. No, James would sit on that idea like a royal flush in poker—it was something to be used at just the right moment.

James had, however, contacted Patterson almost immediately. He sent a frantic email detailing the situation and asking for advice now that his cover was blown. The second the email was sent, James deleted the copy from his email account, then changed his passwords for everything on his tablet.

This morning James got up with the rest of the crew. They exercised, performed their adjusted duties, ate breakfast and lunch together, then reported to this meeting once Harrison had announced that he and Aaron had figured out the problems. And here they all sat in the meeting and auxiliary room, sitting around the crew table which had James' deconstructed suit laid out over it.

"Something doesn't make sense to me though," Mike said thoughtfully. "You said that James' alarm didn't even go off, right?"

"That's right," acknowledged Aaron. "And it's for a stupid reason, too. This wire, the disconnected one, it's not just a control wire. It supplies power as well. See, there are two little wires inside the rubber. Two separate solder points, too. That power doesn't just run to the rebreather system itself. It also runs the CO_2 sensors."

"Power didn't make it to the CO_2 scrubbers and it didn't make it to the sensors," Harrison continued. "And the damn programming wasn't set to trigger an alarm for that particular sensor's power failure, just for CO_2 buildup. Which is stupid."

"Houston is working on a software patch to fix that now," said Aaron. "It'll be done by tonight. As for the wire breaking, it shouldn't happen again. We'll just have to make sure everyone follows the buddy system, no wandering off alone, and keep your buddy tubes close—that's what Houston recommends."

"You're saying we're good to go?" asked Gonzalez skeptically. "Are you sure about this?"

"Houston concurs," nodded Harrison. "I'm sure they'll give us the go-ahead by tomorrow morning, as soon as the software patch has been applied."

Gonzalez paused and looked at the suit thoughtfully. He looked up at James, then back down at the suit. "Gang, this can't happen again," he concluded.

"Agreed," said Jordyn.

"Seriously," nodded Aaron.

"This was too damn close," Gonzalez said softly. Then, suddenly pounding his fist on the table, he shouted. "TOO DAMN CLOSE! We can't lose anyone else, team. We just can't."

"We won't, Commander," stated Mike.

James stared at Gonzalez as he quickly regained his composure. He wasn't shocked by the sudden outburst—in fact, he found it hard to believe that he'd be shocked by anything else this entire mission.

The crew sat in somber silence for a moment, until Jordyn finally cleared her throat. "I think we need a day off," she said. "Not like a fake day off like today, I mean a real day off."

James nodded again, though once again his mind was elsewhere. He had been trying to figure out who had the capacity to tamper with the suit in such a precise way. Harrison was the first to come to mind, and James was finding it almost irrefutable that he was becoming his number one suspect—though that was useless without real evidence. Harrison managed all of the surface equipment on Mars, and he was well-versed with every electric system in the whole mission, from the suits to the space toilet. He could have known about the odd wiring configuration, and his day of tinkering to find the problem could easily have been faked. But Aaron, the crew's official flight engineer, would have become suspicious. He too had intimate electrical knowledge. The fact that the two men seemed to be in complete agreement seemed to acquit both of them—unless they were in it together, which seemed unlikely.

Come to think of it, nearly everyone on the crew had some knowledge of the electrical systems, even Mike, the biologist, and himself, the doctor. Everyone knew how critical systems worked, and how to repair them in a pinch. Besides, *anyone* knew that disconnecting *any* wire on a space suit would be dangerous. Anyone in the room could have just pulled a random wire and gotten lucky.

The meeting adjourned. Harrison and Gonzalez both headed towards one of the computer terminals to communicate with Houston, while Mike, Jordyn, and Aaron left to go prepare dinner. That left just James alone with the suit.

The bodysuit itself was fine. The flexible, reinforced fabric didn't show the slightest sign of wear other than the brownish-red dust that covered nearly all of it, from the built-in boots to the helmet seal on the neck. The dust had stained the parts of the suit that were white, and the colored stripes around the elbows and knees—lime green to identify him from the others—were a little off-color.

The rigid part of the suit that surrounded the wearer's chest and back had been completely dismantled by Aaron and Harrison. James recognized the major components, and wondered how everything fit into such a compact package. He had a brief thought about collecting fingerprints or something— perhaps someone who had fiddled with the suit would have left fingerprints— but that would be useless. Everyone had been poking and prodding the suit all day, including himself.

The helmet sat on top of the suit, and seeing it again sent chills down James' spine. He hadn't even stopped to look at it from the outside before, and he wondered how he had even survived. The glass visor was cracked and deformed, and the built-in camera mounted on top of the helmet was crushed and crumpled. That camera had been recording everything since he'd turned it on upon exiting the rover—the video of him falling and being rescued was surely intense. It had already been beamed back to Earth, and James hoped they wouldn't show it to Claire. He'd better write her tonight. Should he tell her his suspicions? She'd go to NASA immediately, even if he begged her not to, which was as good as James shouting that someone in the SIM was a murderer. It wouldn't do any good. Not now anyway.

James sighed. He felt particularly alone. Claire seemed so far away right now. Hell, Earth was so far away right now. Getting back was starting to look like a terrifying, daunting challenge. He'd have to figure this out before he was killed. That was his only option.

A shimmer of motion caught James' eye. It was Jordyn, returning from the kitchen. She approached the table and stopped to look at the dismantled suit. James didn't bother trying not to look pensive.

"Good thing we have a spare," she shrugged, her jet-black ponytail brushing her dark shoulders under her tank top. She paused for a moment, then reached out and prodded James' helmet with one of her fingers. A small piece of glass fell on the table.

"It's such a weird fluke," James said, intentionally echoing the word Aaron and Harrison had employed to describe the malfunction. "Just a small wire like that."

"If *I* was trying to kill you I'd have just shoved you off a ledge or something," deadpanned Jordyn.

The hairs on the back of James' neck stood straight up.

"I'm sorry," she grinned quickly, noticing James' obvious discomfort. "Too soon, I know."

"It's ok," James explained quickly. "It's just that I think you might not..."

James trailed off, the rest of his sentence dying in his throat. He wanted to tell Jordyn what he was thinking. He couldn't bear this alone. But he couldn't bring himself to do it, either. Why couldn't he trust Jordyn?

"Not what?"

"I don't know what I was saying," James said, forcing a laugh. "I meant to say that you don't fit the killer type."

"Oh, is that what you think?" Jordyn asked in mock outrage. "I've killed for less."

"Don't bother playing along," waved James. "I botched the delivery, let's not prolong it."

Jordyn smiled, her white teeth emerging from behind her lips. James had two simultaneous thoughts: one, that he could very well be looking into the face of a killer; two, Jordyn looked quite beautiful and attractive.

Jordyn walked away, leaving James alone with the suit—an image of his vulnerable mortality. He shook his head and again thought of Claire back home on Earth.

He had been in space for too damn long.

CHAPTER EIGHTEEN

Patterson didn't reply.

It was the first thing that James checked when he awoke the morning after the meeting over his space suit. Shockingly, his inbox was empty, just like it was last night. James couldn't believe it. How could something so urgent be ignored? He quickly compared Mars' time to Earth's—right now, 0800 hours on Mars was about noon back in Houston. No, the time difference didn't explain it.

James drafted another urgent, follow-up message. Up until now James had been purposely vague in his emails just in case they were being intercepted, but he couldn't do that any longer. He explained everything—the bolt, how many prints he had been able to collect, even his suspicions—but then hesitated before pressing send.

He needed help, and he needed advice. But what good was Patterson going to be? He had said that he had how much experience as a police officer? It was months, not years. The guy could be a parking meter attendant for all James knew. Why in the world should James trust the man?

It didn't matter. Patterson was his only contact that knew what was going on, and James was going to need to have some faith. He sent the message, then deleted the copy from his sent folder.

James put his tablet back in its customary space, but only after flicking through the different apps and pages. His tablet was normally right by his cot, meaning that whoever had stolen the bolt and fingerprints could have had access to the tablet. It was password protected—and James had deleted all of

Patterson's emails—but James still worried that it could be compromised somehow. But he didn't know any better way. He'd just have to cycle his passwords weekly.

Leaving his cot, James headed towards the kitchen where the crew was gathering for a quick, standing breakfast. Just as Harrison and Aaron had predicted, NASA had already applied a software patch to the remaining M-suits, and the crew was cleared to continue with their mission duties. Today actually marked the beginning of some interesting operations—with the entire base infrastructure set up and most initial experiments approaching the four-week mark, it was time for some legitimately fascinating science.

James did his best to act normal, knowing that his charade would be more than amusing to whoever had tried to kill him. He chatted with Gonzalez about next week's rover expedition to some interesting water-caused rock formations, then pulled Mike aside to ask about the experiment racks that they'd be collecting and observing together today. He challenged both Aaron and Harrison to a video game when they found the time, then asked Jordyn about her husband back home. He tried to pick up some sign of deception in one of them, any of them, but none came. His crewmates all seemed normal and genuinely upbeat. Who was faking it?

"Oh, I almost forgot," Gonzalez said suddenly, his mouth still full of the tubed maple brown sugar oatmeal he'd been eating. He swallowed and continued. "Houston wanted me to let you know that they went ahead and authorized a name change for our target area. *Marte Vallis* is now *Nicole Vallis*."

"I like that," Harrison said sincerely.

"It's a fitting tribute," agreed Aaron. "We'll have to leave something there, maybe a makeshift memorial plaque or something."

Gonzalez nodded. "I bet we can make that happen. Let's everybody do some brainstorming, and I'll bring it up again next time we have a sit-down dinner."

"It's too bad you didn't die in that crater, James," teased Jordyn. "We'd have made a nice plaque for you too, I'm sure."

Jordyn's ribbing was met by a couple of amused sniffs from the crew. Nikki's death was still fresh and sad, but the crew was beginning to move on. People could joke about death and danger again. At least, everyone but James seemed to feel that way.

Breakfast adjourned, and James went to unpack one of the spare helmets and rigid life support casing that he'd combine with his still-operational M-suit base layer. He carefully drew a large, block number 4—his assigned identification number—on the places where they were on his previous suit, then got busy giving it a careful, thorough inspection. Everything looked fine, but that was just on the outside. James was going to have to trust that whoever had tampered with the first suit wouldn't tamper with this one. And if they did, James was going to have to rely on whoever he was buddied with.

The new, stricter buddy-team rules set in place by Gonzalez and NASA had James both relieved and slightly sick to his stomach. Ostensibly, having every crew member assigned a buddy on every EVA would make sure that someone could help if another suit malfunctioned—however unlikely that would be. It meant that James could rest easy that he wouldn't die alone. Unfortunately, it also meant that James could potentially be paired off with whoever had tried to kill him before. He'd have to trust that his new helmet's top-mounted camera would dissuade anyone from some direct assault.

He was getting better at putting his suit on. James was down to about five minutes from sliding his legs into the skin-tight suit to attaching and securing the new helmet and the rigid life-support casing that rested on his shoulders and back. Even with spare parts the suit felt just like the original. It was like nothing had ever happened.

Mike was his assigned buddy today. While the rest of the crew headed towards the main rover, James and Mike headed out towards the mission's other rover—an unpressurized buggy and trailer that had the range of a golf cart. They'd only be heading out a couple hundred yards—still within view of the SIM—to collect an experiment package that had been set up on only their second day on the red planet. It contained several sealed biology experiments, some with live cultures, which was why Mike, the biologist, and James, the doctor, would share the responsibility today. This particular experiment involved penicillin spores that were being kept in various stages of contained Martian exposure. The potential medical applications fascinated James.

The golf cart ride out was quick and uneventful. *Unity* was intentionally set up in a large, flat plain, a few miles away from the nearest visible ridges and craters. The only thing that the two men had to watch out for during the drive were the periodic rocks and boulders that tended to blend in with the dusty, red Martian soil.

James looked over at Mike, who sat in the driver's seat. He seemed happy to be driving something for once, and his eyes darted back and forth as he looked around at the scenery. James looked back to the ground directly in front of where they were driving and tried to fight off the paranoia that Mike would try to kill him somehow. It took him a moment, but James got a grip on the thought. If anything happened he'd have to tackle it when it came up. That's all he could do.

The two men quickly reached their destination. Mike parked the rover, and he and James disembarked and headed towards the metal station that had been staked into the ground. James did a quick summary inspection of the equipment, then got busy noting this round of measurements on his wristscreen. They'd be taking one of the five sample boxes back to the SIM today, where they'd do some more tests and measurements while the rest of the crew was out.

It took a full hour to verify all of the experiment station's readings. Once that was done, James and Mike carefully removed the selected box from its mounting, then transitioned it to the golf cart. They tied it down carefully, then went back to the equipment rack to make sure everything was left in order.

"Looks good," said Mike. "Let me just check that the mountings are still secure."

The task complete, James took a step away from the rack and turned to look out at Mars' vastness. The SIM was behind him, which meant that all James saw were the desert plains. It was something that James never got tired of looking at. It was exotic, it was wild, and it was untrod by humankind. Most of the steps that he'd taken during this mission made him the first and only person in history to step there.

James took a quick look back to check on Mike, then went back to looking out. For some reason, he saw something else in the Martian desert today: desolation. Mars was beautiful, but it was dead. There were no trees here, no scrub brush, no tiny plants. Even in the American Southwest there were plants and bugs crawling around the desert, but not here. The closest comparison was probably Antarctica or the Sahara—but then again, those places still had bacteria living in the soil.

"It's pretty, isn't it?" asked Mike, stepping next to James. "I notice you staring out like this a lot when you're on EVA. I can see why you do it."

"It's so...unique," James answered. "And pictures will never do it justice."

"They never get the color right, do they?" nodded Mike. He was right of course. Some pictures made Mars look almost crimson red, others made it look burnt orangey-brown. In reality, the surface was a complex mix of colors that blended together. Black specks of ancient lava, red bits of iron-soaked dust, and light brown patches of dirt all made up Mars' muted colors.

"You know the one thing I'll never get used to?" followed-up Mike rhetorically. "The sky. I mean, you could almost see something like this on Earth, but never with this sky. It's either completely black or like it is now."

James voiced his agreement and looked up. It was one of the hazier days they'd had so far—NASA had indicated that the planet was experiencing a somewhat windy year, which meant that plenty of dust was in the thin atmosphere. It gave the sky the same brown-red hue as the dirt, and made the horizon a little hard to discern sometimes.

"It's like that old rhyme," continued Mike. "How does it go? Red sky at night, sailor's delight...red sky at morning...wait, how does it end?"

"Red sky at morning, sailors take warning," finished James. He'd heard the rhyme before.

"That's right," nodded Mike.

It was an old saying involving the weather, that much James understood. Long before modern weather reports and radios, isolated seamen would look to the skies to make predictions from the weather. A red-soaked sunset meant high pressure and good weather, but a crimson sunrise implied that the high pressure was passing, giving way to low pressure and impending rain. That was the scientific explanation that James had learned, anyway.

The words of the rhyme ran through his head again. *Red sky at night, sailor's delight. Red sky at morning, sailors take warning.* It was easy for James to understand how a bygone sailor must have felt as he sailed across a vast, empty ocean. It would be terribly lonely at times, even if he knew his crewmates well. And the thought of an impending storm would have been terrifying. James instantly identified with the mental picture he'd just constructed. How fitting it was that scientists thought that Mars was once covered in massive oceans.

"You're awfully quiet lately," Mike said after a moment of silence. "You alright, James? Still thinking about the other day?"

James didn't reply right away. He was overcome by a deep sense of being alone, even with Mike standing right beside him. Finally, he cleared his throat. "I'm all good," he lied. "Just thinking about all this," he finished, gesturing towards the dusty wilderness.

"Got it," nodded Mike. "But seriously, James. If you ever need to talk, I'm here."

James nodded. There was much he needed to talk about—but no one he could trust.

Their work outside finished, the two men returned to the cart and turned back towards *Unity*. They followed the tracks that the cart had left behind on the drive out, leading them straight back to the SIM. James and Mike carefully grabbed the experiment box and headed towards the airlock, sealing the door tight behind them, then entered the SIM, not bothering to change out of their suits until they had put the heavy box down in the lab. James turned to go back to the airlock to change out of his suit, then sighed to himself in frustration. He had tracked red dust into the SIM.

"Ha," laughed Mike. "Forgot to wipe your boots off as you came inside I see."

"I was a bit preoccupied with the box," answered James. "Weren't you?"

"Cleanliness is next to godliness," shrugged Mike. "At least, that sounds like something Aaron would say. Anyways, I wiped my feet when I came in— I'm not an animal."

"Very funny," replied James.

The two men both headed back to the airlock to change out of the M-suits, then returned to the lab to get to work. Mike began carefully unpacking the experiment box, while James grabbed a broom from the storage compartment. He started sweeping up his dusty footprints, starting in the lab and retracing his steps.

Only he had made the mess. Only his footprints stained the floor with red dust. James swept up the solitary steps—steps as lonely as the man sweeping them.

CHAPTER NINETEEN

Days passed, then days began to turn to weeks. Soon, the Ares I crew had been on Mars for a month and a half—a month and a half of frenzied science and exploration. But for James, it had been a month and a half of pure hell.

There were two different kinds of hell to choose from. The first centered around routine and slow-burning tension. On these days, James would wake up a half hour earlier than the others, just to be safe. He'd check his tablet for an email from Patterson, an email that never came.

Patterson. His silence was as sudden as his initial email accusing someone of murder, and in a way, it affected James more. He had held up his end of the bargain, why had Patterson gone silent when things mattered most? Had something happened? Had he stopped trusting James? Or was it something more sinister? Perhaps someone was blocking their communication. Perhaps someone had gained access to James' email. He changed his passwords daily now—but it clearly wasn't doing any good. Every time James checked his email his heart filled with dread—dread of finding nothing again, or finding something worse.

With the initial excitement of a Mars landing over, the only person who really emailed him was Claire—and her emails were growing shorter. She and the kids were obviously busy, and James understood how hard it must be on her to run everything by herself. He longed to tell her about his suspicions, but he knew he couldn't. Nothing had happened in weeks. There was no evidence.

Claire's emails also served to add stress to James' life—even though it was surely unintentional. Hearing about his wife and kids' problems when he couldn't help them—couldn't even communicate live with them—tore at his heart.

The near-constant hell of isolation and routine continued with lab work, physical examinations, and EVAs within sight of the SIM. When he was alone—which had only happened twice so far—James searched the SIM high and low for the missing bolt, the missing fingerprints, or any kind of clue. There was nothing, absolutely nothing to justify his suspicions of murder. James felt like he was slowly losing his grip on reality.

Sometimes the monotonous hell would lift, but only because of what James liked to think of as spontaneous hell. These days weren't really spontaneous—every detail of them was meticulously planned—but they put James in new situations. Day-long rover missions to far-off craters and formations, maintenance work on the far-flung beacons, and even simple long-distance exploration out of sight from the SIM meant that James was out of his element, paired off with a buddy, terrified of some sort of "accident" that might kill him. On these days, he arrived back at the SIM far more exhausted and tense than the day before. This tension had never really left him—James' body was continuously tense and sore—and it was starting to take its toll. The biggest toll, however, wasn't on his body. It was on his mind.

By now, James was starting to doubt and question everything. He'd been paired off with every single member of the crew, and nothing had happened to him. In fact, the mission seemed to be going better than ever. There were no more suit malfunctions, no technical problems with the SIM, and the crew morale seemed to be at an all-time high since Nikki's death. If it wasn't for the physical items that acted as evidence of Nikki's absence—an extra M-suit tucked away, a tightly packed cot in the sleeping module—it would have been easy to forget everything that had happened.

Fortunately, however, Nikki wasn't forgotten—the mission made sure of it. Her expertise as a geologist was sorely missed, and even with NASA's supervision the crew found it difficult to complete her tasks and experiments. Her simple presence was also a noted absence. Nikki, at least the Nikki that James knew before, was easy to talk to, and quick to bring up conversation. Every quiet moment during dinner reminded James of that. He still felt strangely guilty that he had missed the signs—even as his mind and heart both screamed that this was murder, not suicide.

The crew had indeed left a makeshift memorial out in the Martian desert, right next to the American flag that stood near the MDV's landing site. NASA had also sent the crew a draft of a memorial that they wanted to put outside the Vehicle Assembly Building in Florida. It was a small fountain, flowing constantly with cool water, surrounded with flowers. It was a direct contrast to space, Mars, and the way Nikki had died.

The way Nikki had died. That was what kept James from letting go of his fears. It still didn't make complete sense, even now. James' near-miss with a similar fate, then the fact that his collection of "evidence" was stolen, only cemented things. But that was all James was holding on to now. He felt like a modern-day pilgrim, barely hanging on to some obscure religion.

The SIM's morning alarm rang, this time a classic rock and roll song from James' childhood. It was time to get up, even though James had been awake for a half an hour. As expected, there was no email from Patterson. Claire's daily email had been little more than a tweet about the day's events.

Today was going to be another day of routine hell for James. Yesterday had been a hard day of work at a geologic excavation site fifty miles south of the SIM, and James was beat up and sore. Turns out shoveling for hours at a time in Mars' low gravity was just as dreary and painful as doing it back on Earth, even with the help of the rover's crane. However, the hard work brought the promise of a day inside, which would be nice. In fact, since today marked the halfway point in the Mars surface mission, NASA had halved their work assignments. James might even find time to take a nap.

James ran through his morning routine quickly. He didn't bother to change clothes—the only clothes that were allowed to be washed in the SIM's chemical washer were the sweaty EVA undergarments—and he had already showered the night before. A quick splash of water to the face would have to do, followed by a quick electric shave and teeth brushing.

The entire crew gathered for a joint breakfast—real pancakes and syrup courtesy of Mike and Aaron. It was a double rarity—the crew was seldom all together at the same time for breakfast, and freshly cooked food was uncommon. Pancakes were a first on this trip, and they wouldn't be able to have any once they were back aboard *Perseus.* There would be no making pancakes without gravity.

One of the hardest parts of James' self-imposed loneliness was pretending that nothing was wrong, and this morning was no different. He forced himself to wear a smile, and joked along with Gonzo and Harrison as they ribbed Jordyn for doing nothing other than running the crane yesterday. He caught both Mike and Aaron looking at him thoughtfully on two separate occasions during breakfast, but James didn't really care how convincing he was being. His ruse of tranquility only served to make the killer feel more confident that James had nothing on him or her, that much James knew for certain.

James finished off his pancakes, then left to do his half assignment of tasks. Today he'd be working with Mike to run blood samples from all the members of the crew. NASA was interested in how the human body was holding up to life on Mars, especially to the cosmic radiation that Mars couldn't protect from. Radiation and its consequences was just something the crew would have to live with for the rest of their lives. NASA did it's best to mitigate the risks through technology and timing, but there was no foolproof protection. James knew full well that every crew member had frozen some sperm—or eggs in Jordyn's case—back home on Earth, just in case.

James slid into his customary lab station and booted up the computer terminal, then flicked on the power for the blood chemistry analyzer and the accompanying microscope. James hated the microscope—every time James saw it he was reminded about his investigative failures.

The blood samples were already ready in their vials, and James decided to do his own sample first. He used a small dropper to suck a drop or two of blood out of his most recent sample, then placed it on the machine's tiny reader plate and slid it into position. It wouldn't take long for the machine to do its job, and James was curious about the results. He was especially interested in his red blood cell counts—NASA had the crew using two separate drugs to help prevent red blood cell loss, and with the mission's true halfway point coming up, NASA wanted the entire crew switched to the more effective pill.

"You doing cell counts?" Mike asked as he entered the lab and took his customary seat. "Will you let me know when you're done so I can take a look?"

"You got it," answered James. "Do you want me to do blood sugar and all that good stuff too?"

"It wouldn't hurt," nodded Mike. "Oh, and did you hear the good news? NASA is going to send us a copy of the new 'Star Wars' movie, even before it's released."

"I hope they don't blow it again," remarked James. "They got greedy last time, and a remake of the originals is just asking for trouble."

"I know it," laughed Mike. "But I can't help it. It's the nostalgia man. I'm telling you, I-"

The lab's main light flickered suddenly. It was unusual enough that it stopped Mike in the middle of his sentence.

James stared at the light, waiting for it to waver again—but it held. "Weird," James mumbled.

"Hey gang!" Gonzalez' voice rang from one of the other rooms in the SIM. "Hey, I want you all to put your computers in low power mode for a second.

Main computer is telling me we had a main bus D spike, followed by an undervolt. It's still giving me a warning."

"What's that again?" Mike asked James, looking worried as he booted down his computer, mere seconds after booting it up to begin with. "Bus D, what does that cover?"

The top light flickered again. James, not wanting any stray electrical problems, flicked the nearby switch and turned it off.

"Commander?" James shouted. "Should we go to action stations?"

"Everyone in the meeting room!" Gonzalez shouted back, his voice authoritative.

James and Mike headed straight towards Gonzo, joining up with Harrison on the way. Aaron and Jordyn were already seated next to Gonzalez, who sat in front of *Unity's* main computer terminal. Jordyn was now sending off a message to Houston, relaying information that Gonzalez pointed out on the screen.

"Sir?" Mike asked nervously.

"We're fine, we're fine," said Gonzo, waving for people to gather around. "I've already shut off that block, it's all good."

"Just an electrical fault," reassured Aaron. "I've honestly been surprised that we haven't had this happen already with all this sand and dust everywhere."

"Bus D is general linkage," Harrison said, looking at the schematics that Gonzalez had pulled up on the screen. "That's just main lights and the long-range communications antennae. Life support isn't even close to that."

James relaxed, but only slightly. The crew wasn't in any immediate danger, and he doubted that any killer would want to take everyone, including themselves, out.

"Damn, you scared me," Mike said. Only James heard him. The rest of the crew was already troubleshooting.

James took a deep breath, trying to get his stress levels under control. He told himself that this was nothing more than a technical inconvenience—though he wasn't totally convinced. He looked for a chair and got seated for what would doubtlessly be a long exchange between *Unity* and Houston.

CHAPTER TWENTY

James was right. It took nearly three hours for the crew and Mission Control to get on the same page. All the instrumentation was in agreement—something had faulted out near the communications antennae, and the fuse had tripped. It was something that the crew had rehearsed dozens of times. The complicated part was finding the fault and making the repair. That had to be done before swapping out the fuse inside *Unity*.

"How is your signal?" Gonzalez asked Jordyn again, making sure that the astronauts were still in contact with Houston.

"Five-by-five, all good," she answered quickly. "The beacon relays are nominal."

"Is it even worth dealing with?" Aaron wondered out loud. "Why don't we just use the beacons for communication? We only have a month and half left."

"I'm more worried about a stray electrical fault than I am the comms," replied Harrison. "I don't want some loose wire sparking around somewhere. I'm in charge of the technical well-being of this base, and I think we should fix it quick, Commander."

It took twenty minutes, but Houston eventually agreed with Harrison, and an EVA for that afternoon was tentatively authorized. It was a curse for James, as he was left to his own thoughts for a few hours while a plan was agreed upon by the more engineering-minded crewmembers. It was time that James spent watching the others warily—even though James saw this as an accident or an electrical fault, he couldn't shake the spreading feeling of unease. Today was turning into a day of spontaneous hell.

After several hours, Houston finalized their EVA approval. To find and fix the problem, Gonzalez assigned himself the difficult task of climbing up the outside of the SIM, with Aaron and Harrison by his side in case of emergency. That left Jordyn, Mike, and James inside.

"I want Mike on the video feeds and bio monitors," ordered Gonzalez as he put on his helmet and joined the others in the airlock. "Jordyn, I want you on comms with NASA. James, why don't you try to make yourself useful? Seriously, you don't do a damn thing around here."

James couldn't help but chuckle and shake his head as the three men shut the airlock and began depressurizing. Gonzalez, his voice now piped over the SIM's speakers, had a good laugh at his own joke as he headed outside. James just hoped his true skills weren't needed—that would mean there had been an accident, or worse.

His heart starting to pump again, James took a seat next to Mike at the main computer terminal. He already had the video feeds for the three men outside set up, so James could watch every move from their helmet-mounted cameras.

"This was supposed to be an afternoon off," Jordyn said with mock bitterness as she made room for James. "Hey, just help Mike look over the video feeds. You're on standby if anything goes wrong."

James nodded wearily.

"Alright, let's get this done," Gonzalez said over the speakers. "Aaron, I want you on the ground, and keep a visual of me wherever I am. Harrison, let's you and me start climbing. You have your voltage meter?"

"And the splicer," replied Harrison quickly, his voice also coming in over the speakers.

"Houston wants you to start near the comms dish," Jordyn said. "And work your way down. Be sure to hook up."

"Be careful what you wish for, you're the only woman on board to hook-up with," teased Gonzo. James thought he caught an audible sigh from Aaron's open mic.

The three men outside got to work, every action visible to James from their helmet-mounted cameras. Aaron picked a spot a few meters away from the SIM where he could stand and watch as Harrison and Gonzalez climbed the exterior ladder to the top of the SIM's rigid center module. The communication dish, which looked conspicuously like an upside down, opened umbrella, was clearly seen from Aaron's vantage point.

"Hook-in here, Harrison," ordered Gonzalez, pointing towards one of the SIM's external rooftop rungs. "And pass me that voltage meter. I'll look for the fault."

Harrison did as he was ordered, and Gonzalez continued on his way, hooking his safety harness in occasionally. The SIM wasn't that large, but with its landing struts and reasonably spacious interior, the top of the rigid center of the SIM was a good 25 feet off the Martian ground.

"All suit systems look good from in here," updated Mike. "No problems."

James watched Gonzalez' video feed as he approached the communications dish, holding the voltage meter out in front of him as he searched for the potential fault. The electric systems in the area were shut down for the moment, but that didn't mean that Gonzo was free from danger.

"I've got what looks like burn marks by exterior panel...what is that, one double-a?" Gonzalez said, making sure that his helmet camera got a good view of the panel at his feet, just a single foot away from the antennae. Sure enough, James noticed some blackening around the panel's edges.

"No excess voltage detected," Gonzalez continued. "I'm going to open up the panel, please advise, Harrison."

"Should be fine if the voltage meter says so," answered Harrison. "There should be four six-sided bolts, one at each corner. You see them?"

"Roger," answered Gonzalez as he kneeled down. James watched his video feed as he carefully clipped in his safety harness, then extracted the electric screwdriver from his work bag. One by one, Gonzalez unfastened the bolts, then carefully lifted the panel off. James squinted, trying to make out just what Gonzalez' camera was seeing.

"Ha!" laughed Gonzalez. "No wonder the damn thing shorted out. It's totally full of dust. Screw you, Mars."

"The dust here is so fine," remarked Aaron. "And we *have* been having some extra winds this week."

"I'm relaying," Jordyn said. "Just sit tight."

James took a step away from the computer monitor and reached his arms into a stretch. He was relieved to see that this was definitely an accident, and not something nefarious. The problem found, it would take only minutes to fix.

"I'm going to try to clean this thing out with my hand," said Gonzalez. "Voltage meter still reads zero."

"Hold on just a second," Jordyn said. "Let's see what Houston says."

"Hang tight," agreed Harrison.

"I'm just poking around a little bit, Major," replied Gonzalez, his gloved hand visible on his video feed as he brushed out some of the dust. "Look, it's not even a big-"

A loud popping sound suddenly rang out, audible from James' position inside the SIM. The monitor's screen flickered violently, but didn't cut out. James froze.

"Watch it!" he heard Harrison's voice shout over the feed.

Gonzo's video cut out suddenly.

James watched him slip off the edge of the SIM's roof from Aaron's point of view. There was another loud bang, again audible inside, as his body slammed against the side of the SIM and his emergency harness stopped his fall.

"I've lost him!" shouted Mike frantically. "I've lost his signal!"

Harrison acted quickly. He reached down and unclipped his safety harness, then bolted towards where Gonzalez had fallen. Being careful to avoid the exposed panel, he dropped onto his stomach and looked over the ledge. Gonzo, his face visible behind his visor in Harrison's camera, was clearly panicking. He was alive—for now.

"What the hell are you doing?!?" yelled Jordyn. "James! Get the hell out there!"

James sprinted towards the airlock, tripping and falling hard against the door as he tried to slow his momentum. His M-suit was on in less than a minute, and the second his helmet was secure, he was depressurizing the airlock. Everyone on his radio was talking over each other.

It took an agonizingly long thirty seconds for the airlock's emergency depressurization. James' heart was racing, and he struggled to fight off the panic welling up inside of him. If Gonzo's suit had depressurized, he could be dead by the time James made it out.

Fortunately, that wasn't the case. James bolted outside, only to run into Aaron and Harrison, who flanked a standing Gonzo. Harrison had his buddy tube already connected to Gonzalez' suit. Gonzo gave James a weak thumbs-up.

"Let's get inside," grunted Aaron as he helped support Gonzalez' weight. "Harrison, how you doing on oxygen?"

"All good here," replied Harrison, his voice still trembling.

The four men re-entered the airlock and started the emergency pressurization sequence. By the time the computer chirped that it was safe, James had calmed down enough to assume his practiced mannerisms of a professional doctor. He swooped into action, disconnecting Gonzalez' helmet, taking off his own gloves, and reaching in to search for a pulse.

"What the hell happened out there?" cursed James as he found an elevated pulse. Gonzalez was breathing heavily, but otherwise looked ok.

"He just fell," Aaron said as he removed his helmet, also out of breath. "I watched him go over the edge."

"Damn idiot got himself electrocuted," cursed Harrison.

"Watch who you're calling an idiot," laughed Gonzalez weakly.

"Sorry, Gonzo," apologized Harrison immediately. "You just scared the shit outta' me."

"I didn't feel anything," Gonzalez said. "But my suit just wigged out. I lost all my systems. I swear, the voltage meter said..."

"WHAT THE HELL HAPPENED OUT THERE?!?" Jordyn shouted, charging into the airlock. "Gonzo, why the hell are you so freakin' impatient, you idiot!"

Gonzalez looked up at Jordyn, genuine hurt in his eyes. "I'm s-sorry," he stuttered. "Really, I don't...I don't know..." Gonzalez trailed off, taking a deep breath to regain his composure. "You know, you were all a lot more upset when James almost died," he joked weakly. "Do I at least get some cobbler?"

It was enough to elicit a laugh from the crew. "Go to hell," Jordyn muttered, fighting to keep her lips from breaking into a full grin.

"I'll get some coffee," added Mike.

Once Gonzalez had taken a moment to rest and calm down, he headed straight for the computer terminal with Jordyn and Mike to report in to

Houston before they panicked again. He dropped his tool bag, but didn't bother to take off his M-suit as he tracked more dust into the SIM.

"Seriously though, what happened out there?" James asked the two remaining men as he got to work taking the rest of his own suit off.

"I'll have to go up and take a closer look, but I think the damage up there is more severe than we suspect," Harrison replied bitterly, his voice shaking as he took off his M-suit. "I mean, that was some serious scorching on that panel. And that was a lot of built-up electricity."

"How the heck did Gonzo not see that built-up electricity on his meter?" asked Aaron. "I mean, that would have killed him if he wasn't in his suit."

"It almost killed him anyways," Harrison spat. "Maybe the dust insulated it. I don't know. I'm sure I'll be up on the roof again in like an hour anyways. Half-day-off my ass."

With that, Harrison left the airlock in a huff, his M-suit tossed on one of the benches. Aaron picked it up, hung it up in Harrison's locker, then turned to James. "If I didn't know better I'd think this mission was cursed," he said with a pained smile.

"Seriously," mumbled James. He had had an idea—an uncomfortable one.

James finished undressing and wandered over to look out the airlock window, acting thoughtful until Aaron left. There was some more shouting and arguing from the opposite side of the SIM, and James thought that he heard his name mentioned a few times. His time limited, he stooped down and retrieved Gonzo's tool bag. It was still chilly from being outside, and it was coated in a fine red dust. James reached in and pulled out the voltage meter.

It was exactly the same as the meter James' had used on various spacewalks and trainings. It could detect even small electromagnetic fields, and it really should have detected the built-up energy that shocked Gonzalez.

James pressed the button and turned it on. The display read zero, as expected.

James turned it off and on a few times. It looked and functioned just fine, which came as a relief to James. But as a final test, just to erase any fears, James turned the meter on and approached the airlock's control panel. Its constant electric current would certainly elicit some sort of response.

It didn't.

James stomach dropped. He tried it again. He even left the airlock and put the meter right next to one of the USB outlets in the SIM's lab.

The meter read zero. It was definitely malfunctioning. No wonder Gonzalez had said the meter was reading zero. It was broken.

James sighed on the inside. It wasn't broken at all.

It had been tampered with.

CHAPTER TWENTY-ONE

James needed to bring someone into his confidence, and he needed to do it right away. The fact that Gonzo was targeted changed everything. In a twisted way, James understood why he himself was being targeted. He was actively trying to figure out what had really happened to Nikki, and he had stupidly kept all of his evidence in a place that was easily accessed. But why was Gonzo targeted? Had he been close to figuring something out? Did he have suspicions?

James was worried that the answer was no. If that was the case, then that meant that the killer was acting sporadically and irrationally. It meant that the killer wasn't a rational being acting out of fear of being discovered. It meant that they were a psycho.

But no one on board was a psycho. That was the block that James kept running into, over and over again. He had known these people for years. They had trained together, lived together, shared their lives together. No one could do this. But someone had.

Anyone could have messed with the voltage meter, but some people were more likely than others. Harrison, the chief recipient of James' suspicions, had passed the meter to Gonzo mere seconds before the accident. Aaron, who worked with computer systems and flight systems, used a similar meter at least once a week. James, Mike, Jordyn, and even Gonzo himself had all used similar meters more than once.

That night the crew was up late as they worked with NASA to plan an emergency spacewalk for the next morning. James spent the entire time trying to determine who he should bring into his confidence. He had narrowed it down to Gonzo, Jordyn, and Aaron—though his trust in Jordyn was built on the strength of their relationship alone. Aaron had risked his life to save James' a few weeks ago, and Gonzo had just had an attempt made against his life—he just didn't know it yet.

James also had another worry: what if they didn't believe him? NASA was convinced that Nikki's death was an accident. James' suit malfunction was also another "accident," according to not only Houston, but Aaron and Harrison too. Gonzo's accident was also a stretch. It's not like anyone had time to go cause an electrical failure, or time to go fill a rooftop panel with Martian dust. Fiddling with a voltage meter was something subtle and opportunistic.

James, however, had an ace up his sleeve. The fact that his collection of evidence had been stolen effectively proved that something malicious was going on. If they didn't trust his word on that, well, he'd once again be on his own. And he'd been on his own for a while now.

James looked up from his seat near the main computer terminal and looked over the faces of his crewmates. Jordyn and Mike both looked exhausted, with the latter's eyes drooping obviously as he rested his head in his hands. Harrison and Aaron also looked tired—though that wasn't getting in the way of their spirited debate over the best way to fix the electrical problem. Harrison was adamant that they should follow NASA's instructions, but Aaron was concerned about a few technical details. Gonzalez seemed content to let the crew's most qualified engineers duke this one out for a while. Finally, after a few minutes of impassioned arguing, Aaron conceded defeat. "I know this goes against what I was saying before, but I just think we should try a more permanent solution," he said. "If we don't seal the panel in a better way it could just happen again."

"I get it," Harrison said, taking on a conciliatory tone. "But we're only going to be here for another month and a half. No one will use this base again, ever."

"This isn't a base, it's our home," yawned Jordyn sarcastically. "Now can we be done for the night, Gonzo? I'm sure you'll have us up early tomorrow."

"NASA still wanted Aaron and Harrison to look over my suit to see if the systems are salvageable," began Gonzo, but the volume of his voice faded quickly as he took withering stares from everyone in the room. "Alright, alright," he said quickly. "I get it. And you're right. We'll do it tomorrow. Everyone is dismissed, but plan on being up early."

There were a few groans and audible sighs as the crew filed out of the room, heading into the kitchen, bathroom, and sleeping quarters. Gonzalez stayed behind to give a final report to Houston.

James started to leave, but paused in the doorway, looking back at Gonzalez. His forehead bore the creases and wrinkles of stress and concern. His eyes, illuminated by the computer screen, were tired and bloodshot. It was the million-mile stare, plus a little recognition of mortality. James knew this because he had seen it before—in his own eyes after he was almost killed.

James made up his mind that same instant. He was telling Gonzalez.

"Rough day, huh?" he asked, pulling up a seat next to Gonzo after checking that no one else was around. "It sounds cliché, but I know how you feel."

Gonzalez didn't respond right away. His eyes were transfixed on the screen, but there was nothing important to be looking at. James opened his mouth to say something else, but Gonzo suddenly sat up straight, then shook his head as if clearing away a bad memory. "Yeah, man," he replied. "Though it hasn't been my worst day so far. I think I'd need a little tequila for things to really go south."

James grinned and shook his head. Gonzo really was unflappable—that's what made him the perfect mission commander.

"I'm serious," Gonzo continued. "Ask me sometime about my honeymoon in Cabo San Lucas. Estefani almost divorced me on our wedding night."

"I'm being serious though," replied James. "I'm glad you made it through alright. That's a stupid accident to have happen."

"Oh, it wasn't an accident," said Gonzalez.

James was taken aback. "Wha-wait, really?" he stuttered.

"Of course it wasn't an accident," grunted Gonzalez in reply. "It was my own damn fault. I stuck my finger in some live wires like an idiot. Like a kid shoving a knife into a toaster. I'm an idiot," he finished, pulling the jet-black hair on the sides of his head in frustration.

James just stared at Gonzalez, unsure of what to say, or how to even begin. He was surprised when, out of nowhere, Gonzo started to tear up.

"I was totally fine," he said, sniffing and wiping his eyes with the back of his hairy forearm. "Harrison got to me in like ten seconds. I didn't even have trouble breathing—it all just scared the shit outta' me."

"I know," replied James simply, putting a hand on the commander's shoulder. For a moment, James considered saving his message for another time, but rejected the thought. He had to do it, before something worse happened.

"Erm, Gonzo," he began slowly, clearing his throat. Before continuing he again looked cautiously over his shoulder to make sure no one was watching. "Sir, I actually wanted to talk to you about something."

"Of course," replied the mission commander, sniffing once before sitting up straight again. "Sure thing, Doc. What's up?"

James hesitated again, the gravity of his upcoming accusation weighing far more than that of Mars.

"Sir, I don't think Nikki's death was an accident."

"What?" asked Gonzalez, clearly surprised. There was no trace of crying in his voice now. "What do you mean, James? What does this have to do with anything?"

"Gonzo," stuttered James. "Well, I...uh, I..."

"What?" snapped Gonzalez.

"I think it was intentional," James replied hoarsely as he forced the words out. "I don't think it was suicide. And I don't think my suit thing was an accident. And I think today-"

"That's enough," Gonzalez rebuked sharply, his voice rising. "James, what the hell do you think-"

"Please," begged James in a whisper. "Gonzo, please just hear me out. Please."

Gonzo stared at James, anger apparent in his eyes. "Do you hear what you're saying?" he finally asked, though his voice was now quieter. "Do you have any idea what you're implying?"

It was all James could do just to nod.

"Do you have any proof of this?" Gonzalez asked, his voice dangerous.

"Well, I...uh..." faltered James.

"So let me get this straight," hissed Gonzalez. "You mean to tell me that you think someone on here is doing this on purpose? Someone, someone you and I both know *intimately,* is trying to kill us off one by one. Is that it?"

"Look," began James defensively. "Nikki's death has never sat right with any of us. And then my suit fails in just the right way that I don't get a CO2 alarm? What kind of coincidence is that?"

"A crazy one," Gonzalez answered, though by the tone of his voice James knew that he wasn't jumping on board. "And you probably think that my accident today has something to do with this?"

"Why didn't your voltage meter pick up anything?" James asked rhetorically. "Don't you at least see where I'm coming from?"

158

"Where you're coming from?" asked a flabbergasted Gonzalez. "James, you're saying that someone here is a killer—a serial killer! You know everyone here! Who even has the capacity to do something like that? Do you even have evidence of such an accusation?"

James hesitated once again. Gonzalez wasn't taking this well, but if James was honest with himself, he wasn't expecting him to. "I got an email from someone who claimed to be Nikki's fiancé back home," he explained quickly. "He said it was impossible that Nikki had committed suicide. I've been looking into it, Gonzo. I actually...well, I actually..."

"Actually what?"

"Remember the bolt that was jammed in the door?" James asked. "I kept it. I thought maybe, maybe there were fingerprints or something that I could-"

"Just stop," snapped Gonzalez. "Stop now, Doctor Lake. We're millions of miles from home in a place that could kill any of us instantly. You mean to say you've been living in total distrust of us for months now? You stole a bolt that Houston rode my ass about for a week without telling anyone?"

"Commander, I can explain. Patterson's email—he thinks it's murder too!"

"Patterson?" growled Gonzalez. "Of course Nikki's damn fiancé doesn't want to think this was suicide!"

"But Gonzo, he-"

"James, we need to trust each other up here," Gonzalez interrupted forcefully. "If you thought that I was a killer, would you save my life if my suit malfunctioned? Would you come after me if I was floating away from *Perseus*? If you think Jordyn, or Aaron, or Harrison, or Mike, or me...if all of us have your suspicions, how can I trust you to do your job when everyone's lives are on the line? Explain *that* to me."

James was taken aback. Gonzalez' words and reaction, though not completely unexpected, hurt. And they hurt bad. James would give his life for anyone on board—at least, he would have up until the last few weeks. The fact that he really believed someone was a killer tore him up inside. Couldn't Gonzalez understand that?

"Well?" challenged Gonzo.

"My things were stolen," James blurted out. "The bolt, the fingerprints I had collected-"

"You were collecting our fingerprints too?" Gonzalez asked softly. His voice was icy.

"They were stolen," repeated James. "Someone knew what I was up to. They found my stash, they stole them. Why would anyone steal something like that if they weren't guilty?"

Gonzalez locked eyes with James for a minute. His deep brown-black eyes peered into James' soul, and it was all James could do to keep from blinking. Finally, Gonzalez stopped and looked down at his hands.

"Who do you think is behind it?" he asked softly, not bothering to look up at James. James opened his mouth to voice his suspicions about Harrison, but he was cut off before he could get started. "No," said Gonzo flatly. "I don't want to know, and I don't want to hear it."

"Please, Gonzo," begged James. "You have to trust me on this."

This time it was Gonzalez who hesitated. James watched his face with anticipation, searching for any clues of what the man might say next. He'd like to think that he had gotten good at reading his crewmates from their years spent together, but Gonzalez' face was blank.

"Have you told anyone else?" he asked finally. "Houston?"

"I don't have any real evidence," James admitted. "And we're still a long way from home."

Gonzalez nodded thoughtfully, putting a hand on his chin. "James," he said finally. "I'm going to try to forget we had this conversation."

"But Gonzo!" exclaimed James, briefly forgetting to keep his voice down.

160

"You're under a lot of stress," he continued. "We all are. And Nikki's death hit us hard. Real hard."

James opened his mouth to interject, but Gonzalez cut him off instantly. "No," he said with finality. "James, I've bled and suffered with these people, just like you. I refuse to believe any of them would do what you're implying."

James couldn't believe what he was hearing. He had failed. Defeated, he stood up quickly and turned to leave. Gonzo, however, stopped him in his tracks with a single clearing of his throat.

"I'll keep my eyes open," Gonzalez said bluntly. "But I'm doing it because I trust you, James. I don't want to hear anything else unless you have something tangible, or someone else has an accident. And quite frankly, I doubt we'll have either of those happen again. I think you're wrong, James. That's all there is to it. Are we clear?"

James sighed, a mix of relief and pent up anxiety. He felt physically lighter, like he had relieved himself of a heavy burden. Commander Gonzalez' response wasn't perfect, but it was the best that James could hope for given the circumstances. Were the roles reversed, James would probably have reacted even more poorly.

"Yes, sir," James answered.

Gonzalez forced a smile. "I sure hope you weren't expecting us to go all 'Starsky and Hutch,'" he joked.

"I was thinking more along the lines of the crew in 'Alien,' but I'll take what I can get," replied James before turning and leaving the room.

James was satisfied with how the conversation had gone, although he had hoped for more direct support from Gonzo. At the very least, he'd enlisted another pair of eyes and ears.

Unfortunately, James knew it was a somewhat hollow victory. Gonzo had called him out on his lack of evidence and motive, and James was well aware of the importance of those two things. What made it worse was the fact that two months of snooping around hadn't gotten him any closer to finding any answers. The weight that had briefly been lifted from James' shoulders was starting to return.

James walked through the dark kitchen—all non-essential electronics were shut off until repairs could be made—hoping that he had made the right decision in telling Gonzalez. He entered the sleeping compartment, only to collide with Aaron.

"Hey James," he said pleasantly. "Is Gonzo still back there? I wanted to ask him what he thought about an idea I had for tomorrow."

"Yeah, he's back there," James answered, making room for Aaron to pass. Suddenly, an idea popped into his mind. "Hey Aaron?" he asked quickly.

"Yeah?" asked the flight engineer.

"Don't forget to take a look at Gonzo's meter," James said. "I think it's still in his tool bag back in the airlock."

Aaron nodded. "I'm way ahead of you, James. I grabbed it a couple hours ago to take a look at it. It was definitely on the fritz—it hadn't been recalibrated from being used on the solar panels I think. Should be fixed now."

"Good," replied James. "I just didn't want us to use it tomorrow on accident."

"No kidding," Aaron agreed solemnly.

Aaron passed James by, clapping a hand on his shoulder as he continued on his way to go meet with Gonzalez. James headed to his cot and sat down, putting his head in his hands. He was overwhelmed, but he still felt a little better knowing that he wasn't alone.

James pulled out his tablet and checked for any new emails. There weren't any, not even from Claire.

James was exhausted. It was 0122 hours, but James wouldn't allow himself to sleep. He sat in his sleeping bag, eyes open, listening and watching carefully until everyone, including Gonzalez, was in their cots asleep. Then, and only then, did James allow himself to drift off into a dark, dreamless slumber.

CHAPTER TWENTY-TWO

The damage was more severe than expected.

The electrical problem that had led to Gonzalez getting zapped had done more damage than initially thought. Harrison and Aaron spent the better part of six hours working to clean out and repair the damaged wiring, and were for the most part successful. The problem, however, was that the SIM's primary long-range communications antennae had been fried, almost beyond repair.

It wasn't a huge deal—NASA had designed duplicate systems for nearly everything—that's why the beacons the crew had erected earlier were such a big deal. The SIM would just use its separate, short-range antennae to link up with one of the beacons, which would be receiving the relays from Earth. NASA was confident that the primary antennae could be fixed on station if necessary, but with less than half of the crew's time on Mars remaining, Houston decided to work with the backup system in favor of keeping the crew on task. After all, the only negative from using the beacon system was a small drop in signal reception and uploading speed.

That was fine with James, until he heard some of Houston's proposed changes to account for this decrease. In order to make room for large science transmissions and data packets, Houston was going to limit personal data usage. That meant that just like on *Perseus*, personal data dumps would only be coming in once a week, effective immediately.

It was devastating news for James, helped only by the fact that Gonzalez was in on his little secret. Patterson hadn't responded in forever, and Claire seemed to have started writing only every other day. He wouldn't hear from either of them now for a week at least, and vice versa.

Fortunately, there was plenty to do on Mars still, and James was kept very busy along with the rest of the crew. There were experiments to be run, samples to collect, and data to be acquired. With the obvious exception of Nikki's death, the Ares I mission was becoming a resounding success. They had become the first humans to set foot on Mars, they had conducted valuable science, and the rocks and samples collected from the Martian surface seemed destined to unlock countless secrets from Mars' past. Apparently, the members of Ares I were quite the heroes back home on planet Earth, and NASA and the US government were both thrilled to have beaten the Chinese to the red planet.

Another week passed, then another. Patterson never replied, but Claire did faithfully. The change to weekly emails meant that Claire's messages were more detailed, improving James' morale. She didn't hesitate to remind him that he'd be on his way home soon. There was only a month left before the crew departed for *Perseus*, and James was eager to start the trip home—even as he dreaded being cooped up again. He was grateful that being the first mission meant only a three-month stay on Mars—future missions would spend up to a year at a time here.

The days started to tick by a little faster for James. He was still paranoid and on the hunt for clues, but just knowing that he wasn't entirely alone anymore helped ease his mind. He still waited until the others had fallen asleep before letting himself sleep, but he was at least sleeping soundly now, and boy did he need it. Each day—or sol—was full of work from sunup to blue sunset. James did physicals, ran samples in the lab, and participated in the exploration of Mars. He was still cautious and wary, but his body and mind were starting to adjust to the tension. He could handle it now. Sure, it was like an old injury—always nagging, always threatening to flare up—but it wasn't going to paralyze him. His attitude started to change from constant terror, to sort of a nervous confidence. If there were clues to be found, he was going to find them eventually. If something was going to happen, James would have to act on it then. As long as he was careful to avoid any "accidents," he'd be the master of his own fate.

Something strange happened to James in the two weeks since telling Gonzalez: he actually started to find joy in his work again. Tempered joy, but joy nonetheless. Other than his marriage and family, this was the pinnacle of his life. He was at the top of his career, doing something he loved in a place so wild, so far away, that he was destined to be remembered for it. He was a modern-day Columbus, even if he was too modest to admit it in his own mind. Nevertheless, he *did* take great pride in being part of something greater than himself.

He found himself pondering that concept as he sat in the backseat of the rover one morning. He, Gonzalez, Harrison, and Aaron were headed on what would be the second longest expedition of the entire mission. They had all woken up at 0400 hours, and they had been driving for four hours. Their destination was now only a dozen miles away—an area of hills that NASA suspected had once poked out of an ancient, dying sea. Satellite imagery had shown what looked like the markings of flowing water, and the crew was going to get some up-close observations and samples.

Rover missions were a little dangerous, especially the further they got from the SIM's relative safety, but James wasn't overly worried. The rover had been one of the most trustworthy pieces of equipment that they'd had, and there were clearly established procedures to follow in case anything broke down. Plus, the fact that there were three other people with him, including Gonzalez, put his mind at ease regarding Nikki's potential killer.

There was no denying that Harrison had been James' number one suspect. There he sat in front of James, his brown hair sticking up a bit in the back. He didn't quite look relaxed due to his burly shoulders, but he was clearly thoughtful as he looked out the window. James wondered what he might be thinking about. Harrison's behavior in *Perseus* was odd, and his not-quite relationship with Nikki seemed to supply a ghost of a motive. James had been watching him closely, however, and thus far he'd stood up to the extra scrutiny. James was starting to wonder if he'd been focusing on the wrong person.

"We're getting pretty close if you want to go ahead and put your helmets on," Gonzalez said from the driver's seat. "We've got a lot to do. We'll drop that mini-beacon and the unmanned rover first so that NASA can run a system's check on it before we leave. After that, they want a core sample, and any rocks that look remotely weathered."

"Wish we had Nikki here," commented Aaron. "I don't even know what I should be looking for."

James nodded in agreement as he cast a glance over towards where Aaron was seated. He was pulling his Snoopy cap on over his blonde hair in preparation for putting on his helmet. James had felt a growing bond towards Aaron ever since he had saved his life, and the two had talked more on Mars than they ever had during their stay in *Perseus.*

In a way, James pitied Aaron. He seemed to be lonely sometimes, when people weren't looking. While friendly and outgoing, Aaron also seemed quieter than the others. James had run into him staring absentmindedly out windows, or at his pocket bible or that other religious book in his hands. It probably didn't help that Aaron's religious beliefs made him stick out. He wouldn't drink coffee with the rest of the crew, he almost never swore, and he always seemed uncomfortable when the crew's conversation became a little crass.

James knew that Aaron's parents had passed away a few years ago in a car accident, and Aaron had admitted that he didn't have many friends or family writing him back home. James had been considering something for a while now, and he thought he'd give it a shot.

"We're here," Gonzalez said, braking gently until the rover stopped. "Everyone got your helmets on? Suit checks please."

James put his helmet on, rotating it slightly clockwise until in snapped into position. He checked the seal, then made sure his heads-up display was working right. Lastly, he checked that his life support systems were working properly—something he'd grown accustomed to doing repeatedly. "Ready to go," he said confidently.

"All good," said Harrison.

"I'm set," affirmed Aaron.

"Alright, *Unity*, you reading us?" asked Gonzalez.

"All clear, Gonzo," Jordyn replied, her voice coming in James' headset loud and clear. "We hear you fine. Mike wants you to keep your chatter to a minimum, says he's trying to work."

"He doesn't mean that, I'm sure," replied Gonzalez.

Gonzalez tapped a button on the rover's console, and the interior was suddenly filled with the sound of hissing air. An energy bar wrapper that James had forgotten to stow flew through the air suddenly, getting stuck against one of the interior vent grates. Harrison snagged it and put it in one of the sealed garbage containers.

Harrison and Gonzalez opened both the main doors simultaneously when the depressurization was complete, and the four men climbed out of the rover and onto the Martian surface. Unlike where the SIM was located, this part of Mars consisted of low, rolling hills that occasionally peaked up out of the dusty flatlands. There were fewer large rocks here, and the ones that James saw were flat instead of chunky and volcanic.

Gonzo was James' buddy today, which meant that James could afford to relax a little. The two men hadn't even mentioned their private conversation since it happened, and James wouldn't mind never bringing it up again. That would mean that nothing else had happened. Besides, they couldn't talk in private now even if they wanted to—everything that was said over the radio would be heard by everyone.

168

Aaron and Harrison got to work setting up the mini beacon that would be used to help the rover they were leaving to communicate with Earth. The mini-rover project was actually a German addition to the mission. NASA had agreed to carry it up in exchange for a sizable donation to the Ares missions. It would stay here long after the crew had left, collecting data and exploring what the crew couldn't get to today.

"I'll operate the crane," Gonzalez said, grunting as he hooked the hoist to the mini-rover's attachment point. "Will you just make sure I let it down gently?"

"Are you sure that's a good idea?" Jordyn teased over the radio. "I still don't get why you didn't let me drive this one, Gonzo."

"You drive all the damn time," Harrison grunted back as he and Aaron lifted the beacon off the rover and placed in on the ground. "How come I never get to drive, huh? Everyone but me and Mike have gotten to do it."

"I haven't either," James said. "And no, the golf cart back at *Unity* doesn't count."

"That's because we don't trust you, James," Gonzalez deadpanned. "Simple as that."

James gave an amused grunt, then got busy helping Gonzalez get the mini-rover off the trailer safely. It had to be done slowly and carefully—the mini-rover was heavy, even on Mars—but after a few cautious minutes the rover was down on Martian soil. Gonzalez quickly told Jordyn to tell Houston that it was ready, but there was no rush. They'd have to stick around for a few hours before Houston allowed them to leave the mini-rover by itself.

That was fine, because there was plenty to do. James and Gonzalez struck out with some sample bags, hunting for rocks and dirt samples that looked at all interesting. They spent most of their time in the shallow valleys between the hills, finding a few interesting rocks that looked like they had wave patterns on them. After returning their first bag to the rover, they grabbed another and climbed to the top of one of the other small hills to get a look around. James looked across the landscape, getting a good view of his surroundings. This part of Mars was far more interesting than where *Unity* was, though landing something here would be treacherous.

"Is it worth coming up there?" Aaron asked, waving at James and Gonzo from by the rover, which looked a little small from where James was standing.

"I think so," Gonzalez replied. "Come on up you two, take a break."

"Gladly," Harrison replied, and the two men started their climb to join Gonzalez and James. This hill had more solid footing than the one James had tumbled down, and the two made quick progress in the low gravity.

"Hey, A?" James asked, suddenly remembering his idea. "I have a question for you."

"Go ahead," panted Aaron as he reached the top of the hill.

"Well, look buddy," James began. "Claire has a younger sister. She's like your age, maybe a year or two younger."

"Whoa now," Gonzalez said quickly. "This is a slippery slope, James."

"Seriously, why would you insult your sister-in-law like that?" Harrison joked.

"Hey," said Aaron defensively.

Gonzalez laughed heartily. "Not even that, Harrison. I was more concerned with James losing his wife's sister to a cult. You know Aaron would just try to convert her."

"That's fair," agreed Aaron. "The conversion part anyways."

"At least she'd be wife number one," laughed Harrison. "I have a sister too—she could be number two."

"That joke is like two hundred years outdated," defended Aaron weakly.

"Hey now, I'm being serious," James said, though he was struggling not to laugh at Gonzo and Harrison's teasing. "I could give you her email address if you wanted it."

Aaron was silent for a moment as Gonzalez and Harrison enjoyed a few more jokes at his expense. James was starting to regret bringing it up over the radio when Aaron finally responded.

"Is she as pretty as Claire?" he asked sheepishly.

"WHOA NOW!" Jordyn shouted over the radio.

"I don't think I should answer that on the record," laughed James. "But I'm not trying to set you up with my ugly cousin. Promise. She's a good girl too— my wife's family was raised Methodist."

"I'll think about it," answered Aaron. "In fact, sure. Why not?"

"It's not like you're getting any younger," quipped Harrison.

"Shut up," laughed Aaron. "You're like ten years older than me! And twice as single."

"Not a virgin though," Harrison retorted mischievously.

"I'm fresh off the lot—low miles, no previous owner," shrugged Aaron. It was a solid comeback. The crew shared a laugh as they took in the view from the hill.

There was plenty more work to be done, and it took the four men all day to do it. The mini-rover was up and running, the mini-beacon was working fine, and there were more places to explore and more samples to collect. The men drove around from place to place, pausing at interesting sights and Houston-ordered waypoints to collect samples, take pictures, and leave markers.

Finally, just as the Martian sun was turning blue and settling low on the horizon, Gonzalez declared the work done for the day. The day's mission had been a resounding success, and Gonzalez even offered to let Harrison drive back to *Unity*. James and Aaron did a quick visual inspection of the rover's wheels and cargo trailer, then climbed in for the ride back to base.

The rover took a minute or two to re-pressurize, and the four men didn't waste any time getting their helmets off the second they could. James was especially relieved—he had had an itch for three hours now, and his bladder was definitely full. He'd much rather go on the tiny portable toilet in the back of the rover then in his awkward suit diaper.

The trip back to base went by quickly, even though it was a four-hour drive. The rover could skip along at nearly fifty miles per hour at full jaunt, but safety was more important than speed. The rover's powerful lights illuminated the Martian surface for almost a hundred meters in front of them, and Harrison was careful to avoid any obstacles. One by one, the hours ticked by.

James' mind started to turn to what he'd eat when he got back to the SIM. He was starving, and meal bars and water had gotten old a long time ago. He also wanted a nice, hot shower. In fact, he was also considering challenging Aaron to a rematch of last week's football game. He was confident that this time he'd defin-

"Gonzo, this is *Unity*," Jordyn said suddenly, cutting off James' thoughts. "Commander, you there?" repeated Jordyn, her voice piped through the rover's speakers.

Something was wrong in the tone of Jordyn's voice—James could tell immediately.

Gonzalez quickly turned down the music that had been playing, then punched something into the rover's computer. "Yeah, Marx. Go ahead," he said.

"Commander, I've got a priority message from Houston," she answered quickly. "It's a video message."

"What did it say?" asked Gonzalez tensely.

"I haven't opened it," Jordyn replied. "The attached message says to wait for you."

"When did you get it?" demanded Gonzalez.

"Just now, the priority code interrupted one of my uploads," responded Jordyn. "Commander, how far away are you?"

"Fifteen minutes," Aaron said, looking over Harrison's shoulder at the GPS map. "We're close."

"Commander, this is really weird," Jordyn said nervously. Why would they want to wait for you? Do you think something happened back home?"

"What would have happened?" James asked nervously, his heart speeding up.

"I don't know," Jordyn said exasperatedly. "I have no—hold on guys, I have another priority one message coming through."

"Step on it, Harrison," ordered Gonzalez.

"Commander, this one is just text with a file attachment, it looks like a...hold on a second."

"What is it?" demanded Gonzalez.

"Shit," Jordyn said, her voice out-of-breath.

"What is it?" Gonzalez growled again.

"Commander, I think these are launch updates," Jordyn said. "Coordinate adjustments, window adjustments."

"Is that it?" asked Gonzalez, relief obvious in his voice. "Damn, Major, you had me pissin' myself here."

"Sir, I'm not done," interjected Jordyn. "Houston has moved up our Mars departure date—you're not going to believe this!"

"So we leave a few days early," Harrison said. "Big deal. That still gives us a couple weeks to finish everything. It can't be that hard to add a few hours of extra work a day."

"It's not a few days early," Jordyn said, her voice sounding completely incredulous over the radio. "Sir, it's the sol after tomorrow."

CHAPTER TWENTY-THREE

Gonzalez led the rover crew through the connecting tube, through the secondary airlock, and into the SIM, an air of authority that he rarely carried—but easily managed to—exuding from his confident step. He hadn't said a single word in the last ten minutes of the drive, but the way his brow was furrowed clearly showed just how seriously he was taking all this.

James tucked his helmet under his arm and followed Gonzalez, all the while wondering what was going on. He was trying to think that this was some elaborate joke that Jordyn was playing on Gonzo and the crew, but he couldn't think of any reason why she'd do something like that. No, this was real. Very real.

"Maybe it's a coming dust storm," Aaron postulated. "Maybe a meteor shower or something like that—something that we need to leave early to miss."

"More likely it's a problem with *Perseus*," Harrison replied. It was clear from the tone of his voice that he was nervous, and James could understand why. *Perseus* was their only way back home, and there was no means of rescue if something went wrong. The Ares II mission wouldn't launch for another two years, and half of their ship wasn't even built yet. If anything went sideways, this crew would be alone until they died together. It was a fact that James had learned to mindfully suppress even before Nikki's death.

"Do you think we'll just sit in orbit for the last couple weeks?" Aaron asked. "I mean, we have enough fuel for an early transfer burn, right?"

"To an extent," replied Harrison flatly.

"We'll probably have to start deciding who we're going to eat first," joked James. It was as much for his benefit as for the others—he was getting more nervous by the second. The fact that no one laughed at his joke only made it worse.

The four men entered the kitchen module, where they were met by Mike. "I made coffee," he said, gesturing towards the counter. "I have a feeling we're going to need it. Aaron, that water is for you."

"What's going on?" Gonzalez asked, speaking for the first time in several minutes. He grabbed his mug without stopping and took a quick sip before pressing on towards the inflatable command and meeting room. James had to grab his cup and hurry to catch up.

"We've told you everything, sir," Mike explained quickly, running a hand nervously through his thinning red hair. "The only reason we know about leaving early is because Jordyn looked at the maneuver log updates. It didn't say anything about it in the attached email. It said to wait for you, sir."

"Stop calling me *sir*," Gonzalez said, his voice sounding artificially upbeat. "You're making me nervous. Why don't we see what we're dealing with first, eh?"

James entered the room right after Gonzalez. He had just taken a swig of coffee, but the look on Jordyn's face instantly stopped him from swallowing. Her dark brown skin seemed paler than he thought possible, and her eyes were wide with fright. It shocked James. He had never ever seen her like this before.

"Damn, major," remarked Gonzalez. "Do you know something *else* we don't know?"

"No, sir," she answered crisply. "I just, something has got to be wrong, right?"

"If things were as bad as you're making them look, I'm pretty sure Houston would have just said it straight up," Gonzalez said. "Do you have the message cued up?"

"It's just about to finish parsing," she replied, gesturing at the screen. The loading bar read 98%, with just a minute remaining. Download times were slow this far away from Earth.

Gonzalez took one of the three chairs in front of the monitor. James—still dressed in his M-suit like the commander, Harrison, and Aaron—was content to stand in back next to Jordyn. He reached out and gently touched her bare forearm with his gloved hand.

"Are you ok?" he asked softly.

"I'm fine," she said sharply. "I just hate waiting for bad news."

"We don't know it's bad," Mike said kindly. Jordyn just gritted her teeth in reply, as if bracing for an impact.

"We're ready, gang," said Gonzalez. "Settle down."

The loading screen faded to black. There was a quick flash of light as the video commenced, then a brief image of the NASA logo, the Earth date, and mission sol. A face suddenly appeared on the screen. It was familiar.

Julianna Scoville was the Ares I flight director. Every critical decision went through her, but that didn't mean that she was some distant authority figure. With over two years' experience in space—including time on the International Lunar-orbit Station—Julianna was essentially an extra member of the crew. She had sat in trainings with James and the others, met each of their families, and had developed some level of friendship with each of them. During the first few months in space, the crew video-chatted with her and Houston regularly, but as transmission times increased, the chats were done via email. James knew that per protocol, Gonzalez still emailed her on a daily basis.

The mission's success or failure rested squarely upon Julianna's shoulders, but it was a burden she bore well, even today. Her face carried a reassuring—

although tired—smile, and the pencil tucked behind her ear made her look calm—almost casual. The hoodie she wore and the messy state of her hair, however, indicated that this was no normal video message. It was two in the morning Earth time, and she'd been woken up in a hurry.

"Hi Commander Gonzalez," she said with artificial pleasantry, readjusting her glasses. "I know this has probably alarmed you a bit, Alejandro, and I'm sorry. I want your crew here with you, so if they're not here, go ahead and pause it."

Julianna waited for a moment before continuing. She smiled, then fidgeted with her glasses again. "Hi everyone," she said. "I hope I haven't alarmed you, but I've got an important message for you all. You've probably received a data set as well—I hope Major Marx hasn't looked at it yet, or she's probably panicking without knowing the context."

"You can say that again," grunted Jordyn.

Julianna looked away from the camera for a moment, giving some order to someone in Mission Control. She looked back into the camera and smiled wearily.

"There's no easy way to say this," she began again. "I'm not sure where to start. I'll be blunt."

Julianna paused yet again, this time taking a deep breath. Suspense was welling up in the pit of James' stomach, and it wasn't a pleasant sensation.

"We found Nikki," said Julianna.

James' stomach instantly dropped. There was an audible gasp from several members of the crew, and Aaron spit up the drink of water he was trying to swallow.

"God," choked Jordyn.

"As you know, we've been trying to track down her body ever since it disappeared," continued Julianna. "Without a lot of luck. It's like trying to find a needle in an enormous haystack, and it doesn't make it any easier that nearly everything we have in orbit is geared towards long-range galaxies and...I don't need to explain this to you," she sighed. "Anyways, we've been crunching numbers, potential trajectories of her body, and borrowing time from nearly every telescope we could get our hands on. Well, we finally got a window to use some of the bigger asteroid tracking stuff, NEOWISE and the like. And there she was—it was a trajectory actually hypothesized by MIT."

Julianna smiled again, but it was clearly bittersweet. "Obviously, we can't get a clear picture of something as small as a human body," she continued, "but it's definitely her. We found our girl. She's not lost anymore."

There was a moment of silence, both from Julianna and the crew. James stared at the screen in slack-jawed surprise. What did this mean for him? What did it mean for the others? Maybe he should try emailing Patterson again, just so he'd know...

"Here's the thing," continued Julianna. "Her body is in Martian orbit. Her orbit is highly eccentric..."

Julianna trailed off as tears started to well up in her eyes. She cleared her throat and tried to continue, but was unable.

"She must have followed us right into orbit," Jordyn said softly, her voice sounding hollow. "Her lower mass, the force of her ejection from the airlock..."

The thought made James sick, but that was completely eliminated as a revelation hit James in the chest with the force of a freight train. If Nikki was found, if she was in orbit, if Houston was telling them this...

"We want to bring our girl home," Julianna said, smiling through her tears. "We've worked out an orbital trajectory, and figured out her nearest pass of *Perseus.* Guidance thinks it's doable."

"Wait, what?" Harrison said, completely shocked. "I mean, how the hell is this even possible? I mean, hell yeah, but...damn."

"The data packet we sent you consists of rough launch coordinates," continued Julianna, oblivious to the crewmates' reactions. "In order to get *Perseus* on the right trajectory you'll have to leave Mars early. We feel it's worth it, and so does both the Administrator and the President."

"Of the United States?" Mike asked out loud.

"Of course, the final decision is up to Commander Gonzalez and the rest of you," said Julianna. "And I mean that. This involves a level of risk—one we're comfortable with—but it's your lives on the line, and I'm giving you the option. I know what you'll say, I just want you to know you have it."

Julianna paused yet again. This time she removed her glasses, then dabbed away some tears with a Kleenex. She sighed and smiled again. "Let's bring her home," she repeated. "I'll expect a full response from you, Gonzo, within the next three hours. And if you have any questions, please ask. We'll get you all the answers you need, I promise."

The image faded to black, leaving a NASA logo before switching to the video player's home screen. Nobody said a word.

"Well, we're going to go get her, right?" Harrison asked finally, breaking the silence. "We've got to. She'd have done the same for us."

Jordyn, Aaron, and Mike immediately voiced their agreement, but James didn't reply. He was too busy thinking about what all this might mean. If Nikki was out there, if her body was preserved out in space...could there be...evidence?

"I think it's obvious what we're going to do," Gonzalez said. "But I want to run through all the risks, now, before we hold a vote. This is serious. I want a list of threats from each of you. Jordyn?"

"Alright," she replied quickly. "I'm sure Houston and Guidance are on it, but we've got fuel concerns if we're adjusting *Perseus'* orbit extensively. And even if we set up a rendezvous, Nikki's...I mean, the velocity of our target could be really high. I don't know how they expect us to catch it, er...her."

"Aaron?" asked Gonzalez.

"It'd be an extra couple weeks on *Perseus*, but it's designed for it," Aaron shrugged. "If Guidance is adjusting our course, I don't think there's anything system-related we need to be concerned with. My only concern is the rendezvous with Nikki—any kind of collision at high speed could do some serious damage to the ship."

"Guidance thinks it's doable," Gonzalez said, acknowledging Aaron's report. "Mike?"

"I just don't get how this is even possible," remarked the biologist. "How the hell did she end up in orbit?"

"It's actually not that crazy if you think about it," replied Jordyn, pulling out a stylus and drawing on the touch-sensitive screen. "Look, our trajectory from Earth was the most efficient one possible. It practically dropped us right into orbit without us even needing to decelerate. That orbital insertion burn was really just to get us circularized."

"I'm a damn astronaut, I know the mission plan," Mike said tersely.

"The airlock faces the rear of the ship," Aaron shrugged, as if that was answer enough.

Jordyn nodded towards Aaron before elaborating. "The airlock does point aft. We know the exterior airlock door opened in the middle of depressurization. The force would push her directly backwards—but she'd still be following *Perseus*' general trajectory. It'd be the body's—Nikki's—own orbital insertion burn. She would have slotted into orbit, just like the ship did, even if her orbit isn't clean and circular like the ship's. There's more margin for error than you'd think."

Mike pursed his lips.

Gonzalez, who had been waiting patiently while Jordyn explained the situation, cleared his throat before repeating his question. "Mike," he said gently, "as mission biologist, what concerns do you have with this plan?"

"I have no concerns," Mike sighed. "We're exposed to radiation either way, and I think it's worth it to get her."

"Harrison?" Gonzalez continued.

"Seriously, Gonzo, are you kidding me?" Harrison sputtered. "We've got to get her, man."

"I want your concerns first," Gonzalez reminded kindly.

"Well, we'd be leaving stuff incomplete on Mars," replied a flustered Harrison. "I mean, all the permanent sensors and beacons are set up, but some of the experiments are incomplete, and there are still rover expeditions and research area left to cover. But honestly, we've already done nearly everything we were supposed to do here."

"James?" asked Gonzalez, his eyes turning to James.

"Everyone here seems healthy and fine," James began, racking his brain for any reasons why they shouldn't get Nikki that didn't involve possibly incurring the wrath of a murderer. He'd have to talk to Gonzalez about that in private.

"Doctor," Gonzalez chided gently.

"I guess I'm mostly worried about what we do after we get her," James replied slowly. "I mean, she wasn't in a suit or anything. She's...well, she's frozen out there. Mummified, probably. We don't have the equipment to keep her on board *Perseus* without...without her decomposing. We'd have to keep her outside until right before we reenter Earth's atmosphere."

James' morbid prognosis incurred a hush that fell over the entire crew. It was nearly a full minute before Gonzalez finally spoke up.

"There we have it," he said, his voice cracking slightly. "To be blunt, I think we can overcome all the things we've listed. I vote yes."

"Concur," said Jordyn.

"Yes," added Harrison.

"Let's bring her home," said Aaron.

"Agreed," nodded Mike.

"Of course," James said, confident in his answer, but nervous about what it all meant. "Let's do it."

"Ok," smiled Gonzalez. "I'm glad to hear it. I'm going to draft a response real quick, and then I want Jordyn to give us a flight briefing on what we're dealing with. Each of you, I want you to think of any pending experiments you're assigned responsibility for, and think if they can be completed or partially recovered in the time we have left. Mike, James, can you two cover anything you've been covering for Nikki?"

"Of course," answered Mike. "We'll take care of it."

"Good," nodded Gonzalez. "James, Aaron, Harrison, go ahead and get out of your M-suits. I'll be right there too."

James nodded, then turned to follow Harrison and Aaron towards the airlock. He actually didn't have many experiments left to worry about, but he expected Houston to want a final round of physicals to be done before they left Mars. As far as Nikki's geology tasks were concerned, he and Mike really just needed to make sure all the collected samples made it into the MAV before they left the surface. Everything was already tagged and catalogued.

James checked his wristscreen before taking off his M-suit. It was getting late, and like Gonzo had said, he knew they'd be up late sorting everything out. He'd have to email Claire and let her know what was going on—she'd need to know. James paused and looked out the airlock window at the dark Martian desert. He was nervous to be back in *Perseus*, all cooped up. Mars was just as deadly as deep space, but it didn't feel so confined.

James' thoughts turned to Nikki, and the idea of recovering her body. Decomposition wasn't his primary concern, however. He was more worried about other things he might find. What if Nikki's body held some sort of clue, or something that would reveal what had happened to her and who had done it? If the killer knew that such evidence existed...

James gritted his teeth, exhaling slowly and letting his breath escape through tense lips. If that were the case, if the killer had something more to hide, then things were going to go straight to hell.

CHAPTER TWENTY-FOUR

There was much to do, but little time to do it.

The return to *Perseus* was scheduled for 1800 hours, less than two sols from when the crew first received the news about Nikki. That only gave the crew 48 hours, give or take a few, to get the maximum number of things done as possible. There were experiments to finalize, launch preparations to be accomplished, and a whole host of other things that needed to be done before the crew could depart from the red planet.

Gonzalez, with supervision from mission control, began prioritizing what needed to be done first. The first item on the agenda was putting the entire crew on a temporary sleep schedule, with everybody being assigned a rotating shift. Only two people would be allowed to sleep at any one time, with the other four working. Someone would always be awake, and the buddy system would be maintained.

The number one priority set by NASA was making sure that the crew made it back to Earth safely, which meant that Jordyn was immediately assigned to go give the MAV a thorough inspection. She headed out that very night with Gonzalez to make sure that the MAV's systems were up and receiving the launch instructions that were constantly being updated, tweaked, and adjusted by Houston. If things weren't ready to go, Houston would just cancel the early launch. Recovering Nikki was important, but the crew wouldn't get themselves killed doing it.

Leaving Mars made James nervous for a number of reasons. The launch would be the most physically demanding thing any of them had done since leaving Earth, and there were very real worries that James had as a doctor. Everybody's bones, including his own, were naturally weaker after so much time in zero or Martian gravity, even though the crew kept a rigorous exercise schedule. A forceful launch could actually break ribs. Then there were the psychological concerns of being back inside a tiny ship. Sure, Mars was just as hazardous, but at least there were places to walk and things to explore. Going back to *Perseus* felt like going back to a college dorm room and not being allowed to leave for nine months.

None of those concerns, however, had James as worried as the prospect of Nikki's killer making another move. Things were coming to a head, especially with the mission to recover Nikki's body in full swing. If whoever killed her felt that they were about to be discovered, they could do something rash. And deadly. They could sabotage the MAV, damage *Perseus*, or even make an attempt on somebody else's life. They could even just decide to kill everyone at once. That'd be sickeningly easy in space.

James decided to make one more play for evidence here on Mars. Whoever had stolen his fingerprints and the bolt would have had to have hidden it somewhere. James had already looked, sure, but there were plenty of places he hadn't been able to check. Now, with everyone packing up every last thing that would be returning to *Perseus*, James had the excuse he needed to poke around even more without raising suspicion.

James got started that very night. He and Mike were assigned to sleep first while the others worked. He crawled into his sleeping bag, but once Jordyn and Gonzalez had left to go check on the MAV and Harrison and Aaron began prepping the exterior of the station for its abandonment, he quickly crawled out. He'd have to wait until Mike was asleep to search the sleeping room, but he could get started in the kitchen and lab.

The kitchen and lab were surprisingly neat and orderly considering the chaos of the upcoming departure. The rows of equipment and scientific instruments would be staying here on Mars. There was a chance that the base would be revisited in the future—it was designed to be modularly expanded by future missions if the funding materialized—but the odds were slim. NASA had only secured money for three Ares missions, and the expansion mission was listed as number six or seven.

James started by the door and worked his way around the module clockwise, quietly opening every drawer and checking their contents. Nothing was out of place. All of the tools, chemicals, and even the first aid kit were packed away neatly.

James proceeded around the edge of the module, which led him to the kitchen. It was a little messy, with dehydrated meal pouches and drink mix packets strewn about, but there was nothing to be found here either. James grabbed an energy bar—there was no need to ration food that wouldn't be going with them anymore—took a bite, then headed into the bathroom.

The bathroom on Mars was probably something James was going to miss the most. Mars' gravity meant that the crew could enjoy a proper shower, a normal sink, and above all—a traditional, sit down toilet. It was the toilet that caught James' attention first. While it looked like a traditional toilet, it was very different. It used almost zero water, and the human waste from the crew didn't go into a sewer or septic tank. Liquid waste was removed, filtered, and transformed back into fresh drinking water, while the leftover solids were automatically packaged in sealed bags that then went into a sealed container.

A thought entered James' mind. If someone had stolen his items out of fear of them being used as evidence, wouldn't they have disposed of them rather than hiding them somewhere they could be found? James sighed out loud to himself. That certainly made sense, and it could mean that his carefully acquired evidence could be anywhere. It could be buried out in the Martian emptiness, it could be slowly being buried by dust, and it could even be sealed in some waste-containing baggy right here in the SIM. There was no way James was going to find it, not in the time he had.

James knew that it was useless, but he searched the rest of the base anyway. The inflatable meeting and work room had nothing to be found, and

James knew that the others would be coming back inside at any time. He wanted to check the sleeping and rec room, and then he'd better get some actual sleep. No one could afford to be tired and out of it when they launched—he couldn't be murdered if he was already dead from some stupid accident.

Only fifteen minutes had passed since James had left his cot to search the SIM, but by the time he got back Mike was already fast asleep and snoring. James considered just going to bed too, but he wasn't going to get a chance like this again. The crew's things would be either packed up or left behind, and he'd never be alone—or almost alone—with them again.

As quietly as possible, James headed towards the wall that contained the crew's cubbies of clothes and personal items. He glanced over his shoulder to check that Mike was still sleeping soundly, then slowly slid out the first tray he could find. It was Jordyn's.

James instantly felt guilty. Privacy was rare on any space mission, and the small things were near-sacred. Going through his friends' things was a complete violation of trust, and James knew it. But he also knew that in order to protect the innocent, he had to figure out who did this. He silently unclicked the lid of Jordyn's things and got busy searching.

The first box was nothing more than clothes. James gingerly flicked through the handful of shirts, socks, and underwear, finding nothing. Hurriedly, he moved to Jordyn's second box. This one contained a rubix cube, a few pictures of Jordyn's family, and a journal. James guiltily thumbed through a few pages, but found nothing suspicious.

James moved on. The next box was Gonzo's and it was pretty similar to Jordyn's. His clothes box contained, well, clothes, and his personal box had a small bible, a tiny metal cross, and a picture of his family. James paused at the picture for a moment, wondering how Gonzalez and his wife were doing. So much time apart would strain any relationship.

Mike's snoring suddenly increased in volume as he snorted, then rolled over onto his side. James froze where he was standing, his hand caught in the cookie jar, but Mike didn't wake up. Being more silent then before, James slid Gonzalez' things back into place and moved on to Aaron's box.

James flipped through Aaron's clothes box, finding nothing different than Gonzalez' other than a few pairs of his special Mormon undergarments. Feeling especially guilt-ridden now, he proceeded on to his personal box. It was sparse like the others—religious effects, a family photo, a journal—except for one item. It was a letter—laminated to help fireproof the paper—addressed to Aaron from some woman named Haley. James quickly read it—it didn't seem like anything more than a simple letter from a friend, even if the worn creases from folding and unfolding implied otherwise.

James cursed silently to himself. How could he be so stupid? Why was he wasting time with the others? His prime suspect was Harrison, and Harrison had something that could be considered prime evidence: a letter, from him to Nikki. James had caught him trying to retrieve it shortly after Nikki's death.

James skipped Mike's bin and went straight to Harrison's, passing over the clothes bin and going directly to the personal items. There was a handheld videogame, and a picture of Harrison at the Atlanta Falcons' Superbowl win from two years ago. There was no letter.

There was a noise from outside, a metallic clank that James' recognized as the airlock opening. Someone was coming back inside, and it didn't matter who. He had only minutes to finish up here before he was discovered.

James slid the personal tray back into place and pulled out Harrison's clothes. They were identical to the ones James had been given by Houston. There was a light full-body suit meant to be worn under an M-suit, a pair of gym shorts, a t-shirt, some underwear and socks. The letter wasn't here either.

About to give up, James rifled through the bin one last time, doing his best not to disturb Harrison's neatly folded clothes. Just as he was about to quit,

James' hand brushed across one of the folded shirts at the bottom. Something about it felt off. He carefully reached in, and his fingers felt something other than synthetic fabric. It was paper—mission-specific, flame-resistant paper.

The air pump that repressurized the airlock turned on, its chugging noise vibrating throughout the SIM like normal. James had a minute, maybe more if whoever was coming back paused to take off their suit.

James pulled on the paper, his hands fumbling as he tried to unfold it, and sliced his finger on the edge of the letter. He stuck the papercut finger into his mouth to suck off the blood, then unfolded the note.

Nikki,

I just wanted to say that I'm sorry. Really. I went too far, and you were right to do what you did.

Look, I'll be honest here. I know you felt it too. How was I supposed to act after what you said to me on Monday? I thought it was pretty obvious. I know you were being obvious on purpose.

You didn't have to get after me like that though. I mean, I'm not saying I was right in what I did, but seriously. Why would you say what you said, and then the next day reject me like that? It's not right, Nikki.

I really care about you and I won't apologize for it. I know you feel the same, and you're being pretty stupid about it. You need to decide what you want, and if it's not me, well-

The air pump shut off suddenly, the sudden silence louder than a thunderclap. James wasn't finished reading the letter, but he was out of time. He quickly folded the letter back up, shoved it back in the envelope, and stuffed it back in the correct shirt. He could hear voices now, voices from kitchen, coming this way.

James put the lid on the bin and shoved it inside, then turned around quickly to head back to his cot. Before he could move, however, his eyes caught movement from Mike. The man rolled over, yawned, then looked right at James with bleary eyes. "What are you doing, James?" he asked groggily.

"I went to go get a drink," James lied quickly, stepping away from the wall. "I was thirsty, and with all the noise going on…" he finished, letting his voice trail off as he sat down on his cot. He was just sliding his feet into his sleeping bag when Harrison and Aaron entered the room.

"What are you guys doing up?" Aaron asked. "We're not going to have much more time to sleep."

"Can't sleep with all the noise you guys made coming in," yawned Mike as he rolled back over. "Now if you'll all excuse me, I have three more hours to be unconscious."

"Gonzo and Jordyn are probably coming back in soon," warned Harrison. "And we've got to pack up the rest of the geology samples, so there'll be some noise. I'll shut the hatch if you want."

"It's fine," James replied. "Just don't expect any mercy when it's your guys' turn to sleep."

Harrison looked at James and laughed, his burly shoulders shaking up and down. "It's on," he laughed. "Aaron, you hear that?"

"Maybe I'll go pack up the pots and pans," Aaron joked.

"We don't have pots and pans," complained Mike as he pulled his sleeping bag up over his ears.

Harrison and Aaron left, leaving James and Mike to get some rest. James wasn't sure he'd be able to get any. He wanted to read the rest of the letter, but he couldn't risk it again. He'd almost been discovered.

What had Harrison meant by what he had written? He was apologizing for something—maybe a physical, romantic advance he had tried to make on Nikki? But the letter also implied that Nikki was leading him on or something. Would she do that even with someone—Patterson—back home? He doubted it, but it wasn't impossible. They were a long way from home, both in time and distance. If Nikki *had* given in to Harrison, even if it was just a little...

But Harrison had been spurned. He was angry, that much was apparent in what James had read. And the fact that he had snuck into Nikki's sleeping compartment to get the letter back meant that he was afraid of what someone finding it would think after she was killed.

It was motive. Weak and incomplete, but it was motive. A romantic entanglement gone wrong. Rejection, betrayal, and physical attraction meshed into a powder keg. Was that what had happened? Had a spurned Harrison snapped after months cooped up in space?

James had a sudden flashback of Nikki's face on board *Perseus*, the night before she had disappeared from the airlock. Her blonde hair framed a look of concern on her face, and her eyes...her eyes were painfully familiar. James instantly understood why. His mental picture of Nikki matched the face that James saw when he looked at himself in the mirror. There was undeniable fear. Hopelessness. Loneliness.

The pieces were coming into place. They weren't complete yet, and the image they formed certainly wasn't enough to make an accusation—not yet. James, however, grinned to himself in his sleeping bag. It was a grin of grim determination. He wasn't on the wrong track at all. Harrison had motive. Means were easily present. All James needed was cold, solid evidence. And once he had all those together, the only question left was how a crew could hold a man captive for nine months, millions of miles away from home.

CHAPTER TWENTY-FIVE

Leaving the SIM would have been bittersweet under the best of circumstances, and looking back at the now empty base made James' heart twist in his throat. The SIM was empty of people—but the evidence of their being here would stay for millennia. The equipment remained behind, as did the rover, the array of solar panels, and even the MDV that the crew had ridden down in. The base's life support systems were in standby mode—just in case NASA did decide to return here after all—and the communications network would still be used as an active relay. But that was it. The odds were that this place wouldn't be seen again by mankind for hundreds of years.

The crew had already loaded the MAV for its ascent, and Houston had given their approval of the launch preparations. All that was left now was to get everyone seated and await Houston's final approval. Then they'd be on their way—first to *Perseus*, then on towards Nikki.

James stood a few meters away from the MAV, looking back towards humanity's outpost called *Unity*, a few hundred meters or so away. Everyone but Aaron—who was busy adjusting the automatic camera that would record their departure for people back on Earth—had already climbed the ladder into the MAV. James was grateful for the extra time.

The back of James' mind was full of dark thoughts of worry and despair. He dreaded the thought of being cooped back up in *Perseus* with Harrison, and he was worried about the fight and danger that he knew would inevitably come. James had considered telling Gonzalez about the note, but he knew it wouldn't be enough to convince him. "I'm afraid this doesn't prove anything,"

James could hear the conversation going. "It doesn't even make me suspicious."

Right now, however, James didn't care. He'd never see the surface of Mars again in person, that much was certain. It was an unfamiliar thought. James was an avid hiker back home, but even in the most remote areas, he knew he could somehow find his way back if he ever wanted to badly enough. This was different.

"Almost done," Aaron said over the radio. "I'm just making sure it's linking to *Unity's* commslink."

James ground his boot into the Martian soil, revealing a few blackish pebbles in the reddish-brown dust. He took a few steps away and found an even finer patch of dirt, which he pounded his boot into, leaving an almost perfect footprint. It would be gone soon—swept away by the MAV's thrust or the Martian wind—but that wouldn't change the fact that he had left it. He considered taking a picture of it with his helmet camera, but he didn't want to cheapen the moment.

"Alright," Aaron said, silently clapping his hands together. "We're ready to go. Who wants to be the last person on Mars?"

"Why don't you play rock paper scissors for it?" Jordyn asked sarcastically from the MAV's cockpit.

James looked to Aaron, who shrugged in acknowledgment. "Two outta' three," James said.

James won. He watched as Aaron climbed the ladder, then grabbed on himself. He put a foot up and paused, one foot on the ladder, one foot on the ground, and took a moment to look around. Red dirt. Red rocks. Red sky. But in a way, it had become home.

James scaled the ladder quickly, then waited for it to retract before sealing the bottom hatch. He then climbed the small internal ladder that led into the actual cockpit, where his crewmates were already seated. His assigned spot was next to Aaron, with Nikki's empty seat being on his opposite side again.

"I have the go-ahead for launch," Jordyn said from somewhere behind James. "Houston just sent me a final data packet for a 1824 hours launch. That's t-minus fifteen minutes, fifty-two seconds. Just waiting on final approval from back home."

"Roger," answered Gonzalez. "Team, are we all here?"

James fiddled with his restraints as the others all voiced their readiness. He gave his shoulder straps a final tug, then rested his head backwards as far as it could go. "I'm ready," he said when it was his turn.

James hated the waiting, although 15 minutes was blessedly short. Prior to the launch from Cape Canaveral, James had been stuck in a seat for over an hour. Some of the same thoughts were running through his mind. Being strapped atop a rocket was unnerving, no matter how brave one was. The only comfort to James was knowing that if he was going to die today, it would be mercifully instantaneous.

"Thirty seconds," Jordyn said sharply as time counted down. She was clearly in her zone. "If you're not tightened up, do it now," she warned.

James tightened the straps over his M-suit yet again, overdoing it just a little. It was too late to risk loosening them back up, so he just left it like that.

"Ten...nine...eight..." began Jordyn.

"It's been a hell of a stay," Harrison said.

"I'll miss it," agreed Mike.

"Four...three..."

"Ignition," Gonzalez said tensely as the MAV started to vibrate. A deep rumble instantly filled up the space.

"...one...liftoff confirmed," said Jordyn, her voice stressed by the rising forces of acceleration. "Engine state nominal."

James started to feel the crushing forces of acceleration. It was initially mild, but grew quickly until his breathing became labored. It was like going on a rollercoaster loop for an extended period of time. He was shaken around like a rattle, his body tossed to and fro as the MAV rocketed upwards, automatically steering and making adjustments as it rapidly gained altitude.

A minute passed, then two. The forces on James' body started to diminish as the MAV stopped accelerating and its velocity leveled out. The sky outside the window started to darken, and the reddish haze of Mars gave way to the inky blackness of space. James felt himself start to float up against his straps. He was getting a little dizzy too.

"Initiating orbital burn," Jordyn said calmly. "All systems remain nominal."

"Commander confirms—all systems nominal," agreed Gonzalez.

James was pushed into his seat again, but not as forcefully as before. He took a deep breath and did his best to relax. According to Houston, the rendezvous with *Perseus* was going to take five hours, and this capsule wasn't all that big.

Fortunately enough, time passed relatively quickly. The crew stayed seated for the duration of the flight, and everyone managed to keep their lunch down. Except for the slight discomfort of needing to use the bathroom—the M-suits didn't have anything other than a diaper to deal with human waste, and the MAV didn't have anything other than bags—the ride was comfortable and smooth. Mars glowed beautifully outside the small windows.

Finally, after a long while, James caught a glimpse of *Perseus* in the window, its solar panels and windows glinting sunlight. The final approach took a half hour, with *Perseus* slowly growing larger and larger until it filled all of the forward-facing windows in the MAV. Jordyn and Gonzalez kept rattling off numbers and distances as they lined up for their final docking. There was a slight banging sound as the two craft met up, then a mechanical grind as the docking was safely sealed.

"Pressure's been equalized," Mike said, pausing to tap on his computer terminal. "We're good to open the hatch."

"Go ahead and take your helmets off," Gonzalez ordered, pausing to twist off his own. "Welcome home everybody."

"It's like showing up at a cabin before the blizzard hits," commented Aaron. "Prepare to get snowed in for nine months."

James happily removed his helmet, letting it float in midair for a moment as he freed himself from the seat's restraints. His stomach was still churning a bit being back in zero gravity, but he was handling it better than he had before.

"Hey, I call bathroom first," he said.

"We'll have to cross streams," answered Aaron. "Hurry up and open the thing, Gonzo."

Gonzalez laughed as he opened the hatch, revealing the inside of *Perseus.* It was like they had never been gone. The ship was still dark like they had left it, and it felt a little chillier than James remembered. The biggest difference, however, was the smell. The air was stale and dry from being cycled on the life support system's lowest setting.

There was a lot to be done. The crew would need to run a full system check, transfer the samples in the MAV over to *Perseus*, and prep for the maneuver to line up with Nikki's body. It was the latter that was starting to weigh upon James' mind. In less than a day or two, he'd likely be face to face with Nikki's body, which meant that the killer, who James suspected might be Harrison, might act.

James pulled himself through the hatch and floated into *Perseus*, leaving the others behind him. He'd worry about Nikki after he had beaten Aaron to the restroom.

CHAPTER TWENTY-SIX

Life back aboard *Perseus* got unpleasant quickly.

Sure, the first few days weren't too bad. There was plenty to do—more orbital adjustment burns, moving the samples out of the MAV—and there was a magic about floating weightless that never quite went away. But the novelty wore off quickly, and the other things that came with being back in space—more confined quarters, the lock-step routine of a NASA-mandated schedule—all added up to put a lot of psychological stress on James. It was only made worse by his fear of what might happen in the coming days.

Perseus had made an initial orbital correction burn less than four hours after the crew had arrived back on board. The burn only used about a quarter of *Perseus'* emergency fuel reserves, but the efficiency was paid for with time. It had been a week since the burn, and the actual rendezvous with Nikki's orbiting body was still a day away. That was ok for everyone, however, given the complexity of what they were planning. Getting two orbiting bodies to line up in orbit was an extremely difficult task made all the more difficult by the difference in scale. Nikki's dehydrated corpse couldn't be much more than 100 pounds back on Earth, but *Perseus* would have weighed more than a jumbo jet. *Perseus* wasn't exactly nimble, and there was no margin for error in space.

"James," said Jordyn at dinner that night. "Hey, did you even hear Gonzo?"

James looked at his crewmates and smiled weakly before shaking his head. "I'm sorry," he said, pausing to sip some water out of his water bag. "I guess I was a little distracted by everything."

"I know it's not going to be easy," Gonzalez said kindly. "But you're still good to do it, right?"

"Of course," James said. "I was just thinking...thinking of her."

All the crew members nodded somberly. James didn't have to describe anything. The others all knew exactly what he was thinking.

James had been chosen by Houston to be the one to retrieve Nikki's body from space. It wasn't going to be easy—in fact, it would be quite dangerous. Houston, however, felt that the mission's doctor should bear the responsibility of dealing with a crewmember's remains, and James was eager to get the first look at Nikki's body for the purposes of his investigation. As a friend and fellow human being, however, James was dreading it. It would be morbid and more than a little disturbing. It didn't help that some members of mission control back on Earth seemed to think of this as a science experiment on what happens to the human body in space.

"I'm still willing to do it," said Harrison. "Really, if anyone is uncomfortable with it-"

"I can do it," James reaffirmed. Harrison was the last person he wanted getting near Nikki's body.

"I've already made assignments, let's stick with them," Gonzalez mumbled through a bite of food. "Seriously though, I'm not shuffling things for Houston again. They've got enough on their plates."

"And I'm the one who's going to have to eat it all," Jordyn said.

"You're the best pilot in the space program, and I wouldn't have anyone else doing this," Gonzalez replied. "I know you can do it."

There was a brief moment of silence amongst the crew. Gonzalez, who for the past week had been desperately trying to keep the crew loose and relaxed, unceremoniously let out a loud burp. No one laughed.

"Hey guys," he said, sticking his spoon back on one of the wall's Velcro spots. "Look, I know that this is some heavy stuff. But we've got to look at this like a mission. We only have one shot at this tomorrow."

"Is Houston still saying 1223 hours?" Aaron asked softly.

"That's right," replied Gonzalez. "So we'll all be in position by 1200. Although Mike, I've changed my mind about having you in the airlock. I want you backing up Jordyn in the command module."

"Are you sure?" Mike asked. "Gonzo, if you're trying to protect me or something-"

"It's nothing like that," waved Gonzalez. "I want safety to be the number one priority. Nikki is family, but she's gone. It's just her body. We're not getting anyone killed for this."

"We'll be fine," said Jordyn confidently. "With today's course correction Houston says we'll be meeting up at seven meters per second, with about forty meters of separation. I can get both to half and still have more than half of the emergency fuel left. That's in addition to the scheduled fuel for our return."

"Good," nodded Gonzalez. "Aaron, Harrison, you'll both be in the airlock, suited up."

"Right," nodded Aaron. "Harrison's got the tethers, I'll be back-up."

"And then Gonzo and I will be outside, tethered to *Perseus*, using the EVA packs." James summarized. "We'll catch her—especially if Jordyn can get us down to four meters per second like she said."

"We've got fifty meters of play on each tether," Harrison said. "Me and Aaron checked this morning."

"I still think this sounds like a cheesy movie scene," joked Gonzalez. "Seriously though, it's like the most overused cliché ever. Maybe I'll disconnect myself from the tether and float off to my doom. I'll make great sci-fi."

"That's not funny, Gonzo," said Jordyn seriously.

"Just trying to keep the pressure low," Gonzalez sighed, sounding a little exasperated. James knew that he was trying hard.

"Is Houston still wanting to leave her outside?" Mike asked solemnly. "I mean, I get it, but it just seems wrong."

"You know there's no place to store her," James said.

"I'll have the bag with me," Gonzalez added. "We'll gently strap her just outside the airlock. Then we'll move her and the Mars samples into the command module right before we re-enter the Earth's atmosphere."

"At least she'll be back home," Mike said slowly, nodding to himself. "We could even have a proper funeral for her."

"I think we'd all like that," agreed Aaron. "Maybe if Houston lets us we can..."

Aaron's voice started to trail off as James zoned-out yet again. He was staring outside the small window next to the kitchen area. The horizon of Mars was beneath the ship, its hazy atmosphere clearly defined against the blackness of space. It was hard to see any stars from their current position.

"Do you think it was bad?" Harrison said, his voice cutting through James' mental fog. "The way she died?"

"At least it'd be quick, right?" asked Mike.

"Not really," James heard himself say. He really didn't want to talk about it, but here he was anyway. "Quick is relative, I guess, but if she was conscious when she left the airlock, she could have been conscious for up to a full minute, maybe more. She wouldn't freeze instantly, explode, or anything like that—she'd just basically suffocate, hopefully before she felt her blood boil."

James' brutal description instantly killed any and all conversation. Jordyn just raised her eyebrows as she put more food into her mouth.

James was too anxious to feel bad. He knew that he would only have a few seconds to look Nikki over for clues before he and Gonzalez put her in the body bag and strapped her to the ship. He didn't know what to expect, and he didn't really know what he would be looking for other than obvious signs of violence and foul play. He was also scared of how Nikki would look. Would she be mummified by so much time in space? Scarred and deformed beyond all recognition? The thought made him sick to his stomach.

James excused himself from dinner and headed down towards his sleeping compartment. There were no experiments or other assignments on the agenda, as NASA wanted everyone well-rested for the morrow's recovery operation. The free time was giving James' mind too much time to worry and wander, but he didn't really feel like fighting it tonight.

He floated down into the sleeping module, passing the various compartments—including Nikki's. Her accordion door was shut tight, just the way James had left it last night. He had searched the room twice since getting back to *Perseus*, finding nothing. There was no point bothering anymore— there was nothing there.

James pulled himself into his compartment, drew the door shut, and began to cry. The weight of his situation was more than he could bear, and the thought of plucking Nikki's deformed body from space—and then frisking it for clues pointing to murder—was the last straw. James curled up, floating between the door and his sleeping bag, and cried silently for a solid five minutes.

Gradually the tears began to slow, and his emotions returned to the point just beneath overflowing. He wiped the tears from his eyes, sending droplets flying through space, and blew his nose into his washable handkerchief. James knew that he had to stay focused for tomorrow—and not just so that Nikki's body could be recovered. The next few days were going to be pivotal, and James' life was going to depend on how sharp and focused he could be.

James checked his tablet, first to see if either Patterson or Claire had replied to his latest emails—they hadn't—and then to use the camera to make sure his eyes didn't look too puffy. Believing that he looked close enough to normal, James decided to go for a quick "walk" around the station.

James opened his door and pulled himself out, then pushed himself upwards towards the kitchen. He weakly said hi to the others that were still there, then used a handhold to propel himself towards the exercise module, where he stopped by grabbing onto one of the weight machines. Someone was showering in the bathroom module above him, so James headed down into the auxiliary lab module.

The auxiliary lab was the least-used module in the station. Most of the main lab work was done on the equipment between the exercise module and the kitchen in the front. This module was used mostly for storage and long-term experiments that didn't need constant observation, but the walls were lined with the mission's organic experiments—vegetables and other plant life being grown under various kinds of special light bulbs—and the sizable window at the end made it a perfect place for thinking.

James stopped himself by the window and gazed out upon the Martian surface, analyzing the familiar topography. Thanks to the years of training and study that led up to this mission, James could recognize and name Martian landmarks, identify general geography, and even recognize the landing zone far below. He wondered if during the nighttime the SIM's lights could have been seen from space.

James stayed by the window for a while, contemplating life, death, and the fragility of the line that divided the two. He wondered if there really was a heaven and hell once that line had been crossed. He'd be seeing Nikki's body tomorrow—could it be that the soul was somewhere else? And if he were to be the victim of something sinister in the coming days, would his own consciousness carry on?

A half-hour passed, then an hour. James' concentration was broken when Aaron came into the module, book of scripture in his hand.

"I'm sorry," Aaron said quickly. "I didn't know you were in here."

"I was just getting ready to leave," James answered, pulling himself away from the window to make room for Aaron.

Aaron took a place next to James, and the two men sat looking out the window. "I like to come here to think," Aaron said. "The view makes me feel small, but important at the same time. You know what I mean?"

"Yeah," nodded James, who understood the feeling.

"You worried about tomorrow?"

"Yeah," replied James. "All of it. I'm scared to see her, A."

Aaron nodded solemnly, then paused to look at James with his blue eyes. "She really is in a better place," he said. "I know that's a cliché, but it's true."

"Is that what your Mormon book says?" asked James, gesturing towards the book in Aaron's hands.

"Oh, this is just the bible," Aaron said, turning the book over in his hands. "But yeah, both of them say that. She's not gone, James. Not forever. None of us are lost and alone forever."

Aaron's words struck James as odd, especially how he slotted *alone* in. It made sense though. Heaven wouldn't be worth much if you were all alone— alone like James was right now. "I hope you're right," James said.

Aaron laughed. "I am," he said confidently with a smile. That smile, however, faded quickly. Aaron put a hand on James' shoulder. "I hope I'm right, too," he said thoughtfully. "Either way, let's stay safe tomorrow, eh?"

James smiled, the sensation feeling a little foreign. "We can do that," he said, faking as much confidence as he could muster.

CHAPTER TWENTY-SEVEN

The recycled air in *Perseus* was heavy with tense anticipation. It was clear on everyone's faces just how nervous they all were—and James could see the fear in each of them, including himself. Gonzalez didn't laugh, he didn't joke, he didn't tease. His face was set like stone. Jordyn kept to herself in the command module, getting ready for her upcoming mechanical dance. Aaron, Harrison, and Mike all carried a sort of hollow, resolute stare.

As for James, he just looked exhausted. He hadn't been able to sleep at all last night, and his eyes had large, dark bags under them. A few pouches of instant-mix coffee had helped him shake off the grogginess, but the caffeine only made him feel more nervous and jittery than before. He went for a brief run on the special treadmill before breakfast to try to get his mind straight, but that just left him sweaty, cold, and shivering during the morning's special briefing and breakfast.

Once Gonzalez had finished recapping the day's intricate mission, James headed straight to the bathroom to clean up. Instead, he ended up vomiting into the bathroom's suctioned toilet. Sighing, James grabbed a moist towelette and got busy wiping up the areas where his breakfast had missed the toilet and clung weightlessly to the walls. He had to get a grip on himself today.

And get a grip he did. The hours leading up to the appointed time of the recovery operation ticked away, and James was able to get his emotions under control. His fear and nervousness were replaced by a grim determination, and the repulsion he felt towards recovering a deformed corpse was replaced by a sort of professional calm. He had trained to be a doctor all his life. He had seen much worse in the Air Force. This was his job right now, everything else be damned.

It was with that attitude that James left the command module after bidding good luck to Jordyn and Mike. He made his way through the kitchen, then through the main lab and exercise module as he headed back towards the rear node and the airlock. He floated forward slowly, doing his best to keep his head straight.

James reached the rear node, stopping himself gently on the sealed docking port that connected *Perseus* to the engines and service module, then looked down into the airlock where Gonzalez, Harrison, and Aaron were getting suited up. From James' angle he could just see the red surface of Mars through the window on the rear-facing external airlock door—the same door that Nikki had been ejected from months prior.

"Hey man," Aaron said, abandoning the upper portion of his EMU suit and pulling himself up into the node to meet James. "How you feeling?"

"Ready to go," James said doggedly. "What about you guys?"

"Same," Aaron replied simply. "You feel comfortable with the SAFER?"

"I've used it once or twice during the training flight," James replied. "I'll be fine."

"And I'll be right there with him," Gonzalez said, his voice muffled as he wrestled himself into the top portion of his EMU suit.

"You mind if I finish suiting up in here with you?" Aaron asked. "It's cramped down there."

"No prob," answered James.

James pulled his EMU suit out of the storage closet and got to work putting the pants on. Unlike the slim, tight M-suits, the EMU suits were large and bulky. They were essentially self-contained spaceships equipped with life support, heating, cooling, and even a drinking straw. The only thing it didn't have was a proper way of using the bathroom, but James didn't bother wearing the awkward adult diaper today. This would hopefully be quick.

His bulky pants in place, James next put the top half of his suit on. This part was more awkward than the pants, since it involved sticking his arms up in the air and shimmying his body up into the suit. By the time he had poked his head through the top, he was spinning around lazily, colliding softly with Aaron as he struggled too. James stopped his spinning, took a quick look at the lights to orient himself—the main lights were all mounted on the ship's "ceiling" to help give a sense of direction in weightlessness—and reached for his Snoopy cap.

"Comms check," he said after plugging the cap into his suit's communications jack. "Am I clear?"

"All good up here," Jordyn said, her voice coming in over the headset. The others all replied to the affirmative too.

James checked that the top and bottom portions of his suit were sealed together, then went ahead and put on his gloves. The gloves were one of the most advanced things on the whole EMU suit—they were powered and articulated to allow for easy movement in spite of the air pressure in the suit. With their help, James put on his helmet and twisted it to the locked position.

"I want full systems checks from all of you," Gonzalez said. "Check pressurization, oxygen, everything."

"I checked them this morning, twice," protested Harrison.

"I know, and I trust you," answered Gonzalez. "Just do it."

James didn't need to be told twice. He checked through all the items on his helmet's heads-up display, then used the wristscreen on his left wrist to cycle through all the systems. Everything looked good, and there were no signs of tampering. Besides, if Harrison—or whoever it was—wanted to kill someone, this would be the wrong time to do it. Everyone was on alert.

Mike floated back from the command module to help give everyone a quick visual inspection. With that accomplished, he went back to one of the storage closets and pulled out two SAFER packs, one for James and one for Gonzalez. The SAFER packs were really just little emergency jetpacks that were strapped to the EMU suits just below the backpack-looking life-support systems. They were worn by anyone who spacewalked outside *Perseus,* and were only to be activated in the case of an emergency—like if a safety strap or harness snapped. Today, however, Gonzalez and James would be using them to maneuver freely out in space while connected to *Perseus* via tethers. If they ran out of the limited fuel, they would just be pulled back by Aaron and Harrison.

"Didn't they do something like this in 'The Martian?'" asked Gonzalez, unexpectedly trying to inject some de-stressing humor. "And 'Lost in Space?' And 'Mission to Mars?' And 'Apollo 13?'"

"'Apollo 13,' are you kidding me?" asked Harrison with a laugh. "Come on, Gonzo."

"I still think this is clichéd," replied Gonzalez. "Seriously, can't you just park us closer next time, Jordyn?"

"This coming from the guy who crashed his Corvette in the parking lot at Cape Canaveral," ribbed Jordyn over the radio. James laughed nervously at the memory, his breath briefly fogging up his helmet's visor.

Mike finished securing the SAFER to James, then moved on to make sure that Gonzo's was connected properly.

"Harrison, you check these things, too?" asked Gonzalez.

"Yessir," he replied. "Everything looks good...I mean, they've never been used."

"All set!" shouted Mike, raising his voice so that the four suited men could hear him through their space suits. "Let's get her back, you guys!" With that, he turned and pulled himself out of the airlock and back towards his position with Jordyn in the front.

"We've got about fifteen minutes," Jordyn said. "We're right on target, I've got her on the short range and everything. Mike will cue up the light when we're close."

"How close will we be?" asked Gonzalez. "What's the latest estimate?"

"We're looking at 35-40 meters," Jordyn replied confidently through the intercom. "With about two meters per second being the intercept speed. NASA thought we'd trade range for speed."

"Two is what, five miles an hour?" asked Aaron.

"About," answered Harrison.

The four men crowded into the airlock, with Aaron sealing the interior hatch behind them. After a final system check, Aaron initiated the depressurization cycle. There was the sound of hissing air that slowly faded away to nothing. James was in a vacuum.

"Ten minutes," Jordyn said.

Gonzalez reached for the large touchpad and pressed the "open" button. The exterior door swung open slowly and silently, revealing the rear of *Perseus* and the bright red horizon of Mars beneath. *Perseus'* orbit was much higher than it was before, but Mars still dominated the view.

"Alright," Gonzalez said, his voice sounding almost breathless. "Just like we talked about. James, I want you to line up right in front of her, and I'll be offset just a little in case you miss."

"You'll probably need to catch both of us," James said. "She's going to knock me backwards with her momentum."

"I've got your back," Gonzalez replied confidently. "Aaron, Harrison, you two ready?"

"Yes sir," the two men replied simultaneously.

"Alright. Let's get in position, James."

James pulled himself forward slowly so that he was just inside the large hatch, right next to Gonzo. He felt a slight tug as Aaron grabbed him from behind.

"You're both clipped in," Harrison said. "The winch is ready too, and the tether is threaded properly so it doesn't catch on the edge. We'll just give you slack and push you out all the way."

"Whenever you're ready," answered Gonzalez.

James felt a slight push on his shoulders as Aaron pushed him downwards—towards Mars and away from the ship. He had to fight the urge to panic. It was an odd sensation, floating away freely from *Perseus* into space. He'd never been five meters away from the nearest handhold, much less fifty.

"Thirty meters out," Aaron said. "Thirty-five."

"Alright, James," said Gonzalez. "Stabilize your position."

James reached for the two small control sticks on either side of his SAFER pack. He pulled them both back slightly, and felt his momentum being slowed, although he was starting to spin. It took a few puffs of propellant, but soon he was floating perfectly alongside Gonzalez.

Knowing he had a few minutes still, James treated himself to a look up at *Perseus* from this view—she really was a magnificent ship. James felt a detached sense of momentary pride upon seeing one of humanity's most wondrous creations floating placidly above the red surface of Mars.

"Five minutes," Jordyn said from inside. "You should be able to see her any time now."

James looked in the general direction of where Nikki's body should be coming from, but he couldn't quite seem to find her. He knew why—unlike the brightly colored EMU suits, Nikki had been flushed from the airlock wearing nothing but shorts and a t-shirt. She'd be harder to spot. A small part of James hoped that they'd somehow never spot her, or that Houston would be wrong, and it would just be a small asteroid they'd found. That wasn't going to happen though.

Tense seconds passed. Then a minute. Suddenly, Jordyn called out over the radio, her voice unusually shrill.

"I see her, right there!" she shouted excitedly. "Mike, get the damn light on her."

James' heart seemed to stop in his chest as he squinted out into the black of space above Mars.

One of *Perseus'* bright spotlights moved, briefly casting James in light as Mike directed it towards its target. There was no beam of light to be seen—in space there was nothing for light to reflect off. Until...

"Got her," Mike said.

"Ohhh," Gonzalez said reverently. James saw it too.

It was clearly a human body, a bright silhouette lit up by the light from *Perseus.* Slowly, James could begin to make out some details. Nikki's body wasn't uniformly illuminated—tiny sparkles of light, almost like diamonds, reflected back from what James knew was the exposed skin on her bare legs.

Nikki was drawing closer, a little faster than he had anticipated. James flicked the control sticks on his pack to make sure that he was in front of the approaching body. It was hard to gauge without any easy reference points.

"To your left," Gonzalez ordered. "To your left, James."

James responded by adjusting his position yet again. Nikki was getting really close now, close enough to make out the shape of her body. Her legs were straight, with a slight bend at the left knee. She was curled forward, one arm across her stomach, the other extended out as if shielding her eyes from something. Her hair, once a golden blonde, radiated wildly from her head. It didn't move. It was frozen in time.

"Adjust up!" shouted Gonzalez. "Up one meter!"

"Five seconds!" called out Jordyn.

"Holy shit," he heard Harrison mumble.

James was in the perfect position. Nikki's body collided with him at the speed of a brisk walk. Her legs impacted first, hitting James somewhere near the knees, pivoting her frozen cadaver upwards and sending her head and frozen hair straight into the glass protecting James' face. Her solid hair seemed to explode, splintering into a million pieces and flying into all directions like a cloud of dust. James instinctively closed his eyes and wrapped his arms around Nikki's waist. There was a slight, sickening, crunching sensation.

There was another bump from behind, this one less forceful than the one from Nikki. "Got you!" Gonzalez cried out. "I've got you!"

James held on tight to the body as Gonzalez worked to stabilize their motion. He finally dared to open his eyes, but couldn't see anything other than hair—and what looked like Nikki's ear. It was discolored, wrinkled, and shrunken.

"Hang on," Gonzalez said. "I'm putting a tether around her chest…oh…Nikki…" he said, his voice going soft. "Damn, man. Nikki…"

"Do you have her?" James asked, his voice an octave high.

"Yeah," grunted Gonzalez in reply. "She's secure."

James didn't want to see, but he needed to. He released his tight hug and let Nikki go. He gently floated her around face up, until she was between him and Gonzalez, her face illuminated by their helmet lights. The two men just looked at her for a moment, saying nothing.

It was simultaneously better and worse than James had expected. Nikki stared back at them, both her eyes open, her long eyelashes frozen. Her eyes, however, weren't really there. The whites had turned completely red, and they seemed to have frozen and contracted into her eye sockets. Her hair—what hadn't been broken off by the collision—was no longer blonde. The rest of her face looked unnaturally tight. She wasn't quite mummified, per se, but her skin had turned brown and cracked, and it had sunken up against her cheek bones. Her lips had curled back, exposing her teeth in an unsettling snarl.

James expected himself to be nauseous or sick, but the only thing he really felt was sorrow. Nikki must have been conscious outside of the ship, and she surely died in incredible pain—that much was clear from the position of her body. Her fingers were bent unnaturally, and even her toes were twisted and curled beneath her socks. James knew that at least some of the contortion was caused by the freezing vacuum of space, but not all of it.

"I'm going to get the bag out," Gonzalez said softly after what seemed like forever. He released Nikki's body for a moment to pull the body bag from his tool bag, leaving her suspended in front of James.

James felt the strange urge to touch her, as someone would touch the face of a departed friend in a casket. He reached out slowly with a gloved hand, pausing before touching her shrunken cheek. Nikki's dead eyes were stopping him. What had she seen with those eyes in her last moments?

James needed to be looking for something, for her sake. While Gonzalez worked to pull out the makeshift body bag, James quickly looked Nikki over one more time, starting from her twisted, socked feet and moving upwards. Frozen crystals of ice glinted in the light from his helmet anywhere that Nikki had exposed skin. She was still wearing the shorts that James had seen her in the night she had come to him with a question, and it was the same t-shirt. The t-shirt, however, was torn slightly, revealing her midriff. She was bloated and misshapen, and there was a small icy patch of frozen blood near her belly button.

"James, can you give me a hand?" Gonzalez asked reverently. James let go of Nikki and reached out to take part of the black, makeshift body bag, but he was having trouble taking his eyes off the gruesome scene. His eyes were particularly drawn to the torn shirt. Why was her shirt torn? Why the blood?

"James," repeated Gonzalez. His voice was commanding, but not impatient.

"Yes, sir," replied the doctor, finally tearing his eyes away.

The two men started at her feet. Her legs were close enough that they were able to get them both into the bag's opening, but her arms proved to be more of a struggle. Being careful so as not to break or crack Nikki's body, the two men carefully maneuvered the bag over her torso and up to her neck. James looked at her face and what was left of her eyes one last time before pulling the bag up the rest of the way. Gonzalez repositioned the tether connecting him and the body so that it fit around the bag.

"We've got her," he said softly. "Reel us in."

James felt the slight tug on his tether as Harrison and Aaron started pulling him back towards *Perseus.*

The pull swung James around so that he was facing the back of the ship, with Mars beneath. He looked over to Gonzalez and the black body bag, watching as they too were pulled back. James was overflowing with emotions—sadness, pity, worry, and fear.

"Nice work you guys," Jordyn said finally, breaking the silence that had been kept by the rest of the crew. "She deserves to be home."

"I'm sure her family will be happy," Aaron said.

"I think so, too," James heard himself reply. He wasn't sure why he was speaking—it just sort of seemed to come out of his mouth without him controlling it.

"Harrison," began Gonzalez. "Can you make sure that those straps are-"

There was a sudden jerk from the tether connecting James to *Perseus*. Before James could react, he was spun violently to the right, away from Gonzalez and the body.

"James!" he heard Gonzalez and Jordyn shout out simultaneously.

The force was brutal, and James couldn't fight it. He was spinning wildly now, faster and faster. *Perseus* then Mars flashed before his eyes as he fought to get his hands down to his jetpacks controls. It was hard to tell in the brief flashes of visibility, but *Perseus* was getting closer and closer. An alarm was screaming in his ear. His crewmates were shouting unintelligibly.

There was another tug from the tether, then a shout from Aaron as he fought to get James back. James made another attempt for the controls, but this time his arm was stuck to his side. It was pinned there by the tether, he was spinning, wrapping and tangling himself up. *Perseus* was getting closer now, he was going to hit...

With a sudden blast of strength, James ripped his left arm free just in time to put a hand out to break the impact. He slammed into the side of one of *Perseus'* inflated modules, the impact knocking the wind out of him and sending him spinning wildly in the other direction. He could see the tether unraveling, spooling out and floating in space as he flew helplessly towards another collision, this time with one of the solar panels. He reached out his hand again, but he didn't need to. There was a sharp tug on his tether again as it reached the end of the available slack. He started to spin again.

"KILL YOUR SAFER!!!" he heard a voice yell. "JAMES, KILL THE JETPACK!" It was Gonzalez.

James' right arm was now free, but the newly accelerating spin in the opposite direction was making it hard to move again. He forced his hand down by where the shut off switch was, and started tapping madly, hoping to find the right button. Suddenly, the invisible force spinning him in circles was gone.

"I got it!" he shouted, his voice instantly hoarse. "I got it!"

"Reel him in, dammit!" he heard Gonzalez shout.

James was still spinning, but it wasn't getting any faster. There was yet another tug on his tether that pulled him backwards. James was finally able to take a full breath and focus on his suit's systems.

"James!" Jordyn cried out. "James?!?"

"I'm good," he answered, his training kicking in. He checked his suit pressure, his oxygen, his other systems. All were functional. He heard Gonzalez give some sort of order to Harrison and Aaron, but he didn't care. He just wanted to get back alive.

The spinning slowed as James was pulled backwards by the tether. It felt like an agonizingly long time, but finally he was pulled back into the safety of the airlock, where Harrison, Aaron, and Gonzalez all floated in waiting. The black body bag holding Nikki floated outside the hatch, still tethered to Gonzalez. James looked at the faces of his crewmates and opened his mouth to say something, but nothing came. His mouth was too dry.

"Damn," he heard Gonzalez say. "James, what the hell was that? What the hell happened with your pack?"

"I don't know," James replied, shaken.

"It just started going off," Gonzalez continued. "The left thruster. Did you have it stuck in the tether? Aaron, did you not check-"

"No way," Aaron interrupted defensively. "I was watching him the whole time I was pulling him back."

"It just went off?" Gonzalez said. "Harrison, I thought you checked them?!?"

"I did!" he replied defensively. "How the hell was I supposed to know-"

Gonzalez cut him off quickly, shouting something about how James was almost killed, but James was already tuning them out. He was just starting to get his breathing under control, and he looked out towards Nikki, his breath fogging up his helmet with every shallow breath.

The tear on Nikki's shirt, the frozen blood—James had seen all he needed to push his suspicions beyond any shadow of a doubt. And he had almost been killed, again. Killed by a malfunctioning jetpack. A jetpack that had been "checked" by Harrison.

James gritted his teeth as his crewmates shouted and argued. His blood was boiling, but not from the vacuum of space.

CHAPTER TWENTY-EIGHT

James sat for ten minutes in the airlock, fully suited, while Harrison and Gonzalez secured Nikki's body to the outside of the airlock. Her body would stay there until they were about to re-enter Earth's atmosphere.

"Hey, James," said Aaron. "Talk to me."

James didn't reply. He was full of rage and hate. He had had enough of this. He was nobody's tool, and he was going to make it home alive no matter the obstacles. He wasn't going to be the one in a body bag strapped to the outside of the ship.

He had almost been killed again, this time by a "malfunctioning" jetpack. Harrison had been the one to check it over this morning. Harrison was the one in charge of the equipment on Mars. Harrison was the one James had caught rummaging through Nikki's things. Harrison was the one who stole his evidence. Harrison was the killer.

And there he was. Harrison followed Gonzalez into the airlock, his face grim behind his visor. Gonzalez pressed a button, and the external door swung slowly shut. The pressurization cycle began, and the air began to hiss in.

"She's all set," Gonzalez said.

"Was it bad?" Aaron asked softly.

"You can watch the video feed if you want, but I honestly wouldn't if I were you," answered Gonzalez. "Harrison took a look, and I think he'd agree."

Another splash of gasoline was thrown on James' mental fire of rage. Harrison had seen the body?

"Just her face," Harrison replied hoarsely, as if reading James' mind.

There was a final hiss of air, then a friendly sounding chime indicating full pressurization in the airlock. James reached up and removed his helmet.

"James, how are you doing?" asked Gonzalez, his voice full of concern. "Damn, here we are talking. Are you ok?"

James bit his tongue, ripped off his Snoopy cap, and got busy wriggling out of the top of his suit. He was starting to breathe heavily now. The adrenaline from before was only being compounded.

"James?" Gonzalez asked again.

James finished taking off the top of the suit and shoved it upwards towards the storage area. He clenched and unclenched his fists.

There was a sudden hand on James' arm. It was Harrison, pulling James around to face him. He was already out of his suit.

"I'm really sorry," Harrison began from where he floated in front of James.

"The hell you are," growled James, shaking his arm loose from Harrison's grip.

"Hey!" Harrison snapped. "Look, man. I checked the SAFER packs this morning. I checked the suits."

"And you checked out Nikki's body too," snarled James. "Didn't you?"

"What the...what the hell are you talking about?" Harrison asked, his voice rising.

"Whoa, guys," Gonzalez—who was still getting out of his suit—said weakly. "Guys, let's take a step back he-"

"You know exactly what I'm talking about!" James responded, shouting now. "You did this!"

"Go to hell you damn idiot," Harrison shouted back, his face flushed. "Don't be an idiot, James! Why don't you calm the f-"

James let his clenched right fist fly, connecting solidly with Harrison's nose before he could finish his sentence. There was an audible crunch of cartilage, and the force of James' blow was enough to send both men flying and spinning out of control. James felt Aaron try to grab him by the leg, but he shook himself loose and used Aaron's chest as a push-off point for his next lunge at Harrison. He coiled up, ready to throw another punch.

Harrison caught himself just in time to block James' blow, but James had the momentum. He slammed Harrison against the side of the module, grabbed him by the collar, and let another punch fly. This one caught him just below the eye.

James reached back and punched again, then again, then again—each blow progressively harder. Harrison was helpless, and his weak attempts to parry James' punches were useless. James coiled back yet again, but before he could strike someone latched onto his wrist with a grip of iron.

"I SAID STOP IT!!!" roared Gonzalez as he forced his way in between the two men. James struggled to continue attacking, but Aaron had grabbed him from behind, putting him in a loose chokehold.

"GET A GRIP!" screamed Gonzalez, his voice echoing around the entire ship. "JAMES, KNOCK IT OFF!"

James stopped struggling and looked towards Harrison, rage and hatred in his eyes. Gonzalez immediately got in his way again. "James!" he yelled, putting his face right up to James'. "Hey, what the hell is the matter with you?!?"

"What's going on?" said a voice from behind. It was Jordyn, followed closely by Mike as the two entered the space. James realized suddenly that he wasn't in the airlock anymore. The fight had carried them into the rear node.

"James punched Harrison," Aaron said incredulously. "He just, uh…"

"James!" Gonzalez shouted again, shaking James roughly. "What is it?"

James looked over Gonzalez' shoulder to where Harrison was floating near one of the walls. His left eye was already swelling, and a tiny, floating sphere of blood clung to his nose and was getting bigger. Harrison wiped his nose, sending blood droplets flying towards one of the walls.

"James?" Jordyn confusedly asked.

"Don't look at him!" Gonzalez shouted, shaking James again. "Look at me. What is it, James? Talk. NOW!"

James sniffed, and was instantly aware of his own bloody nose. Harrison had managed to get in a few punches after all. James tried to wipe his nose with his hand, but Aaron had a tight grip on both arms. James didn't bother struggling.

"It was him," James coughed, a few specks of blood floating from his mouth. "Gonzo, it was him."

"What are you...what are you talking about?!?" Harrison sniffled nasally.

"You killed Nikki!" James shouted, more blood flying from his mouth. "You bastard! You killed her!"

Gonzalez released James' suddenly, clearly shocked at the accusation. Aaron, however, still held fast to James' wrists.

"What did you just say?" Mike asked disbelievingly.

"He killed her," James sniffled. The emotions were overwhelming him now. Hot tears of fury were starting to come from his eyes, flying away from his face every time he blinked. Harrison just stared at James, his face completely still.

"Harrison killed her," James repeated. "He killed Nikki. He tried to kill me just now, he tried to kill me on Mars—he's a murderer, a killer! Now let me go!"

"Bullshit!" Harrison retorted, finally coming to his own defense.

222

"Let me go!" James shouted again, trying to fight his way from Aaron's grip. "You've got to believe me, you've got to stop him, restrain him before he-"

"ENOUGH!" Gonzalez shouted. "NOT ANOTHER WORD OUT OF ANYONE ON THIS DAMN SHIP!!!"

"But-" began Jordyn.

"NOT A DAMN WORD, MARX!!!" Gonzalez roared again. The commander was furious. His face was twitching, and the veins on the side of his head were threatening to pop out.

James opened his mouth to say something, but he caught a glimpse of Gonzalez' hands. Both were balled up into fists.

The entire crew went completely silent for a moment. Everyone just floated there, with only the constant sound of *Perseus*' life support systems making any noise. Harrison sniffed again, another droplet of blood floating into the air in front of his face.

James locked eyes with Gonzalez. Gonzalez stared right back, his dark brown eyes peering into James' soul. James knew he could lay out his evidence, but he needed a chance. He needed Gonzalez to trust him.

"Major Marx, Specialist Syracuse, please flank Specialist Larsen," Gonzalez said finally as he nodded towards Harrison, his voice barely above a whisper. "Specialist Samuelson, you and I will take Doctor Lake."

"Gonzo," James whispered.

"SHUT UP!!!" shouted Gonzalez. "Marx, Syracuse, what the hell are you waiting for?"

"Nothing, sir," replied Jordyn. She was completely shocked—her eyes were wide with fright. Both she and Mike pulled themselves towards Harrison, who didn't bother moving. Mike offered him a rag for his nose.

James opened his mouth to say something, but closed it immediately upon seeing Gonzalez' furious stare.

"Oh come on!" Harrison cried abruptly. "You can't be serious about this! What the hell is going on here?"

The veins near Gonzalez' temples bulged again, but he didn't say anything. He grabbed a hand hold, spun himself to look back at Harrison, then back at James.

"Sir?" Aaron finally said slowly.

Gonzalez inhaled deeply, then exhaled slowly. "I want everyone to listen carefully," he said, his voice nothing more than a dangerous whisper. "Tempers are obviously high. We can't do this. Not here. Not now. One mistake up here and we're all dead. We all know that."

There was another moment of silence. The rage inside James still simmered as he stared at the face of Nikki's killer, but his blind aggression was being replaced by a cool, calculating assessment of his ability to convince the others of Harrison's guilt. He could do it given the chance. He had enough pieces of the puzzle.

"James, Harrison, both of you will report to your sleeping compartments to cool down," said Gonzalez. "Mike, I want you to confiscate their tablets for the time being. I don't want anyone outside of this ship to hear a word about this. At least, for now."

"What's that for?!?" exclaimed Harrison. "What, you're going to keep me prisoner for defending myself?"

Gonzalez waited before responding, his silence quieting everyone again. "I'm doing this as a favor to the two of you," he began, pointing at James and Harrison. "I'm going to wait to report this to Houston. This isn't leaving the ship until we get to the bottom of this."

"Are you sure?" asked Jordyn. "That's against protocol. I think we should-"

"I'm sure," interrupted Gonzalez. "Now. I want you both to stay in your quarters for an hour. Aaron and Mike, you'll be on watch. We're all going to take a breather, and cool down. Then, and only then, we're going to talk about this. We're going to be calm, we're going to be cool. If anyone gets out of line again I'll tell NASA immediately, and you'll lose your wings and compensation, I can promise you that. Does everyone understand?"

James nodded slowly, his eyes locked on Harrison's face. Harrison glared right back and nodded too.

"Good," nodded Gonzalez. "And if anyone else so much as sneezes in the other person's direction, I'm going to lock you in the MAV and spend a few hours deciding whether or not to jettison you. This is *my* damn ship, and I'll have order."

"Sorry, Gonzo," James said, still glaring at Harrison.

"Sorry isn't going to cut it for either of you until I get some damn answers," Gonzalez replied coolly. "And James?"

"Yes, sir?"

"It's your ass that's on the line here, not his," Gonzalez said matter-of-factly. "So you better have one hell of a reason for what you've accused Specialist Larsen of, or I *will* make sure you never fly again."

CHAPTER TWENTY-NINE

Gonzalez' articulated threat meant little to James, who had no desire to ever fly in space again after all this. What did worry James was the thinly veiled threat underneath what Gonzalez had said. If James couldn't explain himself, Gonzalez had every power to make his life hell both on the ship and off. He'd be disgraced and ridiculed back home, and Claire and his children would be dragged through the mud along with him.

Claire. James cursed himself for not writing her, not trusting her. He would have liked to finally tell her what was going on before he made an accusation like today's, but the die had been cast. He had lost his cool, and here he was—stuck in his sleeping closet without any means of communication back home. It wouldn't matter anyway—the next data dump was a few days away still.

There was still the question of Patterson too. The man hadn't replied to James in ages, and James had long since exhausted himself trying to think of all the possible explanations. He thought his emails were going through, but that was about it. Did Patterson change his mind? Was NASA intercepting his emails? Was it something worse?

James shook his head silently to himself for the umpteenth time as he floated by himself, his arms folded over his chest. An email to Patterson, Claire, or even Houston would have worked—he should have tipped someone off before stupidly throwing out an accusation in the heat of the moment. If his smattering of circumstantial evidence was a poker hand he'd been collecting in hope of a royal flush, today's events were the equivalent of him getting flustered into gambling on a three-of-a-kind.

James wished he had been more patient, yet he didn't regret his actions today—not one bit. Seeing Nikki's withered corpse had galvanized him in a way that speculation and suspicion never could have—email from Patterson or no. He only wished he had landed some of his punches harder.

James grabbed his tiny mirror from its Velcro on the wall and used it to look at his face. Harrison had landed some good hits, too—James didn't even feel them in the rush of the fight. The beginnings of a black eye were forming under his right eye, and he had some small cuts and scrapes around his mouth, including a tender scratch on the gums above his top teeth. So that was the source of the salty taste of blood in his mouth.

There was nothing for James to do in his sleeping compartment. Other than a few pictures, his clothes, and his sleeping bag, the room was empty. With his tablet gone he didn't even have a way to know the time. So, James waited, floating with his arms crossed, running over in his mind what he'd say once given the chance.

After what felt like more than an hour there was a soft knock on the flimsy door. "It's me," a voice belonging to Jordyn said. "Gonzalez wants everyone in the rec-room. Harrison is already up there."

"Am I allowed to open my own door?" James asked bitterly. "Or do I need to wait for the muscle to arrive?"

Jordyn didn't respond. James reached out and opened his door to find her floating outside all by herself. She was wearing a white, long-sleeve tee with a NASA logo emblazoned across her chest. Deep furrows marked the brown skin on her forehead.

"You look like hell," she said finally.

"You should see the other guy," replied James flatly.

Jordyn sighed and readjusted her ponytail, all without breaking her gaze. Her brown eyes seemed to be analyzing him, scanning him for potential threats. "You want to tell me what the hell happened back there?" She asked finally, keeping her voice down.

"Nikki was murdered," James replied. "And I think Harrison did it."

"How long have you thought this?" followed-up Jordyn.

"Well, I started to really suspect him while we were back on Mars, after my suit-"

"Not Harrison—Nikki," interjected Jordyn. "How long have you suspected foul play?"

James hesitated. "Jordyn..." he began slowly. "Look..."

"How long?" she repeated.

"Since a few days after it happened," admitted James. "I thought...I thought..."

"Why didn't you tell me?" Jordyn asked, her voice flat.

James sighed, stalling for time as he searched for an answer. "I didn't know who to trust," he shrugged finally.

Jordyn stared at James as she analyzed his answer. Her beautiful face seemed to be set in stone, but there was a storm underneath—James could tell. Then, Jordyn winced.

"I thought we were friends," she said, genuine hurt in her voice. "James...I thought we were close. I thought..."

Jordyn trailed off suddenly. "Come on," she said gruffly. "The others are waiting."

With that, Jordyn turned and pulled herself away. James felt guilty, but he'd just have to hope that Jordyn would believe him after he explained himself. He pulled himself out of his sleeping compartment, grabbed the outside handhold, and pulled himself upwards towards the kitchen.

James floated into the rec room to find all of the others already gathered around. Harrison—who was definitely looking the worse for wear—floated near the rec-room window, flanked by Mike and Aaron. James floated in and took the space between Gonzalez and Jordyn—who wouldn't make eye contact with him. Everyone was floating in a wide circle, and everyone could see one another.

The rec-room was one of the most open spaces in the ship. Like every other module, its walls were covered in storage areas and equipment, but there was nothing large in the middle of the room. A big, thin TV took up a fair portion of the starboard wall—this was where the crew would watch movies and play games after a hard day of work. It was currently turned off, but the tiny camera just above the screen was on, as indicated by a tiny flashing light.

"It's not a live transmission," Gonzalez said, noticing James' gaze. "It's just in case. I can delete it the second this is over."

Nobody said a word.

Gonzalez looked around, his gaze sticking to Harrison and James for a second or two.

"I want to talk business first," he said matter-of-factly. "Our departure burn is scheduled for 0735 tomorrow morning, so when we're done here I want everyone to make sure everything loose on this ship is secured. After the burn, we'll be back on Earth time too, so we'll have a weird day of jet lag since Houston's ahead of us."

Gonzalez paused and looked towards Aaron and Mike as if asking them to say something, anything. They didn't. Gonzalez sighed.

"Alright," he began. "We obviously had a pretty bad day today, and stress is high. I'm thrilled we got Nikki back, but it's clearly been hard on all of us. So, what I want to do is have everybody here talk and just get things out on the table. We need to be ok with each other if we're going to make it back alright, and I don't care what it takes. We can screw Houston on this—make some unofficial schedule changes, increase personal time, whatever. I want to think of some ways we can handle stress better, some ways we can handle interpersonal conflict-"

"This isn't some damn stress thing," James said bitterly. "Gonzo, I'm not taking back what I said."

Gonzalez trailed off, and the module went completely silent for a moment.

"Wait," Harrison said. "Wait a second here, am I getting punked? Is that what this is?"

"Shut the hell up!" growled James menacingly.

Gonzalez turned and looked at James. "I was afraid you'd say something like that," he said. "Alright then. Everyone is going to have a turn, and we're going to hear each other out. But I'm the commander here, and if it gets even the slightest bit out of hand I'm going straight to Houston with this. Ok?"

Silence.

"I'm going to start with the accuser," Gonzalez began slowly. "Alright Doctor Lake, let's hear it."

James' heart was pounding, and his breathing was shallow. He'd been struck with sudden trepidation, and he didn't know where to begin. He swallowed hard.

"He doesn't have anything," Harrison sneered. "See, this is some stupid-"

"Enough!" Gonzalez said sharply. "James?"

James took another deep breath to try and collect his thoughts. He'd just have to start at the beginning, and be as detailed as possible. This was his testimony—his crewmates were the jurors.

"Nikki was murdered," he said bluntly. "I mean, I thought it was suicide too, just like everyone else here."

Nobody said a word. All eyes in the room were trained on James, and the pressure almost made James wilt.

230

James cleared his throat awkwardly and continued. "I mean, at first, suicide made sense," he said. "I had seen she was acting weird, especially the day before. She was distracted. She almost lost her tools, she lost one of the bolts on the electrical panel too. And then that night after dinner, after she snapped at everyone, she cornered me by the bathroom. She looked really concerned. She said she had a question for me...but then she sort of...changed her mind. She made up some question about sleeping pills and caffeine. Something about dessert."

"The tiramisu we had that night," Mike said. "I remember."

"Yeah," nodded James. "And then she was gone. The hatch was open, she was gone. The only reason we knew about it was because the door jammed open. Otherwise she'd have been gone all night before we realized it. It all seemed wrong—and then I found what had jammed the hatch open."

"The bolt," Aaron said. "The bolt she had lost."

"That's right," continued James. "And it just didn't seem to add up for some reason."

"Of course not," Harrison said defensively. "It's a crazy coincidence, and a tragic suicide. We all feel the same!"

"Quiet down," ordered Gonzalez. "Get to the point, James."

"So I had doubts," James said after swallowing hard again. "And then I got the email."

"What email?" asked Jordyn. She was clearly upset—upset that she was finding this out for the first time.

"I got an email from a guy—Victor Patterson," explained James. "Nikki's fiancé. Said he was a police officer, that something didn't add up, that something was wrong."

"Oh come on!" exclaimed Harrison. "A family member doesn't want to believe it's suicide—so what? This makes me a murderer?"

"NASA never said anything about this," said Mike. "Why wouldn't they tell us? Don't you think Patterson would go to them?"

"NASA knew Patterson had concerns," Gonzalez said. "I actually checked with Houston on this a few weeks ago. It checks out."

"Wait, *you* know about this?" asked Jordyn, dumbfounded. "You didn't tell us either?"

"James came to me with his concerns," admitted Gonzalez. "But no accusations and no evidence. I didn't think it was worth jeopardizing our trust and mission. I'm just as curious to know what's changed to justify all this."

"Patterson said NASA didn't believe him," James continued. "He asked me for help. He asked me to look into things. And that's where my suspicions started. You see, just days earlier I caught Harrison rummaging through Nikki's things."

"What?" Harrison asked, his face going instantly pale. "James, you don't think-"

"He said that he was looking for a note," James continued. "A note that he'd written to Nikki before her death. Harrison had feelings for her."

"You didn't tell me this part," Gonzalez said quickly.

"You didn't really give me a chance, sir," replied James. "And earlier, when I wasn't so suspicious, I promised Harrison I'd keep it quiet. I didn't consider it to be groundbreaking evidence at the time."

"Where is the note now?" demanded Gonzalez, turning his full attention to Harrison, whose face was pale with horror.

"I...I tore it up and put it down the SIM toilet just before we left Mars," he stuttered. "I felt guilty about it all. I thought I had made Nikki do it somehow, like I had scared her or made her sad."

"I read the note," continued James. "I found it in the SIM earlier and read part of it. It implied a relationship."

232

"Nothing happened!" claimed Harrison. "I didn't touch her! She was flirtatious, I was flirtatious back. I told her I cared about her, told her I wanted a chance when we got back home, and then she changed from one day to the next. Nothing would have ever happened!"

"But she had a fiancé back home," Mike said. "The Patterson guy."

"Nikki seemed flirtatious with everyone," Jordyn shrugged. "It was kind of her personality. I don't see the big deal here."

"That's just one thing," James said. "It was just the first piece of the puzzle. Anyways, Patterson and I decided to try to see if there was any chance of foul play, and I had something that might prove it. You see, the bolt that jammed the hatch open. I thought I'd check for fingerprints. If there weren't any, great. It was just a coincidence. But if there *were* fingerprints, it would mean Nikki had brought the bolt in the ship."

"So prints would either belong to her, or someone who had been with her right before she was killed," Mike said, filling in the blanks.

"That's exactly right," continued James. "I thought if there were fingerprints on it, well, if they didn't belong to Nikki, they might belong to who killed her, right? Either the bolt was floating around space outside *Perseus* for a day, or Nikki had it in her possession the whole time. And which is more probable?"

"Point taken," Aaron nodded thoughtfully.

"So once we got on Mars I started collecting...well, I started collecting your fingerprints," continued James.

"WHAT?!?" exclaimed Jordyn. "You've been spying on us? Collecting fingerprints off of us like we're a bunch of traitors?"

"I still wanted to believe that it was suicide, or an accident," James explained hurriedly. "I was going to send your prints, plus any prints from the bolt off to Patterson for analysis. I was hoping nothing would match. I was going to save the bolt analysis for last, but then..."

"I can't believe this," Jordyn spat. "I've been lied to, we all have."

"Let him finish," chided Gonzalez.

"Then everything happened," said James, his eyes fixating on a random spot on the wall as he was forced to relive what had happened. "I was almost killed. My M-suit, the suit maintained by Harrison, malfunctioned. I almost suffocated, and then I fell and almost died. If it weren't for Aaron, I'd be dead. He could have died saving me, so I knew he was innocent."

"Well, I'm glad to hear that," said Aaron sarcastically. "But seriously, I was there when we autopsied your suit, James. It didn't look like it had been tampered with."

"Yeah, but that's only half of it," James persisted. "You see, when I got back, I went to my sleeping bag. I had been storing the bolt and the fingerprints there. They were gone. Someone had stolen them."

"Did you know about this too, Gonzo?" demanded Jordyn.

"Yeah," he replied, his voice sounding far away. "But I didn't think...I didn't..."

"Then there was Gonzo's accident," continued James, his voice speeding up as his confidence increased. "He got electrocuted because a voltage meter wasn't working. A voltage meter handed to him seconds earlier by Harrison."

"No," whispered Harrison hoarsely. "No, that's not-"

"And then what just happened today," continued James. He had a full head of steam now and no one was going to stop him. "My SAFER, my jetpack, the one *Harrison* checked, the one *Harrison* made sure was safe malfunctioned. I was slammed into the side of the ship. It could have shattered my helmet. It could have killed me."

"Is this true?" asked Mike incredulously, looking at Harrison. Harrison opened his mouth but choked on his words, leaving his mouth agape.

"Nikki's body had signs of something other than just space exposure," James continued. "I saw it just now. Her shirt was torn. There was blood from a cut frozen to her stomach. Harrison killed her. He was in a relationship with a woman who was off-limits, a woman who was playing with him and leading him on. Hell, for all we know it was more than just flirting and smiling. And when she ended it, Harrison was mad. Furious."

"No, I can explain," Harrison pleaded. "I can-"

"You killed her!" shouted James. "I don't know if you suffocated her before or not, but you dragged her into the airlock. You locked her in there and then you opened the outer door. You ejected her into space, Harrison. You murdered her! And when you knew I was onto you, you came after me. But that wasn't enough. Then it was Gonzo. And then it was me again when you realized we'd be retrieving Nikki's body and the evidence that could still be on it! You even tried to convince Gonzalez into letting you go out after her. You practically begged!"

"I loved her!" choked Harrison. "I won't deny it! But I didn't do this! I didn't kill her!"

Harrison's shouts echoed around *Perseus*, then were replaced by complete and utter silence. The six remaining members of the Ares I crew looked back and forth at each other, all of them clearly taken aback. Harrison started to stutter something else, but didn't bother finishing his sentence.

"Sir?" Mike asked finally, directing himself towards Gonzalez. "Commander?"

Gonzalez looked at James, then at Harrison, then back at James. He slowly crossed both arms, then released his right hand and crossed himself.

"Sir?" asked Jordyn.

"I believe James," said Gonzalez, shaking his head in disbelief at his own words.

James was ecstatic inside. He'd been successful! He did his best to keep his face straight and determined.

"I want to know what the others think," Gonzalez said. "I want to hear from everyone before I make the call."

"I want to hear why James thinks it was Harrison," Aaron said. "Why not someone else? It's all circumstantial. I'm sorry James, but I'm not willing to believe it just yet."

"Aaron saved me," James said, nodding in acknowledgment towards Aaron. "A killer wouldn't save his own victim. Gonzalez was a victim too."

"But I saved him!" exclaimed Harrison.

"Only after you knew he was still alive," continued James. "Jordyn…I trust Jordyn with my life, even if she doesn't believe it. Plus, she was in the command module all day today. She didn't have any interaction with the SAFER packs, nor the M-suits, nor the electrical equipment. Mike has a similar alibi. He's the biologist."

The crew was quiet for a moment as they took in James' logic. Gonzalez cleared his throat and spoke first. "Harrison, do you have any defense?"

Harrison looked completely flustered. His face was pale, and he was sweating profusely. "I didn't do it," he gasped. "I know I can prove that, I just need a minute to think…I just need a second to think…"

"Is what James says true?" asked Jordyn.

"That I manage the M-suits?" Harrison asked rhetorically, his voice shaking. "That I handed Gonzo the voltage meter? That I inspected the SAFER pack? Yes. And yeah, I had a thing for Nikki. I can't deny any of it. But…"

"But what?" sneered James. He had won.

"But I didn't do it," Harrison sniffled weakly.

"I've heard enough from you," Gonzalez said. "I still want to hear from everyone else. Jordyn?"

"The emails from Patterson?" she asked. "Do you still have them?"

"I deleted them," replied James sheepishly. "And he hasn't replied to me in months. I don't know why."

Jordyn looked at James. There was clear hurt in her eyes. She quickly looked away. "I trust James," she said finally. "Which is a hell of a lot more than what I got from him. I'm still with James and Gonzo on this, though," she finished, looking down.

"Mike?" asked Gonzalez.

"The logic tracks," he shrugged. "Although I still don't think anyone here is capable of such a thing. I still think it was-"

"What is your verdict?" Gonzalez interrupted. He was like a judge presiding over a jury.

"I guess I'm with you," replied Mike. "The evidence points that way. Though I want to get more from Houston about this Patterson thing."

"That gives us a majority if we don't count James or Harrison," Jordyn said. "What do we do, do we tell NASA? Do we tell them now? What do we do with Harrison?"

"We'll have to hold you somehow," Mike said, looking warily at Harrison floating next to him. "I'm sorry Harrison. I really hope I'm wrong."

"Alright," sighed Gonzalez. "Major Marx, I'm going to have you message Houston, and James is going with you. Mike, Aaron, you two are going to help me restrain Harrison. Let's grab some duct tape from the lab and bind his wrists."

Harrison started to protest, but his words turned into unintelligible sobs. Nobody moved for a moment until Mike reached out to grab a handhold.

"Wait," Aaron said suddenly.

"We skipped you, didn't we?" Gonzalez acknowledged. "I'm contacting NASA either way, but did we miss something?"

"You might say that," Aaron said thoughtfully, his brow furrowed.

"I can answer any questions you have," James offered. "I'll do my best. And maybe you can undelete my emails from Patterson somehow if that helps."

"I don't need Patterson's emails," Aaron replied. "But I do have a question."

"Spit it out," Gonzalez replied. "Let's hear it."

"You said this bolt was key evidence, right?" began Aaron. "That if it had other fingerprints, it would show someone else had been with Nikki. We're assuming the bolt was either in space or in her direct possession in-between your spacewalk and her death, right?"

"That's right," answered James.

"I think we're missing something," Aaron said. "Something obvious."

"We don't have time for 'Twelve Angry Men' in space," said Gonzalez when Aaron didn't continue right away. "What is it?"

"There was someone else on the original spacewalk with Nikki," Aaron said. "Someone else that could have had access to the bolt."

Aaron reached into his right pocket, his hand emerging with a plastic baggy pinched between his thumb and forefinger. He raised it up for all to see. Inside the baggy was a bolt. The same bolt that was stolen from James.

"There are definitely fingerprints on here," Aaron said. "Two sets, actually."

James was confused. He opened his mouth to ask Aaron something, but he couldn't. It was as if an icy hand had latched onto his windpipe. If Aaron had the bolt, if Aaron had kept it, that meant...

"There *is* a fingerprint from Nikki," said Aaron. "So she definitely had that bolt between the spacewalk and her death. The other fingerprint..."

238

"Who?" James croaked.

"You, James."

CHAPTER THIRTY

James was caught completely off guard. He just hovered there for a moment, completely silent, staring at the bolt that floated gently in the bag held between Aaron's fingers. None of this made sense. He had trusted Aaron, absolved him of any potential guilt. But if he held the bolt in his hands...

"James?" he heard Jordyn ask. Her voice seemed to come from far, far away.

"Are you serious about this?" Gonzalez asked. Surprisingly enough, he didn't look at all shocked, just the opposite. His face was expressionless, and didn't convey any emotion.

Aaron nodded slowly. He wasn't smiling, he wasn't happy, he wasn't vengeful. He was the exact opposite of what James was when he had accused Harrison of murder. He looked...disappointed.

"I didn't want to say this," Aaron said quietly. "It's not like I have loads of irrefutable evidence. But if we're about to tie up a man I believe is innocent, I had to say something."

"What, exactly, *are* you saying, Aaron?" James asked, doing his best to stay calm as his mind raced. He was confident Harrison was the killer, but if Aaron had stolen his things, if Aaron held the bolt in his hands...

Aaron made eye contact with James, then quickly looked away. "Look, my evidence is incomplete," he shrugged, turning his gaze towards Gonzalez. "But I think James is the one who did this. Nikki's death wasn't suicide. But it wasn't Harrison. The evidence points towards James."

James' heart dropped. He couldn't believe what he was hearing. The tables had been turned somehow, but how? What had happened?

"What are you talking about?" was all James could muster to say.

"Explain yourself quickly," Gonzalez said, his voice icy and sterile. "And nobody move. No one."

Aaron looked around at the others, though his eyes seemed to pass over James quickly. It was almost as if Aaron was ashamed to look at him, ashamed to accuse him directly to his face.

"Let's hear it," James said finally. "I have nothing to hide. Get it out so we can get on with things."

Aaron gave a fleeting look at James, then cleared his throat. "I got an email too," he said finally. "An email from Victor Patterson. It sounds like it was a similar email to the one James got. He said the same things. That he was a police officer, that Nikki was his fiancé, that there was no way this was suicide. I didn't reply to him for a week. I didn't want to believe it, but I couldn't fight my suspicions. I didn't think it was suicide either. It never made sense."

"Did everyone on this damn ship get an email?" demanded Jordyn. "And how the hell does James tie into this?"

"Well, James is the reason I finally replied to Patterson, in a way." said Aaron. "It's the bolt, this bolt I'm holding. The one that was stuck in the airlock hatch. I remembered it, but I couldn't remember where it had gone. When I looked for it, it had disappeared, vanished. Something important like that shouldn't have just gone missing."

Aaron paused to look at the baggy he was holding. He pushed it gently towards Gonzalez, who snatched it from the air to take a closer look.

"You say there are two sets of fingerprints?" Gonzalez asked, squinting at the bolt.

"That's right," Aaron answered. "Patterson and I had the idea to look for fingerprints. In hindsight, it makes sense what Patterson was doing. He didn't know who to trust. What if the person he contacted was the killer? He had to contact two people. He was running two investigations from Earth at the same time. I, too, collected fingerprints—and Patterson found plenty of Nikki's back on Earth. I'm sorry for not telling anyone, but I didn't know who to trust at first. Anyways, I sent everything back to Patterson for analysis—and he barely got back to me about the bolt."

"The bolt you stole!" James said defensively, his voice rising. "How the hell does that-"

"Can it, James," Gonzalez ordered. "Let him finish."

"You said it had two sets," Mike said. "And a set from Nikki means she had it between the first spacewalk and when she was killed. She had to have had it inside if she touched it with her bare hands. She had it on her inside the airlock when she was ejected—that's the only explanation."

"That's right," James said impatiently, defying Gonzalez' order. "And it shows *my* hunch was right. But I'm not sure how that implicates me in all this. Of course it has my fingerprints on it—I held on to the thing for months! I was trying to take fingerprints too!"

"That's the point!" shouted Aaron, his voice rising suddenly. He turned and looked at James, locking his eyes onto James' and giving him a fiery stare. "That's the point, everybody. That's why I replied to Patterson. He got me thinking about foul play, got me wondering. And that's when it hit me. The bolt. It was missing."

"Because I had it to investigate it!" growled James.

"It didn't seem important at first," Aaron continued. "But it bothered me. It was a key part of what had happened to Nikki, but the physical bolt was nowhere to be found. That's because James had pocketed it. From the second we got back from making the repairs and searching for Nikki's body, James had the bolt in his possession. He took it, and he hid it."

"I was investigating!" James repeated exasperatedly.

"Do you honestly expect me to believe that you immediately suspected foul play?" demanded Aaron fiercely. There was no more timidness or sorrow in his voice, only righteous fury. "That in the heat of an emergency, after spending nine months plus years of training with the same group of people, that you instantly suspected foul play and decided to pocket and hide a key piece of evidence? And then, once you *supposedly* started an investigation, you didn't bother telling Patterson about the bolt until it went missing?"

James opened his mouth to reply, but his mind suddenly drew a blank. He couldn't explain why he took the bolt in the first place. Aaron was right. He hadn't truly suspected foul play. It was more of an impulse. And it was true that he hadn't explicitly told Patterson about the bolt in the beginning either. James had been concerned that his emails were being watched.

"That's what I'm talking about," Aaron continued, pointing adamantly towards James before he could say anything. "You're hesitating, because you know I'm right. You took the bolt because you were afraid it implicated you somehow."

"Then why didn't I chuck it out into space?" challenged James. "Huh? If I was afraid of that bolt so much, why didn't I get rid of it like Harrison got rid of the letter?"

"It's a fair question," Mike nodded.

"I don't know," Aaron said bluntly. "But that's not everything. That's just why I started to get suspicious. With that, I contacted Patterson and my investigation began in full. I kept an eye on James—I watched what he did, and I reported it to Patterson. I gained his trust."

"And what did I do, huh?" demanded James. "What implicated me?"

"Well, you rummaged through Nikki's sleeping compartment right before we departed for Mars," said Aaron. "After lying and saying you were looking for a family picture or something like that. You were afraid you had left something in Nikki's quarters."

"I was suspicious of Harrison's letter and relationship," explained James. "And that letter existed—Harrison admitted it."

"The only thing that letter proves is that Nikki's relationship with her fiancé was tenuous at best," Aaron replied right back. "But that doesn't mean Harrison murdered her. Besides, if you knew Harrison had already retrieved his letter, why did you rummage through Nikki's things in secret?"

James hesitated yet again, and instantly cursed himself for doing so. "I was looking for clues," he replied. "Something else that indicated foul play from Harrison."

"Did Harrison ever search Nikki's things again?" Aaron asked. "Because as I recall, you've gone through her things multiple times since we got back on board *Perseus.*"

James hesitated yet again. He didn't know that Aaron had seen that. He had tried to do it in secret.

"Is that true, James?" Gonzalez asked.

"I was looking for evidence," James repeated. "I was worried something would happen if we were going to recover her body. Really, I..."

James trailed off. There was something in the eyes of a few of his crewmates. They were looking at him funny. They were starting to doubt him.

"Can we stop bouncing around?" Mike asked. "I'm sorry, but I'm just getting confused by all of this. I'm not convinced that anyone did anything anymore."

"I'm sorry," Aaron said quickly. "So James hid the bolt, then rummaged through Nikki's stuff before we left. Then we got on Mars, and stuff started happening. First there was James' so-called accident, which I think was a suicide attempt from guilt."

"Oh come on!" exclaimed James. "You can't be serious!"

"I still find it unlikely that a wire simply broke," Aaron replied. "The damage to your suit could have been caused by the fall, or it could have been tampered with before."

"Yeah, by Harrison!" James argued.

"I saved you because I still wasn't sure it was you," Aaron continued. "And you're lucky too, because your little accident only convinced me that I needed to be more aggressive in my investigation. I searched everyone's stuff again— that's when I found the bolt. Too bad it was *after* your fall. I should have said something then, but I didn't. And *then* we almost lost Gonzalez."

"I wasn't even outside when that happened," James countered. "The meter was faulty, you even checked it yourself! Harrison handed it to Gonzalez before it happened!"

"THAT'S ENOUGH!" Gonzalez roared suddenly, making everyone flinch with his shout. "Look, I've had enough of this damn crap," he said. "Aaron, your evidence is no better than James'. It's all circumstantial."

"I know, sir," Aaron replied. "Just let me finish. Here, look."

Aaron reached into his pocket yet again, pulling out yet another tiny plastic baggy. This one, however, never belonged to James, even though he recognized it instantly. Inside it was the yellow voltage meter that had malfunctioned.

"The broken meter," Gonzalez said impatiently. "So what?"

"It wasn't necessarily broken, just improperly calibrated," explained Aaron. "An easy and fast error to make. But that's not what matters. This meter has fingerprints on it too."

"Someone fiddled with it without gloves," said Jordyn.

"That's right," nodded Aaron. "There's just one set of fingerprints, and guess who they belong to?"

"James," croaked Harrison. It was his first word since Aaron had begun.

"That's right," Aaron nodded. "The meter was brought back with Gonzalez in his tool bag. I went back for it about an hour later to test it, and to check it for prints. Why were your fingerprints on it, James?"

An icy chill ran down James' spine. He knew he could answer the question honestly, but he also knew that it sounded like a stretch. He looked quickly at his crewmates. All eyes were on him again.

"I was checking to see if the meter worked," James replied slowly. "I suspected foul play, so I checked the meter."

"But you didn't bother to tell us that it was broken," Aaron said. "I mean, you tipped me off that it might be broken, but only after you knew I had checked it. You were trying to cover your tracks."

"None of that proves anything other than the fact that I was running an investigation, just like you," James stated flatly. "Besides, what about the SAFER pack? What about the shit that just happened today?"

"Another attempt to cover your tracks, just like an artificial investigation?" Aaron postulated. "Or perhaps the faulty pack was intended for Gonzalez."

James shook his head in exasperation. None of Aaron's evidence was enough to prove that he was somehow guilty, but he knew that it was making him *sound* more than a little guilty—at least as guilty as he was making Harrison sound earlier.

"Please believe me," James said, turning to his crewmates. "I'd never do this. I was investigating, too. I swear. I have no motivation—there's no reason for me to have done this. This is all ridiculous, it's all circumstantial."

"It's no more circumstantial than what you levied against Harrison," Mike said flatly.

There was a brief moment of silence. James looked at Aaron, still not believing how the tables had turned in such a short amount of time. He was surprised to see, however, that Aaron's face had changed yet again, back to the look of disappointment and solemn resolve. There was something there that James recognized, even if he wasn't quite sure how. Something inside told him that Aaron was being sincere. He was wrong, but he was being sincere. Aaron wasn't the killer. James was more sure than ever.

"I know it's not much," Aaron said slowly. "But this is what I've found. I hadn't brought it to anyone because it isn't proof of anything. But I can't float here and watch us all decide to hold Harrison prisoner or something. Not if the real killer is free."

"If there *is* a killer, you mean," Jordyn said. "Because I'm not sure I'm on board with any of this."

Aaron pushed the baggy with the voltage meter towards Gonzalez, who caught it in his free hand. He looked at the meter, then the bolt, then the meter again. He looked at James, then Harrison, then James again.

"What do we do now?" asked Mike. "We've got to go to Houston with this. We've got nine months until we get home. Nine months up here together."

Gonzalez hesitated. "I'm not...I, uh..." he stuttered. "I'm not sure."

"Someone killed Nikki," James said. "If anything comes of this it should be that. And if you think it's me—well, we're all in danger."

"We can't get this wrong," Mike added. "We can't wait for Houston to tell us what to do. The cat's out of the bag now."

"There are three people who haven't levied an accusation," Gonzalez nodded. "Three people who haven't been accused. That's me, Jordyn, and Mike."

Another heavy moment of silence engulfed the crew. No one seemed to want to look at each other. No one moved. The tiny green light indicating that the camera was on blinked steadily.

"Should we do a private ballot?" Mike asked.

"I think our reasoning should be out there," Gonzalez replied, gesturing towards the camera. "I'll go first. I'm still with James on this one."

"Commander," Aaron pleaded.

"No, look," asserted Gonzalez. "James came to me with this weeks ago, and I didn't believe him. I just don't think that he'd fake an investigation to cover his tracks. And honestly, I find Harrison's constant connection to the accidents we've had to be too much."

James breathed a sigh of relief at the exact moment Harrison inhaled nervously.

"Mike?" Gonzalez prodded.

Mike nodded that he heard, but he took a moment to respond. "I'm afraid I disagree," he said finally. "I'm sorry, Gonzo. And I'm sorry, James. But I'm more convinced by the evidence from Aaron. The fingerprints on the voltage meter did it for me—as long as we can confirm them."

"I'm sure NASA can," Aaron said. "I haven't told them yet, but I've been in constant communication with Patterson, especially since I presented my case against James. I'm sure he'd be more than willing to collaborate."

So that's why Patterson hadn't replied. Aaron had apparently convinced him with his evidence—even if James found it to be no better than his own. Still, James was glad to have an explanation—although it wasn't quite the one he would have preferred.

"That just leaves you, Major," Gonzalez said, prompting Jordyn.

James looked directly at Jordyn, doing his best to lock eyes with her. She looked at him briefly, then dropped her gaze. James' heart dropped along with it.

"I...I..." stuttered Jordyn. "I can't..."

"I need an answer, Jordyn," Gonzalez said gently.

James kept staring at Jordyn, mentally begging for her to trust him. She had to trust him. She had to pick Harrison as the guilty one, she had to know that James would never do something like this. They were friends—they were close.

"I don't know who to trust," Jordyn said finally, her voice sounding hollow and defeated. She looked towards James with tears in her eyes, but they weren't tears of sorrow. They were tears of anger, betrayal, and hate.

"Jordyn?" Gonzalez asked again.

"No," Jordyn said sharply, her voice rising slightly. "No. I'm not picking between them, Gonzo. I'm not picking anyone. You're my friends and my crewmates, and I don't think anyone did this. I refuse to believe it."

Gonzalez sighed. "I suppose it's for the best anyways," he mumbled.

"No, no, no," Aaron rebuked. "Gonzo, we're millions of miles away from Earth. I know what you're thinking, but we can't wait on this one. We need to act now and let Houston know immediately."

"I know," replied Gonzalez. "You didn't let me speak, Aaron. This is my ship, and I'm getting everyone home alive one way or another. Harrison, James, I'm putting both of you under arrest on my authority until Houston has a chance to review this footage and make a decision. Major Marx, would you go get that duct tape, please?"

James expected Jordyn to say no, but she didn't say anything at all. She simply slipped away silently into the module below. There was the sound of a compartment being opened, then closed.

James couldn't believe what was happening, but at least Harrison was being restrained as well. James knew that he'd be able to vindicate himself with time. His friendship with Jordyn could be repaired, and his reputation could be restored. What mattered is that he'd make it home alive. As long as Harrison was the subject of suspicion as well, everything was going to turn out all right. James was so confident of the fact that he didn't bother protesting when Gonzalez asked him to turn around and put his hands behind his back.

"Thanks for trusting me," he said softly to Gonzalez as the tape was wrapped tightly around his wrists.

"I'm not sure I trust anyone right now," replied Gonzalez.

CHAPTER THIRTY-ONE

Perseus was already small, tight, and cramped. Now it was a prison, too.

In a way it had always been a prison—a tiny bubble of pressurized air that isolated James just as much as it protected him. Up until this point, however, he had crewmates and friends to talk to, plus frequent emails to Claire back home. Now James had no one to talk to. Not a soul. All he had were the walls of his sleeping compartment—a space that seemed to grow smaller by the hour. At least, it would seem that way if James had any idea of what time it was.

His tablet had already been confiscated by Aaron and Gonzalez when he had first accused Harrison of murder, and they hadn't returned it. It was making James sick. Not only was he worried about what Claire would start to think if she went a long time without receiving an email from him, but he worried that she would find out what was going on without her hearing it from him first. He cursed himself constantly for being so proud and untrusting. Sure, his logic for not telling her made sense, but he should have trusted her. Out of all the people he could have trusted from millions of miles away from Earth, it should have been Claire.

James had no idea of what time it was, but he finally fell asleep, even with his arms unnaturally pulled behind him because of the tape that bound his wrists. He hadn't bothered trying to stretch or escape from them—he didn't want to look at all guilty. So he just floated there in his sleeping bag, sleeping fitfully for an hour or so until he'd wake up with his arms asleep. He'd readjust, then repeat the process. Finally, he got to the point where he couldn't sleep any longer.

James yawned, then moved to look at himself in the tiny mirror stuck to the wall. His dark hair was unkempt, and his eyes were bloodshot. More pressing, however, was the growling in his stomach. He hadn't eaten in hours—at least, he thought it had been hours. Desperate for some human interaction, or at least some food, James banged his head against the door. No one answered.

James sighed. As long as Harrison was detained James knew he was safe, but that didn't change the fact that the tight space and silence of his tiny sleeping quarters were starting to drive him crazy. There was no way he could spend nine months in here. But then again, for the first time in a very long time, James felt like he was at least a little bit safe.

More time passed. James knew that it had to be at least a day, and he was starting to wonder when he'd be ushered to the command module for the departure burn. His question was answered when he heard the deep rumble of the rear engines igniting. The acceleration was gradual, but it was enough to force his floating body up against one of the walls for a solid minute. He was surprised—accelerating without being restrained could be dangerous. Apparently Gonzalez and the rest of the crew were spooked enough to keep him down here. But why would Houston allow that?

Eventually the burn ceased, leaving James floating around his tiny room, more hungry than before. He banged his shoulder into the wall to draw attention. "Hey!" he shouted. "I know someone's out there. Come on, I'm freaking starving in here, and I need to piss!"

No one replied.

James flexed his bound wrists, testing the strength of the duct tape. Gonzalez had been sure to not bind James too tightly, but that didn't mean he had skimped on the tape. There was no give to the tape, and James had the feeling that even if he really intended to escape, it would be near impossible to just twist his arms free.

"James?" a voice said quietly from outside the door. It was Jordyn's voice. Without waiting for a response, she opened the door.

James blinked in the bright lights from outside his dimmed compartment. "Jordyn," he said. "Boy, am I glad to see you."

"I'm just here to bring you some food," she replied curtly. "Here."

It was a tube of oatmeal. Jordyn opened up the top and pushed it towards James' mouth, but he closed it quickly. "Come on," he pleaded. "Please let me know what the hell is going on."

"Just give him the food already," another voice—Mike—said. James tried to wiggle his body around to see where Mike was, but Jordyn grabbed him by the shirt and pushed him back into his compartment.

"Just take it, James," she said, trying again to shove the open bag towards James' mouth. It was almost humiliating.

James was desperate for information. "Jordyn, please," he begged again. "Look, I know you don't trust me right now. I get it. But I didn't do any of this, I swear."

"That's not up to me to decide anymore," Jordyn retorted angrily. "Houston has taken control of the investigation."

"Major Marx!" shouted Mike impatiently. "Come on, give him the damn oatmeal and come back. We still have to feed Harrison."

"Shut the hell up, Mike," Jordyn shouted back, looking upwards. "Just give me a second."

Jordyn looked back at James. Her eyebrows were slanted sharply, and she was obviously angry with James. "Look," she whispered menacingly. "I know you didn't do this. That's just stupid. I don't know what Aaron is thinking."

"Thank you!" James exclaimed.

"But I don't know what the hell you're thinking either," she continued. "Accusing Harrison of something like that—it's reckless and idiotic."

"Lives were in danger," James shrugged awkwardly, his mobility severely limited. "I wanted to find more, but I was almost killed again getting Nikki. You have to believe me. You owe me that, considering I'm stuck here because of you."

Jordyn stared blankly at James, then shook her head in frustration. She left the oatmeal tube suspended in midair in front of James, then moved to leave. "Wait," James begged. "I'm sorry. Just tell me what's going on. Please. Please, Jordyn."

Jordyn paused. "Fine," she said. "I'll have you know I actually changed my mind and argued with Aaron for your release a few hours ago, but Gonzo shut us both down. He's already transmitted the recording of yesterday to Houston, and they're trying to get things straightened out. Scoville actually reprimanded Gonzo pretty hard for not reporting things before detaining you and Harrison. They've assumed full authority."

"If they were so upset about it, why am I still here?" asked James.

"Because the so-called evidence you and Aaron fought over demands attention," Jordyn replied, looking over her shoulder. "Plus, the stuff about Patterson checks out. I guess NASA has initiated a full investigation, in secret. Nobody knows but a handful of FBI agents and mission control, and for your sake, I hope it stays that way."

"The FBI is involved?"

"People are accusing each other of murder up here," Jordyn said flatly. "Seems pretty serious."

"But they think there's a case?" asked James. He was just glad to know he wasn't crazy.

"How the hell should I know?" scoffed Jordyn. "Maybe they don't want the first astronauts on Mars to punch each other to a pulp and get everyone else killed."

James swallowed his pride and accepted Jordyn's pointed criticism. "But you trust me, right?" James asked.

"I trust *you* didn't kill anyone, but that's as far as it goes," Jordyn said. "So don't expect any other favors from me. Eat your damn oatmeal."

With that, Jordyn snatched the tube and shoved it into James' open mouth before he could react. She pulled herself out and shut the compartment door. James sighed through his nose, then sucked out a mouthful of oatmeal. It was ice cold—it hadn't even been warmed.

James was so hungry that he finished eating the oatmeal is spite of its temperature and flavor. With that done, he was left to float aimlessly again, with the empty tube floating next to his head.

There was nothing to do and no one to talk to. That left James with time to think. He was grateful to hear that NASA's investigation was under wraps for now. He was grateful to know that at least one other person on board thought he was innocent—even if Jordyn didn't believe it was Harrison either. The catch, however, was that his prosecution of Harrison and his defense of himself was now out of his hands.

Another hour or two passed, with James alternating between fatigue from boredom and sheer restlessness from being cooped up with a full bladder. Finally, after what seemed like an eternity, James heard more voices from outside his sleeping compartment.

It was Gonzalez' voice, accompanied by Harrison's. James couldn't make out the words, but it sounded as if Harrison was being taken from his sleeping compartment directly across the module from James. James' heart dropped.

James' own door slid open suddenly without so much as a knock. It was Aaron, his face grim, his brow furrowed. In the background, James could see Gonzalez gently pulling Harrison from his compartment.

"James," Aaron said flatly.

"I didn't do this, Aaron," James replied, still looking over Aaron's shoulder. Gonzalez was cutting Harrison's bindings now. He was setting him free!

"Tell that to Houston," shrugged the blonde engineer. "Come on, I'm going to cut your tape first."

So they were both being set free. But why? James let Aaron turn him around and felt his bindings suddenly give way. James slowly brought his arms around front for the first time in forever and painfully peeled the tape off, pulling out his arm hair.

"What's going on?" he asked, looking over Aaron's shoulder again. A ball of fear had settled inside of James' stomach. Why was Harrison being set free too? What was going on?

"Houston has decided we can't lawfully hold either of you," Aaron said flatly. "Gonzalez argued that since space is technically under international law he was in charge, but Houston threatened him with his wings."

"That's no good," James said nervously. "We can't let Harrison go. We can't-"

"I'm not happy about it either," Aaron said, though his tone obviously indicated that he was talking about James. "But that's our orders. In the meantime, Houston wants both of you to make a detailed recording answering some of their questions, right now. I already did the same."

James pursed his lips in thought.

"I'll be keeping an eye on you though," Aaron said. "That's a promise."

"I didn't do this, Aaron," replied James. "We're on the same side."

Aaron did something strange. He opened his mouth, clearly ready to throw back some retort, but then hesitated unexpectedly. He looked at James thoughtfully for a moment, saying nothing, then looked down as if ashamed. "I'm just following the evidence," he said quickly before turning away. "It's nothing personal."

So Aaron had his doubts too, even if he wouldn't admit them. That knowledge pleased James, but it did little to alleviate his concern that Harrison was being released, too. With an investigation pending, would Harrison be more or less likely to do something rash? With everyone suspicious, with everyone watching, could it be that the danger was behind them? It was starting to seem likely that James would find himself vindicated of any potential guilt, but that meant nothing if the true killer was falsely resolved of guilt too.

James pulled himself from his sleeping compartment, stinging pain shooting through his wrists as he twisted them too far. He floated up into the kitchen, where Mike and Jordyn floated as they chatted over bags of coffee. Both of them grew silent as he entered the room.

"Hello," James said awkwardly. "I'm, uh...supposed to do some sort of report?"

"Command module," Jordyn replied. "Harrison is up in the rec room."

"Going to use the head first," muttered James, turning and leaving the kitchen.

James' quick detour to the bathroom complete, he went back towards the command module where he entered to find Gonzalez waiting for him. "Hey, James," he smiled weakly. James could tell instantly that he hadn't slept since the events of last night.

"Sir, we can't let Harrison go like this," James began. "We can't-"

"It's not my call, James," Gonzalez said quickly. "I'm sorry. You know I trust you on this, but it's out of my hands now. I do what Houston tells me to do. That's my job."

"But sir," complained James.

"No," Gonzalez interrupted flatly. "We'll keep an eye on him, James, but that's all we're gonna' do. This isn't a prison, and we can't spend everyone's time keeping an eye on you two anyways."

James opened his mouth to protest some more, but he knew it would be useless. Gonzalez nodded, acknowledging James' restraint, then pointed towards one of the Velcro lined panels on the side of the command module, near one of the windows. Stuck to it was a tablet.

"That's yours," Gonzalez nodded. "You'll find a message from Houston in your inbox. But James, I need to tell you the same thing I told Harrison. From now on, every email we all send is getting inspected by Houston. I'm under strict orders to tell you that you're not to say a word about this to anyone, not even Claire. They told me they'd cut out personal emails entirely if that happens. Is that understood?"

The stipulations made sense to James, even if he didn't like them. "That's fine," he said. "Should I just film in here?"

"I'll leave," Gonzalez replied. "Good luck."

James made his way over to the tablet, powering it on. It looked just the same as it always had, but James knew that whatever tenuous privacy he once had was now gone. NASA would never look at personal emails in normal circumstances—but these weren't normal circumstances. Every piece of communication went through NASA's servers, and there they stayed—easily accessible and within NASA's purview, with or without a warrant. James felt himself blush. He hoped no one would go through Claire's anniversary message.

The questions from NASA and the FBI were simple enough. In his recording, James again explained everything that he remembered from the night Nikki died. This time, however, he was asked for details about each safety incident that had occurred recently, and then outline his evidence and "investigation"—it was NASA that had put that word in quotations. It took James a full hour, and by the time he had uploaded his transmission to *Perseus*, his stomach was growling again. Tablet in his hands, he pushed himself out of the command module and towards the kitchen. He was starving. When he entered the forward node, however, he ran right into Harrison.

"What the hell?" James shouted, shoving Harrison away and throwing himself backwards in the process. "Are you listening in to my report?" demanded James.

"I was just waiting for you to be done," defended Harrison. "James, I want to talk to you. Please."

"Is there a problem up there?" Gonzalez shouted from the galley.

James looked at Harrison. He floated on the other side of the node, eyes locked on James as if pleading with him. James had no reason to trust him, no reason to listen to him. Yet, something in the back of his mind told him to give Harrison a chance.

"No," answered James. "Nothing's wrong, Gonzo."

Harrison exhaled in relief. "Can we go back in the command module?" he asked timidly. "I want to talk in private."

James tensed up. There was no way he was going to isolate himself from the rest of the crew, not with Harrison. "No," James answered. "We stay right here."

Harrison looked around, checking to make sure no one was too close. "Look," he began softly. "I know you don't believe me, but please hear me out."

"I hope it's a confession," growled James.

Harrison looked hurt, but he continued anyway. "James, where were you when the alarm went off?" he asked. "You know, the night Nikki died."

"Sleeping," James replied flatly.

"Well, I've been thinking," began Harrison. "The alarm only went off when the hatch opened manually, right? When the regular depressurization was thrown off. So the alarm went off at almost the exact moment Nikki was ejected, right?"

James nodded begrudgingly.

"James," Harrison said, his voice carrying a strange tone of hope. "James, you saw me. You saw me getting out of my sleeping compartment. Remember?"

James stared at Harrison, not wanting him to think he was winning as James racked his memory. He remembered waking up to the alarm. He remembered pulling himself out of his compartment. He remembered...

Harrison was right. James *had* actually seen a groggy Harrison emerge from his sleeping compartment. Most of the others just sort of appeared in the chaos of the emergency—which made sense to James considering that he was focused on more pressing matters—but that didn't change the fact that Harrison was right.

"You do," Harrison said quickly, noticing James' hesitation. "You do!"

James shook his head. "That doesn't mean anything," he said. "It took me at least a few seconds to wake up and come out. You could have snuck back in the time it took for me to come out."

Harrison didn't argue. "You can believe what you want," he said. "But James, if you are right about this, right that Nikki was killed, it wasn't me. You have my word even if it means nothing to you, but now you have some evidence—a sliver of evidence. I didn't do this, James."

James just shook his head. "I've heard enough," he said before exiting the module.

James floated his way through the kitchen, passing a silent Jordyn and Mike yet again as he headed back to the exercise room. Gonzalez was running on the treadmill, his face set in a scowl as he ran off steam. James pressed onwards into the rear node without interrupting.

James entered the node, and pulled himself up to the closed interior airlock hatch window, looking inside. It was the airlock that Nikki had died in, or at least begun to die in. His gaze passed over the small computer screen located just next to the door.

The alarm had gone off when Nikki interrupted the regular depressurization cycle and opened the hatch early from the inside. All the scientists in Houston had said as much. James looked down at his watch and made note of the time. He waited until the second hand was on the twelve, then began.

He kicked off of the rear node with all the force he could muster, throwing his body through the hatch into the exercise room, through the lab, then into the kitchen. He arrested his momentum on one of the handholds right next to where Jordyn was floating—she looked quite shocked—then pushed himself downwards towards the sleeping quarters. He pulled himself into his compartment and shut the door quickly, then looked at his watch. Only eleven seconds had passed.

Eleven seconds. It wasn't a lot of time, but it wasn't instantaneous either. James didn't want to believe it, but in the back of his mind he felt that he had been out of his compartment in less time than that during the emergency—after all, he was the first person to the computer terminal. If Harrison had killed Nikki, he would have to have been really fast in order to pretend that he was sleeping. It was doable, maybe. But difficult.

James shook his head in frustration, unsure of what to believe anymore. He *had* seen Harrison come out of his sleeping compartment. But did that mean anything?

There was a small ember of doubt that formed inside of James' head. He tried to extinguish it immediately, but a single question fanned it back into a flame. What if it *wasn't* Harrison after all?

There was only one way to find out. James needed to know the amount of time that had passed between the alarm sounding and him getting out of his own sleeping compartment and being at the computer terminal when it was silenced. If the amount of time was less than eleven seconds or so, it meant that Harrison's alibi was true.

CHAPTER THIRTY-TWO

"You expect *me* to trust you?" Aaron asked incredulously. "You can't be serious."

It had been a day since James had been released. NASA and the FBI were still running their investigation, but for the crew of *Perseus*, things were just starting to get back to the routine—as routine as things could be given the circumstances, of course. Tempers were still as high as ever, and *Perseus* felt more cramped and claustrophobic than ever before. Yesterday's dinner was especially awkward. No one spoke other than Gonzalez, who quickly gave up trying to make casual conversation.

James looked over his shoulder, making sure that there was no one else inside the auxiliary lab room. He had waited for Aaron to come here to his favorite place by the window, and sure enough, he had found him during personal time just after dinner.

"You don't need to trust *me* yet, but you should still hear me out," James replied. "Look, even if this is totally wrong, you'll still clear Harrison."

"How in the world would it still clear Harrison?" Aaron asked. "If you're his alibi, how can I trust you?"

James sighed and rubbed his left temple. "Let's say I did it," he said. "I didn't, but let's say I did. Would I lie about somebody else's alibi, especially after I accused them of murder?"

Aaron sighed too, closing his book of scripture and putting it into his pocket. "Fine," he said. "Run it past me again, but this time slow down a bit, ok?"

"Ok," James nodded. "Look, we both think Nikki was murdered, right? Someone ejected her from the airlock, but something went wrong for the killer. Nikki opened the lock manually, after already suffering during a standard decompression. That's what the computer says. So, the killer thought he'd have plenty of time—he or she isn't even expecting an alarm to go off. Instead, the alarm gets tripped and everyone goes berserk."

Aaron nodded his understanding.

"Now, when I woke up I was the first person to the computer terminal in the sleeping module," explained James. "Gonzalez and Harrison can both back me up on that."

"Maybe it's because you weren't asleep," Aaron said, an accusatory tone apparent in his voice.

"Think what you want, that point stands," James said with a wave of his hand. "Point is, I saw Harrison open up his sleeping compartment and come out, just before I made it to the terminal. Well, I timed how long it would take to get from the airlock to my own sleeping compartment and shut the door. I did it like five times. My fastest time was ten-ish seconds."

Aaron opened his mouth to say something, then closed it with a click. He looked at James curiously. "So what you're saying is that-"

"That if there are less than ten seconds between the alarm going off and me accessing the terminal, then Harrison is innocent," James said, finishing Aaron's thought. "It means he couldn't have made it from the airlock to his sleeping compartment before I saw him. It means I was wrong."

"But that doesn't prove *your* innocence," Aaron replied confusedly. "Why would you do that?"

"Maybe because I didn't kill anyone," James said dryly. "I'm worried about the truth, Aaron. It's not me, and if it's not Harrison...then it's someone else."

"Or it was just suicide."

James nodded, though he knew it couldn't be suicide. It just couldn't be. Not after all this.

Aaron paused thoughtfully, a hand on his chin. "That only proves Harrison's innocence if we assume that you weren't in on it together," he said slowly. "But I'll be honest, I find it hard to believe we'd have two psychopaths on board. One is already a stretch."

"Watch who you're calling psychopath," quipped James. "But please. I'm literally begging you. Just check the computer reports for me. Please?"

Aaron nodded to himself as he stared out the window that showed nothing but space and stars. He turned and looked at James, his lips twisted as he tried to decide whether or not to trust James. Finally, to James' relief, Aaron reached for a nearby handhold and pulled himself up towards the auxiliary lab computer terminal. James followed.

"Ten seconds?" Aaron asked as he typed commands into the touchscreen display. "I'm going to verify that myself, you know, before I believe it. Let's see if I even need to bother."

James didn't reply. He just watched as Aaron typed in a few commands and navigated through the ship's archives. With time, James could probably have done the same thing, but he had come to Aaron in order to reestablish a small amount of trust. James still didn't think Aaron had done anything either—though he was still cautious—and if he hadn't, then James would eventually need him on his side.

"Alright," Aaron said, moving over to make room for James. "Here's the report for that day. We've got the time the depressurization started, and the time the hatch was overridden inside."

"Can you tell where the depressurization was started from?" asked James. "If we could prove that it was initiated from outside the airlock itself..."

"No," Aaron answered shaking his head. "I mean, I tried right after Nikki died, but I couldn't figure it out. The alarm tells us depressurization was interrupted from inside the airlock, but doesn't tell us where the regular depressurization was initiated. From what I see the computer simply doesn't record whether the inside or interior or exterior terminal started it. Basically, as long as the hatch between the airlock and the node is sealed, it'll depressurize, regardless of which terminal is used."

"There's got to be a way to tell, though," James said thoughtfully. "I mean, if the whole ship is wired..."

"You're probably right," Aaron shrugged. "In fact, I think the FBI has people on it already. But I'm not sure they've had any success, or we'd know."

James opened his mouth to argue, but something stopped him. Aaron's explanation didn't quite sit right with him, but there was nothing that could be done right now. Besides, a potential détente between the two men was worth more than another argument at the moment.

"Anyways, here are the time reports," continued Aaron. "I have the alarm going off at 0202 hours, 35 seconds. Now, let's see when the alarm was silenced...whoa."

"What is it?" James asked, his eyes darting around the screen as he tried to find what Aaron was looking at.

"It was silenced at 0202 and 43 seconds," Aaron said, surprised. "That's one-two-three-four...eight seconds."

"So, Harrison is innocent!" James cried, barely able to contain his excitement at being right. The excitement however, disappeared instantly as James realized what that meant.

"If you're telling the truth, then that's enough time to get from the airlock to the terminal, but not from the airlock to the sleeping compartment then back out to the terminal," deduced Aaron. "So yeah. This would clear Harrison, but not you, James."

"I don't give a damn," James replied, his eyes following Aaron's finger as he pointed out the number. "Aaron, someone else on board this ship did it. They think they're home free! They think..."

James trailed off quickly. Why was he talking to Aaron about this? If Harrison wasn't the killer, then that meant that the other four crewmembers were potential suspects yet again. James didn't believe it was Aaron, but then again, he used to be positive it was Harrison.

"I need to tell Houston about this," Aaron said. "They'll need to know."

"Yeah," nodded James, giving Aaron an awkward pat on the back. "Send an email now."

"I think I'm going to time myself first," Aaron said absentmindedly. "See how long it takes me."

"Fine, I don't care," James said. "But I'm telling the truth. You'll see."

Aaron nodded absentmindedly again, still staring at the computer terminal. His point made, James decided to leave Aaron to himself.

James was pleased with himself—but that didn't squelch his nervousness. He was back to square one. He'd acquitted Harrison—and owed him an apology—but that wasn't much of a victory. Someone else on board was the killer. To James it seemed it couldn't be *any* of the four remaining, but it almost had to be. Maybe Aaron even had a point about people working together—but that did seem like a stretch. James felt his fear-gnawed stomach churn again.

He needed to write Claire. It had been over a week since he last wrote her, and he needed to let her know that he loved her. If anything were going to happen, she needed to know that. James headed towards his sleeping compartment and went straight to his returned tablet.

James opened up his email and browsed it for anything new. There was a letter from Claire from yesterday.

Hi James! I love you!

I'm so happy that you made it off of Mars ok. It was kind of a shock to hear that it was going to be early, but I don't care! You'll be home a few weeks early, and that's great! And with the dangerous parts over, you just need to make it home!

On a serious note, Jason from flight ops called me today and let me know the real reason why you were leaving early. I guess you recovered Nikki's body yesterday. I'm sorry—that must have been really horrible to have to do that. I'm sure her family really appreciates it though. Jason said that they might break the news to the press sometime next week, so people will start talking about it.

Anyways, the kids are good. I'm good. Missing you, mostly. I'm really proud of you, but this has kind of sucked. Get home soon—I'll allow you a week with the kids, but then you and I are going on a cruise. No arguing.

-Claire.

The letter made James smile, though it also worried him. He was glad her email made it in with the most recent data dump, but he wondered if someone back in Houston had gone through it. At least she didn't know anything about what had happened *after* they recovered Nikki's body. He hoped for her sake she wouldn't find out until he was home safe, and the real killer had been discovered. Even better, James still prayed that this was all some horrible mistake, and that Nikki had just committed suicide, even though he didn't believe it. The thought made James give himself a grunt of chastisement. "Just committed suicide"—what a horrible thing to hope for.

James tapped the "reply" button and crafted his own message. He had to be careful, knowing that he wasn't allowed to mention any of the craziness that had been going on.

Claire,

It's so good to hear from you. I've missed you far more than I've let on. I'm grateful to be coming home to you.

James paused. Did implying that he missed her more than he let on sound bad? Would NASA or the FBI agents looking into this think he had some secret message there? No. He decided to leave it.

It was hard to get Nikki. She was a good friend.

James left that part simple. Best to keep clear of anything else there.

The crew is doing well. A little stressed, but fine. With Mars behind us, I think everyone is eager to just get home.

I love you. Sorry for the short letter, I've got work to do. Maybe I'll sneak in another one before this week's data dump gets sent out.

Say hello to the kids for me. Tell them daddy got some Mars rocks for them. I love you more than you know. So, so much.

A cruise sounds pretty damn incredible right now.

James

James went to press the send button, but stopped with his finger hovering over the screen as he re-read everything that he had written. He didn't want to ruffle any feathers—not now, not when he apparently was a prime suspect. Finally, after determining that it was sterile enough, James pressed the send button.

Almost immediately, there was a loud pounding on James' flimsy door. It startled him and made him flinch.

"What the hell-" he started to ask.

"It's Aaron," a voice on the other side replied. James stuck his tablet to the wall and opened the door to see Aaron there. His blonde hair was disheveled, his eyes were wide with fright.

"What is it?" James asked. "Did you time yourself?"

"Yeah, yeah, you were right," Aaron said, waving a hand impatiently in the air. "This isn't about that. Gonzo wants us in the rec room, now. Something about Nikki."

"I'm coming," James said quickly. Aaron gave him a hand to help him out of the compartment, then James pushed himself upwards towards the module. There were a lot of agitated voices coming from up there. How was it that he hadn't heard anything?

The two men floated upwards passing through the kitchen before entering the rec room. Gonzalez and Mike were already there, and Jordyn and Harrison entered right after. Gonzalez looked deadly serious.

"What's going on?" asked Jordyn. "What happened with Nikki?"

"Why don't you see for yourself," Gonzalez replied, tapping the tablet he carried in his hands and turning on the large television screen on the wall. The face of Julianna Scoville, the flight director, appeared. It was another recorded video message. This one, however, was far different than the last one.

If Julianna had looked tired in the last video, she now looked exhausted. She had dark bags under her eyes, and her eyes were bloodshot. Her hair was somewhat frizzy, and her blazer was slightly crooked. Next to her in the frame sat a man that James didn't recognize, wearing a dark suit and a gold tie. He wasn't smiling.

Gonzalez paused before starting the video.

"Gonzo, what is it?" Mike asked nervously. "Did you already watch this?"

Gonzalez replied by just pressing play.

"Commander Gonzalez," Julianna began. "This is Agent Smithfield from the Federal Bureau of Investigation. What I'm about to show you is a little disturbing, but we feel you and your crew should know. Bring them in after you've watched this.

After a moment's pause, the FBI agent cleared his throat and looked into the camera, checking to make sure that he was in frame. "Hi Commander," he began, his voice deep and authoritative. "I'll cut right to the chase. As you know, we've been given permission to look through the emails of yourself and your crew. Nothing in them seems to indicate foul play."

"This is good," Jordyn said, but Gonzalez waved for her to be quiet.

"At least, that's what we thought," the agent continued. "This morning our experts were able to access Nicole Prince's email account. We've been able to download her emails, both sent and received, as well as her draft folder."

"I wonder if Patterson helped them access that," Aaron said to himself. "Maybe he helped them figure out passwords."

"The following email that I'm going to show you on screen is a draft email," the agent continued. "It is the only suspicious thing we've been able to find, but we feel it's disconcerting. Here."

The screen changed to show a copy of an electronic document. James began reading.

Hi mom,

Mom, I know this letter might sound off, but I needed to let you know how much I love you and dad. I can't shake the feeling that something bad is going to happen to me. I don't mean to sound negative, but...

Mom, I worry I've made a mistake, and I'm worried I'm going to pay for it. It's probably not a big deal, but I just needed to get it off my chest.

Anyways, I'm going to try to talk to someone on board to figure things out so hopefully this gets resolved.

Please don't freak out. I'm sure I'll write you in a week and everything will be fine. Regardless, I love you and dad so much.

Nikki

James finished just before the agent started talking again. "This email was never sent," he reaffirmed. "It was a discarded draft, dated three days prior to Ms. Prince's death. As you can see, it's fairly suspicious."

"Um, yeah," Jordyn grunted.

"So that's where we currently stand," concluded the FBI agent.

Julianna started to talk, but James was already thinking about the letter and what it meant. It was certainly strange, and hastily written. Nikki was definitely worried, but what was she worried about? Was it Harrison and his advances? Because if so, James had just proved his innocence. Who was Nikki going to talk to? Was it him? Was that what she had come to him about?"

"So that brings us to the real reason behind this message," Julianna said. "Agent Smithfield?"

"Commander Gonzalez," the agent said again. "We're concerned about the safety of your crew given these recent circumstances. Quite frankly, Director Scoville and I disagree on what I'm about to ask of you, but my team feels like the threat is imminent enough to require immediate action."

James turned his full attention back on the screen. Julianna's lips were pursed tightly as if she was sucking on something extremely sour. Whatever this FBI agent was about to say, she didn't like it at all.

The agent sighed. "Our first priority is to get you all home safely. Ideally, we'd get you home first then worry about this, but we feel that waiting would only jeopardize your lives. In addition, we're concerned that waiting might lead to us losing potential evidence in what is potentially a murder case. So..."

The agent paused. Now his lips were pursed too.

"We want Doctor Lake to run an autopsy on Nichole Prince's body," he said finally.

James' heart skipped a beat.

"Tomorrow morning, actually," continued the agent. "Now, I know Doctor Lake is under some suspicion."

"He can say that again," muttered Aaron.

"But we want Specialist Syracuse and Major Marx observing and recording the autopsy. You'll transmit a live video feed. We'll have our men here verify all of your results."

The FBI agent continued to talk, but James wasn't entirely focused. He was starting to feel sick to his stomach. An autopsy in space? Cutting open the half-mummified corpse of his friend was too much. It was all too much.

But James wasn't only feeling sick at the thought of dissecting a body—unbelievably, there was something worse. The FBI wasn't just trying to get evidence, and they weren't just trying to get the crew home safe—Julianna's face made it clear that she had deep concerns with what the FBI truly wanted. They wanted to force the issue. They knew full-well the killer would be listening to this message, and they were trying to draw them out. The innocent members of the crew weren't just in danger.

They were being used as bait.

CHAPTER THIRTY-THREE

James slept fitfully that night. His mind was racked with nightmares, all variations of the same terrible fear. For the first half of the night, he was killed over and over again by varying members of the crew. Jordyn stabbed him with a knife, Gonzalez shot him in the chest, and Aaron laughed as he ejected James out of an airlock. James jerked awake at least a half-dozen times, clutching at his own throat, cold sweat beading on his forehead.

Then there were the dreams about Nikki. At first they were only gruesome, but they gradually became worse. He dreamt about the upcoming autopsy, about cutting open her disfigured body. In every variation, her body was more and more mangled, and what he found was more and more disgusting. The last one, however, was by far the worst. He had found himself alone in the auxiliary lab with Nikki, who was as alive as ever. Her blonde hair floated behind her beautiful tan face, and she smiled seductively at James, beckoning him to come closer. He did, and she grabbed him by the hands, forcing them to touch her, forcing them to feel her. He undressed her, leaving her floating naked before him. She grinned erotically as James pulled a scalpel from his pocket.

"I'm glad," she smiled, her white teeth gleaming. Then, as she willingly laid her body against the side of the module, James rammed the scalpel straight into her stomach. Claire suddenly entered from behind and let out a blood-curdling scream.

It was a scream that still rung in James' ears as he woke up for the final time the next morning. He was sweating again, and it made him shiver almost uncontrollably. His mind was instantly wracked with both fear and guilt, and he shook his head forcefully to clear it. It was just a dream—an unconscious, unwanted construct created by stress, fear, and separation from his wife. He just hoped the reasons behind it would all be behind him soon, though he wasn't overly optimistic. James let out a sigh and let his arms limply float back out in front of him.

The alarm on his tablet rang out loudly, jerking James to full alertness and ensuring that he wouldn't fall asleep again. He deactivated the alarm and checked the time. Was it already 0700? It couldn't be.

James sighed yet again and moved to unzip his sleeping bag. He had better try to at least eat something small—doing an autopsy on an empty stomach while floating around weightless would only lead to bad things. He opened the door and pulled himself out, just as Jordyn was doing the same.

"How'd you sleep?" James asked weakly.

"Nightmares," Jordyn replied weakly. "I really don't want to do this."

"You and me both," James said ruefully.

The two floated silently up to the kitchen where Aaron and Mike floated with pouches of breakfast. The two men had been tasked with keeping watch on the other two pairs of astronauts—Jordyn and James as they slept, and Gonzalez and Harrison as they guarded the airlock. Houston and the FBI were adamant that nobody be allowed near Nikki's body until James was ready to go.

Go-time was rapidly approaching. James had already been briefed on what the FBI wanted from his autopsy, and most of it was simple enough. He had been involved in a couple of dissections during medical school, and his basic training was more than enough to let him find his way around a cadaver— even if he lacked the expertise of a professional forensic pathologist. All he had to do was follow the checklist he had been given, and the people back on Earth would handle the rest. At least, that's what James kept telling himself.

James fished a breakfast packet from one of the storage containers and put it into *Perseus'* special microwave. Nobody bothered saying anything to him, and that was fine by James. He grabbed his now-heated cinnamon sugar quinoa and headed back towards the lab to check through all the equipment.

Perseus' main lab was found in one of the central modules, the same one in which the exercise equipment was found. Unlike the auxiliary lab module, which really was just glorified storage and a few pieces of equipment, the lab was fully equipped for a number of different uses, including simple emergency surgery—like an appendectomy. There was a foldable table equipped with straps to keep an unconscious person in a stable position, plenty of surgical tools, and even vacuum and water hoses to clean out wounds. The other equipment, including microscopes, electrocardiographs, blood pressure monitors, and various compound analysis machines, was up against the walls and out of the way.

The table was already set up, though Nikki's body wasn't here yet. It would be, soon enough. The cameras were also in their correct positions—one directly above the table, a backup, and one that would be held by Jordyn as she recorded every single move James made.

James pushed himself towards the side of the module and made sure the stirrups—two straps on the wall that he could jam his feet into—were adjusted properly. He couldn't afford to go floating around in the middle of an incision. He checked everything, finishing his quinoa as he did so.

Satisfied that everything was functional, James headed towards the bathroom where he used the facilities, brushed his teeth, and used a towel to "splash" some water on his face.

"Hey team," a voice said suddenly over the ship's intercom. It was Gonzo, who clearly sounded tired and weary. "James, are you up yet?"

"Yeah," James replied, speaking loudly so the module's intercom would pick up his voice. "I'm just in the bathroom. I've checked everything out—it all looks good. I'm ready for 0900."

"Good," Gonzalez replied. "Then we're ready to bring the body in. I want everyone in the rear node please, soon as you can."

James gave his face one last wipe with the towel, then pulled himself towards the exit to the bathroom module. Houston wanted everyone present when Nikki's body was brought in, for safety's sake. If everyone was watching, the killer would be dissuaded from trying anything rash. That was the idea, anyway.

James was the last person to arrive in the node. Harrison and Gonzalez were already beginning to suit up, and Aaron was tasked with being the third person suited up in the airlock with them. Odd numbers would make sure that a potential killer was outnumbered, whether they were in the vacuum of space or inside the ship.

Gonzalez gave a brief summary of what was to happen, but nobody said anything else until all three men were finished suiting up and in the airlock. Mike, Jordyn, and James—the three who would be running and filming the autopsy—were left in the pressurized node, watching through the window. The airlock began quietly venting air, and then the exterior door was opened.

James watched through the window as Gonzalez, his double safety tethers fastened securely to hooks inside the airlock, climbed outside towards the back of the ship. He wasn't wearing a SAFER pack, just in case. Neither were the others.

"Alright, I'm there," said Gonzalez, his voice broadcast over the station's intercom. The open mic was now mandatory as another safety precaution.

"Roger," Aaron replied. "Your tethers are both good. I'm going to have Harrison come out halfway to observe you."

"Understood," Gonzalez replied curtly.

Harrison, also secured by tethers, climbed halfway outside of the airlock to make sure that Gonzalez correctly attached the body bag containing Nikki to yet another tether. Gonzalez grunted audibly a few times before reporting a successful attachment. "Just got to undo the straps holding her to the ship now," he said, his voice reverent.

A minute passed, then two. Finally, Gonzalez gave the all-clear. Harrison climbed back into the airlock, followed shortly by Gonzalez. A few gentle tugs on the tether by Aaron and the black body bag soon floated into view.

"I forgot my gloves," James said, backing away from the window as the exterior hatch closed. "I'm going to head over to the lab-"

"Gotcha covered," interrupted Mike, reaching into his pocket and pulling out a couple pairs of latex gloves. He handed a pair to James and Jordyn, then got busy putting on his own. James began pulling on his own gloves, wondering if Mike thought he was trying to sneak off or something like that.

"Make sure there aren't any holes," cautioned James.

"It's not like there's anything infectious left to catch," said Mike. "Her body has been out there for a long time."

"It's not the germs *I'm* worried about," Jordyn said weakly.

The airlock pressurization pumps fired up, filling the node with noise as air was pumped back into the airlock, providing life-sustaining pressure and oxygen to the men inside. There was nothing audible from the outside, but James saw the makeshift body bag ripple and move from the air. At least, James hoped it was just from the air. Nikki's body had been in a vacuum for quite a long time.

"Shit," James swore, remembering something that he'd forgotten. "Guys, I didn't adjust the life support thermostat."

"What's it supposed to be at again?" Jordyn asked.

"I think the minimum we can set is five Celsius," replied James. "We...well, we need to keep the body frozen as long as possible, or it'll get...messy. I should go make the adjustment."

"Not yet," Mike snapped. "Wait for the others to get inside."

278

James didn't bother arguing. It was clear that Mike didn't trust him, and he didn't blame him that much. Hopefully the autopsy would provide some answers for everyone. As of right now, the only person James knew was innocent was Harrison. And it was nearly impossible to truly suspect any of the others. Jordyn, Mike, Gonzalez, Aaron—each had circumstantial evidence that suggested they were innocent. So who was it? James prayed they were all wrong. He prayed that it was Nikki. Just Nikki.

The airlock pump stopped, signaling that the pressure had been equalized. Aaron reached for the door and opened it, then proceeded to remove his helmet.

"We forgot to lower the temperature," he said, repeating what James had said earlier.

"I'll do it," sighed Jordyn, who pulled herself out of the module before anyone could protest. To James' irritation, Mike didn't look at all bothered by Jordyn leaving his sight.

The three men took off their space suits, all while the black body bag floated ominously near the exterior airlock door. James was struck by the realization that the last time Nikki had been there, she had been alive.

Gonzalez finished getting his suit off first, and he was followed shortly by Aaron. "I'm going to make sure our reception is clear," Gonzalez said, gesturing for Aaron to follow him. "Wait for me to get back before you bring her in."

"Yes, sir," answered James.

Harrison took a little longer to get his suit off. He seemed paranoid of the bag that floated nearby, and he bumped into the opposite wall as he tried to get his suit off while maintaining his distance. James grabbed each part of his suit as he got it off, pushing them into the storage area in the node. "Thanks," Harrison said hoarsely, pulling himself through the hatch and into the node.

Gonzalez, Aaron, and Jordyn all returned at the same time. Gonzalez reported that all communication lines were nominal, and Aaron held a camera in his hands. Jordyn would take the camera once she had helped get the body in place.

"We ready?" Gonzalez asked, glancing at the black bag containing Nikki that still floated ominously in the airlock. Everybody nodded, but no one answered out loud. A chill ran down James' spine—it was already getting colder in here.

"Lead the way, Doctor," Mike said finally.

James looked at his crewmates—they all looked disturbed—then turned to face the black body bag. He grabbed onto the sides of the hatch and pulled himself through slowly, floating gently towards it. Jordyn and Mike followed right behind.

James carefully stopped his momentum on a handhold, then reached a gloved hand out towards the body bag. He gripped it gingerly in his hand, grateful that the plastic collapsed on itself, as opposed to his hand grabbing something solid. Mike did the same, but Jordyn wasn't as lucky.

"Dammit," she cursed, recoiling backwards after grabbing the bag. "I-I-I felt..." Jordyn looked at James, her expression slightly ashamed. "Sorry," she said, grabbing back onto the bag and shuddering. "Let's go."

The three astronauts slowly shepherded the bag containing Nikki's body out of the airlock and into the node, their every move being recorded for Houston and the FBI by Aaron. Then, carefully rotating the bag, they pushed it slowly into the module containing the exercise equipment and the lab. Once there, the astronauts gently positioned the bag over the operating table in the lab.

"The wider end is where her legs are," James said, doing his best to keep his voice calm and confident. "Keep her head towards the wall. There, now let's bring her down so she's just touching the table. Good, easy does it."

"Should we strap the bag down?" asked Mike.

"Loosely, so that we can get the bag out of the way once we cut it," replied James. "There, just like that. Jordyn, go ahead and take that camera from Aaron."

"I can stay," Aaron said.

"No," Gonzalez answered. "Harrison, Aaron, let's give them some space. Let's at least stay back in the kitchen."

"Alright," answered Aaron, a faraway look in his eyes. He handed the camera to Jordyn, then turned to leave. "Good luck," he said, his voice sounding hollow.

James looked at his crewmates. Jordyn had the camera in front of her, making sure that everything was included in the shot. Mike was just staring at the bag somberly—though he nodded when he noticed James looking at him. James looked over everything one last time, checking to make sure that the cameras were recording and that all the machinery was ready to go. He inhaled deeply to calm his racing heart.

"Alright," he said finally. "Let's begin. Mike?"

"Yeah?"

"Scalpel please."

CHAPTER THIRTY-FOUR

James inhaled slowly once more, savoring his last breath of fresh air before things got bad. With his socked feet firmly secured to the wall via the stirrups, James quickly identified the best place to begin cutting the bag open. He chose the void created by Nikki's still bent leg, above where her stomach would be.

"You got the camera on?" he asked, looking towards Jordyn, who nodded.

James took one more glance at the small lab screen that currently showed his checklist, then extended his arm and scalpel slowly. A pocket of cold air was forming around the body, caused by Nikki's deep-frozen tissue.

James slid the razor-sharp blade into the bag and started his incision. He was careful not to accidently cut the body—that part would come later.

Nikki's remains looked grisly, though at least James knew what to expect. Mike and Jordyn, however, both gasped audibly as James began to remove the bag from around Nikki's body, exposing her tight, shrunken skin and the blood-red remnants of her eyes. The last bit of plastic came from under Nikki's head, and in spite of James' best efforts, little pieces of broken hair started floating away from the body. Jordyn dry-heaved.

"Mike, please use that vacuum to get rid of those particulates," James ordered.

"On it," Mike replied, his voice instantly hoarse.

James did his best not to focus on the horrific nature of the body. He forced himself to be professional—to be cold and aloof. Maybe if he was successful on the outside it would transition to the inside.

While Mike vacuumed up the floating pieces of hair, James reached for one of the instruments that he had pulled out of lab storage. It was a mini Geiger counter, meant for measuring the radiation of space and the various experiments on board. Right now, however, it was going to be used to measure Nikki's body.

The machine clicked and crackled—an unnerving sound even under ideal circumstances. "Definitely elevated readings," James said out loud for the camera's sake, turning the machine so that Jordyn could record an image of the display. "But nothing you wouldn't expect from outside the ship. Hey Mike," he said, seeing that he had finished vacuuming. "Grab the measuring tape, please."

"Yeah," he answered hoarsely, grabbing the tape from one of the storage compartments before returning to his own stirrups on the side of the operating table.

James looked at Nikki's body as he wondered how to proceed. She was still mostly frozen in her previous state—one leg bent upwards, an arm extended slightly as if protecting her face, her body twisted slightly to the left—and James knew that they'd have to carefully reposition her body so that he could take proper measurements and make precise cuts. Use too much force too early and they'd break the frozen tissues—wait too long and Nikki's body would become an oozing, liquidous mess. That was something everyone wanted to avoid in zero-g—they'd have to be careful.

Nobody said a word as James reached out and touched Nikki's extended leg. His fingers barely grazed the body at first, but after fighting off the urge to recoil he allowed his fingers to put more pressure on the tissues. The skin was freezing cold through his gloves, but James was surprised to find that the skin gave slightly, almost like crumpled newspaper. He tested how much give the leg had by trying to force it down towards the table slightly. It flexed a little at the hip, but that was accompanied by a sickening crunching noise. Mike coughed noticeably.

"Let's give it a minute or two," James said, his voice quieter than he intended. "I'll cut off the clothing first, then we'll work on getting the body strapped up. Mike, can you pocket that tape for a second and grab a sealable storage bag, please?"

"Yes, sir," Mike said, reaching for the storage compartments from his position.

James placed the scalpel on a patch of Velcro on the wall and grabbed the pair of surgical scissors next to it. "Can you double check all the cameras are recording?" he asked Jordyn as he decided where to start cutting.

"All feeds are good," Gonzalez said, overhearing from his place in the kitchen. "There's a thirty second delay before transmitting, but then everything is live—er, ten minutes off for Houston."

James nodded as he decided to start with Nikki's socks. He did the left foot first, sliding the bottom of the scissors carefully between the skin and the fabric, then cut his way slowly towards the toes. Nikki's toes were curled like her fingers, and the skin was shrunken and pruney. The skin and fabric stuck together a bit, but with some caution James was able to remove it cleanly. He passed it to Mike, who put it away in a baggy.

"She looks...darker," Jordyn said, her first real words since the autopsy began. "Her skin."

James nodded in agreement. "Not sure why," he replied. "Probably just from the exposure. We'll have to see if it holds as the tissues thaw."

"It should," Mike added. "The surface of the skin is mostly thawed already from what I can see."

James nodded yet again. Mike was right, and not just from looking at the body. A smell was starting to fill the module—though it wasn't a particularly foul odor. It smelled—and tasted—like metal. Nikki was partially mummified, but there were still plenty of frozen—and thawing—fluids within her.

"She's all...twisted," commented Jordyn. "Like she suffered."

James swallowed hard as he fought to stay professional. He moved on to the other sock, cutting it just like the first. This one was on Nikki's still-protruding leg, and it made the effort more awkward. It led to James accidentally ripping off one of the toenails when it stuck to the fabric of the sock. "Dammit," James cursed. "Put this in a different bag."

The socks completed, James moved upwards to the pair of short, tight shorts that Nikki had been wearing. Cutting this time was much harder—the shorts were elastic, and they had pulled themselves into Nikki's body as she shrunk and partially mummified. James had to press gently on the skin of the thighs in order to get the scissors in the right place, and that was accompanied by another sickening give of freeze-dried flesh. James had to swallow down his own vomit and keep cutting.

Once James made it to the waistband, the elastic material snapped away from the skin, sending a few frozen flecks of material and tissue flying around. Mike reached for the vacuum without asking as James repeated the process on the opposite leg.

With the corpse now undressed from the waist down, James turned his attention to the cadaver's torso. He was especially interested in the tear on the front of the shirt, as well as the small pool of slowly thawing blood that was on Nikki's stomach.

"Make sure you get an image of that," James said as he cut the shirt off. "We'll clean it up in a bit to see where the blood came from."

The shirt was the easiest to get off, even with Nikki's outstretched right arm. He passed the tatters to Mike, then began cutting off the also-elastic sports bra. The bra had also dug into the skin of Nikki's chest, so getting it off took more caution. Fortunately, James was able to do it without Mike having to use the vacuum again.

James put the surgical scissors back on the Velcro then looked back at Nikki's body. Now completely undressed, the remains of his friend looked even more sad and pitiful. The skin was all discolored, and deep wrinkles crisscrossed the entire body. James knew that the deformations were caused by the combination of liquids freezing and expanding, then slowly sublimating off into space over time.

"Damn," whispered Jordyn as she moved the camera around to capture the full view.

"It's time to get the limbs down," James said, his voice sounding hollow to his own ears. "We'll need to strap everything down so that we can start the incisions."

"Leg first?" Mike asked, to which James nodded his approval. He reached out again, placing his hands just above the knee, and slowly started to push along with Mike. There were more crunching noises, along with what sounded like paper being rustled together. Together the two men forced the leg about halfway down before running into more resistance.

"Should we wait?" Mike asked, looking to James.

"Thawing will damage the tissues anyways," answered James. "Let's get it down."

James increased his pressure. The leg finally gave, along with an even nastier grinding vibration that passed through the corpse's leg and into James arm. Finally, the leg was flat against the table. Mike quickly strapped both legs tightly into position.

"Hang on a sec," Jordyn said, leaving her camera floating in space. She turned around and started rustling around another storage compartment, finding a clear zip-baggy just in time to vomit. James had to look away quickly to avoid the same fate.

Jordyn was quick, and a few seconds later, after disposing of the bag, she was back in position. "Sorry," she said weakly, wiping her mouth with her forearm.

"No worries," James said gently. "Mike, now the arms."

The process was repeated, along with the same sickening noises and sensations. Both arms brought down to the sides, James quickly strapped the rest of the body in place. Nikki was still twisted slightly through her torso, but this would have to be good enough.

"Alright, let's follow the checklist," James said. "Mike, let's get a measurement of her height, then measure around her chest—right across the nipples. Jordyn, can you leave the camera floating for a second and get me three tissue sample containers?"

With Jordyn alternating between filming and getting containers, the two men followed the external examination checklist down to the most minute of details. Nikki's height was recorded, as well as her width in various places. She had definitely shrunk from her time in space, by at least a couple inches in some areas. James then took several tissue samples—a lock of hair, a carefully cut sliver of skin from her arm, and swabs from each of Nikki's fingertips, methodically labeling and stowing each one individually. James then did the same with the undersides of her fingernails—if there had been a struggle there might be all kinds of evidence there. He wondered what tests Houston and the FBI would have him run later. Everything was going smoothly until his last fingernail swab.

"What is it?" Mike asked, noticing James' hesitation.

"The fingernail is loose," James replied, using the swab to wiggle the nail. "It could just be from space. But it could also be..."

"From a struggle," Jordyn finished.

James nodded. "Did you get that on video?" he asked. Jordyn responded to the affirmative.

The last thing for James to do externally was to inspect the spot of thawed blood that still clung to Nikki's stomach. The shirt over the area had been torn, and James felt inside that it was more evidence of foul play. He took a quick blood sample, then asked for a towel from Mike.

James spotted the blood off of Nikki's deformed stomach, then used a fresh towel and some water to clean off the area. Sure enough, there was a small cut, maybe an inch long. It wasn't particularly deep, but it was definitely enough to cause bleeding.

"More foul play?" Mike asked.

"Could be," James answered, using another swab to take a sample from the edges of the cut. "Though it could be from being thrown out of the airlock into..."

"Space?" Jordyn asked, finishing the sentence. James nodded. He hadn't forgotten the word—James was wondering why he hadn't thought to further investigated the airlock itself. There could be blood in there somewhere, or signs of a struggle. He'd have to tell Gonzalez and Houston about the idea once he was done here.

James and Mike both gave Nikki's body one last exterior inspection, trying to see anything that would have been out of place. In particular, James kept an eye out for signs of bruising or other injuries. He found nothing. The body was so deformed that it was impossible to tell anything.

"I think that's it externally," Mike said, using his elbow to navigate the screen down to the next set of instructions. "I think we're ready, James. We starting right away?"

"Yeah," replied James. "The more frozen the better. We can't let the body get in too bad of shape."

Mike didn't reply, and James reached for the scalpel again. He wiped it off with a clean towel that he had stuffed into his own waistband, then paused to look at Nikki yet again. This was the part he dreaded most. Nikki's naked corpse was deformed and inhuman looking, but James still saw it for what it was. It—she—was his friend. And even worse, the fact that the body was female called memories of Claire to James' mind. He shook his head gently to clear his mind, then got ready to make the cut.

Nikki's body was starting to thaw more now, and her body had started to straighten out. Towels placed under the cadaver's back made her back arch forward so that James could most easily access the internal organs.

James swallowed hard and started the first incision near the left shoulder, running the scalpel beneath the body's left breast, then arcing the cut towards the base of the rib cage. He was careful to make the cut deep enough to penetrate the skin and fat, but not deep enough to damage the internal organs. Other than a brief second when the knife caught on a rib, the cut went smoothly. James repeated the process on the other side, then started a cut from where the two side cuts met, slicing down towards the cadaver's pubic area, forming a large "Y" across the body.

The cuts complete, James and Mike both pulled the skin and tissue away slightly, revealing the ribs and internal organs of the body. It was exceedingly gruesome, and James knew that his feelings were making things even more difficult. He had to bury his feelings deep inside himself. He was a professional right now—he needed to be a professional.

It had been a while since James participated in a live surgery, and even longer since he had examined a full cadaver in medical school. Even then, it was instantly clear that something was off. The organs were discolored and contorted, and they didn't seem to be in their proper places. There was also far less fluid than there should have been. James knew that all this was the effect of zero gravity and the freezing, drying vacuum of space, but that didn't make it any easier.

"So what now?" Mike asked, his voice squeaking noticeably.

"In situ examination," James replied, squinting at the computer screen. "We need to take samples from every major organ, but we're not pulling anything out. I'm sure they'll do that on Earth anyways."

"We'd better be quick," Mike nodded. "Everything is just going to get...softer."

"Let's open the chest," responded James. "Go ahead and clear out the fluid you can get, but be careful not to snag any organs."

While Mike pulled the small vacuum hose over to start cleaning the inside of the body, James reached for a pair of bone cutters. The cutters looked like a small set of pruning shears, and the only reason they were on board was in case an emergency surgery of some sort was needed.

James began snipping the ribs, each one breaking brittlely with just a little pressure from James. He cut each rib on the side, leaving the entire rib cage floating loosely atop the organs. James took a quick glance towards Jordyn— she was still filming but her free hand was covering her eyes.

James wished that he could cover his eyes too, but he couldn't. He and Mike proceeded slowly and methodically as they began collecting the different tissue samples. It was a disgusting process, one that instantly made him wish that he hadn't eaten this morning after all. Each organ was still half-frozen, and James was forced to touch each of them as he used his scalpel to collect the samples that the FBI wanted analyzed on board *Perseus*. First came the heart, then the lungs. Jordyn, who still struggled just to look at what was taking place, was forced to get closer to film each organ as James took the sample, then stored each in their own separate container.

In spite of his best efforts, James wasn't handling things well. He was sweating profusely, and he felt clammy and sticky. He desperately wanted to throw up, but he couldn't touch anything with his blood-stained gloves. Besides, time was running out. He had to get the samples, then get Nikki's remains back in a bag so that they could be put outside again before they thawed completely.

Next was the corpse's stomach and intestines. While James thought any foul play was likely physical, the FBI clearly wanted to check for poisons and other foreign substances. That meant sucking out half-frozen sludge with a wide-needle syringe, then using the first aid kit's staple gun to immediately seal the incisions. The fluids—which smelled metallic as they thawed—were again stored in separate storage containers. James knew that he and Mike would likely be testing everything again—he just hoped it would be easier without the body in the room.

The whole process took hours, with the body becoming harder and harder to work with as it thawed. The initial, sterile smell of metal and irradiated blood was starting to turn foul. Fortunately for James, each passing minute made the process physically easier, even if his soul ached. He even started talking under his breath, saying things like "sorry, Nikki," and "we'll find who did this."

This continued as he moved to the liver and kidneys, carefully slicing a sample off each organ. It pained James to desecrate Nikki's body so, but if it helped find out who the killer was it would be worth it. The question of how whoever had done this had killed Nikki had always been in the back of James' mind, but the more he worked on Nikki's body, the more the thought moved to the forefront of his consciousness. Nikki would want the others to know what had happened. Nikki would want the others to be safe from whoever did this. James fixated on the thought—it was the only thing helping him through this at the moment. His nausea dissipated, replaced by a dark resolve.

James was so focused, in fact, that he was almost shocked to hear a voice belonging to someone other than Mike or Jordyn. It was Aaron, calling out from the kitchen. "Guys," he said, doing his best not to look in the direction of the operation. "FBI says you're doing fine, but they've updated your instruction page. Something about testing bile and stuff."

James stopped what he was doing, leaving a piece of fresh absorbent gauze floating above the body. "Jordyn," he said softly, pausing to look at his bloody gloves. "Can you refresh the instruction set, please?"

"Damn, more stuff to do," Mike groaned. "I just want this nightmare to be over."

James squinted again at the now-refreshed screen. There were only two new items on the list, and both were up next. Houston and the FBI wanted a bile sample from the gallbladder, and a urine sample from the bladder. Then they would be done, with James just needing to stitch the body back together so it could be placed in a new body bag and moved back outside.

"Almost done," he mumbled under his breath, half addressing Nikki, half addressing Mike and Jordyn. He stuffed the floating piece of gauze up against the cut he had just made in the left kidney, then reached for the syringe that Mike was handing him.

James had to move around some of the gauze that he had packed around the liver to reach the gallbladder, but it was easy enough to get the needed sample. He put the newly extracted contents of the syringe in another storage container, then stuffed the gauze back into place. That just left the bladder, then they'd be almost done. James knew, however, that the memories of all this would probably never be done. They'd never go away.

Mike handed James another sterile syringe, and James got busy looking for the bladder. It would be tucked towards the bottom of the torso's cavity, below the intestines that James had already sampled. It should have been easy for James to find—but it wasn't.

"The intestines and lower organs have shifted from weightlessness," he said out loud for the recording. "There also appears to be some deforming of the uterus, the lower intestines, etcetera. There it is," James finished as he found what he was looking for.

James wanted this to be over. He quickly took his sample from the bladder, passing the syringe off to Mike for storage. All things considered, the autopsy had gone well, with minimal mess. They had accomplished everything that they had been tasked with, even if they hadn't found any blatant signs of trauma other than a loose fingernail and a small scratch.

"I'll need you to get the suture stuff ready, Mike," James said, grateful that the worst part was over. "Jordyn, you still doing ok?"

"I'm fine," Jordyn said, her voice sharp.

"Alright," James continued. "Mike, a swaged suture is fine, but make it the largest..."

James trailed off suddenly. His eyes had been looking at the edges of his cuts as he analyzed how to best close Nikki's body, but he had seen something. Something strange.

"I can do that," Mike said. "Doc, should I be...hey, you alright?"

"They really are pretty deformed," James said absentmindedly.

"What, the uterus?" Mike said. "Yeah, you got that. Jordyn's got it on video."

"I do," Jordyn confirmed.

James didn't reply. He *was* talking about the uterus, but it didn't just look misshapen. Something was wrong with it.

James reached for the scalpel, accidentally getting some brownish blood on the patch of Velcro in his rush. He briefly looked over the organ, then gently forced the scalpel down into the tissue. He cut only a two inch incision, being careful to make it as small and precise as possible.

"That's not on the checklist," Mike said. "Can we please just be done?"

James tried to open the cut he had made with his fingers, but it was too small. Using the scalpel, he increased the incision by another inch. Doing his best to keep his head out of the way of the surgical light, James opened the hole.

"Shit," he cursed.

"What is it?" Mike asked, clearly taken aback by James' sudden language.

James opened the hole wider while Mike looked in. There was fluid, but there was also something else. Solid tissue, clumped together. It was tiny.

"No," Mike gasped.

James let go of the organ. He was suddenly dizzy, and the hull of *Perseus* was spinning around him. Mike reached into the body and opened the hole James had cut.

"No, no, no," Mike said. "No, no, no, no, no."

James quickly regained a hold of himself and brushed Mike's hands away. He grabbed his scalpel and made the incision bigger, opening up the walls of the uterus entirely.

It was small, barely an inch in length, but it was obvious what it was.

"It's an embryo," gasped Jordyn, looking in with her camera.

"No," James replied. "Not just an embryo—a fetus. Nikki was pregnant."

CHAPTER THIRTY-FIVE

"Wha-what does this mean?" stuttered Mike.

James looked over his shoulder, back towards the kitchen. Aaron, the only one still in the galley, was looking their way, obviously curious about what the commotion was all about, but still unaware. That meant that Gonzalez and Harrison were managing the video feed from the command module. If they were paying any attention they'd be out any second now.

"Doctor?" repeated Mike.

Thoughts were racing through James' mind faster than he could communicate them. This changed everything, and it changed it for the worse.

"Mike, I need more gauze from the auxiliary lab," ordered James. "We need to leave the body open for the camera."

"What, me?" Mike asked, raising his blood-stained gloves. "James, are you-"

"Take the damn gloves off if you need to," ordered James. "Go get it. Jordyn, get that camera closer."

Mike opened his mouth to argue, but took one look down at the body and closed it. He took his gloves off, stuffed them into a garbage container, and took off.

Jordyn moved closer to get another camera view. "Is something going on?" Aaron asked from the kitchen.

"I don't know," James replied quickly before turning his attention back to Jordyn. "Turn it off," James whispered harshly, intentionally mumbling to try to disguise his words.

"What?" Jordyn asked, taken aback. One look at James' expression, however, was enough to make her understand. She quickly turned off the camera. The one in the ceiling was still running, but that one didn't record sound.

James had to act quickly. "This is motive," he hissed, gesturing towards the body with his head. "Jordyn, this is motive. It means you didn't do this."

"No shit," Jordyn retorted. "I'm surprised it took dissecting a frozen space body to figure that out."

"I should have trusted you earlier," James admitted quickly. "But look, it doesn't take a detective to figure out that whoever knocked her up killed her too."

"Harrison?"

"I don't know," James grimaced. "I thought I cleared him, but..."

"So it's between Gonzo and Aaron?" Jordyn asked incredulously. "Neither of them cou-"

"Don't leave out Mike," James said quickly. "All we know is that it's a male."

"What, the baby?"

"No," snapped James. "The killer. I'm not going to disqualify Mike just because he swings-"

"But James," Jordyn interrupted, her face lighting up. "James, the baby. The baby will have evidence. It will have DNA! We have a-"

"We have a sequencer on board," James said, instantly understanding where Jordyn was going with this. "With a sample of everyone's blood we can match it to the killer—sort of. I can sequence it and send it back to Earth, but

296

they'll have to match it down there. I mean, that's what Houston will have us do for sure. But..."

James trailed off suddenly. This meant...

"But what?" hissed Jordyn.

"It means the game is up," James said. "Whoever did this is going to do everything in their power to stop this from happening. We need to act quickly—we need..."

James was out of time. Mike was emerging from the auxiliary lab, his arms full of fresh gauze pads. James took a quick glance at the nearby box of syringes, wishing that he had thought to immediately get a blood sample from the fetus, but it was too late.

"Hey!" a voice shouted from the kitchen. It was Gonzalez, with Harrison right behind him. "What the hell happened to the handheld video feed?"

"That's my bad," Jordyn lied quickly. "I hit the button by accident. It's running now."

"It doesn't matter," James said. "Did you hear the last audio?" he asked. "Gonzo, you need to come look at this."

"She was pregnant," Mike blurted out, a gauze pad escaping from his grip and floating slowly away from him. "Commander, Nikki was pregnant."

Gonzalez froze even as he floated towards the body. He looked shocked for a split second, but his brow quickly furrowed in anger. "What?" he asked, the word blurting out of his mouth.

James waited for the crew to gather around the open body before he began his explanation. There was no use keeping the pregnancy a secret—the video was already on its way to Houston, and everyone was going to know anyway. The best defense was to keep everyone on board *Perseus* together, and keep them on camera for as long as possible. If the five innocent members of the crew—whoever they were—could stick together, perhaps the

297

killer would just confess rather than do something rash and dangerous. James could hope for that anyway.

The grueling autopsy had desensitized James, Jordyn, and Mike to some extent, but for the others it was their first time seeing the bloody, opened, dissected corpse up close. Harrison, Gonzalez, and Aaron all paled to some extent, but it was Harrison who handled it the worst. He barely got a glimpse of the remains before he had to cover his eyes and conspicuously swallow something down.

"Nikki was pregnant," James repeated clearly after checking that Jordyn was recording for Houston. He reached back into the body to open up the incision he had made to show the others, though only Gonzalez seemed to be able to look steadily at the bloody tissues. "See, right here," James continued. "There's the head and the body—both still in early development. She was pregnant when she was murdered."

"*If* she was murdered," Mike added. "I mean, this could add to the theory Houston had about a mental break-"

"I think it's pretty damn obvious what happened to Nikki," Gonzalez interrupted forcefully, instantly silencing Mike. "And Mike, I'd be careful disputing that fact if I were you."

Mike nodded sheepishly, but James could tell that Gonzalez wasn't satisfied. His word of caution sounded more like a thinly veiled accusation.

Aaron noticed it too. "Commander," he said, his voice steady. "I think we should let Doctor Lake finish before we jump to conclusions. And James, I think we need the facts, not speculation."

Gonzalez grunted his tenuous agreement. "Go on," he said to James flatly.

James swallowed hard, releasing his fingers from the incision. "Alright," he began again. "She was pregnant. About two months pregnant, actually."

"But it was so small," Jordyn said in surprise. "I mean, it's barely an inch."

"James is right," Mike replied. "You can tell the difference between the head and body. It's not just a clump of cells—not just an embryo. It's a fetus."

"And people don't just get pregnant," James followed-up. "She had to have had intercourse with a male partner on the ship—that's a fact."

"Her IUD had to have failed or something," Jordyn said. "I mean, it can happen, right?"

"It happens," agreed James. "My oldest came while Claire was still on the pill."

"But why didn't she say something?" Mike asked. "I mean, Nikki would have had to have known, right? Why didn't she talk to anyone?"

A thought hit James' mind like a freight train. Nikki *had* known. That much was clear from the draft email the FBI had recovered. That must be why Nikki had come to talk to him her last night alive. That's why she was so distracted on the spacewalk. That's why she was so moody. She had known, and probably not for long.

"I mean, a pregnancy in space is dangerous to the mother, and maybe even fatal to the child," Mike said, continuing his thought. "If the radiation and weightlessness didn't deform or kill it in the womb, birth and a return to full gravity surely would. She'd have to abort somehow. She'd have known that."

"Maybe she felt a connection to the child," Aaron said. "Maybe she felt like it was her duty to give it a shot."

It was a nice sentiment, but James could tell that even Aaron didn't believe it. Perhaps it was fear that kept Nikki from saying something earlier. Maybe she was afraid of what would happen if her lover—whoever it was—found out. His career would be over, ended in disgrace. He would have been angry. But angry enough to kill?

James pondered the idea for a moment as the others bickered and argued over Nikki's body. Perhaps the murder was a crime of passion, committed in the heat of the moment as Nikki revealed her pregnancy. Then again, if Nikki *was* mentally unstable, if Nikki *was* struggling with something like depression, or high stress—perhaps something like this would be enough to drive her over the edge. No, James had seen too much in the past months. This wasn't suicide.

"Alright, I'm just going to say it," Harrison said suddenly. "Look, there's no denying she was murdered. She was killed over this, guys."

"Says the guy who was trying to get her to cheat on her fiancé," Mike snipped.

"I kissed her once!" Harrison cried out defensively. "And that makes me a killer? Give me a damn break here!"

"You never said you kissed her," Jordyn pointed out.

"True," Gonzalez said, an eyebrow raised.

"Oh come on!" Harrison shouted. "I'm about to prove my innocence on this anyways, just ask James! Besides, who the hell do you think you are, Marx? Who's to say you didn't kill her out of jealousy?!?"

"Jealousy?!?" exclaimed Jordyn. "Is this guy for real?"

"I'm just saying that we don't know who it is!" retorted Harrison. "So why don't you all quit blaming me and look at the facts!"

"WHAT FACTS?!?" exclaimed Gonzalez suddenly. "We don't have any damn facts!"

"He has a point though," James said quickly. "It could be any one of us. There's no real evidence, no real proof, just motive and circumstance. It could be Gonzo, it could be Aaron, Mike, or even me for crying out loud! We need to take a step back here—we're millions of miles-"

"And we're nine months from home while being stuck in a tube with a killer," snapped Gonzalez. "A killer who's tried to kill me, tried to kill James, and could try to kill-"

"Why are we all assuming that Nikki's been murdered?" Mike asked again, fighting against the current. "Why are we just ignoring the original theory-"

"You keep saying that and it's making you sound pretty damn suspicious," Jordyn said, pointing a gloved finger accusatorially towards Mike.

"More suspicious than Harrison?" exclaimed a totally incredulous Mike. "How the hell-"

"STOP ACCUSING ME DAMMIT!!!" roared Harrison. "Who's to say it wasn't Gonzalez, huh? He's the one with a shitty marriage!"

Things were quickly getting out of hand. "Guys," pleaded James. "Guys, please."

"Excuse me?!?" shouted Gonzalez as he postured up to Harrison. "Who are you to say-"

"What about Aaron?" Harrison continued. "Huh? Some backwards Mormon who's been sexually repressed-"

"GUYS!" shouted James, desperate to get things back in order. "Hey, listen!"

"And what about James?" cried Harrison. "Huh? Are you all forgetting what Aaron said?

"Somebody tried to kill James, too," Jordyn snapped, coming to James' defense.

"Oh I see how it is," spat Harrison sarcastically. "We all know whose side *you're* on, Jordyn—wonder what goes on when James gives *you* a physical, don't you-"

Gonzalez was the one to throw the first punch. He tried to hit Harrison square in the mouth, but his blow glanced off his right cheek. Harrison responded immediately by coiling back for a punch of his own, drawing his arm back so quickly that he hit Aaron in the mouth with his elbow. Aaron spun backwards, colliding with the side of the module.

James ripped off his bloody gloves and moved to intervene, but Jordyn was already there. She left the camera floating in midair and fought her way between the brawling Gonzalez and Harrison, taking a blow to the chest in the process. She then shot Aaron a glare that convinced him not to jump into the fray.

"GUYS!!!" James shouted again. "Hey!"

"Whoever the hell did this I'm going to kill you," Gonzalez snarled, his eyes blatantly locked onto Harrison. "I swear, I'm going to make you pay for this."

"LISTEN TO ME!!!" James yelled. "We're in a damn tin can in the middle of space! We need to get it together or we're all going to die out here!"

The crew got quiet. Harrison spat a bloody mouthful of saliva in Gonzalez' direction, but Jordyn intercepted the weightless blob with her hand and coolly wiped it off on her own shirt. Gonzalez growled.

"Just cool down for a second!" James yelled again, making sure he had everyone's attention. He was surprised to find himself so calm and collected, given the circumstances. "Look," he said. "We keep this up and we're all going to die. Every one of us. We're going to boil and freeze in raw space, and it won't matter who the hell did this! So let's take a second and breathe."

James paused for a moment to emphasize his point, then continued. "Look, I can get DNA from the fetus," he continued. "I can run it through the lab and sequence it, then do the same with a blood sample from each of you. We can't match DNA up here, but Houston should be able to back home once we send them the sequencing results. It'll tell us who the father is—if the radiation hasn't ruined all the DNA from the fetus already."

"What about a sample from you?" Aaron mumbled.

"We'll get a sample from me too," James affirmed. "NASA is gonna' want it anyways. We can see who the father is, and we'll go from there."

"You mean who the *murderer* is?" Gonzalez asked gravely.

"We'll go from there," James said forcefully. "That is, unless someone wants to just come forward and admit it now. That way we all get out of this alive. We make it home, it gets dealt with on terra firma."

James paused again to glance at each of his crewmates. Mike appeared fearful, his eyes shifting as he looked at everyone in the module. Jordyn gazed back at James from her position between Harrison and Gonzalez' sneers, and Aaron, his blonde hair matted, looked towards his feet. Nobody said a word.

"Be the bigger man," Jordyn added. "Just confess."

More silence.

James' heart dropped with disappointment. He didn't expect anything from his challenge, but he had hoped anyway. Things were going to have to be done the hard way. One of these people was the killer.

Gonzalez coughed to clear his throat. "We stay in the groups of two at minimum," he said, his voice rough. "Even in the damn bathroom. We'll wait for feedback from Houston. But when we do bloodwork, I want everyone in the same room at the same time, and I want it recorded."

"Agreed," Harrison sneered. "You'll all see."

"And the body?" Mike asked, gesturing towards where the disfigured remains of Nikki were strapped to the table.

"James will get the sample while we all watch, and then we'll bag the body back up," Gonzalez replied. "But it's going to have to stay in here. Nobody is going outside until we figure out what the hell is going on."

CHAPTER THIRTY-SIX

Nobody wanted to be left alone—not when no one could be trusted.

The entire crew stayed in *Perseus'* center modules, where everyone was within sight. Nobody said much to each other, adding an awkward, hollow feel to the claustrophobia that the ship already carried.

With Gonzalez and Jordyn watching, James carefully extracted a sample from the unborn fetus, putting the discolored blood into a vial that he placed in a storage bin right beneath the now constantly running camera. He then did a quick search for an IUD, finding the small device relatively quickly. Given the state of the body, there was no way to tell if it had been misplaced or broken, but it was obvious that it had failed.

Everything completed, and with a nod from Gonzalez, James got busy closing up the body. There was no need for precision now, but James still moved methodically and carefully as he stitched up the body. His heart was heavy with sorrow for Nikki—for everything that had happened. But he wasn't out of the woods yet.

"Sir," Aaron called out. "Monitor says we have another incoming message from Houston."

Gonzalez nodded, his lips pursed. "Aaron, Mike, come with me to the command module. Harrison, stay here with Marx and the Doctor."

With that, Gonzalez left James' side and pulled himself towards the front of the ship, where he met up with Mike and Aaron. He and Harrison passed by each other, not saying a word, not making eye contact.

The autopsy was complete for now. With Harrison watching, Jordyn and James slowly put another makeshift body bag around Nikki, unstrapping and re-strapping the body to the table as they went. The body bag was just black plastic that had been duct taped together, but it would be enough to keep any fluids or smells from escaping while the body stayed inside. It wouldn't, however, stop the body from thawing out entirely. James shivered. *Perseus* was still freezing cold inside, and it would probably have to stay that way for a little while longer.

"I'm sorry," Harrison said once the job was done.

"I think we all are," James answered as he took off his gloves and disposed of them. There were flecks of blood dried on his arms, and he wanted nothing more than to take a shower.

"I mean about earlier," Harrison continued quietly. "I lost my temper, and I was out of line."

Jordyn scoffed audibly.

"Especially after what I said about you two," Harrison said slowly, picking his words carefully. "I mean..."

James had heard enough. "You're damn right you were out of line," he muttered. "I even proved your innocence with Aaron—although I'm not so sure about it anymore."

Harrison's face lit up. "Are you saying you believe me? That I didn't do it?"

"I *did* see you coming out of your sleeping compartment," James said. "And I timed myself and crunched the numbers. You *probably* weren't there when Nikki was thrown out of the airlock. Sorry I didn't tell you earlier. Maybe I would have if you weren't being such an ass."

"Oh great, another thing you didn't bother telling *me* earlier," Jordyn said sarcastically as she shook her head angrily. "Harrison's off the hook?"

"We've had a pretty busy day," James replied flatly. "And no, I don't think Harrison is off the hook yet. But he's closer than some."

Harrison grimaced. "I've told the truth," he replied simply, shrugging his broad shoulders. "You'll see. Anyways, I am sorry for what I said. Jordyn, this does seem to make you innocent. And James, I never really thought it was you. So who do you guys think it is?"

Jordyn responded by rolling her eyes. "Don't get chummy with us yet," she said sourly.

James nodded. Jordyn had accurately summarized his feelings as well. "I need to go clean up," James said finally, gesturing with his head towards the restroom module. "Can I have at least five minutes?"

Jordyn and Harrison looked at each other. Ostensibly, both astronauts had expressed their trust in James, but their hesitation let James know that said trust was weak—and fluid. "We'll wait outside," Jordyn said finally.

"Outside the shower," corrected Harrison. "In the same module."

"Have it your way," James said, reaching for a handhold to pull himself towards the other module. Before pulling himself away, however, he looked to make sure the camera stuck to the roof above the operating table was still running. He didn't want anyone fiddling with the sample he'd just taken.

"What is it?" Harrison asked.

"Just wondering if I should have you two shower with me," James joked darkly. "The way this ship's turned into a damn frat house it probably would be right up everyone's alley."

Both of his two temporary companions grimaced as they followed James towards the restroom module. True to Harrison's word, both he and Jordyn followed him right into the module. Not really caring after everything that he had seen today, James stripped down naked, floated his clothes towards Harrison, and pulled himself into the ship's shower. He needed Nikki's blood off his hands.

The shower was nothing like a shower on Earth or Mars. It was a small cylinder, not even big enough for James to stretch his arms above his head, and there was no shower head or drain. Instead there were two flexible hoses—one for warm water, the other a gentle vacuum hose to suck the water from his body and the air. James quickly turned the water on and off—getting just wet enough to start cleaning—then squeezed some soap onto his hands and got washing.

It wasn't like a shower at home, but it was still a moment to think and ponder as he scrubbed Nikki's blood off his arms. The same question ran through his mind over and over again: who had done this? Who had killed Nikki? Jordyn was perhaps the only one on board that he could trust even a little now—but still not completely.

James wondered what Houston was telling Gonzalez. What would their orders be? Would they immediately want the crew to do bloodwork to determine who impregnated Nikki? Or perhaps they would want James and Mike to somehow run the samples they had taken from Nikki's fingernails to see if there was DNA from someone else on them. Either way, they were going to need Houston's help. They could sequence DNA as much as they wanted up here, but they didn't have the ability to search for matches on board. The data would have to go back to Houston—back to the FBI. It would be a torturous wait—one made worse by the fact that the killer obviously wasn't going to confess. Would they go quietly when they were discovered?

James finished washing and grabbed the vacuum hose. There were other problems to be concerned about, too. How would they keep a killer restrained in space for 9 months? There was no jail on board, no secure room, nowhere that could be locked. There were no zip ties or handcuffs, only duct tape and spare electrical cords. Whoever it was would have to be supervised almost constantly. Then there was a chance that whoever got Nikki pregnant didn't kill her too. What if the crew "arrested" the wrong person? What if the killer went free?

James sighed to himself as he turned off the vacuum hose and gave himself a final pat down with a reusable towel. He just wanted to make it home. He missed Claire and his children, more than ever before. He'd never take them for granted, and he'd never leave them behind for so much as a day. James decided that he'd go find his tablet and write Claire. It was time to tell her what was going on. If NASA censored it, they censored it. He didn't care anymore.

James finished and opened the shower door just a crack, reaching his arm out for someone to hand him his clothes.

They didn't come.

"Hey," James said, opening the door a little wider. "Harrison, can you hand me my…"

The module was empty.

CHAPTER THIRTY-SEVEN

Terror instantly filled James, terror that something very bad had happened.

"Hey!" James shouted.

Harrison appeared suddenly at the entrance to the module. "Sorry," he said, pushing James' clothes towards him even as he looked over his shoulder.

"What the hell happened?" James asked as he dressed quickly. "You scared the crap outta' me."

"Hurry up!" Jordyn hissed as she too arrived at the entrance. "James, there's some sort of commotion going on up front. Shouting and stuff."

James wrestled his shirt on, then pushed himself towards the entrance—pulling on his shorts as he floated. Sure enough, he could hear angry yelling from the front of the ship. It sounded like Aaron's voice.

James led the way, Jordyn and Harrison right behind him. He floated through the exercise room, the lab, and then the galley as he headed towards the forward node and the connected command module. The shouting was growing louder now, and it was coming from all three men now.

James was nearly to the node when Mike flew suddenly out of the command module, twisting wildly in space before slamming into a wall. Aaron was right behind him—he slammed into Mike, then, without pausing, grabbed him by the collar and slammed him into the wall again.

"Hey!" James shouted. He pushed off the wall to readjust his course, directing himself towards the two fighting men. He got there just in time to keep punches from flying.

"I SAID KNOCK IT OFF!!!" boomed Gonzalez as he too emerged from the command module and moved to assist James. "Hey, break it up!"

Jordyn and Harrison were there now, too. The four crewmates pried Aaron and Mike apart as they twisted and floated in midair.

"What the hell is going on?!?" exclaimed Jordyn.

"How the hell could you accuse me of that?" spat Aaron, letting a rare, PG curse word fly from his lips.

"I didn't accuse you of anything!" exclaimed Mike. "I wasn't accusing *anyone* of anything!"

"Mike made some backhanded comment about who knows what," Gonzalez explained quickly, clearly out of breath. "We had just gotten orders from Houston to go ahead with the sampling, and then these two just snapped."

"I didn't just snap!" Aaron exclaimed. "Did you honestly not hear what he said?!?"

"I don't give a damn what he said!" shouted Gonzalez. "Get a grip on yourself!"

Aaron relaxed and stopped fighting against James and Harrison. "Alright," he said finally, shrugging himself loose. "Alright, alright. I can't wait for this stupid thing to be over. It wasn't me."

"No one is accusing anyone of anything," Gonzalez said. The clear irony in his words would have been comical in any other setting, but not here. "Let's finish this," he added. "Let's get this the hell over with. James, can you start bloodwork now? I'm not waiting for Houston to get back to us on this."

James nodded as he looked at the angry faces of his crewmates. "Sure," he said. "Let's just go to the lab. Again."

"All together," Jordyn said. "Everyone in the same room."

"We might want to have people drink something first," James said. "I mean, it's a small sample, but it's-"

"I want it done," Gonzalez said with finality.

James just nodded again. After checking to make sure that Aaron wasn't going to start throwing punches again, he turned and pulled himself back towards the lab. He felt like he had been there forever, and he almost had. It was nearly 1900 hours now—the autopsy had started at 0900.

With Jordyn and Mike accompanying him, James zipped ahead into the auxiliary lab, grabbing 6 disposable syringes and 6 sample vials that could be run through the DNA sequencer. He'd done this several times before—checking DNA in space was a monthly experiment—but this time was clearly different. He couldn't mess this up.

One by one his crewmates came forward. One by one he pricked the inside of their arms with the syringes, and one by one he drew out enough blood to fill the tiny vials. He labeled each one for all to see, then put each vial next to the sample from the fetus.

"Why do you need mine?" protested Jordyn when it was her turn. "It's not like I got Nikki pregnant."

"I don't give a damn," replied Gonzalez. "Everyone does it."

James drew his own blood last—it was difficult for him to put a needle in his own skin, but he trusted no one else right now. He missed the vein the first time, but found it the second. He then pulled the plunger back, sucking just a little of the crimson blood out. His hands were trembling now, but he managed to put his blood into the vial, labeling it with his name.

With the whole crew crammed into the tiny space, James retrieved the sample vial from the fetus, then moved towards the sequencer on the opposite wall. He put the entire vial into the correct slot on the machine, then got busy setting up the sequencing. The sequencer was a modern marvel of compact engineering and automation. It would even extract the needed amount of blood from the vial on its own.

"How long will it take?" Aaron asked, breaking the silence.

"It'll take a few hours to sequence each sample," James answered.

"A few hours?!?" exclaimed Gonzalez angrily.

"Well, yeah," explained James. "The machine uses enzymes and compounds to separate everything. It takes longer, but that's how they made it so small, simple, and light. Besides, that's not including the time the FBI will need to analyze it and try matching. Again, this just sequences DNA. It won't perform profiling and matching for us—that'll be done on Earth. We'll need to be patient."

"So what do we do in the meantime?" asked Jordyn warily.

"Well, we can all sit around and wait, or we can sit around and eat," Harrison said. "I'm starving, and if I'm going to die I'd like to do it on a full stomach."

"No one's going to die," Gonzalez said forcefully.

"Let me just make sure it's working properly," James said, turning back to the machine's connected monitor. It looked like all systems were functioning nominally—it would just take time. James tapped on the screen to bring up the countdown timer, but the screen didn't seem to register his touch. He tapped it again.

"What's wrong now?" groaned Gonzalez.

James tapped the screen again. It flickered, then went black.

"Huh?" grunted James.

All the lights in *Perseus* flickered suddenly, going off entirely before turning back on. The sequencer screen came back on, this time giving an error warning.

"James?" asked Gonzalez.

"Don't ask me," James said quickly as he rebooted the machine. "I don't know what the hell that was."

"It was an electrical spike," Harrison said. "Was it from the sequencer?"

"I've done this dozens of times," James replied. "There's no way."

"Where is everyone?" demanded Gonzalez, swinging his head to check that everyone was present and accounted for. They were.

"We better report this to Houston," Gonzalez said finally. "Aaron, Jordyn, go send a message from the command module—now. While you're at it, run a systems check. See what the hell that was."

"Yes, sir," replied Jordyn. She nodded at Aaron, and the two left.

The machine rebooted slowly, but the screen came on, as did the fans. James gave it a full system check, expecting the lights to flicker again, but everything seemed to be working again. The sample wasn't corrupted either.

"We had like three spikes on our way to Mars, it's not unheard of," Harrison said tensely.

"What about the machine?" asked Mike. "Does it still work?"

"Yeah," James said, breathing a sigh of relief. "But we'd better have Harrison check the electrical on it after this sample."

"I can do that," Harrison nodded.

"As long as everyone is in the room," agreed Gonzalez. "So we can still run this one?"

"I mean, as long as it doesn't have a power short like that again, it will be fine," replied James. "The whole ship is built for little stuff like that. I'm just not sure we want to risk it."

"Just do it," Gonzalez said. "We can always get more blood samples. I just want all of this to be done with. The sooner we know who did this, the bet-"

"Sir!" a voice shouted from the other side of the ship. It was Aaron.

"What's up?" Gonzalez asked without looking away from James' work on the sequencer.

"Sir, I can't get a transmission through to Houston," replied Aaron.

"What do you mean you can't get a transmission through?" challenged Gonzalez. "Pause the incoming downloads and clear the signal."

"I did that," Aaron said quickly.

"Pause all outgoing, even the ship status updates and the video feed," ordered Gonzalez. "Check the frequency and reset the antennae if yo-"

"I already did all that," interrupted Aaron, clearly agitated. "Sir, I'm not getting anything from comms. Not even a linkage signal!"

"What do you mean?" Gonzalez asked, his voice suddenly very quiet.

Aaron looked at the four men floating around the sequencer, his mouth open and his eyes wide. "Guys," he said weakly, sounding oddly defeated. "Nothing's going out. Nothing's coming in."

James heart dropped. "What?" he asked.

"Nothing out, nothing in," repeated Aaron.

CHAPTER THIRTY-EIGHT

The entire crew huddled inside the cramped command module, encircling Aaron as he tapped away at the touchscreens by the commander's seat. He was growing increasingly agitated and frustrated—feelings that instantly transferred to the crew, even if they didn't all understand the black pages of code that Aaron was quickly navigating through.

"Get me the comms checklist again," Aaron snapped at Jordyn. "No, not the tablet, the paper one under my seat."

"Is it an external malfunction?" Harrison asked to nobody in particular. "Maybe we were hit by a micro meteor or something."

"Do you honestly think this was coincidence?" challenged Gonzalez. "Really?"

Harrison closed his mouth and didn't respond.

James felt helpless, much like he had for the past couple months. He lacked the detailed mechanical knowledge of Harrison, and the technical expertise of Aaron. Jordyn and Gonzalez were skilled pilots and commanders who knew the ship inside and out. He was just the doctor. Mike was probably experiencing similar feelings being the biologist.

James' stomach growled audibly. He hadn't eaten in several hours, and the low temperature inside *Perseus* served to augment his hunger. He didn't dare leave the others, however. Someone had done this—the same person who had killed Nikki had somehow ruined their connection with Houston.

"Next step, perform manual restart of comms system, being sure to keep the navigation computers online," Jordyn said, reading the manual out loud for Aaron.

"Is that really next?" asked Gonzalez. "We haven't reset the thing the entire flight."

"Just following the checkbook," Aaron replied.

"Let me see it," Gonzalez ordered, extending a hand towards Jordyn.

Jordyn handed it over without reservation, though James could tell by the look in her eyes that she was slightly miffed by Gonzalez' apparent lack of trust in her. James couldn't fault either of them for their feelings.

James didn't know what else to do other than worry. Aaron continued his run through the checklist as the others observed his every move. James, however, couldn't focus on the unintelligible gibberish that Aaron would pull up on the screen. He was too worried about the things that were flying farther and farther out of his control. There was no way he could fix a comms link by himself, and no way he could get home without the help of the crew. Gone was his lifeline to home, gone was his ability to communicate with Claire. Even if Houston and the FBI somehow figured out who had done this, James would never know it.

And that was only part of their problems. A comms link to Houston was essential to the success of the mission in more ways than one. Fortunately, *Perseus* was already on course towards Earth, but any necessary course correction, any minor RCS burn, any navigational change would be nearly impossible without data from Earth. Being off course by even a fraction of a degree could end up being millions of miles off course in the scheme of interplanetary navigation—the difference between slamming into Earth's atmosphere or being doomed to forever orbit the sun. They needed to fix this somehow if any of them wanted to make it back to Earth.

"Did you clear the cache like step six said?" inquired an increasingly impatient Gonzalez.

"I already did that, too," replied Aaron. "Just shut up and let me work on this."

"If that *is* what you're doing," mumbled Gonzalez.

Aaron stopped tapping on the screen and turned his head to face Gonzalez. "What's that supposed to mean?" he asked pointedly. "I'm not the only one on the ship who can code—would you be more comfortable having Harrison do this?"

"Is what you're doing being recorded?" Gonzalez asked flatly.

Aaron's face turned a deep shade of red. He opened his mouth to argue, but Jordyn intervened.

"I'm backing all changes up on the secondary log," she said. "Just let him work, Gonzo."

"He's just being careful," defended Mike. "Just like we all need to be."

James didn't bother getting involved in the latest disagreement. The shadows of worry were starting to overpower him, and it was hard for him to fight it. He might not see his children again—he might not see Claire. How long would it take her to figure out that something was truly wrong? Would NASA tell her, or would she be left wondering what was going on? By the time she figured it out, James could be a frozen cadaver floating through empty space, just like Nikki. He and the rest of the crew could be the result of some suicidal death wish from Nikki's killer.

His heart was starting to race, and his breathing was getting shallow, but James knew deep down that this wasn't over yet. He had to get a grip on himself—he had to focus on what he *could* control. He could watch the others—he could keep an eye on everyone. He could fight off an assailant, or outsmart the next subtle attempt on someone's life. If he was vigilant, if he kept his wits about him, James knew he could get through the next nine months of hell. Who cared who caused this, as long as he made it home safely?

James grimaced to himself. *He* cared. This was about more than him—more than mere survival. There was something bigger going on here. Justice had to be fought for, and he had to be willing to take up the cause. There was still a way he could get home safely, *and* get justice for Nikki. He just—well, he just had to figure out who the killer was. It had been his plan all along, hadn't it?

"Dammit!" swore Gonzalez, punching the empty seat behind him. "Come on!"

"It's not an external hardware issue," repeated Aaron. "Gonzo, we had no collision alarms or anything like that. Whatever happened took place between the antennae and where we're floating. It could be an internal wiring problem, a power problem, a-"

"I don't care what it is!" exclaimed Gonzalez. "We've got to get this fixed!"

"I could start inspecting the internal wiring," said Harrison. "We could spacewalk out to the solar panels-"

"No," interrupted Gonzalez bluntly. "Absolutely not."

"Then let's start with the software," Aaron said. "Let me work."

"We do just need to start somewhere," Jordyn agreed, tugging on the black hair in her ponytail.

The argument continued, but Jordyn's words had spoken to James on a deeper level. He had to start somewhere, too. Maybe at the beginning? But where was the beginning of all this? Was it in Nikki's sleeping compartment? The airlock in which she was killed? When had she started up her pseudo-relationship with Harrison? Was he the father? Did the body inside the black bag strapped to the table in the lab hold more clues that James had flat-out missed?

James suddenly remembered the vials of blood still in the lab, under the watchful eye of the camera taped to the roof. The DNA sequencer was running as the crew quarreled and squabbled, lining up molecules and acids as it created a genetic fingerprint of Nikki's unborn child. That blood and tissue bore the key to all of this—if only James could figure it out. But he had none of the needed technology without a stable connection with Earth.

The argument in the command module had cooled down once again, but James' mind was still racing. He was probably stuck waiting until a comms link had been reestablished, but there was work he could do in the meantime. He could make sure all the blood samples were sequenced and recorded. He could make sure that the second he could get a message through, it would contain the evidence identifying the killer. He could even go a step further. He could get DNA off the fingernail scrapings he had collected, he could keep searching for clues...

James felt the sudden urge to go check on the sequencer. He needed to make sure that it kept running, and that the samples of blood were safe and secure. He'd have to keep watch over it—he'd have to keep watch over the bag containing Nikki's body.

"Commander," James said, his voice sounding unnaturally clear. "Gonzo, I'm going to go check on the sequencer."

"Just stay here for a minute," Gonzalez replied impatiently. "I don't want anyone getting separated. No one can be alone."

"I don't need to be alone," replied James. "Send someone with me if you want."

"I'll go," Jordyn said quickly.

"No," responded Gonzalez. "Mike, why don't you go with him?"

"Sure," he answered. "But just me? Shouldn't we be in groups of three?"

Gonzalez pursed his lips, pausing to look at Aaron and Harrison as they paused their work on the computer screen. "I don't want any funny business in here," he said finally. "Just yell if something happens."

"What?" Mike asked. He sounded genuinely worried.

"I'm going," James said. Being paired off was the least of his worries right now. If Mike was the killer, James would rather have him be close anyway.

Gonzalez shrugged dismissively. Mike looked for assistance from the remaining astronauts, finding none. Reluctantly, he turned to follow James out of the hatch.

James led the way. He was careful to keep Mike always within sight as he moved through the forward node, then into the kitchen. "Maybe we ought to grab everyone some food on the way back," he said, to which Mike just nodded.

James knew that Mike didn't trust him, and that was fine. He didn't trust Mike either. The two men passed the kitchen equipment and floated back into the lab and exercise module. A spare, clean gauze pad floated aimlessly a few feet above the bagged remains of Nikki. James grabbed it and put it in his pocket.

"What are you doing with that?" Mike asked skeptically.

"We're going to put it away once I'm done here," answered James as he pulled himself up to the sequencer.

The sequencer was running normally. The timer indicated that there were still a few hours remaining before James could remove the sample and start a new one. The results would be saved to the computer—maybe he could find a way to make a copy too.

"Are you almost done?" asked Mike nervously as he ran a hand through his red hair.

"Mike, do you really not trust me that much?" James asked, his words laced with the mild annoyance he was feeling. "If I was going to kill you, don't you think I would have done something already?"

"Shut up," Mike snapped. "That's not funny."

James rolled his eyes as he left the sequencer and pulled himself towards the entrance to the auxiliary lab. The two men tried to enter at the same time, bumping into each other awkwardly.

"After you," James said, gesturing into the module.

"That's ok," Mike replied warily.

James pulled himself into the module and floated straight to the medical compartment. He stowed away the still-packaged gauze in its proper place and closed the compartment as Mike watched. He was about to pull himself back towards the hatch when something caught his eye.

"What is it?" asked Mike.

James didn't answer. He pulled himself to the large window at the end of the module and looked outside. Mars was already considerably smaller than it was when they had made the exit burn just a few days ago, and it was framed by millions of shining stars. James felt a small burst of pride for what mankind had accomplished—even if it was somewhat tainted. In a way, that was ok with James. Everything great accomplished by mankind had been accompanied by something that history wished it could forget. Maybe that's what this mission would be like, too.

"We need to go," Mike said. "Come on, James."

James turned around, fighting the urge to tell Mike to stop treating him like a killer—even if he couldn't blame him. He reached for a handhold to pull himself out, but his hand missed and clumsily hit the smooth glass that housed the auxiliary lab's growing station. Inside were rows of tiny plants, including space-grown lettuce and some non-edibles. James had a sudden thought.

"What's wrong with my plants?" Mike said, genuinely concerned as he pulled himself into the module. "Are they wilting or something?"

"They're fine," James answered absentmindedly. He wasn't looking at the plants—he was looking at the plant lights. There were several different kinds, all meant to simulate different parts of natural sunlight. He had an idea.

James smiled to himself. He needed to start at the beginning.

CHAPTER THIRTY-NINE

James stayed inside his sleeping compartment until he was confident that everyone else in his group was asleep. He was extremely tired, but James knew that he needed to act sooner rather than later—and now was the perfect time. He quietly opened his accordion door and pulled himself outside into the open space in the center of the sleeping module.

The doors for Gonzalez, Jordyn, and Mike's quarters were all shut tight. The remaining two crewmembers—Harrison and Aaron—were on watch, though James didn't know exactly where they were in the ship. The decision to keep two people awake and together at all times was recommended by Gonzalez himself, and no one on board disagreed. James' watch was coming up in a couple of hours, which still gave him plenty of time to do what he needed to do—hopefully.

James passed by the still-sealed door to Nikki's sleeping quarters. That room was definitely one of his objectives for the night, but not just yet. He had other things to do first.

Whoever the killer was, they had somehow killed the ship's communications. Stopping all communication meant that incriminating evidence wouldn't make it back home, buying the killer more time. That much was clear. What wasn't clear was the killer's endgame. James was supremely confident that Aaron and Harrison were going to find and fix the problem eventually, but then what? What would the killer do then? What if one of those two men was the killer?

The only way to end the danger to the innocent members of the crew was for James to resume his investigation. Without communication with Houston or the tools needed to do DNA matching, James was going to have to do things the old-fashioned way. He needed to find evidence on board *Perseus*— evidence that wasn't just circumstance and chance. And to do that, he needed to start at the beginning of that fateful night. Where had Nikki been while James was sleeping? Where had she been attacked?

Nikki had to have been under heavy duress when she was in the airlock as it depressurized. A simple tap on the airlock's interior computer screen would have instantly stopped the cycle, but Nikki hadn't done anything like that. In fact, the alarm suggested that she had actually short-circuited the cycle from the inside. But why? Was it a mistake? Had she come to when it was already too late for her oxygen starved brain to make the right decision?

Then there was the fact that the body still sealed inside the lab had cuts on the midsection and even a torn fingernail. There had to be some sort of struggle. But was it the airlock itself? Was she assaulted in there? Or was she attacked in another module, then dragged into the airlock as the crew slept?

James pulled himself towards the kitchen, his mind still wandering as he kept a look out for Aaron and Harrison. Finding out where Nikki had been attacked was definitely a beginning—but was it *the* beginning? If only James could figure out where this had all started, and with whom. Maybe if he could get Harrison alone, get him to open up about what had really happened between him and Nikki—but then again, what if Harrison was the one behind this all along?

James allowed himself to float confidently into *Perseus'* center module. Peeking through hatches and hiding behind compartments would only make him suspicious, and get him in immediate trouble. Fortunately, his charade was unnecessary—Aaron and Harrison were clearly in the command module judging by the voices echoing softly from the front of the ship. Looked like James wouldn't have to pretend he was using the bathroom after all.

James grabbed a handhold and quickly pushed himself towards the back of the ship before Aaron and Harrison emerged. He passed through the open hatch that separated the kitchen from the lab and exercise room, and floated quietly up to the sequencer. It was still running fine, with only two hours left on the second blood sample—Harrison's. James looked up to check that the camera was still running, flashed it a quick thumbs up, then pushed himself up and over Nikki's body as he continued towards the rear of the ship, passing the entrances to both the auxiliary lab and the restroom modules.

Checking over his shoulder to make sure the coast was clear, James arrived at the airlock. Both the interior and exterior doors were closed like normal, so James put his face up to the window and looked inside. Everything looked normal from a distance, but James needed to get a closer look. That, however, would have to wait until later.

James backtracked to the auxiliary lab, his primary target for the night. After checking yet again for signs of anyone coming, he pulled himself into the module and floated towards the growing station, twisting his body in space so that he arrived at just the right angle.

The plants inside the growing station looked healthy to James' untrained eye, and the lights providing them with vital energy were still glowing strong, even after a year in space. A few months ago, the crew had the opportunity to eat some space-lettuce, and James remembered watching Mike carefully plant the seeds for a new plant. It was already almost fully grown now.

James wasn't here for the plants, however. He pulled himself down a little bit until he was level with the storage container just beneath the clear glass growing box, then slid the plastic container open slowly and quietly.

Perseus was full of containers and storage bins, some large and some small. This particular one was one of the smaller ones on board, and it held relatively little. Inside of it were replacement light bulbs, each one a unique spare for one of the five bulbs inside the planter boxes. There was a traditional florescent light, a couple of experimental tubes, and even a florescent black light tube about six inches long. It was this tube that James carefully pulled from its foam molding.

The glass tube was cold in James' hands. He rotated it slowly, looking for the positive and negative connectors, which he found quickly. Satisfied, James carefully closed the container, then slid the light into his pocket.

If James was completely honest with himself, he didn't know exactly what he was doing. He had never been a police detective—never investigated a murder. He couldn't match fingerprints—nor could he match DNA. He had, however, watched plenty of detective shows on TV with his wife, and nearly every one of them had the same identical scene. A grizzled detective and his beautiful, long-legged partner would enter a room, almost oblivious to the police photographers snapping pictures of the dead body somewhere on the floor. There was always a dark joke, then a quick search for clues. They would poke around for a while before spotting some evidence that nobody else in the room had noticed—often something in plain sight. A flick of the lights, some white powder, a magic flashlight, and there it was: blood, semen, drugs—you name it.

James didn't know if a regular black light would have the same effect, but he thought it was worth trying out. He had been through every room in *Perseus,* and there didn't seem to be anything obvious to be found. If a black light could make the unseen seen…well, James might then have some leads.

The light alone, however, wasn't enough. James needed something to power it. The light tube in hand, he pulled himself back outside and towards the exercise room, where the storage containing spare electrical systems was kept. Careful to avoid any noise, James quickly retrieved a short length of insulated copper wire that was kept for potential repairs to the special treadmill. He then went to the kitchen, where he retrieved a small roll of electrical tape, and one of the small rechargeable batteries that could be used to power the ship's emergency flashlights.

James shoved all the materials into his pockets, then shut the last of the compartments he had been in. He was just about to leave when he heard voices from the front of the ship. They were getting louder. Aaron and Harrison were making a round of the ship.

James kicked off the wall of the module and shot towards the sleeping module, catching himself just outside his sleeping compartment. He floated there for a moment, struggling to hear what was being said.

"You think it was a virus?" Harrison asked, his voice getting clearer as it approached. "From where?"

"It's just a theory," answered Aaron. "Honestly, if it was a virus, it was a sloppy one. It's more likely the power surge caused it—though we don't know what caused that, do we? We're just lucky the comms were the only thing touched. A systems crash like that with the life support could kill us."

"But you think you can fix it?" Harrison asked.

"Hopefully by tomorrow," Aaron replied. "I know what file has been corrupted now, so it's only a matter of time."

James pulled himself into his sleeping compartment and quietly shut the door before he could be spotted. He checked his watch—only two hours until he was supposed to wake up to be on watch. And if Aaron really was getting close to fixing the comms, time was even more precious.

After checking that his door was shut tight, James got to work. It took him longer than he initially expected, given the cramped quarters and his lack of tools, but James worked as quickly as he could. He split the copper wire by twisting it over and over again until it snapped, then used his fingernails to peel off the insulation at the ends. The last wire end gave him the most trouble—he finally ripped the insulation off, but the copper wire slit his finger open like a paper cut. James sucked the blood off his finger and got back to work.

The fact that the light tube and the battery kept floating around was frustrating, but after a few minutes of experimentation and plentiful amounts of electrical tape, James had a glowing black light in his hands. He could even turn it on and off by unsticking one of the wires from the negative end of the battery.

It was time to test it. With the black light on, James turned off the light in his compartment.

At first James saw nothing. The purplish light from the tube illuminated the room almost as much as a normal light, just in a different shade. A few seconds later, however, and James could start to make out little glowing spots.

The spots were nearly everywhere, but they seemed to be concentrated on the door just across from where James' face would be while sleeping. It made sense. The glowing spots must be drops of spit and saliva that would escape his mouth while he was asleep. There wasn't anything else it could have been—James didn't recall ever cutting himself in here, and he wasn't in the habit of any...self-gratification.

James had a flash of thought. He felt confident from TV and the movies that semen would glow, and now he knew that saliva did too. Just to check, James squeezed some blood from his fresh paper cut and dabbed it on the wall. He then held up the black light, and was surprised to see that it didn't glow at all. Not one bit.

James pursed his lips, slightly disappointed. So, his light wasn't going to help him find traces of blood—but then again, that was fine. Blood would be visible to the naked eye if he looked close enough.

There was only a half hour left before James was due to report for his watch. He looked at the black light in his right hand and briefly thought about saving his investigation for later, but decided that he didn't have time. He just needed to do it.

James unstuck the tape from the battery, shutting off the black light, then opened his accordion door yet again. He peeked his head out slowly, checking to see if Harrison or Aaron were anywhere to be seen up above in the kitchen. They weren't. They must have gone back to the command module.

This time, James *was* cautious and sneaky. He silently pulled himself from his compartment, then pulled himself up to Nikki's. He checked over his shoulder to make sure that all the other compartment doors were still shut, then slid the accordion door open. He pulled himself inside, then shut the door behind him.

The compartment still smelled like Nikki, even now. Her clothes were still in her drawers, and her sleeping bag was still stuck on the wall. Nobody had officially searched the room since she had died, though both James and Harrison had been here at least once. Who else had been here? James wondered.

James quietly gave the compartment one last search with the regular light on. Nothing had changed. There was no blood to be found, and all of Nikki's things were in their customary places. Satisfied, James stuck the taped wire back onto the battery, then turned off the light.

Just like before, the bright purple glow of the light tube filled the room, making any glowing details impossible to see. James was patient, and after a few seconds, a few glowing specks started to appear. James' expectations of a breakthrough, however, were quickly subdued.

The room looked just like James'. There were a few isolated specks, and a concentration on the door in front of where Nikki's head would be. There were no giant glowing splotches, no concentrations of stains inside or outside the sleeping bag. There was nothing to see here.

James checked his watch yet again. He was just about out of time. There were other places to be searched—including the airlock—but he'd have to do it some other time. James un-taped the black light to stop its subtle buzzing, then pushed his ear up to the door to make sure the coast was clear outside. He couldn't hear anything.

James reached down and unlatched the door, sliding it open as silently as possible so he could sneak back to his own compartment undetected. Instead, he came face to face with an angry scowl.

It was Gonzalez.

CHAPTER FORTY

Gonzalez scowled at James, his mouth shut tightly, his jaw trembling under the scruff of not having shaved in a while. James knew that he was in trouble. Big trouble.

"Give me one reason why I shouldn't wake everyone up right now," Gonzalez growled.

"I was investigating, Gonzo," explained James quickly, showing Gonzalez the black light in his hands. "Please, Gonzo. I can explain."

Gonzalez looked over his shoulder as if checking to see if anyone was watching or listening. "The hell you are," he said flatly. "I thought I'd wake you up to start our watch, but you weren't in your compartment."

James tried to move out of Nikki's compartment, but Gonzalez reached out to grab some handholds and didn't move. "Gonzo," James pled softly. "Come on. We're running out of time."

"People need to see this," Gonzalez said. "If you're just investigating, why didn't you tell anyone?"

"I didn't know who to trust," James whispered. "You know that. Now come on, let me out. We can talk about this."

"You didn't trust *me*," Gonzalez shrugged. "Didn't bother telling *me*, did you?"

James inhaled slowly to collect his thoughts. Aaron and Harrison would be coming by any minute now, expecting to wake him and Gonzalez up for their planned watch. If they caught him in here they'd assuredly think he was guilty. By the time the comms were fixed, the killer might have already made another move—one that could kill them all.

"We can talk about this on our watch," James said, over-pronouncing his words. "Gonzo, give me a chance. Please? Trust me for a second."

"Would you trust me if the roles were reversed?" asked Gonzalez. His face was totally blank.

James inhaled. "No," he answered bluntly. "But here we are."

Gonzalez didn't say anything for a moment, but he suddenly let go of his handhold and pulled himself aside so that James could exit the cramped compartment. "At least you're honest," Gonzalez said, shaking his head as if he couldn't believe what he was saying. "But you've got a lot of explaining to do."

James exited gratefully, shutting the door to Nikki's room behind him. James quickly tucked the light bar into his back waistband, hiding the crudely-made CSI tool underneath his shirt as Gonzalez just watched.

"You're looking for blood?" asked Gonzalez.

"I don't think blood shows up," answered James. "I've been testing it, and-"

James trailed off suddenly. There were voices coming from above in the kitchen module. He quickly did his best to look like he was chatting casually with Gonzalez, just in time for Aaron and Harrison to come around the corner.

"You guys are up already," Aaron observed from the entrance. "Good. Come on up so we can talk," he finished, speaking in a whisper so as not to disturb the still-sleeping crewmembers.

James looked to Gonzalez, who gestured for James to go on ahead. Twisting his body in space, James grabbed one of the many handholds and pulled himself upwards and into the kitchen.

"Anything to report?" Gonzalez asked.

"Jordyn got up to use the bathroom, but that was it," Harrison said. "We waited just outside the module for her."

"Good," Gonzalez nodded. "What about the comms system?"

"I think I'm getting close," Aaron said. "I've got the system causing problems isolated. I can stay up and keep working on it if you want."

"You two stayed together at all times?" Gonzalez asked, ignoring Aaron's suggestion.

"Well yeah," Aaron said, caught slightly off guard by the unexpected question. "We stayed together the whole time. We made sure the other didn't do anything to the systems and everything."

"Working together is really great when you don't trust each other worth a shit," grunted Harrison. "Is this going to keep up until we get home?"

"As long as it takes," Gonzalez said. He paused for a moment, then continued. "Go on and get some rest. You've each been up for more than 30 hours straight—I don't want anyone getting punchy while they're dealing with broken systems."

"Thanks," Aaron said, sounding relieved. James didn't blame him. Both he and Harrison looked absolutely slammed. Their eyes were bloodshot, their hair was messy, and their eyes looked sunken.

James watched as Aaron and Harrison headed down into the sleeping module, each retiring to their own little space. That left just him and Gonzalez floating in the kitchen, and Gonzalez still looked quite upset.

"Command module," the mission commander said flatly.

James timidly followed Gonzalez towards the forward node and into the connected command module, passing the open hatch to the MAV's upper stage on the way. Gonzalez headed straight towards the computer screens and began checking Aaron and Harrison's work, leaving James floating awkwardly behind him. James didn't say anything—Gonzalez had given him a chance, and he didn't want to ruin it.

"Looks fine from what I can tell," Gonzalez said finally as he spun himself away from the computer to look at James. He crossed his arms across his chest, then gestured for James to hand over his black light.

James hesitated, but only for a second. He passed off the light.

"You were saying?" prompted Gonzalez as he analyzed the crude instrument. "You were looking for blood?"

James sighed. "Yeah," he shrugged. "But I don't think it works for blood. I was barely testing it, but all I got was what I think was saliva."

"At least you got that," Gonzalez said with mild surprise. "I thought that was just TV shtick."

"Apparently not," responded James. "And I'm pretty sure it'll pick up other fluids as well."

"You're thinking semen," said Gonzalez. "This isn't about blood at all, is it?"

James shrugged again. "Honestly Gonzo, I'm not sure what it's about. I was thinking blood at first, but now I'm thinking we could find out where Nikki and whoever it was would hook-up."

Gonzalez grimaced in disgust. "That's nasty, man," he said.

"I know," replied James. "And I'm not even sure where that would lead us. I just figured I'd keep looking for something, since the comms are down."

"Something irrefutable," Gonzalez said thoughtfully. "Something that could incriminate somebody immediately. You're trying to find out who did this *now*, right? Get them in custody before they can do something else, am I right?"

James nodded yet again. He wasn't entirely comfortable talking with Gonzalez about any of this, but it's not like he had a choice.

Gonzalez looked over the black light again, then handed it back to James. He looked at James thoughtfully for a moment, his dark eyes seemingly scanning for anything James might be hiding. "I know it's not you, James," he said finally. "But you haven't exactly done yourself any favors sneaking around all the time."

"I know," admitted James. "But there's no one to trust."

"Bullshit," Gonzalez remarked sarcastically. "Why would you even think that?"

Gonzalez' sarcasm was enough to elicit a weak chuckle from James. "You know what, you're right," he weakly joked back. "We've got nothing to worry about up here."

Gonzalez smiled sadly before clapping a hand on James' shoulder. "I do feel responsible for all this somehow," he said softly. "I just want everyone home. We can deal with this shit there."

"I know," agreed James.

"So where do we start?" Gonzalez asked. "You got her room, obviously. Do you want to check it again? We've got a three hour watch—let's use it."

"I've searched her compartment high and low," James said matter-of-factly. "And not just today. We should start somewhere I haven't looked yet."

Gonzalez nodded vigorously. "Of course," he said. "So where do we start? Ship's not so big. The MAV? The rec room? The sleeping compartments?"

"We can count out the MAV—it was on Mars when this all happened," replied James thoughtfully. "The sleeping compartments would be great if people weren't in them. We might as well work our way back—I'd even start in the auxiliary lab or the airlock."

"Why?" asked Gonzalez.

"There'd be, uh...well, there'd be noise, Gonzo." James said uncomfortably. "Assuming it was consensual and repeated, which it almost clearly was if she got pregnant, they'd want somewhere where they wouldn't be heard doing it."

"Obviously," Gonzalez replied, shaking his head as if he felt foolish. "Well, let's get started. I'll lead out and make sure no one is watching, then you follow. Got it? We'll be quiet."

James nodded, once again tucking the black light into his waistband. He still felt uneasy about working with someone else on this, but if it was going to be anyone other than Jordyn, James would have picked Gonzo.

Gonzalez pushed himself past James and floated up into *Perseus'* forward node. He waited for James to come into the node too, then pushed himself out into the kitchen and towards the lab, watching the hatch below him that led towards the sleeping compartments. James watched as he stopped his momentum on a handhold by the open hatchway that led into the lab and exercise room. "All clear," mouthed Gonzalez.

James grabbed a handhold and pulled himself towards Gonzalez, floating silently through the kitchen and past the sleeping module. Gonzalez reached out an arm and helped James stop, just above the body bag with Nikki's remains.

"How does the sequencer look?" asked Gonzalez.

James was way ahead of him. "It's all done with Harrison's sample," he whispered. "I can start another one now."

"Wait until everyone is here," replied Gonzalez. "I don't want anyone accusing us of tampering."

James nodded. "Yeah," he answered. "That makes-"

There was a sudden squeak of metal from the front of *Perseus.* James spun his head around, expecting to see someone emerging from the sleeping compartment, but there was no movement.

"Just a docking node squeaking," Gonzalez said. "Probably."

The two men stayed put for a moment before Gonzalez finally pulled himself forward and towards the restroom module. James followed, his heart still racing from the noise. The noise itself wasn't at all uncommon, but he was already on edge and low on sleep.

The two men entered the restroom together, and Gonzalez tapped on the module's touchscreen to manually turn off the light once James had pulled out the black light. Both men waited for their eyes to adjust, then began their search.

The module was surprisingly clean. The size of the module meant that James had to float around close to the walls, holding the light only inches from the walls and equipment. There were definitely specks of some glowing liquid, but nothing as concentrated as what James saw in his own sleeping compartment.

"Is this a lot or a little?" asked Gonzalez as he followed James around the room.

James finished his search and turned the regular module light back on. "A little, I think," he answered. "Not enough to convince me it was here, anyways. I guess it makes sense—we clean this room religiously."

"So maybe it's just been cleaned since?" proposed Gonzalez.

"Could be," answered James. "Could be."

"Should we double check?" asked Gonzalez. "Just to be sure?"

"There's no time," James answered. "Come on. Let's check the auxiliary lab."

Gonzalez nodded and again led the way, checking that the coast was clear as he crossed the open exercise module and entered the auxiliary lab. James followed once Gonzalez had given him a thumbs-up, turning off the light as he entered.

The room wasn't completely dark like the restroom module. Light leaked in from the stars outside the large window, and the warm glow of the lights in the planter box cast everything in artificial light.

"If Estefani was up here with me I'd pick this module," Gonzalez said, half teasing, half serious. "A great window, mood lighting, you name it."

James grunted his awkward agreement and again pulled out his black light. The search was far more difficult here—the excess light meant that James had to skim the walls with his light an inch away just to see any specks. Just like the restroom module, the auxiliary lab was fairly free from glowing spots. In fact, the only real concentration of specks was on the drawer where the spare bulbs were kept. "That's from me," James explained when Gonzalez noticed. "It's how I got the black light a few hours ago."

Gonzalez didn't seem totally convinced that the room was as clean as James made it seem. James didn't care. He simply handed the black light off to Gonzalez, and a few minutes later he voiced his agreement. "You're right," he said. "Clean as a whistle. I'm actually surprised."

"There's still the rear node and the airlock," replied James. "Let's move there next."

Again, Gonzalez lead the way while James hung back to wait for the all-clear. With the ship still to themselves, the two men proceeded into the rear node. James looked around, reminded of the time the crew used the node as a makeshift airlock when the real airlock was malfunctioning. Would exposure to a vacuum make it so nothing would be detected by the light?

"I'll be honest," Gonzalez said, handing the light back over to James. "If this was me, I wouldn't pick here—unless I'm into something kinky. I mean, it's totally open. I can see all the way forward into the MAV."

James agreed. "Let's do the airlock then," he said, grabbing the airlock's interior hatch and pulling it open silently before lowering himself down into the relatively open space.

338

Gonzalez followed James down. He reached towards the panel to turn off the lights, but paused momentarily. "You think we'll even be able to see stuff?" he asked. "I mean, it's been exposed to a vacuum a shitload of times."

"Worth a shot," shrugged James, turning his black light on yet again.

Gonzalez flipped the lights off, casting the room into darkness. Like the auxiliary lab, the window in the airlock's exterior hatch let in some ambient light from outside, along with a small amount of light from the various blinking electronics in the advanced module.

James blinked, his eyes adjusting to the change in light for the umpteenth time this hour. Slowly, his eyes adjusted to the darkness and the purple light from the warm light tube in his hands. He held the tube closer to one of the walls.

"Damn," Gonzalez muttered.

James was simultaneously shocked and unsurprised. Everything in the module was covered in hundreds of glowing pinpricks of light. There were specks on the walls, smeared specks on the computer screen, specks on the hatch. Upon closer inspection, James found specks on the window, too.

"Damn is right," James said. "This is disgusting."

"Let's think for a second," Gonzalez said, swinging his head around as he looked at the constellation of glowing fluid remnants. "Are we sure this is...what we think it is? I mean, you said saliva and sweat-"

"There's way too much," interrupted James. "I mean, it's everywhere, and it's not like we regularly wipe this room down. It's not for sure, but..."

"It looks like my college dorm," Gonzalez joked weakly.

James winced at the off-color humor as he looked around. "So what does this mean?" he asked out loud, not really expecting an answer from Gonzalez. "I mean, this is disgusting, but what does it mean?"

"It means they got busy," Gonzalez replied. "This was where they had sex. I mean, this had to have gone on for a while. You think it was Harrison?"

"I think the only thing we know for sure is that it wasn't Jordyn," James responded.

"So, do we try to take a sample or something?" asked Gonzalez. "Run it through the DNA sequencer? Send it to Houston once comms are back?"

"Maybe," James answered absentmindedly. "But Gonzo, I don't know if that's any more effective than the blood samples we already have. I mean, at best it would be…"

"Be what?" Gonzalez asked.

James didn't reply right away. He was wrestling with the ghost of a thought.

"Hey, whatcha' thinking?" asked Gonzalez. "I know that face, James."

James nodded to himself as he mentally affirmed his initial suspicion. "This was probably the place—I mean it's obvious."

"Hell yeah it is," agreed Gonzalez.

James continued to plow through his thoughts as he spoke slowly. "This was their place," he continued. "This is where they would come. It had to be a lot—it had to be frequent. It was enough to get her pregnant, obviously. And damn, just look at this place."

"I'm not sure I'm following," prompted Gonzalez.

"This was their meet-up place," expounded James. "I mean, they were having some affair, right? Breaking NASA rules, Nikki cheating on her fiancé…They'd come here to do it. They'd come here to talk."

"I think we've established that," Gonzalez said impatiently. "What's your point?"

"Gonzo," James said, the excitement in his voice growing. "Gonzo, what if this wasn't premeditated at all? What if they were just meeting up like normal? What if Nikki confronted him on it? I mean...he comes expecting another sex tryst, and Nikki drops a bomb instead."

"You mean she tells him she's pregnant with his child," Gonzalez said, beginning to understand.

"Right!" James gestured excitedly. "She's waiting for him here—maybe she's even nervously fidgeting with the bolt that she must have brought in by accident. Anyways, he gets here all ready for action, but something is different. She tells him she's pregnant, tells him he's the father. And that's...that's bad. She can't have a child in space—it could be fatal to mother and baby. She'd have to abort. He'd know that!"

"So he gets angry," Gonzalez said in understanding.

"Furious!" added James. "Hell, he might have even thought that she had told *me*, the doctor. Maybe that's why he came after me later!"

"Wait, what?" Gonzalez asked confusedly. "I'm not-"

"I'm getting ahead of myself," waved James. "Look, whoever he is, he snaps. If people find out, he's ruined. He'll lose his wings, his compensation, his family if he's got one. He can't be discovered—he can't have his sins sprayed across CNN. He cracks. He attacks her in here, on the spot. It's a crime of passion. It's not premeditated!"

"So what you're saying is-"

"What I'm saying is that he tried to kill her *here*." Continued James. "Maybe he partially strangled her or something, then panicked. He crawls out, shuts the door, initiates a depressurization cycle. But something happens. Nikki is *still alive*. She regains consciousness during the decompression, fights her way to the control panel, and either opens the exterior hatch on purpose, or by accident as she tries to avoid dying. Either way, boom! The hatch blows open, she's sucked out, the alarms go off, and somehow—maybe by some crazy coincidence, maybe from Nikki's last living efforts—the loose bolt jams in the hatch. The killer can't close it, and the alarms start going off. The killer has seconds, that's it."

"So Harrison—or whoever it is—pulls himself back towards the sleeping compartment just in time for us to wake up," Gonzalez said thoughtfully, a hand on his chin.

"I did see Harrison first," James nodded. "Getting out of his compartment."

"Sounds like we need to talk to him again," Gonzalez nodded, his eyebrows furrowed in anger.

"But I'm not sure," hesitated James. "I mean, I timed it out. There's no way he could have done all that fast enough. I mean, you and I were at the terminal before he had even crawled out of his sleeping compartment, remember? I got to the monitor, you shut off the alarm...I'm not sure it was Har..."

"Not sure it was Harrison?" Gonzalez asked angrily. "James, we have our evidence!"

"It was *you*."

The words just sort of blurted out, the impulsive thought escaping James' lips before his brain could force him to contain it.

"What?" asked a shocked Gonzalez.

James choked on his reply. He was suddenly very dizzy, and he was having trouble focusing through the sudden rush of adrenaline that was screaming through his body. He clenched his fists. "Gonzo," he said, his voice quiet. "You were the first one by my side at the computer terminal. You quieted the alarm, not me."

"What are you talking about?" challenged Gonzalez.

"Not Jordyn, not Mike, Aaron, or even Harrison," James said, his voice starting to rise. "You were the first one there. You turned off the alarm as I

342

watched. It's because you didn't come from your sleeping compartment. You were coming from-"

There was a flash of movement and a glint of steel. Gonzalez struck quickly before James could even finish his sentence.

James was thrown backwards slightly, bumping gently into the wall of the airlock. He opened his mouth to shout, but all that came out was a cold exhalation. Shocked, he looked down. A piece of steel was protruding from his abdomen, just below his rib cage. He recognized it immediately. It was surgical, stainless steel.

It was the scalpel he had used during the autopsy.

"Sorry, James," Gonzalez said, his face blank as he pulled himself up and out of the airlock.

James hesitated only for a moment as he stared at the knife jutting out from his gut, but it was a second too long. He came to his senses and pushed himself off the wall, lightning bolts of pain shooting from his abdomen and into every corner of his body as he dove towards Gonzalez. "You bastard!" James tried to shout, nearly choking on the words. "I'm going to kill-"

The airlock hatch leading to the interior of *Perseus* slammed shut just as James reached it, slamming him hard in the face and sending him flying backwards again towards the back of the airlock. He struck painfully, more searing white pain shooting from his stomach. James coughed and sucked in agonizingly as he glanced back down to his stomach.

Blood was rapidly spreading through his t-shirt, and it was starting to bead up and float into space. James put a hand on the knife's handle and prepared to pull out the scalpel, but stopped suddenly upon hearing a familiar sound.

It was the hiss of oxygen venting into space.

CHAPTER FORTY-ONE

James inhaled sharply and painfully.

He had only seconds to respond before he was killed, and he knew it. Gonzalez' emotionless face was in the window of the interior hatch, waiting for the quick depressurization to fully kill James before ejecting him into space. He wouldn't make the same mistake he had made with Nikki.

Time seemed to simultaneously slow down and speed up for James. His mind was instantly filled with memories, but not ones of his wife and kids. They were from his safety briefings and trainings. Words like hypoxia and exposure rattled around his head in the rapidly thinning air. Random reminders like "don't hold your breath" and "don't panic" echoed in his ears. One second had passed now. Two.

James' ears popped painfully as he willed his wounded body to act. He reached down and yanked the scalpel painfully from his abdomen, the two-inch-long blade pulling out a string of floating, beading droplets of blood that hung lazily in the dimly-lit airlock. James fumbled the scalpel into his pocket while using his free hand to try to stop the bleeding. He had no idea how bad the wound was, but it wouldn't matter very soon.

Three seconds. Four. James kicked off the wall and lunged towards the airlock's control panel. Another sharp stab of pain came from his open wound, making him flinch and grimace as he tried to stop the bleeding with both hands now. It was only another second as he flew from one side of the airlock to the other, but it might as well have been an eternity.

James reached the control panel and squinted at the touchscreen commands. He was having trouble seeing now—his vision was blurry and clouded. He tapped what he thought was the abort button, but nothing happened. He pressed another button and the lights came on. He was smearing blood all over the screen—it was getting harder to read. His blurred vision wasn't from his wound—his brain was tripping on the thinning air.

James' ears popped again. He instinctively took a deep breath and held, then exhaled as something distant told him that doing so could make his lungs rupture. He tried to tap on the touch screen again, but it didn't register anything. The blood he had gotten on the screen was interfering with everything.

Eight seconds had passed now. James' head developed a sudden ache, and his eardrums felt like they were going to explode. He took another breath, but didn't feel like he was really getting anything. His vision narrowed, and a strange feeling of peace suddenly overtook him. Part of him struggled against it, but the peace was strong, and hard to resist. James quickly shook his head to clear it away.

James tried to breathe in again, but it felt like he was sucking air from a straw. He was starting to suffocate now—it was going to get him before the vacuum did. His hands seized up against his will as he desperately tried to clean his blood off the touchscreen. He was only smearing it.

With his last moments of consciousness, James focused everything he had onto the touchscreen. The smeared blood on the screen was starting to bubble slightly—boiling in the rapidly thinning air. There were two buttons he could press, but he couldn't make out the words. He picked the top one and pressed it over and over again...Why wasn't it registering? Why?

James' vision went black, and the wooziness he felt left him. The noise from the airlock floated away into near silence...

For a moment or two, the only thing James was conscious of was the labored noise of his lungs hopelessly sucking at thin, oxygen-sparse air. But he didn't pass out—not quite. As he teetered on the edge of consciousness, his lungs suddenly sensed thicker air.

James focused all his energy on drawing one final breath. It came—as satisfying as an ice-cold glass of water in the desert.

James coughed and choked as his clouded mind started to clear. He slowly began to be aware of a strange noise—that of a warning alarm. It started out softly, but suddenly struck James' consciousness as if he were napping next to a church organ. His eyes jerked open, flooding his brain with sensation. With it came the pain.

His lungs screamed. His ears felt like they had been pierced with hot knives. His head seemed to be stuck in a vice. The wound in his stomach felt like it was bleeding molten hot metal through his shirt and all over his stomach. James tried to put pressure on the site to stop the bleeding, but that made it all worse. He got woozy again, almost passing out from the pain.

The airlock, dark when James had been stabbed, was now brightly illuminated by pulsing emergency lights. He found himself floating near the exterior hatch, even though he didn't remember floating there. In agony, James looked up towards the interior hatch. There was no one in the window.

James looked down at his blood-soaked midsection. It still throbbed painfully, but it was bearable as long as he didn't move too quickly. He carefully pulled up his shirt to inspect the wound, and was simultaneously disgusted and encouraged. The bleeding was slow—expanding slowly in a weightless blob that stuck to his stomach—and the location was as ideal as a stabbing could be. The short, stubby scalpel had stuck straight in, leaving what James estimated as a one-inch puncture wound, and James' self-diagnosis was that it had pierced skin, fat, and muscle, but nothing immediately deadly. He was lucky.

James had to get to the others, he had to stop Gonzalez before he did anything else. He floated painfully up towards the interior hatch, leaving bloody handprints wherever he reached out. He went straight to the blood-smeared touchscreen, wiped it off with one of the last clean parts of his bloody t-shirt, and found the button to open the interior hatch—he could read it now, though his vision was still cloudier than normal. He pressed it, and the interior door opened quickly.

Fighting the pain, James dragged his wounded body through the hatch and into the rear node. He was instantly aware of shouting coming from somewhere else inside this ship.

Perseus' middle compartments, however, were empty. The alarm was blaring and red lights were flashing, but other than that, *Perseus* looked like it always had. There was no one in the ship's main central compartments, from the rear node all the way up to the MAV. Something, however, was moving.

James squinted and tried to rub his eyes without getting blood in them. Then he saw it. There were thousands of floating droplets of blood surrounding the DNA sequencer. It had been tampered with.

"Hello?" croaked James, pulling himself forward into the exercise and lab module. "Guys?"

The red lights stopped flashing suddenly. The remaining lights flickered, almost shutting off entirely before returning to full strength. The alarm kept sounding.

There was a flash of rapid movement just as James reached the side of Nikki's body bag. It was Aaron, who zipped into the kitchen module and went straight to the main computer terminal, not bothering to look around. "I've got an airlock malfunction!" he shouted back towards the sleeping compartment. "Electrical malfunction on the port solar pa-"

The ship rocked suddenly, shifting and rolling around James as he floated in the same spot. A deep rumble filled the entire ship with sound.

"Aaron!" cried James, each syllable stabbing his stomach anew. "Aaron! It's Gonzo!"

Aaron turned towards James, his eyes widening even more with shock as he saw James' bloody state for the first time. "James?!?" he cried out in disbelief.

The ship shuddered again. James latched onto the side of the operating table, clutching at his stomach in pain. Aaron just floated there in shock. "I don't...I don't," he stuttered.

Harrison flew into the kitchen, too fast to stop his momentum before slamming into the module's microwave. "Aaron!" he shouted. "That's the main engine!"

"The what?" Aaron and James shouted simultaneously.

"THE MAIN ENGINE IS PUSHING US OFF COURSE!!!" cried Harrison. Without waiting for a response, he kicked off of the side of a storage bin and flew towards the command module's open hatch, disappearing inside.

James clung to the operating table as he shouted agonizingly again towards Aaron—who didn't seem to know whether to help James or to work the emergency systems from his computer terminal. "This is Gonzo!" James cried again, coughing painfully. "Aaron, Gonzo is doing this!"

"What happened to you?!?" gasped Aaron. "What the-"

Another figure suddenly appeared from inside the MAV, emerging into the forward node just behind Aaron. James recognized the figure instantly.

"LOOK OUT!" James shouted, forgetting the pain for a brief moment. Without thinking, he coiled up and kicked himself off the table holding Nikki, flying through the floating blood and towards Aaron's assailant.

It happened almost instantly. Aaron swung himself downwards and to the left, just barely missing Gonzalez' scalpel as it scythed through the air. In the split second before James and Gonzalez collided, James had time to recognize Gonzalez' new, smaller scalpel while also remembering his own knife tucked into his pocket. There was no time to pull it out.

The two men hit like a pair of football players colliding at midfield. Gonzalez and James were almost equally sized, but Gonzalez was traveling a hair faster. The blow instantly knocked the wind out of James, and he only just had the presence of mind to kick Gonzalez backwards before he could make another swing with his blade. It separated the two men, but only for a moment. James was left floating in the middle of the kitchen with nothing to grab on to. Gonzalez caught the edge of the hatch and pulled himself back towards James, scalpel glinting in his fist.

James convulsed in midair, willing his body to somehow twist itself out of the way, but it was useless. Gonzalez flew towards him, ready to strike. James flinched.

A blur of movement shot up from beneath James. It was Jordyn, flying in at full speed. She collided with Gonzalez, hitting him squarely in the chest and sending both of them flying against the side of the module. Jordyn grabbed him by the neck and coiled her right arm back, ready to throw a haymaker.

Gonzalez, however, was too quick. He jerked to the side, jabbing blindly with the blade in his hand. There was an audible slicing noise and a shout of pain from Jordyn.

"NO!!!" James tried to yell, but his own pain cut him off.

Gonzalez shoved Jordyn off of him and pulled himself away. He grabbed a handhold and threw himself back towards the front of the ship, just as Harrison flew out of the command module in a panic.

"Stop him!" James shouted, pointing towards Gonzalez, but it was too late. Gonzalez shoved Harrison backwards into the MAV, then dived downwards and into the command module, slamming the hatch shut behind him.

Mike emerged suddenly, specks of blood covering his face from the blood floating in the air. James had no idea where he had come from, but that didn't matter. He finally caught a handhold and pulled himself towards Jordyn, who was floating in the fetal position, cradling her left arm.

"It's no good!" shouted Harrison as he pounded at the closed hatch to the command module. "I can't get it open!"

"Maybe I can open it from here!" Aaron replied, pulling himself back up to the computer terminal. "Maybe I can-"

"What the hell is happening?" Mike said, his face pale from shock. "James, what the hell happened?"

The ship shook again, this time rolling suddenly to the left.

"I disabled the engines!" shouted Harrison. "It's the directional thrusters now, the RCS!"

"James!" shouted Mike.

James didn't reply as he pulled himself to Jordyn's side. Her teeth were clutched tightly together, her eyes were squinted shut in pain. For a moment, James completely forgot about his own wound.

The ship shook again. "What the hell is Gonzo thinking?!?" exclaimed Harrison. "He's gonna' kill all of us!"

Jordyn was trembling, her right hand clasped tightly on her left forearm. Her dark skin was stained crimson.

"I told you it wasn't me," she joked weakly. "Maybe next time you'll trust me sooner, eh?"

James didn't answer. He gently grabbed Jordyn's hand and pulled it away from the spot on her forearm that she was covering. There was a split second of nothing, then a gush of blood. James clapped his own hand on the spot.

"He got me good," said Jordyn.

"It's an artery," James replied, trying to keep his voice calm. "You're lucky it's in your arm. Mike! Get me some gauze and a...a..."

"A what?" cried Mike, totally overwhelmed. "James, what's happen-"

350

"I need gauze, medical tape, and something like a cord!" ordered James. "Hurry up!"

"Ok, ok!" stuttered the biologist, flecks of blood in his red hair.

The ship jerked again. Gonzalez was controlling it from the command module, thrashing the ship and its crew around helplessly.

"I can't stop it!" Aaron shouted. "I can't get the system to read my inputs!"

James had a quick thought. "Harrison!" he snapped. "Get back into the MAV and counter his movements with the MAV engines!"

"It's not enough!" Harrison replied. "There's not enough-"

"JUST DO IT!!!" yelled James. "Use the MAV's engines! Mike, where the hell is that stuff?!?"

"I'll go help him," Aaron said quickly, leaving the computer terminal behind and disappearing into the auxiliary lab. With Harrison heading towards the MAV, it left James and Jordyn alone in the kitchen.

"It's really not that bad," James said, doing his best to keep his voice under control. There was so much adrenaline coursing through his body now that he didn't feel his own pain, but it made it so his hands trembled and his voice shook. He squeezed down harder on Jordyn's arm.

"Dammit," she swore.

"It's controllable," James explained quickly. "I think it's just one, but if we can't stop the bleeding, you'll die."

"Haven't you ever heard of bedside manner?" wheezed Jordyn.

James didn't laugh. "WHERE THE HELL ARE YOU WITH THAT STUFF, MIKE?!?" he bellowed, instantly regretting it as his body reminded him of where he had been stabbed.

351

Perseus shook yet again, this time pitching upwards violently. It was immediately countered by a force pushing the nose of the ship downwards as Harrison fought back with the MAV's tiny engines.

"It was Gonzo," wheezed Jordyn. "James, we have to stop him."

James looked to Jordyn, then towards the closed hatch that led to the command module. Gonzalez was going to get them all killed—he was going to throw them off course and into space. They'd all die, even if he could stop Jordyn from bleeding out right now.

"Here I am!" Mike cried from the auxiliary lab. His arms were full of medical supplies of all sorts, but James didn't mind.

"Get over here!" he shouted.

Perseus rolled violently yet again, then back as Harrison fought it. The lights flickered once more.

Another alarm sounded, this one far louder and more shrill. It was the ship's integrity alarm—something that only sounded if the entire ship was about to be obliterated.

There was a sudden whooshing noise from all sides. James swung his head around just in time to see the emergency hatch between the kitchen and the lab close swiftly, blocking off Mike and Aaron. The MAV door shut suddenly as well, then the node hatch, then the entrances to the rec room and sleeping module.

The ship shook once more. Jordyn clung to James as he kept his hand clasped on her sliced arm. All the hatches around them had been sealed shut. They were trapped in the kitchen.

The rolling stopped, as did the alarm. Everything suddenly went very quiet.

Jordyn looked at James, her dark eyes full of fear. In them, James could see the reflection of his own eyes.

He looked terrified.

CHAPTER FORTY-TWO

Jordyn and James floated still for a minute as James worked to figure out his next move. Apart from the closed emergency hatches, *Perseus* seemed almost normal. Everything was quiet, all was still.

James kept his hand clasped tightly over the large cut on Jordyn's left arm. He could feel her heart racing, every beat thumping in his hand as he tried to stop the bleeding from what James guessed was her ulnar or radial artery. In a way, Jordyn was lucky. Of all the arteries to have severed, this was the most survivable. In weightless space, however, all bets were off.

The lights in the kitchen turned off suddenly, flicked off by some invisible switch. James froze for a moment, waiting to hear the sounds of some distant explosion or fire on board. There was nothing. James wasn't surprised—he knew that this was Gonzalez' doing.

James was suddenly aware of a faint banging sound. He searched for the source of the noise while still clasping to Jordyn, finally spotting it in the sealed hatch that blocked his pathway to the lab, where Aaron and Mike were trapped. Aaron, barely visible through the blood-speckled window, stopped knocking and flashed an inquisitive thumbs-up. James gave a thumbs-up back.

"That bastard," Jordyn said quietly. "It was Gonzo all along," she repeated.

"Yeah," James answered, carefully gesturing for Jordyn to follow his movements as they floated towards the hatch. All the medical equipment was kept where Aaron and Mike were, and James needed it desperately to help treat Jordyn.

The two crewmates reached the hatch. James considered having Jordyn take over the task of holding her own wound, but that might mean ruining any blood coagulation that was already forming. No, he had to keep his grip.

James tried tapping on the hatch controls, but they were completely unresponsive. "Shocker," Jordyn said sarcastically. "He's probably locked it all down from the command module."

"We'll have to try it manually," James said, grabbing onto the hatch's lever with his free hand and giving it a tug. It didn't budge. He could hear faint grunting from the other side as Aaron and Mike both tried the same thing, but to no avail.

"The emergency procedures probably prevent it from opening," Jordyn said weakly, coughing slightly. "Maybe if we..."

Jordyn trailed off in thought, something that was rather unlike her. It startled James, who reexamined Jordyn's paling face. He used his free hand to check her pulse again—it was racing, but seemed weak.

"I'm fine," she said suddenly. "I was thinking we could re-route the electricity from bus-"

"Not yet," interrupted James. "Jordyn, we've got to get you stabilized first."

"Stop treating me like some stupid patient," snapped Jordyn. "Gonzo could be trying to detach modules from one another, he could be-"

"I know!" James said forcefully, sending a stab of pain through his wounded abdomen. "But if he does that, he's dead too. He needs us all to get to Earth alive, he knows that. He at least needs *Perseus* intact. Now shut up and move with me to the table. I have an idea."

Jordyn opened her mouth to argue, but saw that James wasn't going to budge. Careful to stick together, the two gently kicked off the hatch to propel themselves to the kitchen "table." The table was nothing more than a foldable platform with plenty of Velcro patches for utensils and food pouches, but its position right next to the galley's storage compartments and trash receptacle was the real reason for moving to it. With Jordyn's arm still held tightly in his right hand, James began rifling through the storage compartments. He was looking for a towel, a plastic bag, anything that he could use.

"What about when he got shocked?" Jordyn asked as James pulled out a tiny pouch of washable napkins. "I thought Gonzo was a victim, too."

The napkins wouldn't be enough. James started searching again, blindly sticking his free arm into the storage bins. "So did I," he grunted. "But it'd be an easy enough thing to fake. Yell a little and throw himself off the SIM, and we'd all drop him as a suspect. It worked on me—I'm a damn gullible idiot."

"Shut up," Jordyn said. "It's not your fault. Nobody trusted anyone anyways. Besides, we all knew him. Who'd have thought he'd be some psycho?"

"Aha!" shouted James. He had found two of the microfiber towels. One alone wouldn't have sufficed, but now they were in business.

"And then there's Nikki," Jordyn continued as James prepared the two towels. "She was having sex with Gonzo then, huh?"

Using his free hand and mouth, James hastily tied the two towels together at the corners. It wasn't sanitary or pretty, but it would have to do. "This might hurt," he said, getting ready to let go of the wound.

"I mean seriously," Jordyn continued bravely. "Fiancé at home while she was getting knocked up by Gonzo, and playing Harrison at the same time. What a slut! I was no angel before getting married, but- DAMMIT JAMES!!!"

James ignored Jordyn's cursing as he pulled the makeshift towel bandage even tighter around the wound before tying it off. As soon as he had pulled his hand off blood had gushed out, but he had gotten the towel quickly in place.

"Is that it?" grimaced Jordyn. "You want to put a tourniquet on or something?"

"Only if this doesn't work," James answered seriously. "Tourniquet could do more harm than good."

"What about yourself?" asked Jordyn, nodding towards James' stomach.

"I'm fine," he lied quickly. "Just sit tight for a sec. I want to make sure it holds."

Jordyn obediently held still as James watched the bandaged wound. He made a few adjustments, but all-in-all, it seemed to be holding. The bleeding had been stemmed for now. A proper stitching done as soon as possible would hopefully eliminate the danger permanently.

"We're going to make it back, you know," Jordyn said suddenly, her voice calm. "And I'll buy drinks for you and Claire."

"And Derek?" asked James, satisfied with his work. He reached for the pack of napkins, wiping Jordyn's blood off his hands before attempting to treat his own painful stab wound.

"We'll share a glass," laughed Jordyn weakly. "Between two military salaries and the debt from my father-in-law's cancer treatments, I don't think I can afford much else."

James pressed the remaining clean napkins tightly against his abdomen, as forcefully as his pain would allow. "I'll take you up on it," he said through gritted teeth.

James kept applying pressure, adding additional napkins as he tried to completely stop the slowing bleeding from his torso. Jordyn watched in silence, a look of concern on her face. She looked at her bandaged arm, then back at James.

"James," she said quietly. "Thank you. If we don't make it..."

"We're going to make it," James grunted through the pain.

"I just mean, I dunno," she said. "In another life, maybe..."

"Maybe what?"

Jordyn shrugged. "I'm not sure. I'm not being mushy or scandalous. Just saying that you're a good friend. In another life, I think we'd have made a good team. You know?"

"You're just trying to make me feel guilty about not trusting you before," James said, using duct tape from a just-found roll to keep the napkins in place on his stomach.

"James," Jordyn said seriously.

James paused, looking at Jordyn for a moment. "I feel the same," he said finally. "But I'd like to focus on sticking around in *this* life for the time being."

"I hear that," Jordyn nodded breathlessly.

There was a sudden popping noise that filled the kitchen. James froze in midair, only to relax when he heard the familiar voice of Aaron coming through the kitchen speakers. "Hey, can you hear me?" he asked. "James? Jordyn?"

"We're here!" James said, putting a hand over his racing heart. "Dammit, A. I thought we were depressurizing or something."

"Sorry," replied Aaron quickly. "James, I hacked the intercoms from the terminal in here. Whatever Gonzo is doing, he's controlling it all from the command module."

"No shit, Nostradamus," Jordyn replied snarkily. "Can you stop him? Can he hear us now?"

"It's just between us," answered Aaron. "And I'm not sure yet. I was trying to get the hatches open and just sort of stumbled across the comms linkage. Mike, grab me that spare battery from the auxiliary lab, quick!"

"Can you isolate the command module?" James said, thinking quickly. "What about Harrison, is he ok in the MAV?"

"I said I don't know," replied Aaron. "I'm already close to getting the hatches, do you want me to stop?"

James looked at Jordyn, who shrugged her shoulders. James wasn't sure what to say as he floated in the dark kitchen module. He had no real computer experience—not like Aaron had anyway.

"Whatever you can do, do it," James said finally. "Just keep the ship in one piece while you do it."

"You don't need to tell me twice," replied Aaron over the intercom. "Thanks, Mike. Open that electrical panel over there. No, the other one."

"What's the plan?" Jordyn asked.

"Stop Gonzo," James replied. "Either isolate him in the module or get in there with him all together. Either way, we've got to restrain him somehow."

"Restrain him?" Jordyn asked in disbelief. "James, we need to get that man the hell off the ship, or we'll all die. We're still millions of miles from Earth if you haven't forgotten. I think we're past restraining. Let's jettison the capsule."

James nodded as he looked over his shoulder. "Maybe," he said finally. "But not yet. I'm not a judge, jury, or executioner. I'm just a doctor."

"And I'm just a pilot," remarked Jordyn. "Either way, we're getting home."

James nodded again, this time remaining silent. Truth be told, he didn't know what the endgame here would be. He just wanted to make it home alive.

James pulled himself towards the hatch separating the kitchen from the forward node. He pressed his face up to the glass, trying to see something in the dim emergency lights, but he couldn't see anything. The hatch window to the MAV was empty and dark—James hoped that nothing had happened to Harrison. The hatch to the command module was closed, too—but it was windowless. It had to be for when the capsule burned its way through Earth's atmosphere.

"Aaron," Jordyn said impatiently.

"Working on it," Aaron replied almost instantly. "Give me a sec."

James floated to the other two hatches in the room—the one leading to the inflatable sleeping and recreation modules. Both modules were dark, but looked structurally sound. The emergency hatches definitely hadn't closed because of a depressurization. It was almost certainly Gonzalez.

"I think I've got it," Aaron finally announced. "I've got the hatch separating us—the lab and the kitchen."

"Great!" James replied, floating back up next to Jordyn. "Can you have Mike get those medical supplies ready?"

"Already on it," came Mike's faint reply.

"James, I'm fine," Jordyn said so that only he could hear. "We need to get Gonzo first."

"It'd be nice if the people to get him weren't two hobbled stab victims," James replied flatly.

The two crewmates waited in silence as Aaron worked to open the hatch. Apart from Aaron's occasional mumble to himself, *Perseus* was silent. It stayed that way for just a moment, before being interrupted by the muffled sound of an electronic motor, and the soft whoosh of air.

"Wait a second," Jordyn said. "Shit."

It was the wrong hatch. The hatch separating the kitchen and lab was still shut tightly. The hatch to the forward node, however, was swinging open.

"Aaron?" James inquired nervously, looking over his shoulder to the dark node.

"I don't know what just happened," exclaimed a clearly frustrated Aaron. "James, I'm sorry, I'll keep working on it."

James left Jordyn's side, his eyes still locked onto the dark forward node. He pulled himself towards it, simultaneously extending his right arm into his pocket and pulling out the scalpel.

"James," hissed Jordyn as she came after him. "James, wait."

James entered the forward node and exhaled a sigh of both relief and frustration. The hatch to the command module was still closed.

"Alright, come back," whispered Jordyn. "Let's give Aaron a chance."

James pulled himself up to the MAV's closed hatch and knocked softly on the window. "You want to wait now?" he asked Jordyn as he peered inside, hoping to see Harrison. "You're giving me whiplash, Jordyn."

"*I* was for jettisoning the damn capsule, James," snapped Jordyn. "Come on, we're going-"

Harrison's face appeared suddenly in the MAV window, making James recoil in fear. Jordyn, halfway through her sarcastic response when James jerked backwards, let out a small shriek. Luckily, their fear was for naught—Harrison was alright. James pocketed his scalpel, and the two men shared a thumbs-up through the glass. "Thank God," remarked Jordyn.

"Now what?" James asked out loud. The entire crew was alive, but still separated.

"We could jet-"

"Not yet," interrupted James quickly—though it was less out of concern for Gonzalez and more for the sake of the ship's integrity.

"Fine...maybe we can have Harrison spin the ship from the MAV or something," suggested Jordyn. "Maybe we can break the window with something?"

Jordyn was just spitballing, and James had nothing better to offer. Before he could think of a reply, however, Aaron's voice called out of the kitchen's speaker.

"Guys!" he shouted, fear in his voice. "Guys, I'm getting an airlock malfunction warning. The exterior airlock door is opening!"

"Shit," cursed James. "The interior hatch is still open! It's going to depressurize the whole rear node!"

"But the exercise room is still sealed, right?" Jordyn shot back. "Aaron and Mike are ok."

"If Gonzo can open the airlock from the command module then he can open up the whole damn ship," James said rapidly.

The ship shook suddenly, a metallic squeaking and popping noise radiating all the way up to where James was floating in the forward node. He quickly grabbed onto the nearest handhold to stabilize himself, but Jordyn had other instincts. She reacted instantly, pulling herself from the forward node and into the kitchen while James floated still in shock. "Come on!" she shouted back. "James!"

"Damn!" Aaron swore, letting James know the situation was desperate. "The rear node just depressurized! I'm getting a hatch alert on hatches B and F—the lab and rec room hatches. He's trying to depressurize the ship!"

James clung to the node handhold in fear as the ship squeaked and rocked again. What the hell was Gonzo thinking? He was going to get everyone killed!

"James!" shouted Jordyn from the kitchen. "Get the hell in here!"

James wavered for just a split second, trying to decide if he should follow Jordyn, try to save Harrison, or bang on the command module hatch. His brief hesitation, however, made the choice for him.

Another alarm started blaring in *Perseus*. James, deciding to follow Jordyn, prepared to push himself through the hatch, but it was too late. The hatch separating the forward node from the kitchen swung itself down quickly, only narrowly missing James' head as he propelled himself towards the once-open space. Instead of reaching Jordyn, he ran painfully into the closed hatch.

Panicked, James peered through the window—Jordyn was yelling something to him, but he couldn't hear her. Desperate to find a way out of his unexpected trap, he looked backwards towards the MAV. Harrison too was shouting something, his words not even close to penetrating the thick hatch between them.

James had had enough of this. Pulling himself downwards and ignoring the pain in his stomach, James began pounding on the closed metal hatch to the command module with his bare fist. He knew that Gonzalez would be able to hear his banging. "Gonzo!" he screamed painfully. "Gonzo, stop!"

Nothing happened.

James kept pounding. If Gonzalez was going to kill everyone, he'd have to do it knowing that everyone was struggling and fighting against him. He'd hear banging until James' last breath of life.

The ship trembled again, but James didn't bother checking through the windows again. He just kept pounding—pounding on the hatch.

Suddenly, it moved.

CHAPTER FORTY-THREE

The command module hatch opened inwards, filling the dark forward node with a widening shaft of artificial light. James steadied himself as it swung open, scalpel ready in his right hand. He grabbed a handhold on the far side of the node and blinked in the sudden light.

The hatch clicked metallically as it opened all the way. Every sinew in James' body was tense as he waited to be attacked, making his stomach wound sting and ache. Gonzalez, however, wasn't by the hatch. It had opened electronically.

James could see down into the command module. He could see the headrests to the seven seats arranged facing outwards. He could see the fire extinguisher behind the pilot's seat, and the enormous laminated flight manual behind Nikki's. What he couldn't see, however, was Gonzalez.

James opened his mouth to say something, but he silently choked. He had no idea what he was doing. Gonzo had lost it.

James inhaled and tried again. "Gonzo," James said loudly, hoping the words would come to him. "Gonzo, it's James."

Silence.

James stayed tense, still holding to the handhold in the node. His best chance was to play off Gonzalez' psychology. "Gonzo, you've got to stop," he said, trying to sound confident. "There *is* a way out of this."

There was no reply.

Letting go of the handhold, James pushed himself slowly towards the open hatch. "Gonzo," he repeated. "Gonzo, we can all get home alive, and deal with all this there. You keep blowing those hatches open and it'll kill everyone. You know that."

There was no answer.

James reached the open hatch, stopping himself by putting his hands on the rim of the meter-wide opening. He could see the back of Gonzalez' head now, his jet-black hair framed by the glowing computer screen in front of the commander's chair. He seemed to be floating just at the edge of his seat, his head only inches away from the screen.

James swallowed hard and gripped his scalpel even tighter. "Gonzo, I'm coming in to talk to you, man. Coming in nice and slow. What do you think?"

Gonzalez still didn't respond. James could tell that he was conscious from the way the mission commander's burly shoulders rose and fell as he breathed. His right hand hovered just above one of the touch screens, but he didn't move.

James' arms flexed as he prepared to pull himself downwards, but he hesitated. The command module wasn't nearly as large as any of the other modules—the interior was barely sixteen feet in diameter, but felt even tighter with the seven seats and walls of instrumentation—and James knew that if he were to kick off just right, he and his knife would reach Gonzalez before he'd even have time to react. But something about that idea made James shirk.

"Coming in nice and slow," James repeated instead, doing his best to keep his voice level, calm, and even friendly. He pulled himself slowly into the capsule, grabbing a seat headrest and maneuvering himself down on the side of the tight capsule opposite Gonzalez, the circle of seats between them. James kept his knife ready, but held it low by his side in case Gonzalez turned around suddenly. The last thing James wanted now was to spook Gonzo into doing something rash.

James cleared his throat, hoping that Gonzalez would say something, or at least move. But all he did was breathe, his shoulders rising and falling.

"You've got a lot of us worried," James said. "Gonzo, there's a way out of this. Talk to me, man. Why don't you sit back in that seat? I'll stay over here, and we can talk."

Gonzalez didn't reply, but James caught a glimpse of slight movement. Gonzalez' strong shoulders seemed to relax a bit, and he slowly retracted his right hand from the screen. What he didn't do, however, was move back into the seat as James had asked. He still floated tensely at the edge of the flight chair.

James was encouraged, even though he wasn't sure what else to say. "Gonzo," he said softly. "We can still get back to Earth, all of us."

More silence.

"Hey, we can even do it without me getting stabbed again," James joked weakly.

Gonzalez didn't reply, but James watched as his shoulders started to tremble. For a split second, James thought he was laughing, but then Gonzalez tipped his head forward. His body shook slightly, and there was an audible sniffle. Gonzalez was *crying*.

It was only momentary. Gonzalez quickly seemed to relax a little bit. He moved his hand to wipe his eyes, sending a few floating droplets flying towards the wall of the command module. James relaxed the tight grip that he'd been holding on the scalpel, but kept it in his hand.

"I'm sorry for stabbing you," Gonzalez said flatly, his voice unnaturally calm for someone who was crying.

"Hurt like hell," James replied nervously. "How 'bout we agree not to do that again? We can skip the airlock part too."

"I ruined this shit," Gonzalez said, his voice taking on a bit of a growl. "This whole damn mission was supposed to be everything for me."

James opened his mouth to reply, but couldn't think of anything to say. Being quiet and slow, James peeked over Gonzalez' shoulder to try to see the state of the ship. He couldn't be sure, but he didn't think any more hatches had been opened yet. The others would still be alive. He had to keep buying Aaron time to override the systems so that reinforcements could make it.

"We landed on the damn red planet, and all anyone is going to remember is the shit that damn whore pulled," muttered Gonzalez, raising both hands and grabbing at his hair.

"Nikki," James acknowledged flatly.

"None of this was supposed to happen, James," Gonzalez said, turning around suddenly to look at James. His eyes were bloodshot, his face heavily wrinkled and whiskered. He ran a hand through his messy hair. "It wasn't supposed to happen," he repeated.

James nodded slowly from his spot behind the circle of seats. He was grateful that he had kept his knife low and hidden from sight.

"It was an accident," James said softly. "I get it. Tell me about it, and I can help you."

Gonzalez' expression didn't change as he analyzed James. It was all he could do just to hold his nerve.

"Estefani and I were struggling," Gonzalez finally said, his voice starting out flat and quiet. "But then she decided she was too good for me, halfway through this damn mission, James. Said she wanted a break. As if two damn years in deep-shit space weren't enough of a damn break!"

Gonzalez slammed a fist into one of the headrests, making the whole capsule shake. It took all he had for James not to flinch.

"Two weeks later my brother sees her with some *cabron* at a nightclub outside Dallas," seethed Gonzalez. "Practically having sex on the dance floor during the cumbia. Typical bitch, just like all the others. They'll open their legs for anyone if it makes 'em feel like a damn queen."

Gonzalez shook his head and let a huff of frustration out of his nose before continuing. "I'm no damn better, apparently," he said, giving a defeated shrug. "Neither was Nikki—slut cheated on her fiancé like my wife cheated on me. Hell, we're all the same. You, Mike, Jordyn... Even Aaron would pimp himself for the right price."

In a normal conversation, Gonzalez' words would have stung, but James just listened and watched hollowly as he tried to calculate his next move. He had to talk Gonzo down somehow. "Humans make mistakes," was all James could think to say. "And people like you get screwed over because of it."

"Damn right," snorted Gonzalez. "That's all we humans ever do. Screw each other, and screw each other over. We're no better than animals. I'm just an animal."

James just stared at Gonzalez, his mind racing as he tried to figure out how to respond.

Gonzalez ran another hand through his crazed hair. "Nikki wasn't supposed to die. I didn't mean it," he said.

James wanted to challenge Gonzalez—ask why he left her in the airlock to die, then watched as she was ejected—but he bit his tongue. "I believe you," he lied. "Gonzo, you can still make this right. We can just get back to Earth."

Gonzalez made an odd face. He looked almost shocked. His eyebrows pinched together in bewilderment, he made eye contact with James. The look in his dark eyes sent a shiver down James' spine.

"I can't bring her back," Gonzalez stated.

"No one else has to die," James responded, an unintentional quiver in his voice. He gripped his scalpel again. "Gonzo, why don't you sit back and let me reseal the hatches. No one else has to die—you don't have to die."

"We'll all die someday, James."

"I'd like to die after living a bit," answered James. "Come on, Gonzo. Just move away from your control panel, and I can do it. We'll all get back to Earth—together."

Gonzalez kept staring at James, who tried to maintain his gaze as well. Then, suddenly, Gonzo's flat glare broke. His lips split and curled in a smile. He let out an eerie, hollow, cold laugh.

"There's nothing left on Earth for me," he said, his shoulders bouncing as he laughed.

Gonzalez moved suddenly, spinning to face away from James—who reacted almost instantaneously. He gripped his scalpel and pulled himself through the air, barely clearing the seats, trying to reach Gonzalez before it was too late...

James was a half-second too slow.

In that split second, James watched as Gonzalez pressed an unknown button on the control screen in front of him. There was a mechanical noise from somewhere in the ship that was instantly drowned out as James collided with Gonzalez at full speed.

James led with his shoulder, and not the razor-sharp blade in his hand. The momentum carried both men straight into the array of electronic screens that made up the walls of the ship. James heard a loud crunching noise as he slammed Gonzalez face first into the largest of the screens, destroying it instantly.

Gonzalez fought back with inhuman strength. James was hit hard in the ribs by a sharp elbow, then right in the throat by another one. He swung out blindly with his knife, catching nothing but empty air as he tumbled weightlessly backwards.

James caught himself on the opposite wall, quickly spinning himself around for another dive towards Gonzalez. This time, his knife was up and ready—James had to stop him before he could kill anyone else.

Gonzalez was ready as well. He too held a scalpel in his hand as he crouched with his feet on the broken control panel. A droplet of blood floated out of his nose, which he wiped off with a hairy arm. "Come on James, give me your best!" he sneered.

There was a sudden clicking sound from up above where James floated. Both men looked up just in time to see the command module hatch close—the locking handles both clicking as they visibly twisted shut.

Once again, James hesitated. There were still plenty of working control screens all around the perimeter of the capsule—maybe he could still try to save his friends from here. Had Gonzo only closed the command module hatch, or were his friends suffocating at this very moment?

"COME ON!!!" shouted Gonzalez, pounding his chest with his free hand. "Fight to survive, like the animal you are!"

James shimmied to the side, grabbing the next handhold over while keeping his knife-wielding arm extended. He kicked off the wall—not diving towards Gonzo, but towards the other side of the capsule. The two men were closer now, both parrying their blades defensively as they began to move counterclockwise around the walls of the small command module.

"Come on, Gonzo!" yelled James. "Drop the knife! JUST DROP IT!!!"

Gonzalez dived towards James, his lips curled in a furious sneer as he rapidly closed the short distance between the two men and struck out with his knife. James jerked himself to the left, swinging his own knife outwards just as Gonzalez drove his into the padded Velcro wall right next to James' head. James felt his own knife connect shallowly just before he kicked off the wall and to the other side of the capsule.

Gonzalez looked down at his torn shirt and laughed. There was a thin streak of red on his exposed stomach but nothing more. "Is that the best you can do?" asked Gonzalez.

James kicked himself forward yet again, but grabbed a seat and altered his course to send himself upwards, towards the hatch and out of Gonzo's reach. He grabbed for one of the hatch's manual handles, but had to let go as Gonzo attacked again, swinging his blade wildly. James was just barely able to grab Gonzo's wrist before his scalpel was driven into his own neck—but by doing so, he left himself vulnerable.

Gonzalez jammed one of his socked feet straight into James' gut, right where the knife wound was. The pain was immense. For a brief second, James was completely unconscious to anything other than pain and the tight grip he still held on Gonzo's wrist.

There was another forceful kick from Gonzo. Stars of light filled James' eyes as his grip slipped. Another kick at James, then another. He was driven backwards, flying and hitting another control panel with his right elbow. The glass cracked instantly, cutting James.

James coughed painfully as he tried to orient himself. Gonzo just looked at him flatly, waiting for him to recover before he struck again.

"You kill us, you kill yourself!" cried James in agony.

Gonzalez looked at James without saying a word, scalpel still clutched in his left hand. He tilted his head to the side, then, unexpectedly, looked down at the unbroken control panel he had ended up next to. He was floating right above the pilot's chair, next to the joysticks and flight instruments.

"Gonzo," wheezed James. "Come on, we're friends. Please, stop this."

Gonzalez reached out and tapped the screen.

There were a loud series of bangs that reverberated throughout the entire Orion+ command module. James latched onto one of the handholds just as the capsule lurched strangely. The subtle movement was enough to make James instantly dizzy. Gonzalez laughed.

"Oh shit," swore James as he looked out one of the capsule's tiny windows. The stars were moving.

Gonzalez had undocked the command module from *Perseus*.

"No way out of this now," Gonzalez said calmly. "What's done is done." With that, Gonzalez grabbed hold of another handhold, then kicked one of the capsule's joysticks with his foot.

James propelled himself forward just as the command module lurched again. Liberated from the massive inertia of *Perseus*, the nimble command module rolled eagerly to the right. The whole module shifted around James mid-flight. Gonzo, who used to be right in front of James, swung downwards and out of reach.

James deftly stopped himself on the moving wall, kicking himself back towards Gonzalez. Gonzo replied by kicking the control stick again, altering the spin and making James slam painfully against the opposite wall of the capsule. He tried to push off again, but he couldn't quite do it. The walls were spinning faster now, and the centrifugal force was starting to shove James up against the wall like a spinning carnival ride. It was a strange form of gravity.

Gonzalez sniggered again. Things were starting to break and fly around the capsule now. A checklist held to the wall with Velcro flew off, striking James' arm. A zooming flashlight hit him painfully in the back.

James struggled to his knees, fighting the invisible force as if it were gravity holding him to the wall. Even Gonzalez was struggling now, but he just laughed where he was, pinned against the wall. James glanced at the joysticks, his mind struggling to understand where they were in three dimensions.

With every ounce of strength he had, James jumped off the wall and towards Gonzalez. He hung in space for a microsecond—and to James it seemed he was not strong enough. Suddenly, however, his body seemed to break free of the imperceptible force holding him, and he began falling towards where Gonzalez was. He coiled his arm and led with the scalpel, aiming for Gonzalez' chest.

Gonzalez reacted faster than the blink of an eye. He parried James' blow, deflecting his strike just enough to send the blade not into Gonzo's flesh, but straight into one of the capsule's exposed metal support beams. The scalpel ricocheted out of James' hand, vanishing in the spinning room.

For a moment, it seemed all was lost. James, completely disarmed, felt himself slam into the wall helplessly, right next to his adversary. By some stroke of dumb luck, however, his foot managed to graze the command module's control stick. The rapid spinning stopped suddenly as the ship's control thrusters fought to send it the other direction. Both men were thrown apart violently, suddenly weightless once more as the spinning decreased significantly.

James caught himself on one of the seven seats, barely hanging on as his body twisted from his momentum. Gonzalez floated on the opposite side of the capsule again, scalpel still glinting in his hands. The joysticks were now positioned to James' left, equidistant from both men.

"Dropped your knife," Gonzalez taunted. "You'd lose your head if it weren't attached to your body."

"You're psychotic," spat James.

"Nothing to live for, I guess," shrugged Gonzalez as he flourished his knife proudly. He pulled himself towards the joysticks. James, unarmed, had no choice but to move the opposite direction, keeping the seven seats between him and Nikki's killer.

"What am I thinking?" laughed Gonzalez darkly instead of moving the joysticks again. "Why don't we just end this now?"

Gonzalez came after James again, this time over the top of the seats entirely. Instead of retreating, however, James lunged forward. He reached his hand into the space between all the seats and blindly grabbed onto the first thing he touched.

Gonzalez jabbed his knife forward, going for a clean stab rather than a slash. James, his entire life reflected in the shiny knife in Gonzo's hand, jerked backwards, pulling whatever he had grasped behind him. It was the tiny, metal fire extinguisher.

Gonzalez' couldn't react in time. This time it was *his* blade that struck metal. The force of the blow reverberated through James' arm, and a glint of steel flashed through the air. Gonzalez had lost his knife now, too.

James acted fast. He rammed the heavy metal cylinder straight into Gonzalez' face with a thud, knocking him backwards towards one of the windows. Without pausing, James pulled the extinguisher's pin, pointed the nozzle towards Gonzo, and squeezed the handle. A forceful puff of white powder shot out, spraying Gonzalez completely and sending James flying backwards. The dry, white fire retardant filled the air, briefly blinding both men.

James hit the wall again, then used his strength to surge forward into the swirling cloud. He swung the extinguisher as hard as he could and connected solidly with Gonzo's defensive left arm. He could both feel and hear the crack of bone as Gonzalez screamed out in pain.

His adversary barely visible in the fog of extinguisher powder, James struck again, then again, then again, ramming the metal towards Gonzo with all the strength he could muster. Each blow did more damage, until, by some fluke, Gonzalez was able to lash out with his good arm, knocking the metal cylinder from James' hands and sending it flying away. James didn't stop, however. He grabbed Gonzalez, wrestling with him until he suddenly found himself on Gonzo's back, his right arm in the perfect position around Gonzo's neck. Using all his might, James pulled Gonzo into a choke hold, using his left arm to pull even tighter.

Gonzalez coughed and gagged as he fought and struggled against James. He struck out with his left elbow in spite of his broken arm, hitting James painfully near his stab wound. James inhaled sharply and fought to keep his tight grip. Gonzalez struck again, then again. James' vision narrowed—the pain was too great.

Gonzalez struck once more. The pain was equally debilitating, but James could tell that it came with less force. He held on, not breathing, just holding on. Gonzalez suddenly went limp.

James didn't let go—not yet. He could feel Gonzalez' pulse, feel his body struggle to breathe even though he was unconscious. There was a cold, medical voice in James' head that told him he could finish it now. Denying a few more breaths, squeezing just a little harder, and the threat would be eliminated forever. Nikki would be avenged, James would be safe for at least a little while longer, and Gonzo would pay for his crimes.

There was another voice in James' head, however. This one wasn't cold and calculating, but warm and reassuring. It yelled James' name, screaming for him to let mercy have its place next to justice. James had an odd moment of instant clarity. The capacity for mercy is what made him human.

James let go.

CHAPTER FORTY-FOUR

For a moment, everything was quiet.

There were, strangely, no alarms, no banging, no noises. With Gonzalez floating limply by his side, James quickly pulled his aching body up to one of the command module's small windows. The stars spun slowly as a result of the capsule's slight rotation, and James struggled to identify anything. There was no distant Mars, no speck of sunlight glinting off *Perseus'* solar panels. With all of the crazy maneuvering that just took place, he could be hundreds of miles away from the ship already.

A sharp stab of pain in his abdomen made James wince. The blood from his wound was seeping through his hastily-made bandage, and the duct tape he had used to secure it had lost its stickiness from his sweating and fighting. James worked to get his breathing under control, the stabbing pain turning back into a dull throb as he brought his heartrate down. He needed to get calm and start thinking—or he was going to die out here.

The command module had its own life support system, but it was much smaller than the enormous ones on board *Perseus.* Alone, without service module equipment for support, it was enough to sustain seven people for a little less than a week. That meant there was enough oxygen to supply two people with air for maybe three weeks—giving James a bigger problem. There was no food or water on board, just an unconscious, psychopathic murderer floating next to him.

Gonzo. James floated up to the body and put a finger on his neck to try to pick up a pulse. It was definitely there—though that didn't mean much. As a doctor, James knew just how dangerous and imprecise a choking could be. Gonzalez could wake up any second now, or he might never wake up. It was the former that had James the most concerned at the moment.

The first thing James went for was the knives. Both scalpels were floating around the cabin aimlessly, and the last thing he wanted was for Gonzalez to wake up and grab one. He put both knives in his pockets, then got to work looking for something to bind Nikki's killer with. Fortunately, James quickly found a roll of duct tape—NASA's go-to repair equipment—in the capsule's lone storage compartment.

It took a couple of minutes of struggling to bind Gonzalez' limp wrists and ankles together, and James didn't skimp on the tape. He bound the mission commander tightly, with tape going all the way from his wrists to his elbows—Gonzo's broken arm be damned—then maneuvered him into what used to be Mike's seat. James strapped Gonzo in tightly, pulling the straps down as hard as possible. Gonzalez' chest rose and fell, but he didn't stir. It would have to do.

"Now what?" James asked out loud. In the back of his mind, James knew he was facing almost certain death, but he wasn't going to quit. His last days weren't going to be spent drinking his own piss in space with a murderer. He had a brief mental image of Claire and their children, but he quickly wiped them from his mind. He didn't have time to get sentimental. He had to get focused.

James floated towards the pilot's seat, positioning himself in front of the control sticks and an impressive array of screens. Above him was one of the command module's tiny windows, this one etched with crosshairs for manual docking. There was nothing but spinning stars outside.

The screens were nearly all broken—not that James would have known how to truly use them anyway. He had sat in a simulator's pilot seat alone a time or two, just to know the basics of flight in case of an emergency like this one—but those simulations all had working instruments. At the moment,

James only recognized a single, tiny display, still working despite the web of cracks in the glass. It showed an image of a sphere, spinning slowly against a black backscreen. James didn't even remember what it was called, but he knew that it represented his orientation in space.

James looped one of the seatbelts over his shoulder as he contemplated the pilot's controls. He knew that the stick to his right controlled the capsule's reactive control system, and he thought he remembered how the different inputs would affect his orientation. He eyeballed the rotating sphere, figured he was rolling right—clockwise—and prepared to try to cancel out the rotation. Hoping he was right, James flicked his wrist ever so slightly to the left.

He was right. The ship's clockwise roll slowed a bit, though it seemed to James that he had unintentionally added some forward pitch to the craft as well. Careful not to overreact, James made another quick movement with the joystick.

An alarm sounded in the cockpit. This one wasn't particularly loud or threatening, but it was enough to make his heart skip a beat. *"CAUTION,"* the computer's audible alarm chanted. *"RCS FUEL FIVE PERCENT."*

James reached over towards another small working screen and disabled the alarm. Five percent? Had Gonzalez really used that much fuel in the struggle? James knew there wasn't much fuel on board the command module to begin with—it really only had enough to slow its velocity so it'd drop into Earth's atmosphere once the crew had gotten home. Still, five percent meant nothing to James without context. Was that enough for five more maneuvers? Ten? Would it be enough to push himself back towards *Perseus*, wherever it was?

James swallowed, his mouth suddenly quite dry, and made another adjustment with the joystick. This time, he succeeded in almost cancelling out the roll entirely, though there was still a hint of a flat spin to the left. It would have to be good enough for now. He needed to find *Perseus*, and pray he had enough fuel left to make it back somehow. But how?

There had to be some sort of radar on board, some sort of electronic beacon or navigation. James set out to examine each and every working screen left in the capsule, hoping and praying he'd find something that he'd recognize. He didn't. Most of them were broken—shattered from the fight. NASA had never imagined that these screens would be physically destroyed— and there were hardly any analog buttons or controls. There were the flight sticks, the radio controls, the handles to the main hatch and door...

The radio! James pulled himself towards the communication controls, found the right frequency, then pressed the broadcast button. *"Dove* to *Perseus,"* James called, using the command module's name. "This is James, can anyone hear me?"

There was no reply. It didn't surprise James—*Perseus'* communications had been down for a couple of days now, and James wasn't really expecting them to work now—even the short-range radio. Still, he tried again. He changed to the backup frequency and transmitted again. Once more, he received no response.

James gave up for now. The radio was still an option later, but he had more pressing matters. The command module was drifting further and further away from the rest of the ship—wherever it was—and he needed to keep his priorities straight.

Abandoning the radio controls, James floated to the small porthole window inside the capsule's main hatch. This hatch wasn't the one used to dock to *Perseus*—it was the one that the crew had entered over a year ago when they had blasted off from Cape Canaveral. He stuck his face up right next to the glass and squinted outwards, trying to find the needle of *Perseus* against the hay of millions of stars. There was nothing.

A small kernel of desperation took hold in James' heart—taking hold as the adrenaline rush of the knife fight wore off. He had to figure this out. He just had to.

There was one more window on the opposite side of the capsule. James pushed himself towards it, flying just over Gonzalez—who stirred in his forced sleep. It both pleased James and panicked him—Gonzo was going to wake up, and soon. Before completing his mini-flight to the next window, James paused and put a patch of duct tape over Gonzalez' mouth.

Upon reaching the other window, James again stuck his face right up next to the glass. From here he could actually see Mars—now looking smaller than Earth's moon did from Earth—but there was no way to determine his orientation relative to the planet, nor did it help him locate *Perseus*. Another icy drop of fear fell into James' chest. What if *Perseus* wasn't even there anymore? What if Gonzalez had somehow destroyed the ship? What if he was the only one left?

This time, James struggled to fight off the building terror. It might have consumed him, if it weren't for the muffled grunts that started coming from Gonzalez as he awoke.

"Shut the hell up!" yelled James, nervously checking over his shoulder to make sure the mission commander wasn't able to escape his bindings somehow.

James had to find *Perseus*. He was running out of time. He returned to the pilot's seat and used the joystick again, hearing the fuel alarm yet again. He shifted and stabilized the capsule's position just enough to get a new view from the three windows, and tried looking out of them again. Nothing. James returned to the seat and moved the ship again. Nothing.

"Come on, dammit!" cursed James as he moved back towards the pilot's seat once more. Another grunt came from Gonzalez' direction.

He couldn't give up. James reached for the joystick, lightly tapping it to the left. The ship, however, reacted strangely. Instead of adjusting smoothly, it jerked into another slow spin. James instinctively moved the stick in the opposite direction to cancel out the momentum, but it didn't respond.

The command module was out of fuel.

For the very first time since this mission began, since Nikki's death, since he had almost died on Mars, James felt completely, utterly, totally defeated. Not just terrified, but defeated. There'd be no getting home now, no seeing Claire or his kids again. He'd drift in his spaceship until he died, never to return to Earth.

Gonzalez grunted again, but James just ignored it. A brief thought snuck into his mind—a temptation to just open a hatch now and end things quickly rather than slowly and painfully. James crushed the thought immediately. Claire would be ashamed of him. No, he'd have that mental debate later, when things got worse.

There was nothing James could really do at that moment—nothing but wait. Curiously, that thought seemed to calm him. He had a sudden moment of clarity.

James pulled himself towards the window on the other side of the ship—opposite Gonzalez' bound body—taking a moment to savor the ease of moving in weightlessness. He was truly weightless now—caught in the space between planets, floating through the void. One of the light panels was right next to the window—it was one of the few unbroken screens left. James reached out a finger and turned off the interior lights, ignoring Gonzo's noises, then pulled himself close to the window again.

There were millions upon millions of stars. With the weak sun on the opposite side of the command module, James could see more than he had ever taken the time to see before. Pinpricks of light—some white, some yellow, some blue. James knew that some weren't stars, but distant galaxies—vast nebulas containing trillions of stars and planets—somehow compressed into a single tiny light source.

James marveled at the magnitude of it all. He felt drawn to the stars, just like mankind had always been. They were oases in the middle of the empty desert of space—evidence of God's power for some, evidence of His absence for others. James was just happy to be a part of it all, even for a moment. His heart swelled with joy.

It all hit James again, all at once. His predicament, his family he'd never see again—It all collapsed on James' stomach, like a black hole collapsing in the center of a galaxy. Maybe he could broadcast something again and hope his last words somehow made it back to Houston—and Claire. Maybe...

Dark thoughts enveloped James again. Maybe he could disengage the CO_2 filters and just sort of fall asleep once things got too rough. Yeah, that would be an easier way to go. Maybe he could...no. He had to stop thinking like this. But there was no hope. James was coming face to face with his own mortality. James was going to die.

As James' mind darkened, so to—it seemed—did his surroundings. The interior of the module dimmed as James floated into a corner, arms clasped around his stomach. He was feeling nauseous, his body and mind fighting over whether James should vomit and tremble, or start to sob uncontrollably. A part of him begged him not to give up hope, but that part was losing.

A sharp, metallic clang suddenly rang through the capsule. Ripping James from his self-pity and into full consciousness. He didn't even have time to respond before his metal lifeboat jerked suddenly—but not wildly. In a panic, James latched onto the nearest handhold and swung his head around. Was it Gonzalez? Had he escaped?

There was another banging noise. James winced and waited for some sort of explosion that never came. It wasn't Gonzalez—he was still in his seat, swinging his head around wildly as he tried to grunt through the tape covering his mouth.

Another bang, followed by the shrill sound of squeaking metal. James took a final breath. And then...

*BANG...BANG...BANG...*went the metal hatch at the roof of the capsule. *BANG...BANG...BANG...*

It was knocking.

James couldn't believe it. This wasn't possible.

BANG...**BANG**...**BANG**...louder this time.

James weakly pulled himself towards the metal hatch at the top of the command module. He put his hands on the cold metal and felt the vibrations of another series of pounding.

Without caring about the potential consequences, James grabbed the manual release handles and twisted them sharply to disengage the sealed hatch. He winced, waiting for some sort of instant pain from depressurization, but it never came.

The hatch opened inwards, and the inside of the dark module was again flooded with light. James squinted upwards.

"I don't normally pick up hitchhikers," a voice said. "But I'll make an exception for you."

It was Jordyn.

CHAPTER FORTY-FIVE

Docking two spacecraft in flight was like a delicate dance. For every action, there was a reaction—for every adjustment towards center, a slight creep in the wrong direction. For one reason or another, James was reminded of his marriage with Claire. Two separate entities, fighting their own inertia to simply join together as one.

The outcome was never in doubt. Jordyn flew the MAV straight and true, connecting almost effortlessly with the docking port on *Perseus'* forward node. There was a slight bump, then the sound of the metal docking linkage engaging, then a cheerful chirp from the MAV's computer.

"With eleven-percent to spare," Jordyn muttered, patting the ship approvingly with her good arm.

James put a hand over his wounded stomach and exhaled, relieved that he was finally safe.

"You sure you're alright?" asked Aaron from the seat next to James as he unbuckled his harness. "You look...well, you look like hell James."

"That bad, huh?" James remarked weakly as he undid his own harness. "Yeah, I'll be alright. I just need an aspirin or two. A beer would be nice, too. Jordyn? How you holding up?"

"I'd be a lot better if this asshole hadn't stabbed me," she said angrily, glancing back over her shoulder.

James looked back too. Gonzalez just stared back at him, his eyes cold and glassy looking. There was no remorse there—no feeling. If it wasn't for the rising and falling of his shoulders he would have looked dead.

"I still think we should have left him in the command module," Jordyn said bitterly, starting to unclasp her straps with her favored arm. James broke eye contact with Gonzalez and moved to help her.

"I'm fine," she said quickly, waving his hand away. "I mean it, James."

James wouldn't be denied. He finished undoing Jordyn's straps, then helped get them off her shoulders.

"James," she chided.

"Thank you," interrupted James, putting a hand on Jordyn's good shoulder. "Thank you. You saved my life."

"Hey, I was at least along for the ride," joked Aaron.

James hadn't forgotten. He grabbed Aaron's hand, clasping it tightly. "Thank you, too," James said, his voice croaking slightly. "I thought I was a goner."

"We *all* almost were," Jordyn said quickly. "*Perseus* was about to depressurize and break itself apart before the command module was released. With it gone, Aaron was finally able to hack the controls and get everything stabilized."

"It was nothing," Aaron said sheepishly as he released James' hand. "Honestly, we're lucky *Perseus* was built so tough. Besides, Jordyn is the one that had the idea to use the MAV to come get you. We're just lucky it still had enough fuel."

Jordyn huffed. "Maybe if we had a little less we would have had an excuse to leave this idiot in the command module," she repeated, giving the middle finger to Gonzalez without looking back. "He'd still be floating out there."

Jordyn was right. With no fuel left in the command module, the crew was forced to leave it in empty space after picking up James and Gonzalez—otherwise the MAV wouldn't have been able to make it back and dock with *Perseus*. It would float emptily in space for eons.

James grimaced, avoiding looking back to Gonzalez again. Part of him wished they *had* left him, but none of the crew could bring themselves to do it. None of them were murderers.

Pressure equalized, chirped the computer.

"I got it," Aaron said, moving to open the hatch.

James was fine with letting him do the work. His own blood-stained hands were still trembling. Jordyn noticed him looking at them and put a hand on his arm.

"Hey, you did it," she said reassuringly. "It's done."

"Yeah," replied James weakly, his hands still shaking. He didn't feel like it was done.

The hatch's locking mechanism clicked open, and the door swung away almost instantly. Harrison and Mike were already there, smiles plastered on their faces.

"You did it!" exclaimed Harrison as Mike clapped his hands together for joy. "You did it, you did it, you did it! You got him!"

"Thank God!" Mike shouted joyfully.

James smiled somberly, pulling himself from the MAV and into *Perseus'* front node. "It was either him or me," he explained feebly.

"Not *you* getting *Gonzo*," explained Harrison. "Jordyn getting you! The MAV was never meant for something like that, ever. That was some incredible flying."

"Thanks," James and Jordyn replied simultaneously. One sounded pleased, the other sarcastic.

385

Mike was next in line to offer his congratulations. He quickly swooped in to hug James, who managed not to wince too much as his abdomen was squeezed. "I'm so sorry," Mike said quickly. "I'm so sorry I didn't trust you."

"It's ok," chuckled James. "I didn't trust you either until Gonzo put a knife in my stomach, so there's that."

The crew laughed nervously, but the fear was starting to break. Mike hugged Jordyn, and Harrison gingerly embraced James. Everyone exchanged smiles and hugs in the forward node until Aaron cleared his throat.

"Um, guys?" he said softly. "What do we do with him?"

The entire crew looked through the MAV's hatch, back where Gonzalez was still strapped into his seat. He glared back.

"We can eject him from the airlock," deadpanned Jordyn.

There was a chorus of sniffed amusement from the crew. James, however, only sighed.

"It's a long way back home," he said. "We've got a lot to worry about. We don't even have a command module to get back to Earth in."

"We still don't have radio comms either," remarked Harrison. "But look, can't we just put him away for now? We can talk about this in a bit. I don't like him staring at us."

"Let's do it," agreed Aaron. "Mike, help me out. Let's get him into his sleeping compartment. Harrison, make sure there's nothing in his room—not even a sleeping bag."

Harrison zipped off, leaving Jordyn and James to observe as Aaron and Mike reentered the MAV. James tensed up where he floated, expecting Gonzalez to struggle, but he didn't. Aaron and Mike unstrapped him from his seat, and floated the murderous mission commander into Perseus, his arms and legs still bound with the duct tape James had applied.

The entire crew escorted Gonzalez to his sleeping compartment—just feet away from the stickered door to Nikki's old compartment. Harrison applied another layer of duct tape to Gonzalez' wrists and ankles, then paused.

"Should we take the tape off his mouth?" he asked.

James looked at Gonzalez. Then, almost against his own will, he reached out and grabbed a loose corner of the grey tape. He peeled it off slowly, tearing out several of the mission commander's whiskers.

"Anything to say for yourself?" asked James.

Gonzalez kept his mouth tightly shut. His eyes were still dull.

"Put him away," said Jordyn.

Aaron pushed Gonzalez into the compartment. He checked one last time to make sure there was nothing in there that could be used to escape, then slid the accordion door closed until it clicked shut.

There was a collective exhalation from the crew.

"What now?" asked Mike.

The five remaining member of the Ares I crew looked at each other for a moment, unsure of what to say. Finally, Jordyn—now the officer in charge of the ship—cleared her throat.

"We need to talk," she said. "Everybody up to the galley."

The other members of the crew nodded their agreement, each in turn pulling themselves upwards and out of the sleeping module. James, however, caught Jordyn's attention. "Can I go wash my hands?" he asked, lifting up his still-shaky hands.

"Of course," Jordyn replied kindly.

James followed her out of the sleeping module, not bothering to look back towards where Gonzalez was detained. Instead of stopping in the galley with the others, James pulled himself backwards, towards the restroom module.

"He'll be right back," he heard Jordyn say. "He just needs a minute or two."

Perseus looked almost the same as always to James as he pulled himself back. The lights were all on, and the hum of the life support system and electronics was as constant and strong as ever. There were still signs of what had happened, however. Little droplets of blood still floated near the DNA sequencer, though most had beaded up against the walls of the lab.

More imposing, however, was the black bag that was still strapped to the module's surgical table. James stopped himself, pausing to place a hand on the black plastic. It crinkled inwards until James' fingers found the flesh of Nikki's arm. He didn't recoil, however. Not this time.

"I got him, Nikki," James whispered, giving Nikki's arm a quick squeeze.

CHAPTER FORTY-SIX

James turned on the sink hose and gathered a large, bulbous blob of weightless water in his hands. He held it there for a moment, watching it jiggle as he shook and trembled. It reflected the crimson from his stained fingers. It looked like a giant ball of blood.

James added some soap and got scrubbing. He scrubbed his weathered hands, getting the cracks of his knuckles and under his fingernails, then toweled them off. There was still blood. He repeated the process.

It took several rounds of soaping, scrubbing, and toweling, but finally, James was clean. He sucked the floating water droplets from the air with the suction hose, then paused to look in the mirror. He looked haggard and weary—but something was different. His eyes—bloodshot and wide—were missing something. They were missing the look of fear that they'd carried for months.

It was time to return to the galley, but James had one more thing he needed to do. He left the restroom, glanced back towards the airlock, then proceeded into the auxiliary lab. He grabbed suturing tools, disinfecting wipes, and everything else he would need to take care of both his wound and Jordyn's. Satisfied that he had enough, he floated his way back towards the galley.

"I think I'm close to getting comms back, but I'm not sure," Aaron was saying. "And yeah, we could be off course too. That's not mentioning the lack of a command module."

"But the ship's integrity is intact," nodded Jordyn. "That's what's most important. We'll work the problem from there. Besides, we have…"

The crew quieted suddenly as James entered. Harrison looked at him concernedly.

"You alright, James?" asked Harrison. "You look like you've seen a ghost."

James forced a smile as he floated next to Jordyn, clearly signaling his intentions to begin cleaning and stitching her wound. "I honestly feel like I'm the ghost," he said. "But I'm ok. Can I get some water or something?"

"I'd offer you a beer," shrugged Mike. "But people like Aaron make it so NASA doesn't send proper alcohol on these trips."

"It's not just Mormons," said Aaron as he floated to retrieve a water bag. "Muslims don't drink either, you know."

"Yeah but there're no Muslims on board, are there?" joked Mike.

"There's also no alcohol," Aaron shot back.

The crew laughed genuinely for the first time in a while—including James. He felt himself smile—a feeling that had almost become foreign to him—as he put a water bag to his lips. He swallowed it down gratefully, not taking the liquid—or the smile—for granted.

"Can you imagine if Houston could see us now?" laughed Harrison. "They'd think we were nuts."

"They're probably *going* nuts," James said as he opened a disinfecting wipe and prepared to clean Jordyn's injury. "They're probably in a total panic."

"Let them panic," remarked Mike. "We've been doing all the work anyways."

"Seriously," sniffed Jordyn. "After all we've been through, it's nice to-GAH!"

"Sorry," apologized James as he quickly finished sanitizing Jordyn's wound and got busy applying more topical anesthetic.

Jordyn just gritted her teeth and pressed forward in conversation to distract herself. "What I'm curious about is what they're going to have us do with Gonzo," she said. "I still think we should make the decision without them."

"You've made your point abundantly clear," laughed Aaron. "We all know what you think."

"Hey, I think it'd save the taxpayers a lot of money," Harrison joked, rubbing his jaw in mock thought. "We airlock him, and no one needs to pay for a stupid trial. We have a pretty good jury right here."

"Mission control is in Houston anyways," remarked Mike. "If he gets put on trial in Texas, he'll probably get the firing squad, no joke."

James couldn't help but grin at the grim humor, even as he prepared the suture he was about to use on Jordyn's arm. She was still bleeding, and he needed to get her wound shut. He put the needle next to where he'd begin, but paused for just a moment. His hands were no longer shaking.

"I'm just saying," Jordyn grunted as James began, talking her way through the pain as she avoided watching the stitching. "I swear I remember reading somewhere that ship captains could hold court on their ships in international water."

"Nah, that's just weddings," joked James. "Besides. I just went through all the trouble of detaining him instead of killing him. We don't want to waste that."

"It wouldn't be right anyways," admitted Aaron. "I mean, we're an American-flagged ship, right? He has the right to a proper trial...in America. I guess."

"We could try to land in Russia," suggested Harrison.

James grinned again as he finished stitching Jordyn's stab wound. He cut the thread and applied a fresh bandage as the crew kept talking. He'd have to clean out his own wound, then attend to Gonzalez' broken arm, but that could wait. For just a moment he wanted to relax.

"We could feed him nothing but the plain, freeze-dried spinach rations," joked Mike. "We can split up all his dessert rations."

"What we feed him doesn't matter," Jordyn said. "I'm more worried about where we keep him. We can make the airlock a brig, leave him in there the next time we have to do maintenance. We could even..."

James closed his eyes and grinned as he floated gently in zero gravity—but not at his crewmates' humor. No, their voices had already faded away to the background of his consciousness. His mind was already far away from his friends, Gonzalez, and the cramped interior of *Perseus* itself. James' thoughts were already on planet Earth, with his beautiful wife Claire and his two children.

James smiled broadly to himself. It was going to be a long trip back to Earth, but he was going to make it.

He was going to make it home.

EPILOGUE

In many ways, it was fitting that the Ares I mission's end was postponed by a sudden change in Hurricane Miguel's path. For the crew of Perseus, their two years in space had been a whirlwind of adventure, of danger, and of tragedy. From the powerful launch of the most powerful rocket ever built in human history, to the first proud steps of humankind on the surface of the red planet, to the tragic death of one of their own at the hands of a man who was their friend, the Ares crew had been swung to and fro by their bizarre circumstances.

At long last, the Sparrow capsule, constructed by a private company and hastily modified for a rescue mission in Earth's orbit—all in a matter of months—plunged into the atmosphere. It endured temperatures of over three thousand degrees Fahrenheit as it carved through the Earth's surrounding layer of nitrogen, oxygen, and carbon dioxide. Finally, three enormous parachutes blossomed like a rose, slowing the capsule for a gentle descent into the still-churning oceans of the eastern Caribbean.

The crew remained inside, obediently awaiting the tell-tale knock of a US Navy rescue diver. After two years in space, the last thing they wanted to do was fall in the water alone, left to fight against gravity and the rolling ocean. Even more pressing than that, however, was the fact that their craft contained delicate human remains, and a tightly-bound killer.

Commander Alejandro Gonzalez was the first to emerge, squinting into the sunlight as his duct-tape handcuffs were replaced by ones of steel. "His eyes were hollow," said 2nd Lieutenant Cameron Perry, the first rescue diver to reach the capsule. "He was compliant, but he didn't say much. It was creepy."

One can only imagine how the rest of the crew must have felt during the nine months between their apprehension of Gonzalez and their arrival back on Earth. Using nothing more than duct tape and wire, the five remaining crewmembers had kept their murderous commander isolated in his tiny sleeping compartment, under 24-hour watch.

"It was damn awful," Harrison Larsen said in the crew's first press conference back on Earth. "He even tried to talk to us like normal, but how do you come back from what happened? You can't."

And the jurors of the US District Court in Houston agreed. Gonzalez was convicted of 2nd degree murder, with a sentence of 45 years in prison—essentially a life sentence. While a step towards closure for the family of Nicole Prince, it was really just the beginning of...

"James?" a voice asked. "Doctor Lake?"

James squinted against the bright lights on the stage. They nearly blinded him, but not enough to hide the enormous crowd of people in the auditorium from view. He swallowed hard, his throat dry.

"I'm sorry?" asked James, who had been caught reminiscing. "I missed that."

"No problem," the British host replied graciously. "I was simply curious, could you describe just how mixed your feelings are? I mean, you're certainly very proud to have played such a role—both in reaching Mars, and in apprehending Mr. Gonzalez. But obviously, your feelings aren't so simple."

James reached for the water bottle on the small table next to his padded chair, taking a slow drink as he collected his thoughts. "That's a pretty loaded question," he smiled, laughing nervously. The large audience laughed with him.

James paused before responding, still disliking the sound of his amplified voice in front of all these people. There were way more people than he was expecting—way more people than even the documentary directors expected. Perhaps it was the result of Gonzalez finally being sentenced just two months prior. Perhaps it was because of the successful Mars landing of Ares II just two weeks ago—a crew that included a British astronaut who used to live a half hour away from the auditorium in which James now sat.

"I apologize," the host added, adjusting how her legs were crossed. "I'm afraid that really was a tough one."

"Of course I'm torn," James said finally. "On the one hand, I'm just proud to have been part of something bigger than myself, you know? For a moment, I felt like I represented myself, my family, my own country. In a way, I feel like I represented Britain and the whole world, really."

There was a smattering of applause, and even a whoop from someone in the crowd.

James paused before continuing. "But my friend died," he said somberly— it still ached after all this time. "She was killed by another friend, someone I trusted. I think that's what hurts the most, right? Having trust ripped out from under me like that. I think that callouses a person if they don't have the support they need. I'm just lucky to have such good colleagues—friends. And an amazing family."

The host nodded. "So, was it all worth it?"

The question caught James slightly off guard. He had never had one like it, not in the literally hundreds of interviews he'd had in the past five years. He'd been asked about Gonzo, about Nikki, about his feelings. But never had he been asked if it was "worth it."

"I, uh," he hesitated. "Now *that's* a hard question."

A few people in the audience laughed. The host smiled kindly.

"I can answer that," a voice said. "If that's ok?"

"Mrs. Marx," prompted the host.

Jordyn smiled from her seat between James and Harrison. "It was absolutely worth it," she said, sounding confident and comfortable in spite of the crowd. "Obviously, it hurts. There was evil that took place. Evil. But that's how humanity is, you know? We're a species of contrasts—but it's our ability to choose that makes us special. The capacity to choose the better angels of our nature."

"Something you all clearly did," nodded the host.

"Don't give us too much credit," joked Harrison. The crowd chuckled again.

"Look, everything great has this contrast," expounded Jordyn. "I mean, Columbus discovered the new world. He was nearly a hero. But he was more than flawed. He enslaved, he killed. The American founders had a similar dichotomy, just like the men who wrote the Magna Carta here. In the end, however, look at the good that's come. It sounds strange, I know, but I think that in a really weird way, it fits. It fits that mankind's—and womankind's— first journey to another world followed a similar theme."

"A messy step towards a bright future," summarized the host.

"That's a good way to put it," agreed Jordyn.

"And unfortunately, it also looks like it's a good sentiment to end on as well," stated the host. "But on behalf of everyone here, including myself, I want to thank the five of you—Major Jordyn Marx, Doctor James Lake, Mr. Aaron Samuelson, Mr. Michael Syracuse, and Mr. Harrison Larsen, for being here."

"Thank you for having us," answered Aaron. "And thanks for such a great crowd."

The host nodded emphatically. "Yes, thanks to such a great audience. We're so glad you came to watch this premier of 'In the Void,' and we hope you'll travel home safely—a wish we extend to the Ares II crew currently on Mars. Goodnight to all!"

The audience arose in thunderous applause. James and his crewmates stood politely, acknowledging the ovation that none of them really wanted anyway. Finally, after what James felt like was far too long, the stage lights dimmed, and a suit-clad usher came to escort them back into the waiting room.

"That was enormous," exclaimed Aaron as they entered the tiny waiting room. "Way too many people. I don't know how you seemed so collected, James. I'm so glad you're always the one to field all the questions."

"You did fine too, A," Mike said, clapping his friend on the back. "Better than fine. Were you able to spot your fiancé in the crowd?"

"No," mumbled Aaron, reaching to check his phone. He looked at the screen for a moment, his face lighting up. "Haley said she saw me though, so that's good."

"You don't deserve her," Mike teased good-naturedly.

"Do I get to finally meet her in person?" asked Harrison. "More importantly, does she have sisters?"

"Mormon sisters," Aaron replied mischievously.

"The forbidden fruit," sighed Harrison. "Tempting in so many ways. Not to sound creepy, but if they look like Haley then I might just have to convert."

"I'll hold you to it," joked Aaron. Everyone laughed.

The five friends waited in the room for a few minutes, allowing the crowd to clear. The host and the documentary director came in and thanked them all once more for their participation, then a handful of local VIPs and government leaders were allowed in to voice their thanks. It was nearly an hour before they had the waiting room back to themselves.

"Well boys," sighed Jordyn as she stifled a yawn. "I need to catch an earlier flight, so I can't make it to dinner tonight. But don't forget that you're all invited to our place on the fifteenth of next month for the six-year reunion.

You might want to book a hotel, because we're going to drive out to Nikki's memorial the next morning. Oh, and nobody put Aaron in charge of drinks again. I'm begging you."

"It's *your* fault for putting me in charge of it last time," Aaron said defensively.

"*I've* got drinks," reassured Mike as he stifled a laugh at his friend's expense. "Heaven knows that since my divorce I can sure afford it."

"I'm still sorry about that," said Harrison.

"Don't be," waved Mike. "Honestly, I needed a chance to really find myself. Anyways, I wouldn't miss time with you guys for the world. Come on, Jordyn. You sure you can't stay and fly home with us? You're really that sick of us?"

Jordyn smiled. "It's just that I suspect Derek is already getting a little overwhelmed," she said with a small smile.

"It's what you get for having twins," teased James.

"Ha, ha," Jordyn said. "Very funny. For that, *you* get to walk me out to wait for a taxi. Be a gentleman and grab an umbrella, James."

"Please don't kill him," Harrison pleaded mockingly. "It was just a joke, Jordyn. Let him live!"

"I'll be right back," James smiled as Aaron tossed him his umbrella to borrow. "I can fend for myself, remember?" His friends grinned.

James led the way out the door, holding the umbrella above Jordyn as they stepped out into the rainy night. The street outside the auditorium was still plenty busy, and the bright headlights from the cars glinted on the raindrops as they fell. Jordyn tried to hail the first taxi that passed, but it was occupied.

"We really ought to do stuff with everyone *twice* a year," James said. "It's odd, I was sure I'd hate all of you after being crammed in that ship."

"Speak for yourself—*I* still hate all of you," joked Jordyn. She smiled at James as she quickly adjusted her long, elegant dress. The scar from where Gonzalez sliced her was still visible on her arm's dark skin.

"Fair enough," James laughed.

"Nah, I actually agree with you," said Jordyn. "It's always good when we get everyone together—I really look forward to it every year. We can talk about it."

Another taxi passed by. This time, James was able to hail it. It screeched to a stop by the curb, and the driver inside opened the door.

"We're still on for next week, right?" asked Jordyn. "Derek and I found a killer Mexican place we wanted to show you two."

"Wouldn't miss it," replied James. "And we're doing dessert for the reunion too, right?"

Jordyn nodded. She took a step towards James and pulled him into an embrace. "Say hi to Claire and the kids for me," Jordyn said. "Man, I'm just glad you guys live close by. Travel safe."

"You too," answered James, squeezing his friend back.

With that, Jordyn gave James a friendly kiss on the cheek and climbed into the taxi. "Heathrow," James heard her say as she closed the door.

James watched as the taxi sped off into the night. He was about to turn around and head back inside when another car—an exotic luxury car—pulled up to the curb right next to where he was. The driver revved the hybrid engine, then rolled down the window.

"Hey, are you James Lake, the famous astronaut?" a beautiful woman in a cocktail dress asked. The curled hair that flowed over her bare shoulders was halfway between blonde and brown.

James laughed. "You're the only person I know willing to spring for the sport package on a rental car," he replied.

Claire just grinned. "Why get some boring sedan with autopilot when you can drive something fun?" she asked. "Hurry up and hop in."

"Yeah, let me just return the umbrella."

James quickly stepped back to the entrance and tossed the umbrella back towards Aaron. "I'll see you at the restaurant," he said quickly to his friends before jogging back towards Claire. He almost opened the wrong door before remembering that the passenger's seat was on the driver's side here.

"Hey babe," Claire smiled as he climbed in and wiped the rain from his face. "You really did great in there."

The two kissed deeply, still not taking their time together for granted. Somebody behind them honked their horn.

"Alright, alright," Claire said, pulling back and putting the car into gear. She pulled out into traffic, the wipers struggling to keep up with the rain on the windshield.

"Jordyn and Derek are still good for this weekend," James said absentmindedly as he watched the rain streaking down his window. "We're still good too, right?"

Claire nodded, not saying anything for a moment. James turned to her and squeezed her thigh playfully.

"Hey, what's on your mind?" he asked.

Claire kept her eyes on the road, not replying right away. "I think it was worth it," she said finally.

James groaned. "That damn question sucked," he replied. "I swear, every time I get interviewed the questions get harder and harder. I almost wish nobody knew me."

"Really, though," reaffirmed Claire. "I'm glad you left. You did something that mattered. It made us stronger."

"And the book sales pay for a yearly vacation," joked James.

"Fair enough," laughed Claire. Her expression, however, quickly turned pensive. "You think the kids are going to be disappointed?" she asked.

James sighed. "I know Carter was excited to see Hawaii, but I'm not sure Jane is old enough to really be sad about it."

"You still feel okay going forward with something like this?"

"In-vitro?" asked James. "Of course! I want number three as bad as you do. I just feel bad. I feel like it's my fault we haven't had any luck."

"It's not for lack of trying," remarked Claire mischievously.

"Seriously though," James said somberly. "It's got to be the radiation from my time in space. What else could it be? As if almost getting killed in space wasn't bad enough."

"Stop blaming yourself," Claire said. "I'm just glad you came home to me. That's enough. I promise."

James grimaced silently, looking straight ahead through the windshield. "Maybe we could make it work," he said distractedly. "Maybe I can talk with the insurance guy again. If we adjust the monthly payment, maybe we could squeeze the trip in, too."

"It's ok," Claire said quickly. "Don't worry about it, really. I'm not disappointed, and the kids will be fine. There's always next Thanksgiving. Really though, maybe you shouldn't worry about this so much."

"It's my job to worry," persisted James. "Money's tight, but it's not so bad. Really, maybe we could make both work. In-vitro and the vacation. Maybe I can put more hours in—NASA's been desperate for more consulting since Ares V was approved."

"James, I really think you shouldn't worry about it."

"This is selfish, but what if just you and I went?" asked James. "Save money by not bringing the kids. We could certainly use it."

"James," chided Claire.

"I know, I know. That's really selfish. I'm sorry. Maybe I just like seeing you in a bikini, have you thought of that?"

Claire just laughed.

"Oh, come on," James said. "It's not such a bad idea, is it?"

Claire grinned at James, her eyes sparkling as she glanced his way. "I really just don't think you need to worry about it," she said. "Not about the money, or the vacation. I actually don't think you need to worry about in-vitro either."

"Wish I was paid better," grunted James. "You'd think having been to Mars I'd-"

"James!" Claire exclaimed. "My gosh, how obvious do I need to be? You solved a murder in space, but you're clueless."

"What are you talking about?"

"I've missed," Claire said abruptly.

"Missed what?" asked James. "The turn? That's why you should've gotten autopilot. Look, the GPS says-"

"I missed this month!" Claire repeated loudly. "I'm sorry I didn't tell you earlier, but you were gone for that space research symposium that you were so excited for, and I knew you were going to lecture. I didn't want to wor-"

"Wait, wait, wait," James interrupted, shaking his head. He looked at his lovely wife, her words dancing around in his head. "Wait, *what* did you miss this month?"

Claire smiled incredulously. She took a hand off the wheel and gestured exaggeratedly towards her lap.

"Are you telling me you missed your period?" James asked, his voice quivering. "Is that what you're saying?"

Claire grinned mischievously at James, her blue-grey eyes twinkling as her smile spread. "That's right, *Doctor*," she answered. "What's my prognosis?"

ACKNOWLEDGEMENTS

A special thank you to all the people who made this book possible. I'm particularly grateful to my wonderful, patient wife Haley for her constant support and encouragement. Thanks are also due to my parents, siblings, friends, and extended family members who kindly relented to my constant pleas to read my book and provide honest feedback. And of course, a huge shout out to Jill, my de-facto alpha AND beta reader.

Finally, I also need to thank you, Dear Reader. Thank you for taking the time to read my work. If you have enjoyed Red Sky at Morning, I'd like to ask a favor. As is always the case with modern, online publishing, I am totally dependent on word of mouth for advertising and future exposure. **Please consider leaving a review for my book on whatever site you purchased it from, and don't hesitate to let your friends know about Red Sky at Morning.**

ABOUT THE AUTHOR

An aficionado of space, flight, international politics, and all things seafood, Konner has been writing since 2014, when he decided that he needed to write something that wasn't just another college essay. Four years and a bachelor and master's degree later, Konner writes from the foothills of the Rocky Mountains in Provo, Utah, as he strives for a career in diplomacy. When he's not writing, Konner loves spending time with his gorgeous wife, hiking the American Southwest, and playing the occasional flight simulator.

COMING SOON

The Nightswitch trilogy

The year is 2104. A rare human pilot in a world of drones and automation, 19-year-old William Jackson's world is turned upside down when his homeland is suddenly invaded by an unknown military force. When Will and his friends escape San Francisco and are rescued by the beautiful Camila and her squad of semi-invisible, exosuit-wearing special-ops soldiers, they believe they'll be safe, but nothing could be further from the truth.

Fathom

Water crushes down from all sides, making Fathom's metal walls creak and squeal under the pressure. For Marko and the others on board it's all they've ever known. But what of the Soulkeepers' insistence that this isn't their true home, or the Peacekeepers' constant fear of a war like the one centuries ago? Marko knows only one thing: water will not be his grave.

Made in the USA
Middletown, DE
28 June 2023

34110961R00243